THE CHILD THIEF

BELLA FORREST

PROLOGUE

I stood frozen outside my parents' bedroom.

Staring at the door handle, I tightened my grip around the breakfast tray I had prepared. I could hear the murmuring of the television seeping through the cracks of the closed door, and I wished I didn't feel so nervous. I wished today was just like any other day I treated them to breakfast in bed… But it wasn't.

I had news to share with them this morning. News unlike any I had ever shared before.

And although I had known them for sixteen years and ten months of my seventeen years of living, I feared how they were going to react. They had always treated me as if I were their own child, ever since the day the Ministry of Welfare took me from my birth parents and assigned me to them.

But this… This was big.

I tried to convince myself that everything would be okay. They loved me, didn't they? They wanted me to be happy, right? They had always said so, and yet, with this, I feared I had gone too far.

Still, I drew in a deep breath and moved closer to the door. I had delayed this for long enough already. It was time to come out with the truth.

God knew I couldn't wait longer than a couple more months, even if I wanted to.

I repositioned the tray against my hip to free up one hand and then knocked boldly, thrice, with more confidence than I felt.

"Come in," my mother's musical voice chimed through the cracks.

Swallowing, I gripped the handle and opened the door, then entered with the tray.

My parents were in bed. My mother, forty-five years young, a beautiful woman with long, dyed blond hair and eyes the color of a clear sky, had been watching the television, while my father, a tall, bald man of forty-nine with swarthy skin and a strong black goatee, was holding a newspaper in front of him. Even lying in bed, he exuded the confidence of one of the most important people in the United Nation of America: a governor, whose moral high grounds were as high as they came.

"Oh, thank you, darling. What a treat!" my mother cooed as I approached her side of the bed. I set the tray down in between the two of them, then tucked my hands behind my back and stepped backward.

"Thank you, Robin," my father murmured, lowering the paper momentarily to pick up his coffee and a piece of toast.

I nodded and tried to smile back, but it felt like I was wearing one of my mother's solidifying masks.

As they began eating, my toes curled over the silken rug, and I allowed my eyes to wander to the television screen, unable to resist the temptation of procrastinating a few minutes longer.

"—latest report from the Ministry of Welfare was released this morning. Divorce rates are steady at 79 percent—a slight improvement from 2102—while the number of children born out of wedlock remains at 56 percent of the total number of children born. Government savings are up, thanks to continued implementation of the CRAS, while adoption admin fees continue to improve living conditions for low-income families nationwide. The CRAS has saved the UNA trillions in child welfare and foster services since the system's introduction by President Burchard after the Crisis in 2082—"

"You sleep well, hon?" my mother interrupted around a mouthful of fruit.

And I was glad for the interruption, as the current news topic was doing nothing to help my nerves.

"Yes," I lied.

"Are any of your siblings awake yet?" she asked.

"Um, I think I heard Joseph and Lora. I'm not sure about anyone else." The last thing I'd thought to do this morning was check on any of my seven younger siblings—not when we had two full-time nannies caring for them.

"It's going to be a gorgeous day, by the looks of it." My mother sighed, glancing toward the sunshine streaming in through the wide French windowpanes. "You want to take the dogs for a walk?"

"Um, yes. Sure. I just..." I cleared my throat, forcing myself to look from one parent to the other. I inhaled slowly. "Mom, Dad... There's something I've been meaning to tell you."

They both paused in their eating, their eyes moving to me.

"What is it?" my mother asked, while my father raised a dark eyebrow.

A surge of blood rose to my face, and I suddenly felt too hot, even with the cool breeze wafting in through the window. I balled my fists together, trying to take a deep breath through my constricting throat. And then I closed my eyes and let it out.

"I met a boy last year at summer camp. We... We've kept in touch ever since. He's the reason I've been coming home late from school on some days, recently. I was going to tell you about him sooner, but... one thing just led to another, and I just... didn't. I wish I had told you sooner now, though, because... things got a bit out of hand. I never planned for this, but... I'm pregnant."

It felt like I could have dropped a pin onto the mahogany floorboards and heard it even over the television. My parents stared at me, their jaws slack.

"What?" My mother finally found her voice, her fingers quickly moving to the remote to switch the television off. She gave a nervous laugh. "I'm sorry, Robin. Is this some kind of late April Fool's?"

I shook my head. "It's not," I croaked.

She gaped at me, stunned, while my father maintained his shocked silence.

I was most fearful about what *he* was going to say, and I was so desperate not to be one of the statistics I knew he so disapproved of—which was why I'd waited for Henry to propose before telling them. I'd thought he would... but he still hadn't.

And I just couldn't hide my pregnancy from my parents any longer.

I knew this was a big thing to ask my father to accept. Governors of the Burchard Regime were expected to have the highest moral standards, to be paragons of virtue that set an example for the rest of our lax society. And their families were considered reflections of themselves, their ability to influence and infuse good behavior in others—which, in my father's eyes, was ultimately what defined a true leader.

If he couldn't even keep his own family in check, what did that say about him? He'd be gossiped about, and even if nobody said anything to his face, he'd be subtly looked down upon in his social circles.

I knew the consequences, and I felt bad for letting him down, but what was done was done.

His affection for me just had to be strong enough for him to swallow his pride and accept the situation. I had to believe it. Because I had a baby on the way, and a man I was deeply in love with.

If he didn't accept it, he could ruin everything.

"Who is this boy?" my father asked, dropping the food and cup in his hands onto the breakfast tray and rising to his feet. The bedcovers slipped off him, revealing his full, tall, broad frame, the muscles in his arms visible even beneath his nightshirt.

I hesitated, then glanced toward the door. "Henry," I called softly, and a moment later my boyfriend stepped tentatively through the doorway. His normally tan complexion looked pale as he laid his deep brown eyes on my parents, his handsome face a mask of tension.

At least he had offered to come meet them today. I'd let him in through the back door first thing this morning, and hoped it would help soften the blow of what we had done once they saw that he was a sweet guy. Marriage was a big step for anyone, and while I wished we had come to my parents with news of our engagement, I loved Henry too much to pressure him into it.

"Good to meet you, Mr. and Mrs. Sylvone," he said tightly.

Silence reigned once more over the room, as both of my parents glared at him. It occurred to me then that inviting him into their bedroom might not have been the most sensitive move.

"Henry's eighteen," I said, desperate to break the quiet, "and he works part time at the camp during the summer. He lives on the Meadfield Estate."

My father's gaze darkened as he exchanged a glance with my mother, and I looked anxiously at Henry. He came from a humble background compared to me—very humble, in fact. He'd dropped out of school at sixteen to work in the factories and help his parents pay to keep his two younger siblings, and while that shouldn't be an impediment to us being together, I knew it had to be playing on my father's mind. I was sure he'd had the son of one of his governor friends in mind for me, although he'd never come out and said it.

There would be little to no financial support for our child coming from Henry's side, but that didn't have to be a problem, because my parents had no shortage of money to support an extra child. Hell, they'd been talking about hiring another nanny and doing another adoption recently anyway.

We could pull this off easily. *If* my father could accept the situation for the sake of his grandchild.

The pause that stretched between us seemed endless, as my father turned his back on us and faced the window. His broad shoulders rose and fell as he took deep breaths, and I feared it was all he could do to keep himself from exploding.

I'd borne the brunt of his temper before, over the years, when I did something to irk him. But I'd never done anything like this. I knew how strongly he was against intimacy outside of marriage. He'd told me time and time again.

Still, I couldn't help but feel that sometimes you just couldn't plan love. And since contraceptives had been banned before I was born, situations like mine were hardly uncommon.

But they are uncommon within governors' families, a small voice in my head reminded me. *They train their children well.*

It was true that I didn't know anyone within my social circle who'd been in my position. Which was why I was so nervous about this. Even now that I'd told them, I still didn't know how this was going to go down.

I looked to my mother, but her expression was stoic, unreadable, as she watched my father's back. She was avoiding looking at me, waiting for my father's reaction.

"I'm sorry, Robin," my father said finally, heaving a sigh and turning back around. "We welcomed you into our family with open arms, raised you as our own. But this... this I cannot, in good conscience, sustain. Your stay here is over. You must leave."

I gaped at him. I had feared this would go badly. I'd expected some sort of punishment for my indiscretion. But *leaving*?

My voice choked up and I looked to my mother again, but she was still avoiding eye contact.

"B-But Dad," I gasped. "What do you mean, *leave*? Wh-Where will I go?"

I had not a cent to my name. Everything I owned, including the clothes on my back, belonged to my parents. *Leave?* It was... It was absurd.

I... I was pregnant. This was my home.

Tears flooded my eyes as a surge of panic took hold of me. This couldn't be happening. I had to get him to see reason.

"Sir," Henry spoke up, before I could attempt anything. He had gone pale as a sheet and his own voice was raspy as he hurried toward my father, his palms open in a peaceful gesture. "I'm sorry. I'm sorry this happened, but please, don't ask Robin to leave. I-I'll marry her. We... We'll get married before the baby's born."

His words made my heart expand, and I prayed this would be enough to fix things. Then my eyes returned to my father's face, and I saw the deep scowl that remained there.

"Unfortunately, it's too late," he grated out. "You were more than willing to mess with my daughter behind my back, and you're saying this now only because you're desperate. The two of you have already revealed your mentality to me—and it's one of the ailments of our country. Irresponsible people like you are what led our great nation to crisis twenty years ago." He shook his head bitterly, his eyes returning to me. "No restraint. Despite all I have done to try to mold you, make you into an honorable human being, it's all gone to waste. I can no longer maintain my association with you. You have disqualified yourself from living in our household. I won't have you infecting your siblings with your bad example... So get out. Now."

"No, Dad!" I choked out. I rushed toward him, trying to pull him into a desperate embrace, but he gripped my arms as though I were a stranger, and pushed me backward.

"You've lost the right to call me that," he said, then stalked out of the room.

I followed him out at a run, not knowing what else to do. This couldn't be happening. If I was thrown out, I'd have no means of supporting myself during my pregnancy, and Henry and his family were stretched to the max as it was. If I couldn't get the money together, then...

"No, Dad!" I cried out again. "Please, just stop!"

I didn't even know where he was going as he sped down the staircase to the entrance hall. All I knew was that I had to get him to change his mind. I had to get him to see *reason*. I could hear Henry's footsteps pounding behind me as I raced after my father, who, I realized a moment later, was heading toward his study.

He ran to the door and pushed it open, and when I entered a few seconds after him, it was to the sight of him rummaging through the drawers of his bureau, his face dark, his eyes a quiet storm.

I realized, then, as he pulled out a brown binder, what he had been searching for.

My adoption papers. He tore them from the folder and drew a huge red cross over each of them with a marker, then ripped them apart, one by one, the pieces scattering all about the room.

"I'm sorry, Robin. But we're done here. You've left me no choice. And now you two are as good as trespassers—your boyfriend in particular. I'll have the neighborhood know that you have forsaken me and are no longer anything to me, so I suggest you leave and never show your face around here again. You two have made your bed, and now you can damn well lie in it."

"No, sir!" Henry surged forward, and the next thing I knew, my father was pulling a gun from one of the drawers, his eyes glinting with a rage I had never seen in him before.

He fired at Henry's left leg before I could scream out for him to stop, and then Henry was crying out and crumpling to the floor.

"No!" I gasped and rushed to him, pressing my hands down around his wound to stem the blood flow while he writhed in pain against the carpet.

"I told you to *leave!*" my father hissed. "*Now*, before my children come down here."

"No, wait! I need to call an—"

My father's hand closed hard around my wrist and he yanked me up from the floor, then grabbed Henry by the arm and hauled him up, too. His strength was enough to allow him to drag us both out the front door, and he cast one last glowering look at me before he slammed it shut behind us.

Henry collapsed again the second my father let go of him, and I stumbled to help him back up, even as my whole body trembled in shock. Adrenaline lent me strength I didn't know I possessed, and I managed to support the hobbling six-foot boy down the steps and out onto the street.

I staggered down the sidewalk with him, praying our neighbors were in and would allow us to make a call. It wasn't a fatal wound, and if an ambulance arrived quickly, I knew Henry would be okay.

But I also knew then that, barring a miracle, the baby I gave birth to would never be mine.

1

2 years later

I stared at the girl in the mirror. At her long, dirty-blond hair. At her light hazel eyes. At her narrow bone structure and thin lips. She was me, and yet she was a me I was still getting used to.

Two years can do a lot to a person. And just about everything that could have gone wrong in a person's life had gone wrong in mine.

And yet, here I stood. A survivor.

It would be a lie to say, though, that I hadn't been convinced I would break—more than a few times. The days had been dark and long after my adoptive father banished me from home. I had no choice but to move in with Henry and his family, and it was there that I experienced what life was like outside of my comfy little bubble for the first time. I experienced what life was like for the unprivileged.

I was forced to quit my private school, with no means of affording the tuition, and wound up getting a job at the same clothes factory in which Henry worked during the week. The pay there was a pittance, just enough to cover living and travel expenses, given that I was still under eighteen and had no prior work experience.

And then, when I could no longer work due to my pregnancy, it became a waiting game—waiting for the day my baby was born, and a member of the Ministry for Welfare arrived to inform me that unfortunately, I was not eligible to keep my child.

I became a victim of the same system that had punished my birth parents, all those years ago, when they were forced to give me up. The Child Redistribution Adoption System, the CRAS, aimed at the poorest of society. President Burchard's genius idea to solve the Great Crisis our country found itself in, which was, if we were to believe the news channels, precipitated by the spike in family welfare costs over the past century, thanks to our country's deteriorating morals. When it reached the point where taxes rose to unprecedented heights to meet the expense of welfare, his regime swooped in to solve the problem by instituting the CRAS, whereby only those who could afford it—the wealthy of our society—would shoulder the "burden." They would take in children under the age of three, which allowed for an easier adjustment period than older kids, thus relieving the government, and everyone else, of the expense. The system would work particularly well, they argued, because many upper- and middle-class families with career wives tended to have few or no biological children anyway, and wanted to adopt.

I lit up as a bright red flag on the Ministry's audit system, labelled as someone who would sap too many resources from the government because I didn't have adequate means to support my child. I became part of the bottom 20 percent of the population—those who were in danger of being targeted. In fact, I was probably closer to the bottom 5 percent.

And so a minister arrived the day she was born. My beautiful baby girl, whom, during those few precious hours I got to hold her in my arms, I named Hope.

Because she was my Hope, on that bright, sunny morning. That someday, things would change. That someday, I would live in a world where I could see her again.

I cried and whispered to her that I would find her, though it was a promise that was virtually impossible to keep, given that it was illegal for parents to seek out their children after they had been resituated, and detailed adoption records were kept in cyber vaults.

It was the same reason that my birth parents had never found me—because I was sure they would've sought me out if they could.

If they had experienced anything like I had, that day I gave birth, then it was a certainty. I had never thought I'd be the kind of girl to have a baby before her mid- to late-twenties, with the academic path carved out for me by my parents. But when I held Hope, it felt like a huge piece of my life had been missing until her arrival, and I didn't know how I could've lived without her. Couldn't bear even *imagining* a life without her.

But I had to.

The tears stopped after a week, once the Ministry took her away, and numbness settled into their place. The ordeal took its toll on Henry and me, as a couple. Although, to be honest, I'd felt the beginnings of a crack in our relationship when my father shot him in the leg.

Not that I could blame the poor boy. He was probably afraid to have anything more to do with a governor's daughter after that— even an ex-governor's daughter. And the time he spent with me during the pregnancy and birth was more out of duty than anything else. Henry would never admit it, but it became clearer to me in the months that followed that my father had been right about one thing: he hadn't been intending to commit to me anytime soon. We'd both been caught up in the passion of a first-time, forbidden summer romance, and had let it go too far. I'd thought that maybe our relationship could survive it, but after the baby was taken away, it became clear that she had been the only thing holding us together. Once she was gone, Henry announced that he had accepted a job transfer to another factory up north, and left.

I guessed different people reacted differently to trauma. Some people drew closer together, while others drifted apart. Our relationship was never as deep as I had thought it was, in my naïve seventeen-year-old mind, which was why he hadn't proposed until he'd been guilt-tripped into it.

In any case, we lost touch, and if he'd started seeing another girl in his new town, I honestly couldn't say I would have minded, or even felt the smallest twinge of jealousy.

Hope's absence ate at my soul, and I could barely even think of anything else.

I moved out of Henry's parents' small apartment as quickly as I could, to get away from the memories it held, and managed to get another job in a factory—as I had given up my previous one to have the baby. I found a little cabin in the woods to call home, and it was where I lived to this day.

The sound of barking outside my window made me start, and I turned away from the mirror. I padded out of my little five-by-seven bedroom, over the rough wooden floorboards, and into my only slightly larger living room, toward the front door. I pulled it open with a creak and switched on the lantern outside. The beams illuminated a small pack of local wolves I had befriended, standing in the darkness of the late evening. They had basically become part-time pets—ever since I'd allowed them to sleep in my living room last winter, during a particularly bad storm.

"No food today, boys," I muttered, bending down to stroke their silky fur. They nuzzled against my face, and I kissed them each gently on the nose.

"Nor for you, girl," I added, my eyes falling on the female. I felt particularly bad about having nothing for her, as she was heavy with pups.

But I was earning just enough to support my lifestyle, with only the occasional money to spare, which I tried to save up. I did occasionally give them treats, but it wasn't something I wanted them to get into the habit of expecting.

Besides, my day-to-day diet wasn't suited to them, anyway. I grew potatoes and greens in a small dirt patch round the back of my cabin, and those, along with grains and milk from the local farmer, were basically what I ate. Except when I was in a rush. Then I resorted to Nurmeal, a meal-replacement drink. But I preferred real food in my mouth when I had the option. Living alone didn't exactly motivate me to cook fancy, either way. I just consumed what did the job and kept my food bill as low as possible so I had more flexibility in my budget for other things.

After a couple minutes of back stroking, I closed the door on the animals and retreated back inside, gazing around my little cabin with a sigh. It contained only three rooms: my bedroom, the living area—which was combined with a kitchenette—and the bathroom. It had taken a while to get used to living in such a raw environment, but the months I had spent holed up in Henry's parents' apartment had gotten me accustomed to small spaces. By comparison, I had more room to myself here.

Still, the first few months I'd spent in this cabin had been the hardest of my life. The dark and cold seemed to seep out of every nook and cranny, and it was the kind that no amount of cozy lighting or fur rugs could drive away. The depression had come close to consuming me, and the only thing I had to look forward to every day was work at the factory, to take my mind off things. Not that the mind-numbing work was ever really a distraction...

But then, seven months ago, things had changed. The darkness was still never far away, lurking in the shadows of my mind like a waiting monster, but the bad days were far fewer, the motivated, optimistic ones the norm now. Seven months ago, I found a renewed purpose in life...

The sound of my phone ringing brought me back to reality— and told me that I had been spacing out. I hurried to my bathroom counter, where I had left the small device, and picked it up. After checking that my phone's encryption app was running and the line was secure, I accepted the call and pressed the speaker to my ear.

"Hey, Nelson, what's up?" I said.

"Coordinates have changed for tonight," a low, crackling voice replied, only barely distinguishable as female. "You need to head to the Roundhouse, and we'll launch the mission from there."

"Oh. Everything okay?"

"Yup. Just a slight, unexpected shift of target. So we're gonna have to approach from a different angle. Get over there and you'll get a briefing."

"Okay. I'm leaving now," I replied, and then she hung up.

I hung up too and slipped the phone into my pocket, then hurried to tie my hair back into a tight bun and slide into my jacket. After pulling on my backpack and grabbing my keys, I left the cabin and swung onto my motorcycle, kicking it into gear.

As I drove out through the woods toward the road, I breathed in the crisp evening air, taking a moment to just... *feel* the mix of emotions coursing through me. They came whenever Nelson got in touch, and while I looked forward to her calls, they didn't exactly fill me with light or happiness. Nor could I even say with excitement. No, it was with something much darker than that.

Something deep and burning, almost primal… Perhaps the kind of thing only a broken mother can feel.

If there was one thing I had learned in these past two years, it was that pain can make you hard. But it can also mold and shape you into something you never thought you could become.

And that, I hoped, was what had happened to me.

By day they still called me Robin Sylvone (as much as I disliked the surname now, I had no other to which I could subscribe). Factory worker and upper-class reject.

But seven months ago, my nights had gotten a whole lot more meaningful. Now, by night, they called me Robin Hood.

2

As I rode through the countryside toward the nearest city, where my meeting with Nelson was due to take place tonight, my eyes rested absentmindedly on the hulking shadows of factories that loomed beyond the fields. They were the first signs of the industrial estate where I spent most of my day, sitting in front of an assembly line, quality-checking fabrics.

Our country hadn't always held so many factories. That was another thing that had changed toward the latter part of the last century, due to a push by the government to create more jobs for America's people.

The increase in factories had definitely opened up a lot of jobs... though I had yet to meet a single person who was actually happy working in those cavernous metal shells. Still, the work helped pay the bills. Just about. And that was all most people aspired to in this day and age.

Having been brought up in a prosperous family, where my parents had funded everything in my life, from my hobbies to my education, I had never realized just how good I had it—until I lost it. Back then, I had the world at my feet, by comparison. I could've gone after any career, even in the arts, and my parents would've backed me (although their preference was that I go into politics). The world would have basically been my oyster, with all the opportunities that had been open to me.

Did I sometimes regret what had happened? Yes. I couldn't deny that, on more than one occasion, I had wished I could turn back time. Stuck by my parents' training and withstood the sultry gaze Henry had given me, that night we'd made love by the lakeside.

But being out of that privileged bubble had also taught me things about the world that I never would have realized otherwise. It had woken me up to the reality of the majority. The reality most people in the world woke up to every morning, the daily grind of keeping food on the table and fuel in the tank. The stress of paying bills and keeping a roof over your head. And while it had jaded me, to a certain extent, I also felt like a wiser and more compassionate person for it.

Besides, I had brought a beautiful human being into the world. Wherever she was now...

I veered to the left as my opening in the road came up, and trundled across the industrial estate, past the factories, which were practically a town unto themselves, and then through the surrounding residential area for the workers—skyscraper apartment blocks, all designed to fit as many people into as small a space as possible. I'd lived in one of those with Henry and his family, and I knew, after being packed up in their little matchbox of an apartment, that any other accommodation would be better.

I was grateful that I had managed to find my little hut in the woods, via a contact I had made at the employment office. My landlord let me stay there for a pittance. It was more inconvenient to have to travel so far to work each day, but it was also a journey

I enjoyed. It helped to clear my head on my way to and from the factory, allowed me some space to think about more than just keeping the clothes on my back.

I entered a commercial area filled with storefronts, which marked the beginning of a more affluent quarter of the small mountain city. Opulent mansions sprawled less than seven streets away, mostly belonging to landlords and factory owners, and were quite the contrast to the rest of the town.

I passed along a few more roads, and then stopped at the end of Fraser Avenue, in front of a large, round pub, whose official name was announced on the big, bold sign hanging above the front entrance: the Foxtrot. Raucous laughter and chatter spilled out through the bright, open windows. It was packed, as usual at this time of night, and the noise and general commotion about this place were exactly the reasons that Nelson had a habit of choosing it. That, and the owner was one of her contacts.

I parked my motorcycle and then entered through the main door. Heading toward the bar, I made brief eye contact with Cianna, the porky, middle-aged owner of the place, and she gave me a knowing nod, then gestured toward a door at the back of the pub.

I gave her a brief smile and a nod back, then picked my way through the crowd toward it. Stepping through, I was met with a staircase, which I scaled quickly, finally stopping at the fourth floor, where a small landing connected to a single door. I walked up to it and then knocked three times in quick succession, followed by a pause, and another three quick knocks.

I heard the sound of the lock drawing back, and then the door opened, a pair of bespectacled green eyes peering through the crack.

"Ah, glad you made it, RobinHood21," Nelson "Nelly" Peters

(or NellP, per her handle on the shadow web portal where we had first met) greeted me with a grin.

She was a short woman of five feet, four inches, with a shock of curly brown, shoulder-length hair and olive skin. She looked to be in her late twenties, though I couldn't be sure, as we had never exchanged real details about ourselves—for security reasons. Because with the types of missions we ran, the fewer personal details we knew about each other, the better. Fewer details meant there was less we could spill, if any of us got caught.

She stepped back, allowing me through to a small meeting room with a circular table in the center, and I realized our five other accomplices were already waiting.

"Oh, hey, guys," I said, plopping into a free seat beside Julia Caesar (aka Juicy1), a quiet, pale-skinned girl with bowl-cut auburn hair and dusky gray eyes. She was around my age, and was assistant to Nelson, who was the mastermind and ringleader of our little group. "Sorry to hold up the meeting." I glanced at my watch to see that it had just struck midnight.

"Oh, that's fine," Abe Lincoln (AL1) replied, kicking back in his chair and crossing his arms over his chest. "It's not like we've got anything important to do tonight." He was a tall, lanky young man who looked about twenty-three, with a mop of sandy blond hair and warm brown eyes.

"Yeah, I was just gonna bring up some drinks," his twin brother Ant Lincoln (AL2) added with a wink. He was identical to Abe, except for a rather stupid-looking pencil moustache, which he claimed he maintained solely for the benefit of helping others distinguish between the two of them (and I hoped, for his sake, that it *was* the only reason).

Jackie K (JK007), a girl with Asian ancestry, and in her early twenties, scoffed. "You're hardly late, R. Most of us only just got here." She narrowed her eyes at Ant in a death glare (which, for the record, given the girl's combat abilities, was genuinely unnerving). "And you know what I'd do to you if you drank before a mission."

Ant shrugged, his face deadpan. "How would I? It's not like you've ever threatened me before." He leaned back in his chair in a motion that mirrored his brother's, and put his feet up on the table.

Jackie pursed her lips, tossing her long black braid over one shoulder and then sweeping his feet back to the floor in one swift move of her forearm. "Don't mess with me."

"Speaking of drinks, anyone want a hot chocolate?" asked Marco L. King—a slightly chunky boy with light blue eyes and russet-brown hair, who I figured was in his early twenties, too.

Everyone's hands immediately rose, including mine and Nelson's. We still had a little time before we had to leave this place and it was growing chilly outside.

The boy's round, freckled face fell. "I was just being polite," he muttered.

"Your handle's CoCo-King for a reason," Nelson said with a wink.

"Yeah… that's not what I meant by it." He sighed, then ambled over to the kitchenette in one corner of the room and begrudgingly began setting out seven cups. "This kettle's tiny," he grumbled to himself. "The things I do for you people."

I smiled, looking around the room and taking a moment to appreciate the people who had played such a major role in turning my life around. In the short time I'd known them, I'd come to feel closer to them than anyone in my former social circle, even though I barely knew anything about them, other than the personalities that spilled through from behind their fake personas. Without them, I honestly didn't want to think about where I would be.

I'd heard talk of people like Nelson's team at the factory one day during lunch break—whispers about something called the shadow web, where people were brazen enough to talk negatively about our country and its government. About things they saw as unfair and unjust. About things they wanted to see changed. Things they would never speak about in public, for fear of punishment.

Having just lost my baby, the idea of connecting with like-minded people—people who might have gone, or be going, through the same thing as me—drew me like a moth to a flame. I needed to talk to someone, anyone at that point, to be honest… to make me feel a little less alone in the deep hole into which I was losing myself.

So I saved up and bought myself a small, discounted tablet during a sale and managed to convince the person I'd overheard speaking about the shadow web to tell me how to access these clandestine social networks—and install the necessary software to keep my connection untraceable.

And it was then that I'd discovered a world of freedom. A Wild West, where anything seemed possible.

The networks were all anonymous; people created fake names and profiles for themselves, so they could interact freely. I read many thoughts and stories that mirrored my own, but what was more… I read about people actually *doing* things. It took a while to figure out the codenames and words people tended to use on these forums, but thanks to night after night of feverish reading, I started to get it. These people were pushing back against the government—or so they claimed. On some networks, they spoke of things I would never stoop to, like hacking into bank accounts and stealing money and weapons, and other activities, ranging from shady to despicable. I stayed away from those networks, but there were others—one in particular—buried deep within the web, that grabbed my imagination and refused to let go. It was a closed network called Operation Hood, and, once my registration request was finally approved, I discovered a community of people that spoke my language, and appealed to my deepest, darkest desires.

The network's mission statement was simple—*steal from the rich and return to the poor*—and on it I found discussions about stealing children back from their adoptions, and then either smuggling their families to other countries where laws were different, or hiding them in some way.

At the time, I could hardly believe what I was reading. After all, the amount of risk and danger involved with that kind of operation was *insane*. Not to mention how difficult it would be to track children in the first place, when the government kept those details under lock and key. Plus, it was basically impossible to leave our country without permission. Not to mention the risk you'd run trying to hide a kid *within* our country.

And then, even if they had somehow figured out how to access the records, stealing children from their new families?

In all, it seemed like the operations would involve a crazy number of infractions, many of which would be excuse enough for our justice system to send you to the morgue.

Still, the idea sparked a fire in me that I couldn't put out. A fire that I latched onto for dear life, in fact, because I just knew that it was my way out of the darkness. I needed to contact one of these activist groups from Operation Hood (also known as OH), not only to see if they were real, but to find out if I could get involved.

I created a profile, claimed the handle RobinHood21 (Robin-Hood was an annoyingly popular handle within OH), and started contacting people individually. Most were far too cagey to give me details or locations, given that I was a brand new member. I was also careful not to be too precise about my *own* location. But

I finally managed to get a contact, who put me in touch with NellP, who said she managed a team that operated in my approximate area.

Actually gaining her trust enough to persuade her to take me under her wing was a whole other matter entirely. She'd claimed to be based two cities away and wanted to meet me in a dark alley one Sunday night to see if I was who I said I was.

I traveled to the location at the specified hour and found her waiting with a gun—and Jackie K. Both wore masks and had a vehicle in which to flee at the first sign of anything shady. But after realizing I was alone, they took me to a little café, where we talked. It took several more appointments before Nelson felt comfortable enough to invite me to meet the rest of her group, and even then, for my first few training missions, they kept masks on around me at all times.

Then, after a couple of months, I was finally accepted as one of them, and they became more relaxed around me. I'd been on five missions with them since.

And had discovered just how they were pulling all this off.

Nelson was not only the manager of our group, but a hacker and programmer who had several sympathetic contacts in high places. She'd never tell any of us who they were, of course, but one of them was supposed to be responsible for helping us slip through the cracks of border control.

As for tracking children in the first place… to my disappointment, it turned out that Nelson had no way to break into the government's e-archives. At least, not yet. She was working on it, but it was a highly risky task, as security around those records was dangerously sensitive to attacks or breaches. If the attempt was traced back to her in any way, she'd be as good as dead. She had to play it carefully. But even in spite of all that, I held out hope that she would find a way in. She'd told me that she first joined

Operation Hood out of the frustration of losing her own daughter to the CRAS three years ago, so I knew she had the motivation to crack their defenses.

And if she did, I would stand a hell of a good chance of getting back my own baby... now a toddler.

The idea made my heart clench whenever it crossed my mind —that I was missing out on the most precious period of Hope's life. Especially because Nelson had told me she'd never attempt to kidnap a child older than four. As much as their birth parents might want them back, it would be too traumatic for an older child to be suddenly uprooted by strangers from what they'd believed all their life to be their home, especially for the children who hadn't even been told they'd been adopted. Kids younger than four had an easier adjustment period, but after that, kidnapping just wasn't a humane way of doing things. I didn't want to risk putting my daughter through that kind of trauma either, in spite of how much I wanted her.

So for now, all I could do was be patient and hope I could locate her before the deadline. Nelson's heart was in the right place—her child was even closer to four years old than Hope—so I had to believe she'd find a way. And I would continue to work and set aside as much money as I could, for when the time might come when I could get Hope back.

In the meantime, I was at least helping other families, as long as they met certain criteria. The first requirement being that they needed to prepare in advance.

Parents, or parents-to-be, whose income had dropped danger-ously, or was on the verge of dropping, sought out our services over the shadow portal. Nelson and Julia would do a thorough background check on them, to verify that they weren't moles, and then the parents would transfer a small sum of digital money to Nelson's anonymous account—just to show that they were serious, and also to help us cover the cost of our operations.

Then Nelson and Julia set up an initial meeting with the parents, and in cases where the child was born already, the duo inserted a tiny tracking device behind the child's ear, which allowed Nelson to trace his or her whereabouts for up to eighteen months.

Next the parents had to figure out a way to cobble together enough money for escaping and starting a new life. Occasionally they could achieve that while the woman was still pregnant or before the Ministry came for their kid, and all they'd ask of Nelson was her smuggling services. But it usually took them longer—around a year after the child was resituated, due to their low earnings. Which meant they required the whole shebang: insertion, tracking, kidnapping, and smuggling.

Of course, there was only a very small number of families we could help in this way. Each mission came with a risk to our lives —either from the family whose home we were breaking into, or from the government, which would kill us if we were caught.

Stealing too many children would also turn the heat up on people like us in general, who were running similar operations in other parts of the country. Right now, the number of children going missing could be put down to other causes, like kidnapping in the dark, criminal sense, and we were careful never to target the same area too many times.

In addition, the number of parents who actually knew about services like ours, and dared to hire a group like us over the shadow web to begin with, was small.

Plus, Nelson's contact could only help a very limited number of people across the border.

So yeah... I couldn't see us changing the world anytime soon.

But it was something, and it made my life feel a whole lot

more meaningful, knowing I could prevent the kind of heartache I'd been through in even a handful of others. It brought purpose to my days, and gave me a bitter sense of satisfaction, that I was doing something to rebel against the system that had caused me so much grief. I believed our country's leadership had taken a wrong turn, somewhere in the past several decades, and even if we never managed to correct it, I knew I wanted to be a small part in trying.

"Right," Nelson said, interrupting my train of thought. Her tone turned businesslike as she set her pad down on the table in front of her. "Let's get this party started."

"Yeah, what was that about our target moving?" Abe asked, leaning forward in his seat and adopting a more serious expression.

"Nothing major, like I said. It just seems that Grammy and Gramps have taken the boy and girl in for a sleepover tonight. The kids shifted to Parkdale City, which is why I called you guys here. It'll make for a more direct journey."

We had a brother and sister to kidnap tonight, which was an unusual case. We didn't usually take on two at a time, because most biological siblings didn't end up in the same house, and also, it was more of a challenge. But for whatever reason, in this case, they had been taken together, and given that they were both small —under the age of three—they wouldn't be difficult to carry, so Nelson had agreed to take the assignment.

"How do you know it's Grammy and Gramps?" Marco asked, frowning. He approached the table with two steaming cups and set them down in front of Nelson and Julia, before returning to the kitchenette to continue preparing the others.

Nelson shrugged. "I guess it could be Uncle and Auntie. Point is, I've noticed that the kids travel to Parkdale every now and then, so I'm guessing whoever they're staying with are relatives."

Ant sighed. "Well, I hope they're old fogeys. They'll be way easier to rob."

Everyone snorted—except for Jackie, who cast the twins a dark look. "Yeah, that would prevent a repeat of *last time*."

And I couldn't help but share that sentiment. Our last excursion had been dicey, to say the least. We almost got caught, thanks to a surprise alarm nestled at the back of the property's large yard, which the twins had somehow missed during their initial sweep of the place.

"Well, tonight should be different," Nelson said, taking a sip of her cocoa. "I did a scan on the electronics of both houses personally this time, because I knew there was a chance the kids could be at either one. So listen up. We have about an hour before departure, and we've got a bunch of stuff to cover. Marco, would you dim the lighting, please?"

"Oh. So now I gotta play barista in the dark?"

"Just do it."

He grumbled, but moved to switch off the lights. Nelson then projected her tablet screen onto one of the walls and began going over the schematics of the house.

After an hour of discussion, and finishing up our hot chocolate, we were ready to leave.

We donned our backpacks and left the meeting room, scaling the staircase to the top floor of the building. Nelson retrieved a key from her pocket and opened a door that led out onto the roof, and we all stepped outside into the cool April night.

My eyes fell to the far end of the roof, where our ride was waiting: a small, military-grade stealth aircraft, which Marco piloted—and which had been given to us by another of Nelson's contacts.

It turned out there were more people in our society who were unhappy with the status quo than I had imagined, including those who were high up enough to have access to this kind of equipment. Which helped kindle that small hope in me that maybe, just maybe, things *might* change someday.

For now, however, it was one child at a time. Or two, this evening, as the case may be...

3

M arco, the twins, Jackie, and I bundled into the aircraft, leaving Julia and Nelson on the ground. We carried two small drones with us on the ship, one of which the duo would control remotely once we arrived, to help us keep an eye on the surrounding area as we worked. It wouldn't be a good idea for our entire team to go, especially when it wasn't even required. And especially Nelson. If something happened to her, it would be bad for all of us. Particularly for me. She was the only person I knew who was even attempting to crack into the government's archives, and without her, any hope I had of finding my daughter would basically vanish in a puff of smoke.

So, yeah, suffice it to say I was praying for her long and continued good health, and I was happy for her to stay behind. She did more than her fair share of work in setting up and managing our missions, anyway.

We tended to limit our excursion teams to five members: Marco, as our ever-trusty pilot, and then the rest of us for the ground team. Only two of the ground team would enter the house, with the other two staying in the aircraft to serve as backup in case anything went wrong. We were all trained in basic piloting, though I personally wouldn't feel comfortable with anyone in the pilot's seat except for Marco. Especially me, as I'd had the least experience. It was just important that we all knew some essentials, in case worse came to worst and something happened to him.

Today, Jackie and I had offered to touch down first. Hopefully, all would go smoothly inside the house, and there would be no need to call on the twins for backup.

"Everyone buckled in?" Marco called from the cockpit.

"Yup," the rest of us confirmed.

"Okey dokey. Taking off in three, two, one..."

The engine growled quietly—it was the noisiest the aircraft got during its entire flight process, thanks to its stealthy design— and we lifted off. I watched as Julia and Nelson waved up at us then headed back to the door, their forms quickly becoming small dots as the aircraft rapidly ascended into the sky.

Once they were gone, I turned to my team. "Any of you ever been to Parkdale City?" I wondered, as I had never been.

Abe and Ant shook their heads blankly, while Jackie gave a bitter nod. "Yeah. I worked there once."

I was tempted to ask for more details, as I always was with these friends-yet-strangers, and had to remind myself of our rule. No identifying information. I was *pretty* sure that none of our group would intentionally rat a fellow teammate out, even if they were caught, but who was to say what the government would do to us if one of us fell into their clutches? I wouldn't put torture past our country's current administration, given their liberal use of other violent methods to combat criminals—as well as the death penalty—if they thought they could extract information about a network of dissidents. Could any of us really withstand that kind of pressure? I didn't know. I certainly wasn't sure that *I* could, and while I was obviously hoping nothing like that ever happened, I slept easier at night knowing none of us could identify the others, even if we wanted to. It was also why none of us were allowed to take photographs of each other. The most we could do was describe general features, which wouldn't be that helpful. Especially as I was pretty sure that at least some of our team wore wigs and contact lenses whenever we met... Nelson in particular.

"Let's just say Parkdale is about as bourgeois as you can get," Jackie muttered. "Each family has an average of, like, four kids, or something."

I blew out, leaning back in my seat and thinking of my old neighborhood, which had been about as *upper class* as you could get. There, households probably had an average of seven kids. My adoptive parents had had eight in total, including me, and had been talking about adopting at least one more.

Having grown up in that environment, I honestly hadn't thought much of it. It had just seemed normal, until I moved out, was forced to give up my own child, and saw how the lowest rungs of society lived. It was then that I started asking myself why it happened. *Why* did the wealthier families want so many kids around them, kids who weren't even their own flesh and blood?

The news channels had answered that question for me, telling me that the redistribution scheme had gone smoothly because the wealthy had embraced raising children as a responsibility to our nation. They'd seen it as a way to avoid another crisis and to give those born in lower-income families the chance for a better life. But, still, the scheme was optional for them. No household was forced to raise others' children, and certainly not in the numbers I had seen. Which meant they had to genuinely want them.

Had the wealthy always wanted this many kids, throughout history? I doubted it.

It had started to feel to me like the number of children they took in had become something of a status symbol over the years, thanks to the Burchard Regime. Like kids had become collectibles, and adopting them was akin to owning a fleet of cars, or a selection of vacation homes. Especially as nannies did most of the grunt work involved in raising the children.

It would be unfair to say that my adoptive parents had never shown me love, because they had, but I also couldn't say that they'd ever had a lot of time for me, in between their own careers and all of their other children, none of whom were biological.

I sometimes thought of my younger siblings, back home, and wondered how they were getting on now. If they missed me at all. And what my parents had even told them, given that they'd been so keen to hide my pregnancy. I guessed my father would have thought up some good excuse, and that they'd all then just gotten on with life. It wasn't like they'd been given an option to keep in touch with me, even if they'd wanted to. Plus, they no doubt had at least one other new sibling to distract them by now.

I supposed one could argue that I was just being bitter about this whole subject, having been deemed ineligible to raise even a single child. My *own* child. Jealousy did make it easy to read things into a situation that might not be there—turn something noble into something… less noble.

Still, I stood by my belief: parents should have the option to raise their own children. It was just a course of nature. I'd have been willing to take out a loan and work like a donkey for the rest of my life to pay it off, if that was what it took to keep Hope and avoid being a burden to my country. But no, as a single teen mother, I'd been deemed a potential drag to the system, and hadn't even been given the option.

I sighed, shaking my head and knowing that this wasn't a productive line of thought. I'd been through it so many times already over the past two years, thinking about how the government could work differently. How there *had* to be another way for hardworking people with lower incomes to keep their kids, if that was what they wanted. And I still didn't know what the solution was. I wasn't a politician or an economist. But basic common sense told me that we'd allowed everyone to keep and raise their own kids before, for who knew how many centuries, prior to the CRAS's introduction. And that we could do it again. That the way we lived now was a result of humans overthinking things and meddling with stuff we should just leave alone.

Because this wasn't what nature had intended for us. Couldn't be. Not when it felt so damn *unnatural*.

"So, returning to the matter at hand," Abe said after a pause. He leaned back in his chair and gave Jackie and me a sly look. "I really think you two were being disingenuous when you offered to give Ant and me a break today."

I wrinkled my nose at him, while Jackie frowned. "What do you mean?" she asked.

"Um, if it's only old Gramps and Grammy, then it's hardly much of an offer."

"Oh, that." Jackie scoffed. "Yeah, *if*. Call us disingenuous once we verify that they *are* actually old folks, smartass. For all we know, we could be about to lower ourselves into little Becky and Jason's military uncle's backyard."

I shuddered. We'd hit a military family's house once, on my second mission ever, and the number of Rottweilers they'd had lurking around the grounds had been insane. I'd had a bit of a phobia about dogs ever since, to be honest. Except for my wolves. They were sweetie pies.

"Hopefully this time we'll be faced with an army of cats," I muttered.

"Yeah, kitties I can deal with," Jackie said with a smirk.

"Meow," Ant purred, throwing us a salacious wink.

Jackie scowled at him. "What are you, twelve?"

"Also," Abe added, "that look would sit way better on you without the 'stache. Just saying."

"Oh, thank God someone finally said it!" Marco burst out from the cockpit. "Seriously, dude. Get rid of that thing. It reminds me of Weazeloo, and not in a good way."

Jackie erupted into laughter. "How *can* you look like Weazeloo in a good way?"

Marco shrugged his shoulders. "Everyone has their taste, girl."

Weazeloo was a wizard character from an old fantasy TV series, which had recently been adapted and rebooted for a modern audience. I'd seen one episode of it, and could verify that the comparison was not a compliment.

"Look, I'd grow a full-on beard…" Ant sighed, scratching at the faint stubble lining his jaw. "But I can't, okay? And there's the truth of it. It comes out all patchy and gross."

Jackie threw her head back. "Ha! I knew you were twelve."

Now it was Ant's turn to scowl at her. "Laugh all you want, JK, but the 'stache is staying. It's the best I can think of to maintain my individuality. Which is important, you know. Keeps me from having an identity crisis every morning when I wake up and see him across the room." He jerked a finger at his brother.

"You mean across the bed," Abe added in a low voice.

Jackie clapped a hand to her forehead. "Oh, Lord. Oversharing, people. OVERSHARING."

"Do you guys seriously share a bed?" Marco muttered.

"Nah. We love each other, but not that much," Ant replied. "We have twin beds."

"Do you have matching pajamas too?" I asked.

Abe pursed his lips. "That's personal information."

"Seriously though," Ant cut in. "If it's what you people want, I can shave my moustache. If it's, I mean… if it's really that bad."

"It is," Marco confirmed.

"But then how would you be able to tell the difference between us?" Ant mused. "I guess you wouldn't be able to, given that neither of us wants a change of hairdo. In which case, we could switch names. I always wanted Abe Lincoln, but he nabbed it first and I got stuck with the crappy alternative."

"We could take turns," Abe allowed.

"Honestly, be my guest." Jackie sighed, rolling her eyes. "Like you say, I wouldn't notice the difference."

Abe raised an eyebrow. "Why, because we'd both be just as sexy?"

"You don't want me to answer that," Jackie deadpanned.

I chuckled, then pulled my focus away from the interior of the aircraft and looked out through the small round window near my seat. Judging by the change of landscape—the industrial area we'd left was far behind us now—we'd covered a lot of ground already. Which was another perk to this aircraft: in addition to its stealth, it had sheer speed. These machines were built for spying and had a way of zipping in and out of places incredibly quickly. They were also hard to detect, especially after dark, as the exterior was built to be inconspicuous and blend in with its surroundings. All of which meant it was perfect for missions where we couldn't afford to be discovered.

"How much longer do we have, Marco?" Jackie asked.

I glanced at her to see that she had drawn her attention away from the twins and was looking out of a window, too.

"Um, about eighteen minutes," Marco replied.

A shiver ran through me. That wasn't long. And although I had gone on a number of these missions now, the nerves were always intense. Perhaps even more so, with each additional trip. Because I had started to realize how unpredictable they could be.

"You nervous?" Jackie asked in a low tone, switching seats to get a little closer to me, and a little farther from the twins.

I sucked in a breath and nodded, seeing no point in lying. My cheeks felt like they were flushed with nerves, so I doubted I could hide it anyway, even if I had wanted to.

She gave me a knowing look, then a small, reassuring squeeze of my knee, before withdrawing. Jackie wasn't one for physical contact (well, not in the affectionate sense), and that was probably the first that she'd ever touched me. I gave her a grateful smile, but decided she might not appreciate getting a squeeze back, so kept my hands folded on my lap.

We all went quiet for the rest of the journey, even the twins. I sensed the tension settling around each of us, now that those few initial minutes of levity had passed. I closed my eyes, trying to clear my mind and go over the plan we had discussed before our departure.

Nelson had sent a drone to the location in advance, and it had scoped the place out and given her schematics, so we knew that the building was laid out over three stories and contained eighteen different rooms in total. Her drone was rigged not only with a powerful X-ray device, which provided us with a reliable plan of the property, but also a detector that picked up electronic frequencies, thus letting us know where the alarms were. So we knew where the children's bedrooms were. Theoretically. They weren't too difficult to place, once we had the scans, as they contained the smallest furniture in the house. Of course, given that our target properties usually had several children living in them, it could still be tricky, as we'd have to check more than one bedroom. But in this case, there were only two kids' rooms located on the ground floor, and the lack of children kind of confirmed to me that we probably were dealing with old folks whose own kids had flown the nest.

Which would give us the additional advantage of not needing

to examine multiple children's features to make sure we were kidnapping the right ones. As crazy as that sounded, it was a real danger when the only photographs parents had of their children were sometimes over a year old, and taken when they were still newborns. Some households could have more than one child around the same age, and while we hadn't made that mistake yet, I was always leery of it happening.

As for the alarms, it was a large building and there were several of them. But that would be a problem for the twins to deal with, before we set foot on the ground.

The rest of the journey slipped away quickly, and before I knew it, the aircraft was slowing and Marco was announcing our arrival. I grabbed my backpack and dug into it, retrieving my balaclava/head mask and pulling it over my head. It obscured my entire face, except for slits for my eyes, nostrils, and mouth. We all wore black, unlabeled clothing, and the mask blended seamlessly with the rest of my outfit in the darkness, making me look like one dark, fluid form. Anyone could probably see that I was female, but that was it.

I reached up to an overhead locker and pulled down a wide, black belt and a pair of gloves. The belt was filled with equipment I might need, and I secured it around my waist, then put on the gloves.

My colleagues began to prepare, too—with Jackie donning a belt and gloves, like me—and soon, we were all standing up, tensely watching our descent through the windows as the lawn-speckled city of Parkdale came into focus.

It was quiet now, approaching 2:00 a.m., so hopefully everyone would be asleep. If they weren't, we'd have to hang around longer, which I really didn't feel like doing. My stomach was already tight with nerves, and waiting would only make it worse.

I felt my belt again, double-checking that all the equipment was there, and then straightened and waited as the aircraft descended. Once we were directly above the roof of our target mansion, the aircraft stopped and hovered in place, the side hatch gliding open and letting in a cool gust of wind. The twins pulled the first drone—a small, round, dark gray piece of machinery that was shaped like an oversized beetle, and was also incredibly stealthy— from an under-seat compartment, and once they'd configured the settings, Abe pushed it to the edge of the aircraft's open door. Ant picked up the control console and, pushing a few buttons and levers, launched the machine into the air. Its soft hum was barely noticeable, even in the dead of night, as Ant took it closer to the house and began to navigate it around the perimeter.

"Okay," he murmured. "Zapper's going off in five, four, three, two..."

The zapper was another little apparatus Nelson had rigged to the drone. It sent out a pulse that knocked out electronics within specified physical parameters, disabling the alarms, and also helped us once we got into the house, as the absence of light was obviously a good thing. If someone did wake up, darkness caused confusion and gave us the advantage, since people didn't usually have flashlights or candles on hand.

Also, it prevented them from calling the police.

We just had to always be careful to keep our aircraft a safe distance away when the pulse was going out, because if it reached us... Yeah, that would be bad.

The little red lights that had been flashing at intervals on the exterior walls of the house suddenly winked out, along with a handful of nearby streetlights, and Ant put the drone in hover mode and set the console down before picking up his comm device.

"Pulse activated," he said softly into the receiver. "Ready for your takeover, Nelly."

Her voice came crackling back. "Roger that."

A handful of heartbeats later, the drone was moving again, cutting a wide sweep farther away from the house and then hovering over the neighboring roads, where it would help Nelson keep an eye on the surrounding area.

Abe then pulled the second drone from its compartment and prepared it for takeoff too, before Ant launched it into the air, controlling it just like he had the first. Abe switched on the screen in the wall of the aircraft, near the entrance of the cockpit, and an X-ray, bird's eye view of the house blinked to life, our vision of the second drone's view. The picture was murky, to say the least, and it was difficult to make out details, past the structure of the house and the shapes of furniture, but it was easy enough to tell if there was movement, which was the main thing. A heatmapping tool would definitely be more useful than the X-ray for locating residents, but Nelson didn't have an unlimited budget, and even her contacts only had so many resources they could offer us. So we made do with what we had.

Right now, all seemed still, which was a good sign.

Ant handed Jackie and me earpieces, and we fitted them into our ears. We'd take comms with us too, in case of an emergency, but we needed to avoid talking as much as possible. With the earpieces, the twins would have a direct, quiet connection to us, and could give us a heads-up if anything started moving.

Jackie reached up to the zip line holder attached to the ceiling and extended two lines, handing one to me while attaching the other to her belt. I attached mine, too. The aircraft lowered a little farther.

My heart raced as we cast one last look at each other, and then moved to the threshold of the open hatch.

It was time.

4

We landed on the lawn with a soft thud.

My first instinct was to search for kennels, even though none had shown up on the scan. There weren't any that I could see beneath the moonlight, in the spacious, ornament-filled garden. Another good sign, I hoped.

Jackie signaled for me to follow her, her dark eyes glistening with alertness behind her mask, and we crept to the building. Keeping close to the wall, we moved around it toward the opposite side of the house, where the children's rooms were located. My breathing was loud in my ears, my senses perked for the slightest sound or movement.

Once we reached the other side of the structure, we walked a few more feet and then stopped outside a rectangular frosted glass window, which was supposed to connect to a bathroom. Jackie reached into her belt and pulled out a cutter, then, after one quick glance around us, pressed it to the edge of the window and began to slice the glass. The device cut through it quietly.

The kids were a little farther up, per the schematics, but it was too dangerous to cut directly into their rooms in case they woke up. As discreet as the cutter was, it just wasn't worth the risk, so we always had to try to enter via a room that was near our destination, but less likely to be occupied.

And we were counting on Ant and Abe to warn us if this bathroom *was* occupied.

After two minutes, the windowpane was ready to be removed. We used our gloved fingers to grip its edges and lowered it down together, careful not to let it shatter.

Jackie moved in first. Deftly, like a panther, she swept over the windowsill and into the large, awaiting—and thankfully unoccupied—bathroom. I followed her, much less gracefully. She was already at the bathroom's door by the time my boots touched the ground, and I stepped cautiously over the marble flooring, following after her.

We emerged into a dark hallway and stopped, listening again. After a whole minute of hearing nothing, Jackie removed the flashlight from the belt and switched it on at a dim setting, just enough to show our way. Then we began moving again.

The photographs on the wall caught my attention as we crept closer to the kids. The first was of a young, brown-haired couple on their wedding day, a tall man and a woman just over half his size. The next photo seemed to have been taken perhaps ten years later and was of both of them standing in front of a Christmas tree. And then a decade later, and a decade later, until the last one, at the end of the hallway, showed an elderly couple with pure white hair, clad in ski suits—the man looking about as slim as he had in the first photo, while the woman had gained at least twenty pounds.

Yup. I was pretty sure this house belonged to Gramps and Grammy after all.

I gripped Jackie's arm and pointed at the frame, wanting to

make sure she had noticed that final photograph. She gave me a knowing nod, and then we continued through the house at a slightly more confident pace than before.

Now, I wasn't one to take advantage of the elderly, but in this case, I felt our cause was justified.

We crossed a wide entrance hall, then entered another corridor, and after another half minute, we were stopping outside a pair of pale blue doors.

"Think these are the ones," Jackie said, in a voice barely louder than a breath.

I nodded, swallowing, and then we each picked a door and pressed our ears to the cracks. I couldn't hear anything, but then again, infants could be quiet when they slept. Pulling away from the door, I caught Jackie's eye, and she nodded, indicating that she was ready to move in, too. I returned my focus to the door and gripped the handle ever so gently, and was glad to find it well oiled. It glided downward beautifully, and then I was stepping into a generously sized square bedroom filled with colorful furniture... and a cot at the far end of the room.

Holding my breath, I approached swiftly while doing my best not to step on any of the toys that were scattered across the floor. I was just reaching for the tissue in my belt (smeared with the chemical we used to sedate infants temporarily, to keep the experience from being too traumatic, as well as prevent them from making a noise), when I peered over the edge of the cot and realized that it was empty.

I blinked, wondering for a second if my eyes were deceiving me. But they weren't. There was no kid there.

I backed away and looked around the rest of the room more carefully, wondering if perhaps the child had managed to climb out of the cot and had fallen asleep somewhere on the floor. But there was no kid to be found anywhere.

I cursed beneath my breath, then whirled as I heard the door open behind me.

Jackie stood there, the frustration in her eyes mirroring mine. She moved into the room, pushing the door softly closed behind her, and hurried up to me. "No kid in here, either?" she whispered.

I shook my head.

"Dammit," she breathed. "We gotta call Nelson." She pulled out her comm device, and we both switched to Nelson's channel. Jackie spoke softly into the microphone. "Hey, there are no kids in the children's bedrooms."

There was a pause, and then Nelson's voice came through our earphones. "They're definitely at the house. They must just be in different rooms."

I exhaled slowly. This wasn't good. Nelson's tracking technology was precise to the point of determining which house a child was located in, but not so granular as to specify exactly which room they were being held in—especially when there were multiple floors. I'd been part of a scenario like this once before, when the target hadn't been in any of the rooms we'd expected them to be in, and it had been the first and only mission I'd been on that we'd had to abort. It was just so risky to start venturing deeper into big houses like these, blindly opening doors to rooms where adults could be sleeping, or worse, awake with insomnia.

Jackie and I stared at each other, and I bit my lip. I knew the risks, and yet I was still reluctant to immediately call it quits on this one. Especially when we were both almost positive that this house belonged to two elderly people. There was only one car parked outside on the driveway, too, which was a good indication that they didn't have visitors other than the kids.

Aborting a mission was a terrible blow for the birthparents; it made the chances of us being successful on a follow-up mission much less, because after one break-in, a family went on high alert—brought in extra security, like dogs—and it wasn't as easy to pull off a burglary again. We had to leave a gap of at least six months, to be safe, and let things die down a bit. And I knew better than anyone that that was a long time to wait for your child, even if the second attempt was successful, especially when this family was already geared up and ready to flee to the border this very night. As soon as we delivered their children.

"What do you suggest, Nell?" Jackie whispered, her voice tight. I sensed from the expression in her eyes that she was experiencing the same reluctance as me.

Nelson swore softly on the other end of the line. "Honestly, guys, this one's up to you," she replied after a beat. "You gotta go with your gut. I'm not gonna tell you to keep going, but I'm also not gonna tell you to retreat. Ant and Abe haven't reported movement other than yours yet, and I've also got my eye on their screen, so I guess you could keep going as long as everything's still. But again, do what you feel is right. It's your asses on the line."

Jackie sighed. "Okay," she muttered, then cut the line and turned back to me. "What do you think?"

I swallowed. "I guess we could keep going for now. We both have a pretty good idea of where the other bedrooms are from the map, so we could see if the kids are in any of those. Worse comes to worst, we open a wrong door and make a run for it."

Jackie nodded stiffly. "Okay," she whispered. "Let's keep moving, then."

We headed up to the middle floor and took a left down the hallway, stopping at the first doorway we came across. It was ajar, and a quick sweep inside told us that it was another bedroom, but empty. Retreating, we split up to walk on either side of the hallway to make our search faster, and carefully began opening each door, making as little sound as possible, before shining our lights inside on a dim setting.

By the time we reached the end of that side of the hallway, we still hadn't come across any kids—or anyone at all, for that matter.

We were just moving back the way we'd come to search the other end of the hallway when Ant's voice suddenly crackled in our ears. "Something's moving near the staircase. It's... It's heading toward you."

I looked to Jackie, and she immediately grabbed me by the shoulder and hauled me into the nearest room, a bathroom we'd already verified as empty.

We pressed ourselves up against the wall, Jackie resting a hand on the gun in her holster, and waited for several tense seconds, while my heart did somersaults beneath my ribcage. Then Jackie created the smallest crack in the door and peered through it.

She scoffed quietly. "Quite the intruder," she whispered, then opened the door fully and reentered the hallway.

I stepped out tentatively after her to lay eyes on a large, ginger tabby cat.

It was gazing at us cautiously, its wide, nocturnal eyes glistening in the shafts of moonlight that spilled through a nearby window.

"D'you think we should give him the tissue?" I whispered, deciding it looked like a male. I didn't want to needlessly sedate a cat, but at the same time, cats could be noisy, and putting him to sleep for an hour wouldn't do him any harm.

We stayed still for a long moment, watching the animal, while he continued to watch us. Then Jackie moved slowly toward him, and he ran off. She rolled her eyes. "Let's just keep moving."

"It was just a cat, guys," I murmured into my comm.

"Okay, I see it moving away now," Ant muttered back. "Sorry, it's easy to miscalculate size on this screen." And then the line went quiet again.

We continued exploring the other end of the hallway, but only found more empty rooms and nothing of interest—until I arrived at the door at the very end and found that I couldn't open it. I pressed my ear to the crack, but was met with only silence, giving me no clue as to what could be inside.

I beckoned Jackie over as she finished checking her last door. "Locked," I whispered, pointing to the handle.

We exchanged a look, and she nodded, as if reading my mind.

I retrieved the pick from my belt and began working quietly on the lock. We'd come this far, and it didn't make sense for us to leave any stone unturned. Even though I couldn't think of a reason why they would lock children inside a room at night.

It took a couple of minutes, but the device finally cracked the lock with a soft, satisfying click. I pushed the door open by less than an inch, listening. When I could still hear nothing, I pushed it wide enough to enter and shone my light inside, to discover that it was definitely not a bedroom.

It was a long, rectangular room, the walls of which were packed with shelf upon shelf of expensive-looking weapons, ranging from handguns to heavy-duty machine guns.

"Whoa," Jackie whispered, stepping in behind me. "Seems there's more to Gramps and Grammy than we thought."

"Yeah," I murmured, finding the sight unnerving, to say the least.

Maybe the guy was ex-military, or ex-security, or something. Which wasn't really the vibe I had gotten from those placid photographs down in the hallway. Then again, everyone presented themselves differently in photographs. Still, as I gazed around at the eye-watering array of lethal weapons, I felt a small tug from my intuition to turn back, for the first time. Anyone who owned this many guns wouldn't take a break-in lying down, if they caught us.

But I couldn't let it get to me. I reminded myself that the security on the house had hardly been great so far; we'd broken in easily enough, and there were no killer dogs around. We just needed to find the kids and get out ASAP.

Then, when we stepped back out of the room into the corridor, Ant's tense voice suddenly burst into my eardrums, midsentence. "—your way! Guys? Where are you?! Something else is moving toward you!"

I had no time to unpack his words, as Jackie had already yanked me back into the weapons room and pulled at the door to conceal us. We both pressed our cheeks to the wall again as we peered through the small crack she had left, my head beneath Jackie's, our breathing sharp and uneven. But no footsteps followed Ant's alert. Just the same fat, ginger cat as before, returning to the hallway and ambling down it toward us. He stopped right outside our room, his eyes fixed on the door crack.

"Oh, for the love of…" I grumbled.

We both shifted back into the corridor and stepped around the feline.

"Guys, it's the same freaking cat!" Jackie hissed into her comm.

"Sorry!" Ant shot back. "It's easy to lose track of things on the X-ray, and better safe than sorry, right?"

"Yeah," Jackie mumbled, running a hand over her masked face.

As we took a moment to let our heartrates recover from the false alarm, Ant added, "Also, what happened to you guys? You disappeared for a minute."

"Huh?" she whispered. "What do you mean, disappeared?"

"I mean disappeared. Whatever room you just stepped into, it's not showing up for us."

"Oh," she said softly, shooting me a look that showed she was as confused by his statement as I was.

We peered back into the weapons room and ran another sweep over it with our flashlights. It occurred to me that perhaps the whole thing was some kind of vault. A safe room. Not terribly safe from burglars—well, at least not burglars with a lockpick as advanced as ours—but maybe thieves weren't the main reason they hid all this stuff in here.

Sometimes the government ran aerial scans of residential areas to check on people's weapons inventories, particularly in cities where crime was higher. They had special tech that could pick up on guns and such, similar to how we were able to retrieve information about a house's structure from the air. If our X-ray wasn't able to penetrate this room, and our comms didn't seem to work when inside it, then that meant it had to be insulated with some kind of heavy material our rays couldn't pass through. Maybe lead.

So perhaps the couple didn't want the government knowing about their huge collection, though I didn't know why they'd possess it in the first place.

I pushed my speculations aside. Whatever the case, we needed to keep moving.

And we also needed to stop having stupid distractions. Each minute we stayed in this house was a minute longer for one of the residents to wake up and cause us trouble. My eyes fell on the chubby cat, who was still sitting by the entrance to the weapons room, and was looking utterly unapologetic for the fright he'd just given us. I could tell he'd become more confident since our first encounter, too, as he hadn't run away this time when we passed right by him.

I made a spur-of-the-moment decision and bent down to pick him up, stifling his subsequent meow by quickly plopping him down in the weapons room and shutting him inside.

"Sorry, Chubbo," I murmured. It was either that or drugging him, and I figured this was the friendlier (and quicker) option. If I could, I'd let him out on the way down.

Jackie gave me a look, and I shrugged. "He was just gonna keep setting off false alarms."

The corners of her eyes lifted slightly in what I guessed was an amused expression. "Okay," she muttered. "Let's keep moving."

Having finished on the middle floor, we headed up the staircase to the final floor, where, close to the top of the stairs, we finally found a room with loud snoring emanating from it. It sounded like two sets of adult snoring, in fact, so we figured we could write that room off as the couple's bedroom and search the rest of the rooms for the kids—hoping that they were not in the same room as the grandparents. As that would... not be fun.

Thankfully, we found a room with lighter snoring carrying through the door cracks, too, just a little farther along and across from the grandparents' room. I could only assume that the infants were up here because the adults had wanted them closer, which I honestly didn't blame them for. Having children's rooms on the ground floor of a three-story house had seemed like weird planning to me, from the start.

Stepping inside, we found the two children with curly red hair lying in the center of a wide, side-netted double bed. Little Becky and Jason, both looking blissfully asleep.

My heart clenched at the sight of the little boy in particular. He had to be very close to Hope's age, and I found myself approaching his side of the bed instinctively, while Jackie moved around the other side to be closer to the slightly older girl.

Not wanting to waste another second, we immediately reached for the tissues in our belts and leaned over to press them gently against the noses of the children. They were already sleeping, so there was no noticeable difference; it would just mean that they would stay asleep now, when we picked them up. The sedative acted within three minutes, so we stood there, waiting and watching the time. We couldn't afford to pick them up prematurely and have them make a noise now that we were up here, so close to the—

A blaring siren pierced the quiet. It carried up from somewhere beneath us, but was so loud and screeching, it felt as if it could've been emanating from within the room itself.

Panic shot through me as the sound rattled my brain and eardrums, and I looked at Jackie, finding her eyes wide with alarm.

"Go, go, go," she hissed, and we scrambled to pick up the kids, three minutes' waiting be damned. There wasn't even time to consider what the hell the siren was, considering the fact that we'd taken out all the alarms.

We raced with the children to the door and were on the verge of crossing the threshold when the door to the grandparents' room swung open, several feet ahead of us in the hallway, forcing us back inside.

Feeling the boy stir in my arms, I pressed the tissue back over his nose, while Jackie did the same to the girl. Holding our breath, we gazed through the crack we'd left in the door and watched as a tall, broad-chested, elderly man in dark green pajamas thundered out, a long shotgun clutched between his hands.

"What the devil!" he growled, his voice shockingly menacing for a seventy-something-year-old. "Someone's broken into the armory!"

The armory.

Realization dawned on me, and my stomach dropped. The weapons room. It could've been fitted with alarms that had been protected from our pulse by the room's fortified walls. And Chubbo…

"Seems your friend just caused us another round of trouble," Jackie hissed into my ear.

I grimaced. Never mind an army of cats; we couldn't even deal with one. Or rather, *I* couldn't.

Guilt surged through me, as it had been me who had shut the animal in there. Though it probably wasn't fair to beat myself up about it. We had already entered the room, and no alarms had gone off, so I hadn't exactly had reason to expect that locking a cat in there would set one off. Perhaps he had actually climbed up onto the shelves and touched the weapons, or something similarly obtrusive.

Damn, kitty.

"Guys! There's a bunch of movement right near you, and I don't think it's the cat this—"

I pulled the earphones from my ears with a wince. The alarm was still so loud, and Ant's frantic voice layered on top of it was not something I could handle right now. Jackie did the same, and though I wanted to reply via comm to assure him that we knew the location of the hostiles now, there was no time.

"Lights are out, too!" the old man growled, hitting the switch in the corridor. He stormed toward the staircase, and Jackie and I both knew this was our moment. Our tiny window of opportunity.

We launched out into the corridor the second his frame disappeared from view and raced after him toward the staircase. We stopped a few feet before reaching it, our backs against the wall, and peered out to check his progress on the stairs. He was halfway down this flight, and we waited for him to reach the bottom and turn right toward the armory before dashing down ourselves.

We had to slip past the second landing and make it to the ground floor during his transit to the room—before he discovered it was empty.

Our legs pumping, we had just made it halfway down the stairs when a guttural roar erupted from above us.

"HARRY! I got 'em here!"

I turned to see his stout wife standing at the top of the staircase, her lips pinched, her eyes raging beneath her silk nightcap... and clutching another large gun in her hands. Judging by the huge assortment of weapons they had in the armory, I guessed I shouldn't have been surprised if they slept with guns beneath their mattresses.

"Don't move another inch!" she yelled, pointing the barrel in our direction.

Jackie and I froze, clutching the limp children closer to our chests as Harry reappeared at the bottom of the staircase.

We were trapped.

5

"Put the children down," Harry ordered.

My arms instinctively tightened around the boy, and I stole a glance at Jackie, to see her eyes flitting between the couple, as if calculating our options. Holding the children was likely the only thing stopping them from shooting us right now, so putting them down would be a bad idea.

I held my breath, waiting for Jackie to make the first move rather than trying to make one myself, as she had way more experience in kidnappings gone wrong than me. Something told me, however, from the harshness of her breathing, that she'd probably never found herself stuck quite like this before.

"I said put them down," Harry growled. "I won't ask a third time."

The creaking of a step drew our attention to the top of the stairwell. The woman was descending, slowly but surely, toward us, and I guessed she was trying to get closer so she could get a better shot.

We couldn't let that happen.

As if of the same mind, both Jackie and I shifted the kids to a single arm and slid our free hands to our holsters. We drew our guns swiftly, trusting that neither hostile was going to risk shooting quite yet.

The motion made the woman pause in her descent, though she'd managed to get unnervingly close. I realized with a spike of panic that if she were a risk-taker, she could very well take a shot at us from there.

"We'll lower our guns if you lower yours," Jackie said in a distinctive, slurred accent that wasn't her own, doing a remarkable job of keeping her tone calm.

"Lower your guns *and* the children," the woman shot back.

"Only if you lower *your* guns," Jackie retorted.

I realized then what her plan was. Chances were, they hadn't noticed the other items strapped to the belts around our waists, since the children's bodies were obscuring them. Which gave us an advantage, because we had more weapons than just the guns.

We all remained standing there, frozen, for several moments, waiting for either party to budge, and then, as if a switch had been flicked, we all began to bend simultaneously. I kept my eyes on the woman, while Jackie kept hers on the man. The four of us set our guns down on the floor, and then slowly, Jackie and I made to put down the children.

The second she laid the little girl on the floor, however, Jackie launched upward. Her body became a blur of motion as she back-flipped over me and the children and landed on another stair several feet above us. The next thing I knew, her foot was kicking the gun away from the woman. It fell through the cracks of the banister and landed on the ground floor with a loud clatter and a bang. The man instantly moved to pick up his gun again, but before he could fire it, Jackie had reached for the smoke bomb in her belt and released it, dowsing the entire stairwell with dense plumes of dark fog.

I could tell, from her methods, that even now she was doing her best not to hurt the elders, but rather disable them, and I respected her for that.

Coughing in the sudden deluge of smoke, I scrambled to gather the children, even as Jackie came rushing to me, gripping at my shoulder.

"Go, go, go!" she hissed, before racing past me, down the stairs and toward the man.

He was armed again, but there was no way he was going to start firing blindly in this smog—not with the children and his wife up here.

I picked up both kids, holding each one against a hip and supporting them as best as I could with my shaking hands. I moved to follow on Jackie's heels, though I could hardly see a foot in front of me, and couldn't go as fast as I would've liked for fear of tripping and injuring the children.

Jackie's vague outline in front of me disappeared entirely when she lunged forward, and suddenly I heard a crash and a grunt somewhere to the right of the stairs, a little farther up the hallway. Then came a piercing gunshot. Fear pricked my spine, but I forced myself to press onward, knowing that more than one life rested in my hands. I rushed past the landing and then down the final staircase, praying that Jackie was okay.

My heart nearly leapt out of my throat when I bumped into the tall, black-clad figure who emerged suddenly in front of me from the entrance hall.

"Robin!" one of the twins gasped.

The second twin appeared behind him a second later. "What's going on?" he asked.

"Jackie's upstairs," I breathed. "But be careful. There's a guy up there with a gun."

Though I was praying that she had disarmed him by now.

They gave me stiff nods, their breathing heavy, and then ran up the stairs into the dense fog, their guns held out in front of them. I raced across the entrance hall as fast as I could, then back along the hallway lined with photographs, and into the bathroom with the broken window. I grabbed a towel from a rack and set it down on the cold, hard marble floor, then lowered the little girl onto it, as I could only take one child through at a time.

The boy's head rested against my shoulder as I held him with one arm and used the other to maneuver myself over the windowsill. It took me longer than I was comfortable with, as my body was shaking from nerves, and I was terrified of dropping the child onto the hard cement path that ran directly outside the window or grazing him against the rough-cut glass.

When I finally touched down on the other side, I left the boy on a patch of grass and raced back for the girl. I was halfway through the window when the bathroom door sprang open, and Jackie and the twins came bursting in at a sprint. I cried out in warning that the little girl was lying directly beneath the windowsill, as it was dark and they were moving so fast that I was terrified they might not notice her. They stopped just short of reaching her, and Jackie dipped down to scoop her up and hand her to me.

As the young woman's face moved beneath a shaft of moonlight, I realized that her mask had been ripped, laying half of her face bare for all to see—and that her skin bore a bleeding cut across the cheekbone.

"Hurry!" she urged, before I could think to ask.

I lifted the girl through to the yard and stepped back as the other three bundled out.

"We gotta run!" one of the twins whispered, and I handed him the girl and rushed to pick up the boy. I could hear the angry bellows of the couple drifting through the broken window, followed by the distant sound of footsteps.

We skirted around the house and raced across the backyard to where our zip lines awaited. My chest ached from how hard I was breathing as I attached myself to my line, and then, once everyone was secured, Jackie gave the order through her comm. "Pull us up!"

The zip lines jerked instantly, and I clung both to the line and the little boy for dear life as the automatic winch reeled us up. We shot through the air at a frightening speed, exacerbated by the fact that Marco had already started raising the aircraft, and soon the large house was small beneath us, the trashcans in the street no bigger than ants.

And then we disappeared into a dark patch of clouds, gone in the blink of an eye. Like the thieves in the night that we were.

6

Once the winch had finished pulling us up, we all stumbled into the airship, wheezing and gasping as we collapsed into seats. One of the twins hit the red button by the hatch and it glided closed, banishing the harsh wind and sealing us safely inside.

Tearing off my mask, I leaned backward, my whole body still thrumming with adrenaline, and took a moment to just breathe. I kept the little boy close to my chest, holding him tight, not quite believing that our sedative had been good enough to have kept the kids under through all of *that*. It had to have been the choppiest ride I'd given a child so far, with so much stopping and starting, picking up and setting down—not to mention all that noise: the deafening siren, the gunshot, and the yelling, as well as the smoke bomb.

I sighed, just feeling grateful that we'd all made it out alive.

I chugged down the bottle of water that Abe handed me, then closed my eyes, needing silence and darkness to settle my mind and nerves, while I rested my cheek against the soft head of the infant. My limbs felt heavy, as did my eyelids, and I drifted into a blissful state of nothingness, allowing myself to imagine for just a few moments that it was my own child that I held in my arms.

My chest ached at the thought, and I had to remind myself that one day, it would be. Just as soon as Nelson cracked those records.

At least, for tonight, we had good news for one set of parents.

It was a while before anyone spoke, as Marco continued to carry us away through the night. Then Abe, who was holding the girl on his lap, eventually broke the quiet. "Well, I take back my disingenuous comment."

I glanced at Jackie, expecting her to retort, only to find her staring off into the distance, tension written all over her face. I was reminded then of what had happened to her.

"Hey," I said softly. "You okay? What went on back there?"

She turned reluctantly to look at me, revealing the side of her face that bore the cut, which she had patched up with a Band-Aid —though I could see a dark line of blood seeping through. The wound had to be pretty deep.

She grimaced. "I disarmed him of the gun, but the crazy coot had stowed a pocket knife in his pajama pants." She paused, swallowing. "He saw my face."

"You mean half of it," I said, wanting to bring her a thread of comfort. I'd be just as worried if I were in her shoes. The thought of someone out there having even a vague idea of what you looked like was nerve-wracking, when you were part of a group whose mission statement was basically treason. And also when it was someone you'd just burgled.

"Even so."

"Do you really think he got a proper look, though?" I asked, frowning. "Through all that dimness and smoke?"

She sighed, but still looked annoyed. "I guess you're right. It's probably unlikely he got a good look. But it's still a risk. And it could've been prevented."

"Hey," I said, unable to stop myself from reaching out and squeezing her knee. "You did all that you could back there, okay?"

She gave me a dark look. "No. I was being polite. I could have just knocked them out."

"Yeah, but that wouldn't have been a very nice thing to do to Gramps and Grammy, would it?" Ant cut in.

"Plus, you can't just go knocking elderly people out without risking their lives. They're fragile. Even the badass ones," I added.

She sighed, giving another grimace. "I guess," she muttered.

Nothing could change the fact that she'd exposed herself to risk, but I hoped what I'd said was true. There had been so much going on back there that I had to believe he couldn't have seen her properly. And that everything would be fine.

We passed the rest of the journey in silence, giving in to exhaustion and dozing off. Except for Jackie, who got on the comm with Nelson and filled her in on the details of what had happened. I was so tired, I didn't absorb much of it—just enough to make out that the girl was still tense.

Our arrival felt like it came too quickly, just as I was ready to drop off into a deep sleep. My mind and body were spent, but the thought of what awaited us on the ground was enough to perk me up. The reunion was always my favorite part of a mission.

The kids were still deep under as the aircraft touched down in a small parking area around the back of the Foxtrot. Marco navigated it into a concealed garage, which belonged to the landlady, and which she let us use whenever we needed to. Then he opened the doors, and Abe and I slipped our masks back on, before climbing out first with the children. Already waiting for us in the opposite corner of the parking lot were a redheaded man and woman with large black suitcases sitting next to them and over-coats thrown over their clothes.

A masked Nelson and Julia were standing on either side of them, but in that moment, I could barely spare a glance for my colleagues. My eyes were fixed on the parents' faces, the way they lit up like sunshine, and then the way they burst into tears as they ran toward us to claim their children.

They had no words at first, only deep, racking sobs as they clutched their children to their chests and sank to the floor, holding them as if their lives depended on it.

We gave them a moment, and my heart both expanded and contracted, from the happiness and from the ache of longing. A tear slipped from my own eye at the sheer joy radiating off of them.

Finally they stood, their eyes bloodshot but glistening with relief. "Thank you," the woman choked out, pulling me into a hug with her free hand. She hugged the rest of my team as they bundled out of the aircraft—Jackie was wearing a makeshift mask she'd fashioned with her scarf—and the man did the same.

And then it was time for them to leave. Once Nelson had made arrangements, there was a limited window of time in which her contact could help with the smuggling. Which meant this family had to get going, as it wasn't a quick flight. Marco had a long night ahead of him still, though the earlier part of the mission hadn't been nearly as stressful for him as it had been for us. I was sure he'd remembered to pack extra instant coffee in the cockpit. Knowing him, he had a jumbo pack of sugar cookies, too.

He gestured for the couple to get into the ship with the kids, and we watched them climb aboard and back out of view into the interior, saying thank you again right before they disappeared.

Then Nelson and Julia approached us. "Good job, guys. I'm proud of you for sticking with it," Nelson said, patting us each on the shoulder. Her tone was encouraging, though there was a flicker of worry in her eyes—over Jackie's torn mask, no doubt. I sensed that she wasn't going to bring it up now, though, with all of us looking so exhausted.

"Thanks, Mom," Ant replied with a yawn.

His yawn infected the rest of us, and I closed my eyes as one overtook me. I wasn't looking forward to the motorcycle journey home, but I'd manage it. Tomorrow (or today, rather) was a Sunday, so at least I didn't have to get up for work in a few hours.

"There's just one thing before I leave you," Nelson added, glancing between us.

I raised an eyebrow. "What is it?"

She wet her lower lip, casting a fleeting glance toward the waiting aircraft and then back to the four of us again. "I was contacted by an OH admin this evening. He… or she… said they want a meeting with us."

We all frowned at her, confused. I'd never heard of an admin reaching out to members of Operation Hood's portal like that. The team of admins were renowned for being cagey and aloof, and for good reason, given that they ran a criminal network. Besides, they were just facilitators, stepping in to moderate on forums occasionally, but never getting directly involved with individual members or groups that operated on there.

"What about?" Jackie asked.

Nelson shrugged. "They didn't give me any details. Just said they wanted to meet in person. At Mullen Bridge, tomorrow at 8:00 p.m. I guess they must have analyzed my history on the platform and the reviews I've received from our clients, and figured they could trust me. Enough to meet at a random location, anyway. Julia and I are planning to go to see what's up. Any of you want to come with us?"

"I'll come," I replied immediately. My curiosity was piqued, to say the least, and if this person was an admin, I figured they were unlikely to pose a threat to us. Granted, I guessed none of us actually knew who ran Operation Hood. For all we knew, it could be some grand setup by the government to catch criminals like us. But given that the network had been operating for over six years and was only growing in the number of people that joined, plus the illegal conversations and operations that took place there on a daily basis, I doubted it. There could very well be moles signed up for OH, but I just couldn't see the government facilitating a platform like that for so long.

"Which admin is this?" Abe asked.

"Mr. X," Nelson replied with a smirk. "His profile name is the same as his handle. I guess it could be a girl, though. I've seen their comments around on the forums before, but never had any direct engagement with them."

"I'll come too," Jackie said after a beat, the traces of sullenness from the situation with her ripped mask giving way to intrigue.

We all looked to the twins, who gave us an apologetic look. "Ah, sorry." Ant sighed. "We got... family commitments tomorrow night."

"Girlfriend commitments," Abe coughed, and Jackie scoffed.

"In your dreams," she muttered.

Before either twin could retort, Nelson clapped Jackie and me on the back. "Okay. It's just you two, me, and Julia then," she said. "And Marco, if he wants to come, but I'm pretty sure he'll want a day off tomorrow, too. We'll report back to the boys on how it goes. And let's touch base in the morning to discuss travel arrangements to the bridge, yeah?"

Jackie and I nodded.

"All right." She headed with Julia up the aircraft's ramp but paused when she reached the top. "Sleep well," she said with a smile.

"Good luck," we replied, and she turned and disappeared inside.

The four of us ambled away from the private parking area, back toward the front of the pub, where I'd left my motorcycle. We wished each other a good night's sleep, too, once we reached the pub's entrance, and then headed our separate ways.

I, for one, knew I would sleep well tonight.

1

Nelson got in touch with me at noon the next day. She suggested that we all meet at her office at 6:00 p.m., and that we travel via public transport to the bridge. It was located right in the heart of Samsfield, a town that was notorious for getting crowded on a Sunday evening, and where road traffic could be nightmarish.

So, after a day of mostly lounging around in my pajamas and resting, I headed off on my motorcycle.

My first destination was Nelson's office, which was located in a small industrial town that took me about an hour to reach from my cabin. Her space sat at the top of a grocery corner store on a quiet, inconspicuous, working-class street on the outskirts of the town. I parked in a public parking lot about half a mile from it and walked the rest of the block. Nelson was apparently friends, or at least close acquaintances, with the grocery store owner, who let her use the room upstairs as her temporary workspace. I didn't know where she actually lived, but this was where she kept her equipment safe at least some of the time. I had visited twice before, when I rode along with her to a mission.

Reaching her door at the top of the narrow stairwell that wound up the exterior of the building, I performed our signature knock: three quick ones, followed by a pause, and then another three quick ones. She answered it thirty seconds later, wearing a pair of baggy gray jogging pants and a loose yellow t-shirt. Her curly hair was swept up into a messy bun, and her glasses rested slightly askew on her nose, as she allowed me into the small, crowded room.

I could tell she'd spent the night here; her black backpack was resting on the narrow sofa, which was also strewn with a set of pajamas and a toiletry bag. The shadows under her eyes told me she hadn't gotten much sleep, though her eyes themselves were shiny. One sweep of the collection of cups on her work desk told me she was buzzed on coffee.

"Sorry I'm a bit early," I said, realizing I was the first one here.

"No problem," she said, pulling up a chair for me.

"Everything go okay last night?" I asked.

She nodded cryptically, giving me a wry smile. "Yup. One less family waking up in America this morning."

"Good," I murmured. I would have loved to know the details about how they actually pulled the smuggling off, but I knew she would've shared the information by now if she wanted to. Instead, it was a task she chose to handle personally, perhaps even at the request of whoever her contact was.

She returned to her seat in front of the long desk, where a large, dimmed monitor was set up, a myriad of wires attached to half a dozen hard drives sticking out the back of it. I seated myself at a respectful angle, from which I couldn't see the screen directly. I didn't know what she had been in the middle of doing—it might have been personal or private—so instead of looking at the monitor, I watched her fingers dance over the keyboard as she continued to work.

I then blew out softly, my eyes doing another brief sweep of the small room. Now that we had a moment alone, there was something I needed to talk about. It had been over a month since I'd asked her about her progress on cracking the archives (again, out of respect, because I knew she was juggling a lot of things), but I really wanted an update now. I felt a decent amount of time had passed since I last pressed her about it.

I waited for her to take a pause in typing before shifting in my seat and asking, "Any progress at all on the archives?"

She gave me a canny look, adjusting her spectacles, and then leaned back in her chair. Reaching for her coffee, she took a sip, then replied, "Maybe."

I blinked, hardly daring to believe my ears. Every time I'd asked her so far, the answer had been a clear no.

"Meaning?" I asked, suddenly leaning forward, anxious.

She gave me a wan smile. "Well, I don't want to raise your spirits too high yet, but I think I might, and I repeat *might*, have finally stumbled onto a potentially exploitable loophole. It's still kind of a long shot and will probably take at least another month of trial and error before I can know for sure, but yeah. I do think I've reached a point of progress that I've been waiting months for. Possibly even years."

"Oh, that's amazing," I said, unable to stop the relieved smile from breaking out onto my face, even though I knew nothing was certain yet. It was just the most optimistic I'd seen Nelson about this since I'd first met her, and I couldn't tamp down the surge of hopefulness, in spite of her realism.

"Also," she added, then paused, glancing at the hard drives scattered around her desk. She set her cup down and rose to her feet, picking up three orange-colored ones that were strapped together with a black cord. "Now that you're here and we're on the subject, there is something I've been meaning to talk to you about."

I watched her tentatively as she unplugged the hard drives from her mainframe, then sat down again, placing them on her lap and folding her hands over them.

"These three hard drives are identical backups of basically all the work I've done on the archives project since I first started to access them, three years ago. I've kept a record of every trial and error, every thought and finding. Basically every step that has gotten me to this point. I'm going to tell Jackie and the twins about them, too, but I wanted you to know about them, just in case something... Well, you know, something happens to me."

The very thought made my heart palpitate, and I wanted to dismiss the idea outright, even though I knew that would be fool-ish. With the type of life that we led, none of our futures were certain. Still, I didn't know where we'd be without Nelson, not to mention her contacts.

"Jackie's lost younger siblings, and the twins have lost... Actually, I don't think they ever told me who they're looking for, but I'm pretty sure they all have a vested interest in the archives," she went on. "Of course, even with the information on the hard drives, there's nothing a non-hacker would understand. But at least you could stand a chance of finding a replacement for me, someone who could decipher my notes and build on my work. Now that I feel I might be close, it's really time I let you know about them. I've already told Julia."

"Okay," I murmured, nodding and watching her closely as she stood up again, then moved to one corner of the room.

"Come here," she said, bending down to a bare patch of floorboards.

I walked up and leaned over her crouching form to see her pulling a floorboard loose and revealing a small metal safe with a combination lock.

"Cliché, I know." She smirked. "But it's the best hiding place I've got right now." She pulled the safe out and set it on the floor next to her. "The combination's 8936, and it's the same code to access the drives, to make things simple."

She input the numbers and the safe clicked open, revealing an empty space in which she placed the drives. Then she closed the safe and put it underneath the floorboard again.

"It's where the drives live most of the time," she explained, straightening.

"Okay, thanks," I breathed, focusing on committing the numbers to memory. They were way too important to forget.

A knock at the door drew our attention, then. Nelson moved toward it after hearing the signature six raps, and opened it, revealing Jackie and Julia standing in the doorway. The auburn-haired girl looked just as tired as Nelson, like she'd stayed up all night, while Jackie looked a little more spritely, probably having taken the morning off to rest, like me. She had a fresh Band-Aid over her cut, but it seemed to have gotten quite a bit better already, as it was a thin bandage compared to the one last night.

"Hey, you arrived at the same time," Nelson remarked.

Jackie nodded. "Yup."

"That means we can leave now," Nelson said. She moved back into her room to assemble her phone, keys, and backpack. "I'll show Jackie another time," she mumbled in an undertone, as if more to herself than to me, and then we headed for the door and stepped outside.

It was a good thing we left when we did, because there were

several delays in our train connections. We arrived at Samsfield town station with barely fifteen minutes to leg it to the bridge. But we made it on time, even through the rain that had started to pour.

As we approached the long bridge that ran over the wide, swelling river, we saw that it was thankfully devoid of pedestrians, due to the foul weather, and took the opportunity to slip on our masks, pulling our coat hoods low over our foreheads to cast shadow and prevent ourselves from looking too sketchy to oncoming vehicles. It was important to have the masks for this meeting, to be safe.

The cars whizzed past us, wheels cutting through puddles and splashing us every few moments, and by the time we reached the center of the bridge, one thing was clear: we were still the only pedestrians around. We paused and leaned against the chunky metal railing, waiting and looking in either direction.

And in that moment, the fear returned to my mind that maybe, just maybe, this was some kind of trap after all—even though I knew it wouldn't make much sense—and my throat tightened. Then, a couple minutes later, Nelson's phone rang. She fished it out of her pocket, and I glanced at the screen to see an unidentified caller notification flash up.

"Yes?" Nelson said, answering it. "We're on the bridge. Where are you?"

She put the phone on loudspeaker for the rest of us to listen in, though it was difficult with the cars roaring past us.

"Take the ladder down," came a deep male voice.

We all frowned, gazing around the bridge for something we'd missed—and then Julia spotted it: a rusty service ladder on the opposite sidewalk.

"Okay, heading there—"

The caller hung up before Nelson could finish.

We quickly looked left and right, waiting for an opening in the traffic, then hurried across the road and lowered ourselves down the ladder as inconspicuously as possible. Jackie went first, then me, Julia, and Nelson. We touched down on a wide catwalk that ran the width of the bridge, its base speckled with tiny metal holes that did nothing to make me feel better about the height. I could see the water roiling and gushing beneath us, even as the rain continued to pound down on either side of the bridge.

"Well, this is discreet, I guess," Julia murmured, her gray eyes wide and darting about behind her mask.

Jackie slipped a hand beneath her coat, resting it on her gun, and I did the same, though neither of us drew yet. The place *seemed* empty...

Until something caught my attention near a column at the other end of the catwalk. A shadow moved out from behind the thick post, and we all stalled and stared as the silhouette of a large male came into view. Very large. He had to be at least six foot four, and he was bulky, too. An unzipped army-green overcoat hung over his broad chest and shoulders, which looked like they held plenty of muscle tone.

He definitely didn't belong to the computer geek stereotype that I had imagined for all admins.

As he closed the distance between us, I saw, to my surprise, that he *wasn't* wearing a mask, giving us instead a full view of his face as he stopped a few feet away from us, under one of the white lights that were fixed at intervals beneath the bridge.

My first thought was that he was younger than I'd assumed— maybe just a year or two older than me—and my second was that he looked like he belonged in the wild. His features were rugged, his irises the color of raw honey, fading into burnt umber at the edges, and deep-set beneath a strong brow, while his jaw was angular and shadowed with dark stubble. His lips were a little uneven, tugged upward slightly on one side, and there were two fine indentations in the skin at the edges of his mouth. His midnight-brown hair looked windswept in the damp weather and was long enough for tousled locks to graze his eyes and jawline.

I also realized then that he looked about as suited to the black shirt and pants he was wearing as a grizzly bear. Even beneath his coat, they looked too small for his broad, muscular frame. The seams strained around his chest, and the pants stopped just a touch too high above his shoes.

I frowned, altogether bemused by his appearance. My colleagues appeared to be confused, too, since they were momentarily speechless as they looked him over.

But hey, maybe we were all just being narrow-minded. Who said geeks couldn't work out?

"So you're Mr. X?" Nelson said finally.

He nodded. "Nelson, I take it," he replied, his voice baritone, as he reached out a large hand.

Nelson nodded and took it in a firm shake. "I'm here with Juicy1, JK007, and RobinHood21," she said, gesturing to each of us in turn. "All of whom are linked to my online circle."

His eyes roamed over us and met mine last, lingering on my face for a moment, as if trying to analyze what little he could see of me, before switching back to Nelson as she said, "Don't mind that we came with masks. I'm sure you can understand."

He cleared his throat. "Of course. It's only wise."

"Why didn't you come wearing a mask yourself?" Jackie asked.

He shrugged. "My boss is confident that you're among the top tier of groups and can be trusted, based on your ringleader's activity on the platform and the independent recommendations people have made for her. I would like you to trust me, too, so I figured it was a courteous gesture."

"Well, there's a couple of things to unpack there," Nelson said, gazing at him curiously. "First of all, who's your boss?"

"The founder of Operation Hood," he replied.

"Oh, I see," Nelson murmured, and I could tell she was thinking the same thing as me: *So the network has a single founder.* I had kind of assumed that it was founded by a collective of people, who probably belonged to the team of admins, so it was interesting to hear that there was only one man or woman behind it.

"Is the founder one of the admins?" I wondered.

Mr. X's eyes returned to me, and he nodded slowly.

"I'm guessing you can't tell us which one?" I asked.

"Your guess is correct," he replied stoically. "As you can imagine, they want to stay as anonymous as humanly possible."

"Okay, so why have you called us here?" Nelson asked, bringing the conversation back on track. "Why do you want to gain our trust?"

Mr. X glanced around briefly, then nodded toward the opposite end of the catwalk. We followed him over to it, slinking into the darkness of the shadows out of which he had stepped, until there was nothing but a thin sheet of metal railing separating us from the churning river.

I tried to ignore the height and focus on the man who was leaning against the railing, his torso twisted to face us head-on.

"We're planning to restructure things slightly on the network in the coming months, in order to create a safer and more productive environment for our real, most serious members," he began. "A team of admins, including myself, has begun reaching out to members the founder believes best fit into this category, based on scans of every data point we have on them since they joined the platform. Our job is to vet them in person—meet them to make sure they are real and to get a feel for them—before inviting them to be part of this new initiative."

He paused, looking between us, and at Nelson in particular, as if wanting to gauge our reactions.

She nodded slowly. "Go on."

"OH's founder... for the sake of simplicity, let's say they're male and call them Nathan... initially established the platform to give victims of the CRAS a voice. To facilitate dialogue. Provide them with somewhere they could go that was private and safe. Somewhere they could seek solace and share experiences.

"Nathan never imagined how things would develop over the years. That his network would grow into the community of 100,000 members that it is today. His hope was that the network would spur people to start doing things, but he hadn't actually expected them to have the courage to.

"As you know, you're just one of many groups who are using the platform to organize themselves and take action against what we all believe is an unfair system." His face darkened then, and I couldn't help but wonder what his own story was. "Nathan has been watching this trend for a while, and it's reached the point where he believes the platform needs to take its 'facilitating' to the next level," he went on. "Before, OH's focus was on encouraging conversation; hence all the forum, message, and chat modules that have been there since the beginning. Now, however, we want to shift the focus into encouraging *action*. Hence the network's recent name and mission statement tweak."

I frowned. I hadn't realized that the name and slogan had been changed. It had been titled Operation Hood, with *steal from the rich and return to the poor* as the subtext, since I'd joined. Though, that was barely seven months ago. So I supposed they had been updated sometime before then. I wondered what it was previously.

"All the conversation OH has facilitated has already led to action," Mr. X continued. "But Nathan believes there's a lot more we can do to support people like you who are actually doing things, in smart, organized, and effective ways. Because like most of us, he wants to see an end to the CRAS. It was his frustration with it that drove him to found the network in the first place."

He paused again, giving us all a moment to absorb his words, and we exchanged glances, our eyes wide with the same intrigue.

"This is very interesting," Nelson said. "So, if I'm catching your drift, you're looking to sift out the wheat from the chaff, so to speak. Identify your real and most capable members, and provide some other kind of safer facility for us all to... band together?"

Mr. X nodded. "Nathan is working on a closed, invite-only portal, separate from the main OH network, that only those we have screened will be allowed to join."

"And then what?" Jackie asked.

"At this stage, think of the portal as an incubator," Mr. X replied. "We bring people together and see what comes out of it. More has sprung from dialogue than Nathan could have ever anticipated. Who's to say what could result from a focused, active group of people like you?"

I saw his point, and to be honest, the whole idea sent a burst of excitement through me. Who knew what could be accomplished if everyone united, pooling together all their various skills and resources? The government was strong, but if Nelson had under-cover contacts in high places who didn't support the CRAS, I was betting that at least some other groups did, too.

Who was to say that we couldn't cause a dent in the system, if we organized ourselves under one unified banner? Or at the very least, effect a change in the public's consciousness? I, for one, was convinced that if more people knew about the existence of OH, more people would find the courage to take action like us, and the government could start feeling some serious push-back for policy change. Especially if a subsection of the wealthier rungs of society got involved. If enough people stopped agreeing to take our children, then the CRAS would fizzle out.

The network was currently dotted with lots of little groups, all doing their own thing around the country, and rarely merging due to trust issues. We were united under the OH network, and yet divided within it, which really made no sense. If we could come together…

Still, there were a number of security concerns I had about the idea, which I knew my colleagues would share.

"This seems pretty risky, though," Jackie said, voicing my thoughts before I could. "I mean, I know you have a vetting process, but it's not bulletproof. You can't ever be completely sure that you're only inviting well-intentioned people into the portal. And it would only take one mole to bring us all down."

Mr. X nodded, running his tongue over his lower lip. "That's a valid concern. Of course, we can never be 100 percent sure, just as you can never be 100 percent sure of the new members you accept into your own little groups. Although we'll do everything we can to keep moles out, the risk will always be there. It's up to you if you want to take it.

"We'll advise all of our members to be as cautious within the private portal as they would be within the main network. Maintain your anonymity, wear masks when meeting in the flesh, and so on, until you have built up trust. The point is, it'll still be a big step forward from where we are now, with everyone scattered across one big, disjointed network."

Jackie pursed her lips, considering his words, while Nelson nodded slowly. Her eyes were fixed on the man's face, and yet seemingly distant with thought. "Assuming we do want to be a part of this, what would be the first step?" she asked finally.

"The first step of the entire initiative is to figure out which members we want the group to consist of," he replied. "And for that, we need a trustworthy vetting squad. We have only just started, and since there's only a limited number of admin volunteers, each admin has been advised to build up a small team for themselves out of their initial contacts. I'd ask you to join mine."

"Oh, I see," Nelson said, taking a step back and folding her arms over her chest. "It's very grassroots, then."

Mr. X smiled. "Very."

"How many others have joined your team so far?" Julia wondered, giving him a considering look.

"Currently, it's just myself, because you're the first people I've reached out to," he admitted. "I wouldn't need all of your group at once, typically, but I need more than just myself. Ideally, no fewer than two people should make a visitation, for security reasons, and sometimes more, because Nathan's definitely not as confident about all of OH's groups as he was about you. Which is why he suggested I reach out to you as my first contact. You're in the top rung of members who are most likely to be trustworthy, as I said."

"I see," Nelson replied again, then drew in a slow breath. She paused, glancing at Jackie, Julia, and me. "Mr. X," she said after a beat, "do you mind if we have a word in private?"

"No problem," he replied with a shrug, and the four of us moved away from the man, back toward the ladder on the opposite end of the catwalk.

She turned her back on him once we reached it and looked at us questioningly. "Thoughts?" she whispered.

"I'm up for trying this out," Jackie replied, surprisingly quickly. She was arguably the bravest among us, and definitely the most badass, but she was also usually the most cautious—and definitely not one to barrel headfirst into a situation unless she felt comfortable with it.

Which gave me a boost of confidence about my own decision.

"Me too," I replied. Yes, there would be risks involved. More risks than in our current operation, as we would be coming into contact with so many more people. But I had already resigned myself to a life of risk, and I wasn't about to back out on taking on a bit more, given the potential of this project.

"I'm willing to try it, too," Julia said cautiously.

And then we were waiting for Nelson's answer.

"Me too," she replied finally, with a firm nod of her head. "I think we should all give this alliance a shot."

And with that, she turned around again, and we all followed her back across the catwalk to the man.

"I can confirm that I and my team members present here would like to sign up for this. I don't know about the rest of my colleagues, of course. I'll have to ask them. But you can put the four of us down on your list for now."

A flicker of relief crossed his face. Given that this was his first visitation, which he had made all alone, I could imagine that it must've been pretty nerve-wracking.

"In that case," he said, straightening his back, "is anyone free for a visitation tomorrow evening? Likely after work hours. I only need one for tomorrow, as I'm still working through the higher rung of trusted people."

"Ah, I can't tomorrow," Jackie muttered.

"I'll come," I said, knowing I had nothing to do in the evening except watch my six-inch TV. This would be a much more fulfilling use of my time.

His honeycomb eyes lighted on me, and his lips tugged upward in a small, appreciative smile. "Okay, RobinHood21. I'll send you a message over the network as soon as I have details, which is most likely going to be either later tonight or early tomorrow."

"Sounds good, Mr. X," I replied, returning his smile, even though I knew he couldn't see it properly. "I'll see you tomorrow."

8

I checked my messages on OH before I went to sleep, and then first thing in the morning, but there was still no word from Mr. X. So I left for work, wondering whether tonight's excursion might have been canceled for some reason. The thought made me feel disappointed, because I had been counting on it as my carrot to get me through the day.

This was important stuff. If my occasional missions with Nelson had managed to turn my life around and give it so much meaning, then I could only imagine the impact this whole new project could have on me—on all of us. How much it could change everything.

If we were careful, of course.

I knew things could just as easily go down in flames. It would only take one bad apple, as Jackie had pointed out. But at least, on this morning, the risks weren't enough to overshadow my enthusiasm, and I couldn't wait to get started.

I also wished that Mr. X and I had exchanged numbers, so that he could contact me via my cellphone while I was out. I had a pay-as-you-go SIM that couldn't be traced to me, and thanks to the encryption app Nelson had installed on my phone, I could make and receive calls without my location being compromised, or anyone tapping the call. So no matter who he was or how dangerous this new portal was, a phone call could never lead back to me.

Unfortunately, we hadn't actually exchanged phone numbers. So I had to wait.

When I got home and logged into the network, a message was indeed there, sent a few hours ago, at 3:02 p.m.

"Can you make it to Umberland Station at 10 p.m.?

- X"

A smirk twitched my lips at his signoff, as my brain had registered it as a kiss on first read.

I then blew out, glancing at the time in the corner of my tablet. It was just after 6:00 p.m. now, so yes, I could definitely make it. Ten at night was a pretty late meeting time, and it meant I'd feel like death getting up for work in the morning. But there was no way I was missing this, no matter how much sleep I didn't get.

"I'll be there," I typed back. *"But can we exchange numbers? In case we need to contact each other once we arrive."* He'd contacted Nelson via her personal phone, so I didn't see why it would be a problem. I proceeded to type my number and hit send on the message.

I then left the tablet to scarf down dinner and have a quick shower, and by the time I returned, he had replied.

"Sure," followed by his own number.

I sucked in a breath and entered it into my address book, his becoming the first entry under X. I then hurried to get ready to leave the cabin… while praying this evening would go well.

The journey was almost a three-hour ride, and it ended up being far too long for comfort. At some point during the trip, the excitement I'd felt earlier in the day morphed into nervousness, then sheer angst, and my stomach was feeling quite sick by the time I pulled into Umberland's small station.

I forced myself to take deep breaths as I parked on a road nearby, while trying to convince myself that this was going to go okay. That I could trust Mr. X. He was an OH admin, after all. Or at least, he was supposed to be. Now that my paranoid mind was zeroing in on details of the situation I'd gotten myself into, though, it helpfully reminded me that there *was* something that had felt kind of off about him last night. He really hadn't struck me as your typical admin.

Nerds can work out, I repeated to myself firmly, knowing that this line of thought was not productive. I was here now, and I'd agreed to accompany Mr. X to visit whoever it was we were supposed to be meeting tonight.

And after a three-hour journey here, there was no way I was turning back.

I just needed to try to learn more about the guy, because most of my nerves came from lack of information—both about Mr. X and about who he was taking me to meet tonight. Once I got that, I'd stand a chance of feeling better about the situation.

And if I didn't like his answers... Well, there was still the option of running.

But I hoped it wouldn't come to that, because I really, *really* wanted this OH portal idea to work. It was the only step forward for all of us, if we wanted to have any hope of affecting significant change in our country. Otherwise we'd just remain disjointed, weak, isolated little groups forever.

Plus, it had occurred to me that with so many minds pooled in one place, we might even find someone who had already broken into the government's adoption archives, or was at least further along in the job than Nelson was. And I was willing to risk a *lot* for that. Nelson might believe she was close to cracking them, but she'd told me herself she couldn't guarantee it. The idea of immediate access to my daughter's location, even if it was only a remote possibility, was enough to give me the kick in the ass I needed to pull myself together.

Setting my jaw, I forced confidence into my step and crossed the road separating me from the station.

I climbed the stairs that led up to the entry barriers and was about to walk through them when I stalled, spotting a familiar tall, broad figure, once again cast in shadow, standing in a corner just in front of the barriers.

Balling my fists reflexively, I headed cautiously over to him. Through the gloom, it took him a moment to recognize me, given the fact that he'd only seen my eyes and a sliver of my lips last night. He looked me up and down, squinting slightly. Unless I was misreading things, it seemed that he was feeling as much caution toward me as I was toward him.

"RobinHood21?" he asked after a long pause, his voice low.

I nodded, my neck feeling uncharacteristically stiff. "Yes."

Still scrutinizing me, he unshouldered his backpack and pulled out a pad. Then he glanced down at it and swiped at the screen several times before presenting it to me. "I'm going to need you to confirm that."

Taking the device, I gazed down at the OH portal's login window, and paused for a moment, wondering if there could be any harm in entering my credentials. Even if this was some kind of ruse to steal them, though, I didn't keep any identifying information in my account. And it seemed like a legitimate request, a decent way to verify that I was who I said I was. So I entered my username and password, and a second later, the device was logged on to the network. I handed the pad back to him and watched closely as he glanced at the top of the screen, where it displayed my username, profile, and stats for my general activity, such as how many forum posts I'd made and when I'd last logged in.

"Hm, okay," he muttered after a moment, seemingly satisfied. He moved to replace his pad in his bag, but before he could, I took a step forward.

"Hey, not to be funny, but I'd like to see you log in to your admin account."

He blinked, staring at me for a moment, and then nodded. "Of course."

He brought the pad back to life, and I watched intently as his fingers moved over the screen, then passed the device back to me. My eyes immediately snapped to the top right-hand corner, as his had done, and I let out a quiet breath upon seeing that it was indeed logged in to the right account. This seemed to be at least some proof that he was who he said he was—the admin Mr. X, whom my group had seen frequently around the network before— and it went a fair way toward loosening the knot in my stomach and making me feel better about the situation. At least, a little. I guessed the fact that he'd seemed suspicious of me too helped with that.

"So, now that we have that out of the way," he said slowly, taking the device back and placing it in his bag. "It's good to meet you again, I suppose."

"Yeah," I replied, wetting my lips and trying to restore some of the moisture there. My eyes scanned the length of him again, and this time I was less focused on his face and more on his general appearance. And I couldn't help but notice once again that his clothes looked too small for him.

It gave me another prickle of unease. It was just damn *odd* for someone to walk around in clothes that were too small. But I decided that wasn't the best way to begin a conversation. By the end of this evening, though, I was determined to get to the bottom of why that was.

There was an awkward pause, during which the two of us continued eyeing each other, and then I looked around, flapping my arms against my sides to diffuse the silence. "So, where are we going?" I asked. "Are we going to take a train or what?"

"Um, no, actually," he replied, breaking eye contact and glancing toward the street beneath us. "Follow me."

He took off down the stairs before I could say another word, and I followed him, struggling to keep up with his swift, broad strides, surprisingly agile for a man so big. He led me around the edge of the station and down a deserted alley nestled behind it. Halfway down, he stopped abruptly in the middle of the sidewalk and lowered to a crouch in front of a drain that lay there, his outfit creaking slightly with the motion.

I frowned, wondering what on Earth he was doing.

I knew from last night that he was pretty creative with meeting spots, but when he slipped his fingers around the drain's edges and dislodged it with one forceful pull, I realized I never could have expected this one. I gaped as he swung his legs through the hole, and, within the blink of an eye, disappeared inside it.

"Um, what…" My mouth opened and closed like a fish's as I stared at the now-empty sidewalk. I cast a furtive glance over my shoulder to check that the street was still empty, and then moved tentatively toward the drain, still in disbelief.

I peered downward and saw him standing at the bottom of a ladder, his face tilted up to me and illuminated by the dull orange lighting of the nearby streetlamp, which somehow managed to reach him down there. He was over six feet underground, plus the six and a half or so feet of his personal height. So basically twelve feet to the ground.

"Really?" I said.

A slightly amused expression played at the corners of his mouth as he gazed back up at me. "What?" he asked, giving a shrug.

I closed my lips, concluding that this guy was a little bit insane. What was wrong with meeting whoever we were about to meet on a dark street corner? This street looked pretty empty, for that matter.

But he disappeared from view a moment later, ducking his head slightly and moving deeper into the tunnel, and I had no choice but to swing myself into the damp drain and follow after him. Unless I wanted to cave in to my nerves and go home. Which I had already decided I *didn't* want to do. This was my way forward.

I was halfway down the slimy ladder when his deep voice echoed up the tunnel, the sound waves reverberating all around me in the narrow passage and feeling as though they were vibrating my very stomach. "Please close the lid after you."

I stalled, my eyes going wide as I looked back up at the drain's entrance. "What?" I said, incredulous, my voice echoing as well. "But it'd be pitch black!" I hadn't thought to bring a flashlight with me this evening, as I'd had no reason to think I would need it.

In response, I heard a click, and then a glaring shaft of white light beamed up through the tunnel, blinding me completely when I glanced down in its direction.

I exhaled, closing my eyes in an attempt to rid them of the white spots dancing beneath their lids. "Okay," I muttered. "Point made."

But even when my eyes recovered, I hesitated. I pulled a deep frown as I returned my gaze to the grate. Was I really going to do as he said and close it? I had more than one reservation about shutting myself inside a dark tunnel with a guy who was the size of a bear, and whom I had only just met yesterday.

Yes, he was an admin, but still...

I exhaled, and after a moment, decided to continue biting the bullet. I just hoped I wouldn't regret it.

Moving back up the ladder, I yanked the heavy drain closed above me, then continued my descent, silently praying to the powers of the universe to look after me tonight.

I reached the bottom and winced as my boots landed in a slushy puddle, but dared not look down, not wanting to get a visual of the dreck I must've just stepped into. Ugh. I was going to return home smelling like a sewer rat. Looking to my left, I could see Mr. X's light flashing against the walls about ten feet ahead, still casting enough light for me to make my way toward him. He'd been walking at a slower pace, I realized, waiting for me to catch up.

"So, seriously, X, what is this?" I asked, reaching him. My nerves were too taut for this mystery to stretch out any longer.

He kept his eyes focused straight ahead, on what seemed to be a never-ending tunnel, though his expression turned mildly apologetic. "To be honest, I technically don't have permission to talk about it," he replied. "But you'll see soon enough. It's not too much farther along."

"You're about to take me there, and yet you're not allowed to talk about it?" I asked, incredulous.

He cast me a serious look. "Yes," he replied. "As admins, it's protocol, and part of the oath we take, when it comes to securing the privacy of others. If someone comes with us, they see what they see, but we're not supposed to talk about stuff in advance."

I sighed, feeling miffed. I mean, I supposed it was a good thing they were so respectful of others' privacy. But still, I really would have appreciated him throwing me a bone.

I guessed I was just going to have to wait and see.

Resigning myself to silence, I kept my eyes on the path ahead, trying to make out an end to the tunnel. About three minutes of trudging along later, X stopped abruptly and turned to face the wall on our right—where, I realized, another passageway lay.

We moved down it, following its gentle curves. It snaked this way and that in a winding path before we reached another offshoot and made our way down that one. After another ten minutes, we were deep in a veritable maze of tunnels, and my nerves returned full force. I instinctively felt for the gun strapped beneath my coat, needing to remind myself that it was still there. I didn't get the sense that X was going to try anything with me, but his physique made him a pretty intimidating guy, and I still didn't know enough about him to fully trust him.

Finally, we came to another stop, and this time it was in front of a dark gray metal door etched into the brick wall. X raised a fist and knocked five times in rapid succession, followed by a pause, and then another two loud knocks.

Then he took a step back, and I held my breath, waiting.

One minute went by, then two, and then a creak came from the other side and a small hatch I hadn't even noticed slid open, halfway up the door. I couldn't see who was behind it, however, as it consisted of dark tinted glass, and then the hatch clicked shut again, followed by the sound of heavy bolts being drawn.

The door swung open, revealing a tall, wiry woman with dark salt-and-pepper hair, which was tied back in a severe bun. She wore a long-sleeved navy-blue dress that reached her ankles, and a stethoscope hung around her neck. The floor behind the door was elevated, and seemingly free from gunk, and also made her tower over us. Or at least, me. She looked down at me along her sharp, pointed nose, and although I had no idea who she was, the presence of this mature-looking woman helped steady my racing heart some.

"Doctor," X greeted her, with a respectful nod of his head.

She nodded back, her lips pursing as she looked between the two of us. "You have an appointment with Davine, right?"

"That's correct, ma'am," he replied.

"Very well, come on in." She stepped backward, opening the door wider and allowing us to slip through.

We climbed up onto the raised platform and found ourselves entering another tunnel, except the floor was completely dry, and the warm, orange lighting fixed at intervals to the walls gave it an almost homely feel. Which further helped to calm me.

"Just leave your shoes by the door, please," the woman said, eyeing our filthy boots.

She pointed to a plastic container filled with water, just by the door, and a large shoe rack that had to contain at least thirty sets of footwear, most of them feminine.

What on Earth...

X and I quickly dipped our boots into the water, ridding them of the worst of the gunk, and then placed them on the floor next to the rack, on top of a pile of old newspapers, to dry. X then took off down the hallway with the woman, and I followed after them. The tunnel soon gave way to a well-lit, cavernous space, which I quickly realized was an abandoned subway station. Except that it had been modified and was barely recognizable. There were walls cutting off the track on either end, and three wide, makeshift bridges had been set up to connect the two platforms, built from sturdy wooden beams and lined with pots of cheerful red bromeliads.

The platforms themselves had been sectioned off into small, makeshift rooms, separated by boards and heavy woolen curtains. At least ten women were mingling outside, on the strips of platforms that had been left untouched in order to provide walkways, and all of them had bumps protruding from their bellies.

It hit me then what this was.

I remembered coming across references to places like this on the OH forums soon after I'd first joined the network, as one of the ways people were defying the government. I'd thought the idea sounded so ludicrous at the time that I'd dismissed it as just a rumor, and yet here I was, standing right in the middle of what had to be a "pregnancy factory," as they had crudely referred to them on the forums. It was a hideout for poor women who found themselves pregnant, yet refused to give up their children at birth. After they discovered they had conceived, they supposedly went into hiding and gave birth in secret. I had no idea what happened to the children afterward, but this was supposed to be how they evaded the Ministry's notice.

It was a sobering reminder that not every family had the option to flee the country. I doubted there were many who had contacts like Nelson's at the border, if there were any at all. Which meant that the other groups around our nation had been forced to adapt and figure out alternative methods of pushing back against the CRAS. When escape wasn't an option, they had no choice but to find ways to hide within the country itself.

I had never thought about this in depth before, having become so used to the way Nelson's team did things; I had never given much thought to how other groups on OH might evade the government. Crossing the border had always seemed to be the only option to me, and now my mind felt expanded as I gazed around, struggling to absorb the scene.

It made me wonder how many other hideouts like this were out there, scattered about the country. How many children were born each year "off the grid." And what ended up happening to them, as surely they would have to reintegrate with society at some point. They couldn't live down here forever. And judging by the lack of actual *children* down here—I couldn't hear a single infant sound—they must have definitely figured that part out, too.

"So this is another trusted group," I mumbled to X as we crossed one of the bridges to the platform on the other side. My mind was already mulling over what kind of resources they must have to keep this little show running, and how they might possibly play a role in the grand scheme of things. They had a safe place down here, hidden from the government, which was a very valuable asset in itself.

X nodded.

"And they really don't mind us coming in here, right into their base?" I asked, surprised. From what I understood, this was the first time X was making real-life contact with them, and it took me aback that they'd just let a stranger—two strangers—into their fold, with so many women's and unborn children's lives at stake.

He slowed to hang back a couple of steps, to create a little more distance between us and the woman who was leading us, and replied quietly, "They trust the admins of OH because they've had dealings with us before."

"Oh. What about?" I asked, curious.

"They reached out to a member of my team a year or so ago, asking if we could put them in touch with a reliable black market medical equipment supplier," he explained in an undertone. "We asked around and helped them source one as best as we could, and I guess it worked out for them."

"I see," I muttered. So today's visitation really didn't seem like a risky mission after all, then. I suddenly felt a bit stupid for even carrying a gun, amidst all these harmless pregnant ladies. Then again, I'd had no idea this was where X would lead me.

"Why did you need someone to accompany you today, then?" I couldn't help but ask him, cocking an eyebrow.

He gave me a wry look. "You're right that security wasn't really the reason today. A duo just creates a more professional impression. Plus, I figured having a girl with me would help. In case you hadn't noticed, I'm kind of the odd one out down here."

I allowed myself a chuckle as we passed a group of four pregnant women, who eyed us curiously, particularly X. "Guess that's fair enough," I said, my eyes continuing to scan the closed-off station. "And do they really get all their supplies in here via that little door?" I asked.

"I was told there's another secret entrance around here somewhere, but it would've taken us longer to travel to, which is why I picked the drain outside the station."

"I see," I murmured.

And then I ran out of time to ask more questions, as our escort had stopped at the end of the platform, outside the final makeshift compartment, which was sectioned off by a heavy navy-blue curtain. She gave a cough and then called through, "Davine? It's Mr. X."

"Oh, come in," a soft, younger-sounding female voice answered.

The older woman nodded to us and then drew open the curtain, revealing a small-yet-cozy office space. It contained a slim table with a rather dated desktop computer set up on it, and there were shelves upon shelves of equipment, including, I couldn't help but notice, a little pile of baby clothes and a column of diapers. Perhaps they stocked just enough of those for when each baby was first born, before he or she was taken wherever they went to next.

A brunette woman who looked to be in her mid-thirties stood in the middle of the room, dressed in a pair of worn jeans and a loose, light pink t-shirt, her hair swept above her head in a high ponytail. Her resemblance to the older woman struck me instantly;

she was about the same height, with the same sharp nose, high cheekbones, and thinnish lips. I assumed they had to be mother and daughter.

"Please, take a seat," the younger woman said courteously, retrieving two seats from a stack of chairs that was tucked away against the wall, next to the desk.

X and I sat down in them, while Davine took a seat in front of the desktop. After drawing the curtain again for privacy, her mother opted to remain standing and leaned against the desk, her arms folded over her chest.

There was an intelligence that sparkled behind their blue eyes as they examined us, and I wished I knew what their story was. They seemed to run this place, and I could only wonder how they had managed to find and then renovate it into what it was today, all without being noticed.

As well as how they had the resources to run it. Feeding a small army of pregnant women couldn't be cheap. And what had driven them to do all this? What had the CRAS done to them to stoke such a fire?

"So," Davine said, clearing her throat. "What is it you want to talk about?"

I leaned back a little in my seat and listened as X began the same pitch he had given us the day before. I watched the two women's faces closely, and recognized the same emotions displayed on them that I had gone through yesterday. Surprise, intrigue, confusion, concern, and an undeniable hint of excitement. They even asked nearly identical questions to us, particularly when it came to security, as they had many more lives at stake than our group.

After X had finished addressing their concerns, they glanced at one another, and the little room fell into silence.

I stole a glance at X's face to see him watching them intently, as if gauging their reaction. I was sure that Nathan had vetted them, and they didn't exactly strike me as villains, given all the pregnant ladies they appeared to be sheltering. But, still, nothing was a guarantee, and X was right to stay alert.

"How soon do you think this portal will open?" Davine's mother, who had introduced herself as Noreen over the course of the conversation, finally asked.

"It's expected to be open in about a week for the first wave of invitees, though it'll be a while before it's fully populated. The admins still have a number of visitations to make as part of this initial vetting process."

"I understand," she replied.

"If you confirm your interest in joining," he added, "I will put you down on the list and you will automatically receive a notification and a unique link to sign up to the portal as soon as it's live."

"What exactly would we be expected to contribute to the group, if we joined?" Davine asked.

X shrugged. "What a group contributes is totally voluntary. And it's something that should come out naturally in conversation, as the portal is populated, and people begin to connect and talk. We want this to be an organic process, with everyone offering resources or information only as far as they feel comfortable. So don't worry about feeling pressured. You're both clearly competent women, to run this kind of operation, and I'm guessing just your presence and general input could be a positive contribution to the new community, even if you didn't want to offer anything tangible. Your heads seem to be in the right place, and that's the kind of member we want to attract."

That appeared to put both women at ease, and they both let out sighs, leaning back and glancing at one another again.

"Well, what d'you think, Davi?" Noreen murmured.

Davine looked between X and me, and then nodded firmly. "I think we should join, Mom. As the gentleman says, it's no skin off our noses, as we don't have to commit to anything unless we feel comfortable with it. As I'm sure you understand," she added, addressing X and me, "we have to put our ladies' needs above all else."

"Of course," he said, nodding respectfully.

The women asked about a few more technicalities, such as how many people were expected to join in total (X replied it was hard to know at this point) as well as the confidentiality surrounding our visit (X assured them he wouldn't share their location with a soul), and then the meeting seemed to conclude itself.

We all stood and shook hands, and Noreen was on the verge of leading us out the door when Davine suddenly called us back.

"Oh, I'm sorry," she said. "I almost forgot. While you're here, Mr. X, I wonder if you could take a quick look at my tablet. I've been having problems accessing my messages on OH via the tablet recently, which is really inconvenient, as I can't carry the computer everywhere with me. I figure it might be a problem you encounter on a regular basis with other users, so…" She trailed off as she reached for a backpack on one of the shelves and pulled out a shiny silver tablet. She switched it on, and after several swipes of her fingers against the screen, handed it to X with an expectant look. "Here, you can try yourself."

X's dark brows furrowed as he stared down at the screen, and I wasn't sure if I was imagining it, but I could've sworn his cheeks grew a touch warmer in color. He swiped a couple of times, then heaved a sigh and sat back down in his chair, continuing to frown at the screen.

The silence became a bit awkward after a minute, especially as he didn't seem to be actually doing anything with the device. I shuffled over to him and tentatively peered over his shoulder. He was reading a help file.

After another half minute, he exhaled irritably. "I'm not sure, to be honest," he muttered. "Give me a minute and I'll call a colleague."

"Okay, thanks," Davine said, taking a seat opposite him and watching him with expectation.

He pulled out his cell phone and dialed a number, then stood up and moved over to the closed curtain with the tablet, turning his back on us and pressing the phone to his ear with his free hand. "Hey, yeah, Mr. X here. Look, I'm having trouble connecting to messages on a tablet. When I try to access them there's just this spinning disc thing, and nothing loads."

And just like that, my guard was up again.

Spinning disc thing? That definitely didn't sound like a term a tech would use.

It also hit me then that *I* had encountered the same problem before myself, at the beginning. I hadn't had anyone to ask for help at the time, but had managed to figure it out pretty quickly. Which meant that I was even more tech-savvy than X. Which was saying something, considering I was mediocre with computers at best, and he was supposed to be part of the admin team on a highly technical social network.

Was he really an admin? I'd witnessed him log in, but… this didn't sit right with me. I wasn't sure what else he could be, if he wasn't an admin, but suddenly I was eager to get out of these tunnels again. I tensed in my chair, sitting rod-straight and eyeing him warily as he continued the conversation.

"Huh?" he said after a pause. "I'm sorry, you need to say that again in English. Oh. Geez. That's hardly intuitive. Okay, I'll try that, then. Thanks." And with that, he hung up.

I watched him with suspicion as he returned to his seat and

swiped at the tablet some more, and then, after several additional hard frowns, finally announced to Davine that it seemed to be working.

"Oh, great, thanks," she said, taking it from him and testing it herself. "Yup, it's working."

It struck me that neither she nor her mother seemed fazed by X's lack of tech-savviness, which made me wonder for a moment whether I was overreacting, reading things into the situation that weren't there.

I mean, he hadn't exactly tried to hide the fact that he'd been clueless about what was a pretty basic fix—basic enough for me to know—having held the conversation in here, for everyone to overhear.

Still, I needed to know *how* he had come to be a part of OH's admin team, because he was just odd and out of place, in general. It'd been the first thing I noticed about him the moment I laid eyes on him last night. And I was going to question him about it as soon as we got out of here.

9

After Noreen escorted us back out to the sewers and closed the door behind us, we began making our way through the maze toward the drain exit. I gave X a discreet sidelong glance, watching his rugged face for a moment as his eyes tracked the tunnel ahead of us, and then decided I ought to try to ease into my planned interrogation a bit, figuring he might feel a little easier around me after some small talk.

I coughed softly, then remarked, "Well, you're pretty smooth at this, aren't you, Mr. X?"

He cast me a bemused look, his eyes narrowing slightly. "What do you mean?"

I shrugged. "I mean look at you, charming two groups of ladies into accepting your invitation in a row."

He gave a surprised laugh, a deep, rich sound that did something... unexpected to my insides. And then he shrugged, his expression deadpan as his gaze returned to the tunnel ahead. "I dunno. Maybe I'm just a smooth guy."

"Just like your name," I replied.

He raised an eyebrow. "You think it's smooth?"

I smiled. "Well, not really, actually. Calling you Mr. X all the time feels pretty weird, and X alone is even weirder. Not to mention that every time you sign off a message, it looks like you're—well, I'm sure you've been told before."

His eyes returned to me, and I could tell he was suppressing a smile. "In that case…" He gave me a considering look. "I suppose you could call me Hux instead."

I widened my eyes at him. "Hux?"

He nodded. "Yeah. It's my fake middle name."

I smirked. "Okay," I said, then repeated, "Hux." I decided I quite liked the way it rolled off my tongue. "So, Hux," I said after a pause, coming to the crux of the matter as we entered another tunnel. "Tech doesn't really seem to be your thing, huh?"

"Um, no. It's not," he replied bluntly.

I blinked, appreciating his honesty, but only feeling more confused. I hesitated a moment, then went on. "I guess I'm just curious how you came to be an admin of the network, then."

He inhaled, and suddenly his expression turned unexpectedly bitter. Studying it, I couldn't help but notice traces of grief there, even through the gloom, glimmering in the depths of his amber eyes. I had seen that look too many times in my own eyes, when catching my reflection in the mirror.

He must have lost someone dear to him, just as I had, which had led him to this path of rebellion. And it must have still been very raw in his heart and mind to elicit that kind of reaction, despite his official façade up until now. Perhaps it had even been recent.

"I'm sorry," I said quickly, worried I'd overstepped the line.

He shook his head, though that dark expression remained on his face. "It's okay. It's just…" He exhaled, a muscle ticking in his jaw. "A bit of a long story."

I wet my lips, falling silent, and waited to see if he would go on.

He did, about a minute later.

"I'm crap at technology because, until four months ago, I was basically a caveman."

His statement took me by surprise, and I found myself stalling and staring at him. An involuntary laugh bubbled up in my throat, at the randomness of it, and while I was horrified by my reaction, knowing this was a sensitive subject, I couldn't control it. I tried to tamp it down quickly, but luckily, he didn't seem to mind. On the contrary, his mood seemed to lift as he met my eyes again, and a smile spread across his lips, strengthening the indentations at the edges of his mouth.

I was pretty sure it was the first time I'd seen him smile fully, and it registered in my brain then how cute he was, his appearance instantly going from rugged to boyish. But I batted the thought away as quickly as it had come. It was totally *not* where my mind needed to be right now.

"What?" he asked.

"Caveman?" I replied. He definitely *looked* like a caveman, now that he'd used the term. But... "What do you mean?"

He sighed. "I was born and bred in a community of cave-dwellers, up near the border of Canadia, and off grid. We lived and hunted in harsh conditions, surrounded by ice and mountains and forests. My family fled there, along with a circle of close friends and relatives, just as the CRAS was being introduced. My mother had fallen pregnant with me, and she and my father decided to shun mainstream society to hide out there, hoping they could start a new life, where they wouldn't risk losing their children. Their plan worked... for about twenty-two years."

He paused, all traces of humor now vanished from his face,

and I bit my lower lip, waiting for him to go on as we continued sludging through the tunnels.

"Then our home basically turned into a warzone overnight," he said after a minute, a hard edge coming into his tone. "A group of border patrol agents somehow got wind of our settlement, and struck our caves before dinner one evening. We lost everything."

"Oh," I breathed. "I'm so sorry."

He sighed, shaking his head. "The past's the past," he muttered.

I hesitated, then asked, "What happened after the attack? How did you escape?"

He pursed his lips. "Most of us didn't. The agents were on orders to bring the adults in for interrogation and confiscate any children they found, as we didn't have a license to live on that land and were suspected of being CRAS evaders. But, given the nature of the sting—their surprise arrival as the sun was setting, armed with guns and wearing all black—my people's first reaction was to assume it was an invasion, perhaps by a nomad gang looking to plunder our resources. We'd grown into a harsh and feral people over decades of living in the wild, and our defensive reflexes flared." He wet his lips, swallowing hard. "By the time we realized they weren't there to kill us, it was too late. My people had opened fire with their own guns, and the patrol retaliated."

He paused as his voice faltered slightly, and ran a slow hand down his face, his eyes haunted. When he spoke again, his voice was huskier. "It was a bloodbath," he said. "Most of us didn't survive... my parents and older brother included. Of my family, just me and my ten-year-old sister escaped."

I felt a stab of pain in my chest, and instinctively reached out to place a hand on his forearm. He glanced down at me in mild surprise, and our eyes met.

"I'm so sorry," I whispered. I just couldn't imagine how hard that must've been. I had lost my own parents and my daughter, but as far as I knew, they were still living. His weren't.

He shook his head again. "It's okay," he muttered.

"And this was only four months ago?" I asked.

He nodded grimly.

I blew out. It was no wonder he still looked so cut up about it. And it was also an explanation for his lack of technical know-how. Maybe I had just been wrong in my assumption that all admins needed to be nerdy IT types; some could just be there to moderate community discussions and such, rather than being involved with actual coding and maintenance of the site.

"How did you escape?" I asked.

"My sister and I happened to be out when they swooped in," he replied heavily. "We managed to escape notice and make it to the nearest town. From there, the rest is more or less history."

"But how did you make it all the way down here? How did you become an admin?"

"I had a contact," he replied, a touch clipped. "Who happened to be an admin on the site. They helped me, and I volunteered to help in whatever way I could with the platform."

"I see," I murmured. I wondered which admin that might be, and also where his sister was now, but figured it would be prying to ask. To be honest, he'd already told me more than I'd expected him to.

We fell into a silence as we crossed the final stretch of sewer up to the drain, but as it came into view, I felt the need to try to lighten the mood a little again. I definitely wasn't sorry for digging into his personal history a bit, since I needed to figure out whether I could trust the guy, but I also knew how painful memories could be, and I'd just dredged up a lot of them.

"So, you really were a literal caveman then," I said, stopping short of the ladder.

He sighed. "Yup. Mancave included."

I smiled. "It must've taken quite a bit of adjustment to get you into those jeans."

He shrugged, tilting his head back to gaze up at the drain. "Probably not enough adjustment, given how I practically break the zipper every time I put the damn things on."

I laughed. "Well, I wasn't going to say anything, but…"

He smiled. "It's fine. I have seen myself in the mirror. Unfortunately, it's the largest size I've been able to find around here, so… I'm probably gonna continue looking like a compressed wood bison for the foreseeable future. Back home, my mother used to make our clothes, and sadly, I can't sew for nuts." With that, he gestured to the ladder. "Ladies first."

I considered his words as I climbed, realizing that I now finally had an answer to his odd dress "style" too. And by the time I'd reached the top, an odd idea had occurred to me.

After dislodging the drain and pulling myself up to street level, I stepped aside and waited for Hux. Once he had climbed through and replaced the lid, he stood to his full height, and I gave him a tentative look.

"Um, in case you're interested," I ventured, "I've got pretty mad sewing skills. So, if you want me to have a go at, uh, extending those things…" I suppressed a smile as I glanced over him from head to toe. Though beneath the full light of the street-lamp, my eyes were quickly drawn less by the fabric and more by… him. I felt myself blush. He was a *fine* specimen of the male species. "Just ask," I finished after a moment, forcing my eyes back to his face.

He gazed down at me, narrowing his honey-brown eyes as if considering my offer. "Really?" he said after a moment.

"Really," I replied. "I'd just need to get hold of a needle and thread, and maybe some extra fabric." Sarah, one of my nannies at the Sylvones', had taught me how to knit and sew as a hobby, and while I didn't have the equipment back in my cabin, it was probably about time that I got a sewing kit anyway, for when I needed to mend my own clothes. Plus, I honestly felt sorry for the guy. He seemed to have no one else in his life right now who could fix them for him, and would continue wearing them for the foreseeable future if I didn't offer.

There was a pause as he thought about it. His expression went serious, though his eyes held a twinkle of amusement. "Hm," he murmured. "Well, I'm not sure if that would be overstepping the boundaries of our... colleague relationship. But I'll consider it."

A smile tugged at my lips. "Okay."

And with that, we headed back along the quiet street to the station. When we reached the base of the stairs that led up to the barriers, we stopped again. He pulled out his phone and swiped across the screen several times, a frown denting his strong brow. And then he cleared his throat.

"Uh, I'm planning to make another visitation tomorrow evening, near Lakerville. It'll be an earlier appointment, around eightish." He paused and looked up at me. "You wanna come again?"

"Um, yeah," I replied slowly, not needing to look at my calendar to know I was free. Tonight's visitation hadn't been so bad after all, and although I was tense at the idea of walking blindly into another meeting with strangers, I was willing to give it another shot. I wouldn't have another mission from Nelson for at least two weeks, anyway, as we never did them too close together. So in the meantime, all I had to keep me busy was my day job. "Do you need only one of us again?" I asked.

He nodded. "Yeah, Nathan figures this is another safe one."

"Okay, count me in, then," I replied. I figured none of the others would mind me taking the spot again. Nelson and Julia were always busy with background tasks, not to mention Nelson's work on the archives, and I couldn't see Marco or the twins complaining. Nor Jackie; she'd likely appreciate the downtime, as I sensed she was still a bit shaken up from having her mask torn the other night.

"Okay, well, I'll confirm the exact address via OH message again. And now that I've given you my number, you can just call me if you have any problems."

"Okay, cool," I replied, dipping my hands into my coat pockets and casting him a wry look. "So you're basically at my beck and call now."

He frowned. "I wouldn't go so far as to say that," he replied. "And fair warning: I turn into a grumpy bastard after midnight."

I laughed. "Noted."

He extended a hand. "Safe journey home, Ms. Hood."

I did the same, and his large, strong hand engulfed mine in a firm shake. "And you, Mr. X," I replied with a small grin.

He gave me the faintest smirk back, and then turned on his heel and scaled the flight of steps, his tall, broad form disappearing beyond the station's barriers.

10

I remembered only as I stepped through my front door that I had set my phone to silent. Making my way through to my bedroom, I sat down on my bed and pulled the device out, to see that I had three text messages waiting for me.

The first was from Nelson: "*Hope all goes well. Give me a report as soon as you can.*"

The second was from Jackie: "*Hey R. Good luck with Mr. X.*"

And the third was from the twins: "*Yo, Hood, keep us in the loop. AA xx*"

A grin split my face at the last one. The twins' habit of double signing and double kissing texts always had a way of making me smirk.

Then, although I was ready to drop off to sleep, I decided to pull out my tablet to see if anyone was available for a conference call now; it would be the quickest way to relay information. Because it was unlikely I'd have time to catch them up tomorrow morning, and then I'd be gone again with Mr. X in the evening. I didn't know what each of my colleagues did for a living, but if there was one thing I had noticed since I'd met them, it was that they tended to be up at odd hours, even on non-mission days.

I logged on to the secure conference app Nelson had installed on my device and saw that everyone's avatar was lit up green, except Julia's, which was grayed out. I invited each of them to a call, then waited for them to respond.

Nelson immediately joined, while Jackie and the twins and Marco followed within seconds. That was a ridiculously fast response, even for them, and I suspected they had been in a discussion already, likely about this whole new development with OH and its founder's grand plan. Or about me, waiting for me to sign in with an update—particularly as they hadn't heard back on their texts.

I plugged my earphones into my tablet and initiated the call, and several enthusiastic voices chimed into my ears at once.

"Heyyy."

"Yo, yo, yo."

"Glad you finally joined us."

"Hey, guys," I said, smiling and trying to suppress a yawn. "I'm beat, but I wanted to fill you in on what happened before going to sleep."

"And we appreciate that," Nelson said, adjusting the glasses over her nose and leaning closer to the screen, her green eyes glinting in anticipation.

"How was Mr. Mysterious?" Marco asked, slurping from what looked like a chocolate milkshake.

"He was okay, actually," I replied. "And I think we can trust him." I went on to explain what the trip had entailed—including a summary of X's background, and why he had a grudge against the CRAS—and by the time I finished, they were all staring at me, jaws slack. The only thing I didn't tell them was the exact location of Davine and Noreen's hideout, as X had made it clear that needed to stay confidential.

"Wow, I can't believe places like that actually exist," Nelson said, her fascination still locked on the pregnancy shelter.

If any of us were to know about such a place, I had expected it to be Nelson, as she was the most connected, and the fact that she hadn't known kind of brought home to me that we really *were* all isolated, scattered around the country. With that in mind, Nathan's idea to bring us all together seemed like an even better thing, so long as we took the necessary precautions.

"Yup, they sure do," I replied. "It boggled my mind, too." I leaned back in bed to get more comfortable, positioning my tablet against my knees.

"I wonder what on Earth they do with the children when they're born. And the women, for that matter, suddenly resurfacing from nowhere," Nelson mused.

I shrugged. "I wondered exactly the same thing. I can try asking Hux about it next time I see him."

"Hux?" Marco asked, frowning.

"Oh." I smirked. "It's Mr. X. He said I could call him Hux."

Ant scoffed. "Look at you, on first-name terms with him already."

"Middle-name terms, actually. *Fake* middle-name terms."

"Well, thanks for staying up to fill us in, Robin," Nelson said with a sigh. "Now we know this whole new portal idea is really happening, and we can take admin requests for help seriously. I guess we shouldn't keep you longer."

"Yeah, I'm ready to zonk off. Oh, I forgot to say that I'm going out with him again tomorrow—somewhere in Lakerville. I don't have the details yet, but I'll report back when I return. I assume none of you mind me going again?"

They shook their heads. "Nope, you be our guest," Ant said.

"Well, soon more of you may need to start coming, anyway. I'm not sure how long his 'safe' list is."

The conversation entered a dip as I trailed off. Marco continued to slurp from his drink, the twins began snacking on a bowl of fruit, and Nelson seemed to get momentarily distracted by some other task, the keys of her keyboard clacking.

"So, do you wanna hit the pillow now, R?" Jackie prompted. "I'm guessing you have work tomorrow."

"Yeah, I do." I sighed. The word "goodnight" was once again on the tip of my tongue, but then I felt the urge to say one last thing. In spite of how tired I was, I was finding it hard to tamp down the optimism burning through me, thanks to the evening's excursion. It had started out downright nerve-wracking, but the more I thought about how it had ended up, the more hopeful I felt about this whole project.

"I know we haven't discussed this properly yet, as a group, but after today, I really feel like we might be on to something, with the direction Nathan's trying to encourage us in. It's just... I dunno, maybe I'm just buzzed from meeting other like-minded people today. It brings a certain energy, you know?"

"You mean we're not enough to get you pumped?" Abe remarked, picking up an apple and taking what I guessed was supposed to be a seductive bite.

I rolled my eyes and ignored him, as did everyone else on the call.

They all knew what I meant. The thought of OH's admins recruiting other smart, driven people like Davine and Noreen and assembling them all into one place made me feel jittery—in a good way. Going out today and seeing with my own eyes that there were other real people out there, people behind the stupid profile names, had added a level of fire to my enthusiasm that I hadn't thought possible. Fueled my belief that we really could accomplish something with this. Something significant.

It was hard to describe, and maybe I was just getting carried away, but it almost felt like we were at the start of a storm. A grassroots movement, as Nelson had called it, from which nobody yet knew what would spring. In a way, the uncertainty only made things feel more exciting. The possibilities more far-reaching.

Who knew what we could pull off?

For starters, we'd have a chance to form new bonds and friendships. Forge new allies who could watch our backs. Meet new people we could commiserate with and draw strength from, as well as share strength with. Hell, even just the short time I'd spent with Hux this evening had made me feel a connection to him. We both shared a tragedy that was brought on by the same cause, even if his was much rawer.

I thought back to all the historical figures I had read about who had brought about change. Shifted public perspective. Led revolutions. And I couldn't help but wonder if we might be them now. Even if we felt small and insignificant. I was sure they had felt that, too, at the start. And yet they hadn't let it stop them from dreaming. From *doing*.

Maybe I was just overtired and my imagination was running wild, but I couldn't deny the feeling that Nathan was definitely on the right track. Was leading us all onto the right track. I hoped that I could meet him one day, as he sounded like a brave and brilliant man, or woman.

"I get you, Robin," Nelson replied with a yawn of her own, leaning back in her chair to stretch out her arms. "And I'm looking forward to meeting these people myself."

"Hux actually said that Nathan's planning to open the portal in about a week, so you shouldn't have to wait long," I said with a smile, remembering what he'd told Noreen.

Another yawn then overtook me, and this time, I could no longer fight it. "Okay, guys, I'm signing off now. Sleep well."

"Ciao."

"Night-night."

"Toodle-pip."

I signed out and shut off the tablet with a contented sigh, then laid back and drifted off before I could even brush my teeth. I was soon lost in a lucid dream filled with vast skies and endless possibilities.

11

I took the train to Lakerville the next evening, as I didn't feel like another several-hour-long ride on my motorbike. Honestly, I should have just taken it the day before, too, to Umberland, but the trains at rush hour made me feel claustrophobic, and I tried to avoid them as much as I could. This journey, however, would be too far; Lakerville was a town by the coast, and I could get a direct connection from my nearest station that would get me there within an hour, while it would have taken hours on my bike.

Upon disembarking the train at my destination, I exited through the barriers and gazed around the gloomy station entrance, expecting Hux to be lurking around somewhere in the shadows. But he wasn't. I frowned and checked the time on my phone. It was eight minutes past our meeting time—8:08 p.m.— and he'd said to wait for him just outside the station.

My nerves started to spike again, in spite of how things had gone yesterday. Though this time it was less about fear *of* him, and more about worry *for* him. My mind started dishing out worst-case scenarios, involving him being caught or arrested, and before I knew it I was approaching full-on panic mode.

Then I grabbed hold of the reins and reminded myself that he was only eight minutes late. There could be other explanations.

Taking a deep breath, I walked onto the street that ran parallel to the station and gazed up and down it, though I still didn't spot him. I crossed the road to the parking lot on the other side, wondering if he might be leaning against the hood of a car to rest his legs or something while waiting for me.

As I entered the lot, my assumption proved correct. Except he wasn't sitting. I heard his voice drifting over a row of cars from my right, and turned to see him standing, his back toward me as he paced. His phone was pressed to his ear, so it was probably just as well I hadn't immediately attempted to call him to verify his location; he was preoccupied.

Then, as I began to make out the words of his conversation, I realized his voice sounded oddly strained.

"Wait, what do you mean? Yes. I know how she reacted. I know. But I want to try again. I already told her I'm coming this week. No. No, of course not, but I... I need to get to the bottom of this for both of our sakes. If I keep at it, I know she'll come around. I mean, she has to, dammit. I'm the only family she has left." There was a pause, and I recoiled, chastising myself for encroaching on what was clearly a very personal conversation. I moved to back away instinctively, but not before I caught him saying in a voice that was softer, cracked almost: "She... She really said that?"

I almost stalled to listen further, but then he began to turn, and I was forced to duck out of view, not wanting him to see me eavesdropping. I discreetly made my way back to the other side of the road to wait for him.

Still, my mind couldn't help but wonder what the conversation had been about. From the snippets I'd heard, I guessed the *she* must be his sister. And it sounded like they were having trouble in their relationship.

I tried to stop my musings there, because it was totally none of my business, though the question still played at the back of my mind—even while I assumed a casual pose outside the station, leaning against a wall and pretending I hadn't spotted him across the road yet. I knew he'd come over when he was ready.

About three minutes later, he did. I kept my eyes to the ground as I sensed him approaching, then lifted them slowly to his face when his footsteps stopped in front of me. His hands were stuffed into the deep pockets of his coat, which was zipped all the way up to his neck tonight, and I could tell he was trying to keep his expression neutral in front of me. Though he couldn't hide the storm whirling behind his eyes. Nor his tense jaw and slightly uneven breathing.

"Hi," I said with forced brightness, trying to sound as if I knew nothing.

"Hi," he replied, his voice a couple of tones deeper than usual. He broke eye contact quickly and pulled out his pad, and after swiping a few times, pointed down the road to our left. "We need to head that way," he said, then took off down the sidewalk.

I was forced to move at a half jog to keep up with his long strides, while trying to keep my breathing in check and my mind focused on the task at hand.

Hux cleared his throat. "Hope your journey home last night wasn't too rough," he said, clearly trying to distract his own mind, too.

"Um, it was okay," I replied, glad for the small talk.

"Oh, and something you'll be interested to know: Nathan decided to launch the portal early, since between myself and the other admins who've begun recruiting, we already have around eleven groups on the list. There will probably be a few glitches, as he's launching ahead of schedule, but he wants to start letting people in as soon as they're recruited. Strike while the iron's hot, kind of thing."

"Oh," I said, genuinely excited. "So when will I get my invite?"

"Nathan's going to be sending them out this evening some-time, so by the time you get back home, you'll probably have one."

"I'll definitely check in when I get back," I said. And I also made a mental note to touch base with my team to see if they'd gotten theirs yet. "It feels like everything's moving so quickly, all of a sudden," I remarked.

He gave a dry smile. "Yeah, I know what you mean. It's a big step for the platform."

"Sure is. It's a big step for all of us, really."

"Mm-hm."

There was a span of silence as we rounded a corner, and then I wondered aloud, "What do you think is going to come of it?"

As he was an admin of the platform, I was curious to hear his take.

His expression lightened somewhat as he gave the question some thought. "Honestly, I don't know," he replied after a beat. "I've thought about it a lot, and it's just so hard to say until we have people together and a better idea of what resources will join the pool. At the very least, I'm hoping we can shift more people's perspectives. Remind them that it doesn't *have* to be this way."

I nodded. In the beginning, when the CRAS was introduced, there had been enough people with fires in their hearts for protests and riots to break out all around the country. Many were unhappy with it, and they had the courage to show it. Now, however, it felt like atrophy had set in among the people. The government hadn't responded kindly to the public protests, and they had long since died out, replaced with unhappy acceptance of the status quo.

Except for the people who went underground with their flame of discontentment. The people who descended into the shadow web. There were still protests going on, I reminded myself. There were just fewer participants than there used to be, and they weren't public anymore. It was a new kind of protest, where we had to work harder to get people's attention, while also ensuring that we stayed safe. Safety versus action was going to be a very tricky balance to manage, but I had to believe that where there was a will, there was a way.

There had to be. Because I feared that with each year the CRAS remained in place, it would become harder to uproot. The more we came to accept it in our lives, the less chance we'd have of ever getting rid of it. If change didn't start happening now, then who knew how long this scheme would run? How many more generations would have to bow to it? How many more families would be torn apart?

"Right," I replied, fiddling anxiously with my phone in my coat pocket. "We just gotta make sure we stay safe."

He nodded. "Yes. Especially once we move on to the less-trusted groups."

"When will that be?" I asked.

"Well, I only have five trusted ones left, and I'm intending to meet with them by the end of this week, beginning of next. Honestly, there aren't that many trusted people on the platform— trusted as in, verifiably trusted by Nathan. And we're not expecting all of them to accept our invites."

"Which is why you're planning to take the risk of reaching out to the less-trusted ones?"

He nodded. "We're all pretty sure there *are* a lot of other genuine members out there. Most members just didn't make the top list because their activities are sparser on the platform, giving Nathan few data points and making it harder to detect their positions either way. So yeah, our visits to them will be a bit more… thorough."

"You mean, you'll do some kind of interrogation?" I asked.

He nodded. "Of sorts."

"I see," I replied. I wondered what that would involve, exactly, but then noticed the ocean coming into view at the end of the long station road, and felt the press of a different question. "And who are we visiting today?" I asked, wondering what kind of people or person would want to meet us out here.

He gave me a cryptic look, and I rolled my eyes. "You get a kick out of keeping me in suspense, don't you?"

He chuckled, then shook his head. "Nah. I'm not lying when I say it's protocol, but I actually don't know much about these people, other than that they come recommended on the platform. All I know is they're due to show up at the end of the pier"—he glanced at his watch—"in about ten minutes. So let's hurry up."

He poured on the speed, and I had to move at a slow run to keep up. I guessed his phone conversation had set us back a few minutes, plus I had been eight minutes late myself. When we reached the end of the road, the ocean came into full, glorious view. It wasn't often that I visited the coast, and I breathed in deeply, enjoying the crisp, salty air in my lungs.

The woods in which I lived were fresh and calm, away from the pollution of the towns and estates, but still, nothing could quite beat the ocean in my opinion.

We arrived on a broad promenade and headed straight for the wide pier, which looked like it stretched out for at least half a mile. Moored boats bobbed on either side of it, though the dock in general seemed pretty empty of vessels, and also of people, except for a handful of couples enjoying an evening walk.

I was out of breath by the time we reached the end of the pier, and I dragged in deep lungfuls of air. Waves lapped hard against the base of the pier, sending spray up into my face, and I relished the feeling. It was a surprisingly warm evening, so I slipped off my coat, folding it over my arms and then keeping it held in front of me so that it still concealed the gun I kept around my waist.

I watched as Hux did the same, stripping off his jacket and revealing his broad torso, hugged by another slightly too-small shirt. We were three minutes early, and I thought about reminding him about my sewing offer, as small talk while we waited for whoever we were meeting to arrive, but then I remembered a more pressing topic I had been meaning to broach.

"Hey, I understand if this is confidential information, but I was wondering what happens to the kids who are born at Noreen and Davine's place. Same with the women."

"Ah." He hesitated, his eyes switching to the ocean. "Yeah. I do know, but I don't have permission to share it. At least, not right now."

"I understand," I replied, even though I felt disappointed. "I guess I just wondered if they stay in the country, or leave some-how…" I added, hoping to get at least that little morsel of infor-mation out of him.

If there were other ways people had found to disappear, then that was good news—for all of us. Because if we were going to become bolder in our rebellion against the system, I sensed that having as many ways as possible for people to hide themselves from the government would be useful, in times to come.

"I can tell you that they stay in the country," he replied.

I nodded slowly. It meant they must have some system that was keeping them hidden, and together. Which was very, very interesting. My plan had always been to flee, once I found my daughter, but if there was another way, I was willing to consider it.

The United Nation of America, for all its leadership's faults, was my country, after all, and I didn't want to be forced to leave if there was a viable alternative. I just couldn't imagine what that might be right now.

Maybe, as the days and weeks unfolded, and I came to know more and more people, I would find out.

Suddenly another question hit me, one that was more important than anything I'd asked him so far. "This may be a long shot, but I figure that you're surrounded by hackers and IT people on a daily basis, even if you're not one yourself." I glanced around the pier to verify that we were still alone, before continuing in a lower voice. "Do you know of anyone who's ever managed to break into the state's adoption archives?"

I waited for his response with bated breath. Like I said before, Nelson was amazing with computers, and I had a lot of faith in her, but still. Who was to say that there weren't people who were even more skilled than her out there, who might've already found a way to breach the archives?

Hux shook his head. "I'm sorry, but I don't. Though, to be honest, it's not something I've really asked about. It's possible there are people on the network who have figured out a way in. I guess that's a question you can raise in the portal. The other admins will spend time in there too, to answer questions wherever they can."

His reply sent a pulse of excitement rippling through me and added extra fire to my heels in regard to helping him reach out to as many people as possible. The more minds we had together, the more likely we were to come up with a solution to the archives. I was sure there had to be tons of others on the platform who wanted to break into it, to figure out where their children were. The answer could be out there, and it could just be a question of meeting the right person.

I was about to continue the conversation when I noticed Hux squinting at something over the water. My eyes followed the direction he was looking in, and spotted a small ship heading directly toward us, its dull headlights glowing through the darkness.

12

We both stared at the vessel as it floated over the dark waves toward us. Our eyes then moved along the length of the pier, and, given that there was no sign of anyone approaching from that direction, it occurred to me that the people we were waiting for might be *on* the boat.

I looked to Hux in question, and he shrugged.

We continued watching the small ship as it slowed to a stop, its side brushing gently against the tip of the pier before mooring. Now that it was closer, I could better make out its features beneath the light of the pier's lampposts. It looked large enough to hold fifteen or twenty people, and had definitely seen better days. Its exterior was rust-ridden, the original dark blue paint barely notice-able, as was the painted sign at the front. *The Forebearer*, it seemed to read.

The sound of a door opening drew our attention to the super-structure at the top. An elderly man stepped out, his hair shoulder-length and white beneath a floppy brown cap that hung lopsided on his head. He wore a thick, wooly sweater, and seemed to hold a cane in one hand as he hobbled toward the railing to peer down at us.

"Mr. X?" he asked, his voice gruff.

Hux exchanged another glance with me, and I could tell that even he was surprised by the means by which this person had arrived. He cleared his throat and nodded. "Yup."

The old man nodded back, then retreated into the ship. A minute later, a ramp descended from the belly of the vessel, revealing a dark space behind it, and connected to the edge of the pier.

Hux and I hurried across the ramp and into the open space, which seemed to be some kind of storage chamber, filled with boxes and piles of rope, and reeking of seaweed. The ramp creaked behind us as it closed, sealing us inside the dark chamber, and I shivered as I heard the sound of footsteps overhead.

Who *were* these people?

A moment later, a trap door opened above us, spilling warm light down into the room and illuminating a winding metal staircase that led upward. To my surprise, a young, curious face gazed down at us through the hole. A boy who looked no older than four, with round, pink cheeks and curly, shoulder-length brown hair.

"Move over, Rufus! You're hoggin' all the space!" another child spoke up from behind him, and a small hand closed around Rufus's left shoulder and pushed him to one side. A girl around age six, with the same curly brown hair and round face, appeared next to him, clearly his sibling.

"Now *you're* blocking the way, too!" another child's voice complained. "I can't see!" A third face squeezed in beside the first two. Another boy with curly brown hair, who looked about eight.

"All of you out of the way!" a female adult voice growled. One by one, the children were pulled away from the trap door's entrance, and then a heavyset brunette came into view. She had the same curly brown hair, so I guessed she was their mother. "I'm sorry for that," she said pleasantly, plastering a broad smile across her face as she met our gazes. "Please come up."

Hux and I frowned at each other, and then scaled the staircase, with him taking the lead. We emerged into some kind of living area, lined with sofas and carpets and... people. There had to be over twenty of them standing around the room, all of their eyes fixed on us.

I looked around, slightly dazed, at all the faces. Judging by the similarities between them, I was guessing they were one large, extended family. Eleven were kids, ranging from around one to sixteen, and then there were eight middle-aged adults: four men and four women. Three of the men and one of the women—the large brunette—resembled each other, so I assumed they were siblings, and that the other adults were perhaps their spouses. Then there were four elderly people, including the old guy with the brown cap and cane. Two sets of grandparents, from what I could tell.

"Uh, hi," Hux said, gazing around at them. I could tell he hadn't quite been expecting this kind of reception, either. "Good to meet you... all."

I stared at them as well, still shocked. The kids in particular looked intensely curious. So much so that the younger ones were being held back by their parents, as though they were straining to come up and touch us.

I suddenly felt very much like an animal in a zoo.

"Who're you?" Rufus blurted out, twisting a strand of curly hair between his small fingers.

"Yeah, who're you and why're you here?" a little blonde girl with a rather wonky pixie cut piped up.

"Shush!" a blonde woman, presumably her mother, said. "I

told y'all we were expecting visitors! Now all of you kids go upstairs and play!"

She might as well have said nothing, because none of them budged, not even the three teenagers. Apparently we were far more interesting than anything they had to do upstairs.

"Go," the brunette mother ordered, her growly voice returning. She tugged Rufus and his sixish-year-old sister to the door, while the rest of the adults got to work on the others. To my bemusement, even the teens were manhandled out—though the oldest of the teens managed to slip back in just before one of the men closed the door. She was a tall, thin, mousy-looking brunette girl, with freckles and large blue eyes. And for some reason, she seemed to find me particularly interesting, as she perched on the edge of one of the sofas next to her mother and fixed her eyes on my face with almost as intense a curiosity as the younger kids.

From the way they behaved, you would have thought we were the first people they'd ever come in contact with outside of their family. It occurred to me then that maybe that wasn't far from the truth.

The boat shuddered suddenly and started to move again. Hux and I looked to the adults, who were settling themselves among the sofas now that they'd closed the door on the kids, and I noticed that the grandpa with the cane was missing.

Before we could ask why we were moving, one of the brown-haired men explained, "Best we stay away from ports in general, you know? Don't worry. We'll drop you back off as soon as we're done here. We just don't like to hang around." He gave us a dark, knowing look.

And I looked again to Hux, not feeling at all comfortable about the situation. I hadn't expected us to be more or less kidnapped on their ship. Judging by the tight expression on his face, Hux wasn't at ease with it either.

But apparently it didn't bother him enough to object.

"I understand," he said after a moment. "And I trust that you *will* return us once we're through," he added, and I detected a slight warning in his eyes.

"Of course!" the brown-haired man said.

"Then I guess we'll get down to business," Hux concluded, shooting me a look that told me he felt things would probably be okay.

I wasn't sure what people like these would want with us, but as with Davine and Noreen, we could never be sure. For now, I tried to put it aside and focus on the motley group around us.

"Hold up," a black-haired woman wearing a red bandana said, raising a hand. "Surely you'll be wanting some tea or something first? Wasn't it a long journey to get here?"

"Um, okay," Hux replied, glancing at me tentatively.

"Okay, thanks," I added. I didn't feel like tea, or really any consumable right now, given that we were locked on a boat filled with utter strangers and were sailing away from the shore, but I guessed this woman didn't get the chance to make tea for guests very often. It just seemed polite to oblige her.

"Hot tea it is!"

"And also, how about some introductions?" the blonde woman said, giving us a friendly smile.

The large brunette woman rolled her eyes. "I'm sure that's not what they're here for, Luna," she said, her tone condescending. "They're here to talk business, like Mr. X said in the messages."

The blonde shot her a sour look. "And I'm sure they can reply for themselves."

"Yeah, chill out, Martha," one of the brown-haired men said, presumably one of Martha's brothers. "It ain't often we have guests."

Martha gave him a glare, but before she could respond, the

one grandfather who was left in the room—perhaps Luna's father, judging by the same slight hook of their noses—scoffed. "You can talk, Rick. Usually you're the one pissing your pants over inviting strangers aboard."

"Oh, lay off about that already, you old goat," Rick shot back, looking genuinely irritated. "You admitted yourself I was right to be nervous that time."

And then they started bickering, as though they'd forgotten that Hux and I were even in the room. I watched the exchange with a raised eyebrow. They seemed to quarrel as much as the kids, and I had to wonder how on Earth they got by sharing this small space. Because from the vibe I was getting so far, I was taking a guess that they lived on this boat full time, and I was 99.999 percent sure that they were CRAS evaders, just as Hux's parents had been.

My eyes wandered to the teenage girl, to find her looking thoroughly unamused. Downright embarrassed, in fact. Her head was dropped in her hands, what I could see of her cheeks flushed a dark shade of pink. And I couldn't help but feel sorry for her. I couldn't imagine what it must be like growing up in these circumstances. It had to be a terribly stifling environment for her, as a young woman. If she was in hiding along with her younger siblings, I doubted she ever got to mix with anyone her own age. And even if she did, it would have to be rare.

Which was perhaps why she had appeared to take a particular interest in me.

Looking back at the adults, whose bickering seemed to finally be dying down, I supposed this had just become normal behavior for them over however many years they'd been living like this. Maybe this was what living in a small space with all your family members did to you after a while. They likely didn't realize how odd it looked to outsiders.

"I'm so sorry," one of the grandmothers said loudly, her voice cutting through everything else. "Please, do start."

The bandana woman returned with two cups of tea at that moment and set them down on a low table beside us, and then Hux sucked in a breath, and began to introduce himself.

The teen seemed to gather the courage to look up again now that her family's arguing had stopped, and her eyes once more returned to me, curious. I looked away, as it felt weird for us to be staring at one another, and listened as Hux started explaining the history behind Nathan's new direction for the platform.

About halfway through his pitch, to my surprise, the teen got up from her seat and moved over to me, sitting down right next to me on our sofa. I gave her a friendly, if a bit surprised, smile, and she smiled shyly back. Then she leaned in tentatively and whispered in my ear, "You wanna hang out in my room?"

I stared at her, a bit taken aback by the offer. I found it kind of creepy, to be honest, but looking into her hopeful eyes, I could tell she really didn't mean it to come across that way. She was obviously desperate for company, and I felt a stab of pity for her.

Plus, it occurred to me that this would give me a chance to ask some questions. Figure out who these people were, and maybe get information that the adults would be too careful to let slip.

So I glanced at Hux, who was still busy talking, and then shrugged. I guessed I might as well, as I doubted Hux needed me to sit here the whole time. I wasn't exactly doing anything productive right now.

"Sure," I whispered back.

Her eyes glistened with excitement, as though I had just given her a birthday present, and she reached for my hand and pulled me up. I barely had a chance to note Hux's, or anyone else's, reaction to her gesture before she'd led me through the door and closed it gently behind us.

We emerged in a narrow passageway that contained a short staircase leading up to the higher levels. Out here, I could hear the raucous noise of the children upstairs, their footsteps pounding on the ceiling, an occasional shriek tearing through the boat, as they probably ripped each other's hair out or something. The girl led me along the corridor and stopped about halfway down, in front of what looked like a storage cupboard set beneath the stairs. She opened it and crept inside, turning on a light to reveal a tiny bedroom. A mattress took up most of it, and at the end was a small desk, just about wide enough for her to sit in front of, which held a computer.

The girl glanced at me hesitantly, as if waiting for my reaction, and I managed to pull an impressed face. "Looks pretty cool in there."

She moved her eyes to the computer, shrugging ruefully. "It's not much, but it's all my own. Nobody else is allowed to come in here."

I smiled. "Well, I appreciate your invite then."

She smirked, and then made room for me to step inside. I lowered myself onto the edge of the mattress and sat in a cross-legged position, while the girl sank to the floor in front of her computer. She brushed an errant strand of hair behind her ear, smiling at me nervously.

"So do you all live on this boat full time?" I asked, figuring that was a good, fairly nonintrusive question to start with.

Her smile soured somewhat. "Yeah. Full time."

"For how long?" I asked.

She sighed, leaning back against the table. "Since forever."

I nodded at the confirmation of my earlier suspicion. "And how do you pass your time?" I asked.

She shrugged. "Homeschooling. Just like the rest of my siblings and cousins." She glanced at her computer. "Well, that and I spend a lot of time with George here." She stroked the top of the old monitor.

I smiled. "Oh, you've named it."

"I've named *him*, yes," she replied with a grin.

"And are you some kind of computer genius?" I asked.

She scoffed. "I wish. But nah. I'm still just learning the basics of coding and stuff." She paused, then hit a key on the keyboard, bringing the screen to life. It showed a black window filled with lines of green-and-yellow code. "I'm working on something cool, though," she added with a shy smile.

"What's that?" I asked.

"A network for homeschoolers. It's still pretty ugly, and I've got a lot more work to do on it, but ten people have joined already."

She pulled up a dark web browser and navigated to a plain-looking portal under the name of *Homeskoolers Unite*. The color scheme was a bit all over the place, with lots of pinks and purples, and then some splashes of blues and greens, as if added as an afterthought to make boys feel welcome too. But when she logged in, it looked impressively functional, with all the basic modules of a networking site. The girl was clearly smart and driven, and I could picture her being a valuable member of our group in a few years' time, if not already. She could offer assistance with running the portal, for one thing.

She brought up a list of the ten members, all of them with non-identifying avatars and obviously fake names, and pointed to two of the accounts. "I'm friends with these two. Not really sure about the others, though. They're pretty unresponsive." She puffed out her cheeks, then navigated to a profile under the name of Gabby Sails. "This is mine," she explained, bringing up a page with an avatar image of a cartoon-drawn girl who very vaguely resembled "Gabby."

"Well," I said, "it's impressive. You basically *are* a whiz."

Her cheeks warmed. "Meh. I still got a lot to learn. But yeah, I guess I can do some fairly cool stuff. Mostly, I just wanted to start something where teens like me can hang out. I mean, my family can't be the only underground homeschoolers."

I nodded. "I'm pretty sure you're right about that." Wherever Davine and Noreen's women went with their kids, I was certain they'd have to stay hidden too, which would leave homeschooling as the only option to educate their children. "And all this coding stuff—did your parents teach you, or is it all self-taught?"

"Self-taught. I took a bunch of free online tutorials in my spare time—still taking them, in fact—and I forced my parents to give me George when I was eight. I've been playing around with him ever since. He's been on the ship for like, two decades or something, but he's still chuggin' along." She gave the monitor a warm smile and another affectionate stroke.

I nodded slowly, feeling as though I understood much more about Gabby than I had a few minutes ago. This seemed to be her only way of socializing with anyone other than her family. And while I was glad that she at least had some outlet away from the craziness that was the rest of her home, I couldn't help but feel sad for her. They might've all escaped the CRAS, but the kind of life they lived now didn't seem like that great of an alternative. Better than being separated from their families, yes, but once a child got past a certain age, they needed space to breathe and develop independence. Not to mention, what was Gabby's future going to be? Would she be stuck here indefinitely, even into her twenties?

It was an angering reminder of the lengths the CRAS was driving people to, just to keep their families together. We *had* to find a way to fix this.

"Do you mind me asking why you don't just sail off to a different country and start a new life there?" I asked.

Gabby sighed. "That's not so easy for people like us. None of my siblings or cousins have any kind of documentation. We're basically ghosts, and if we suddenly showed up at a port, we'd be asked questions we wouldn't be able to answer. We could all get deported back to the UNA and handed over to the authorities. It's just not a risk my parents are willing to take."

I nodded, supposing it made sense. Though, how could they even live perpetually on the water? What about fuel, and so on? Satellite Internet charges? Electricity? I guessed they must've figured it out somehow; maybe they had a contact or two on the land who was helping them. And as for food, perhaps they lived off the ocean, and/or the adults made occasional bulk shopping trips for groceries on land.

Whatever the case, I realized they could greatly benefit from this new alliance Nathan was pulling together, too. There were others who had figured out how to hide and live inland—Hux had told me that the women from Davina and Noreen's organization went somewhere after they gave birth. And that it was somewhere in the country. Did that mean that there could be an entire underground society that we didn't even know about? Hundreds of people who lived in the country, but off the grid? And if there were, could they help Gabby escape? Could they help this entire family? And once I found my daughter, could they help me? I put it on the list of things to think about later. The adult members of Gabby's family might be able to hack this lifestyle, but she and her siblings and cousins simply couldn't live like this forever.

Gabby returned her focus to the monitor, and I watched as she minimized her social network and went back to the search browser. "There is also another project I'm working on, by the way," she said, an excited twinkle in her eye.

"And what's that?" I asked, genuinely curious.

"Learning to be a hacker," she replied proudly.

"Whoa. How many other tricks do you have up those sleeves?" I had been right about this girl being driven and smart. And, suspecting she'd wind up helping us sooner rather than later, I made a mental note to confirm with Hux that she would be invited onto the platform with her parents (assuming he decided to invite them, after his discussion with them was done).

She grinned. "Not many more."

"What do you want to hack?" I asked.

She shrugged. "There's a lot of bad stuff going on in the shadow web. People who've become criminals for all the wrong reasons."

"Oh, I know," I said, giving her a serious look. I'd stumbled upon enough of those after I discovered the shadow web, myself.

"So I figured it would be useful if I could cause them a bit of trouble."

I frowned. "What sort of trouble?"

"Oh, like, digging into their admin panels and messing up their databases. Disabling forums, overloading servers, that sort of thing…" She trailed off as she focused on the monitor. "This is one I found the other day," she said after a minute, bringing up a dark gray login screen. She somehow bypassed it, and the screen that popped up next made my eyes bug.

"What in the world?" I breathed, gazing at what looked like some sort of auction site. Except the items on offer didn't appear to be items at all.

The page was comprised of listings containing descriptions of what I could only imagine were kids, judging by the biometric data detailed there—and an "availability status" was attached to each entry. Of the ten that I could see on this page, five were grayed out as "unavailable" while one was "processing" and the others were a bright green "available."

I had come across a lot of forums discussing sketchy stuff, but I had never seen anything like *this*.

"Yeah, it was well hidden," she went on. "I don't know how anyone would stumble upon it without a direct link. I only discovered it because someone mentioned it on a random forum I happened to be browsing. Some guy thought he was being all clever and cryptic, talking about a place where 'some people bought potatoes.' Obviously it was code for something, and I was curious, so I PM'd him and he gave me the link. Looks like it's run by some kind of shady kidnapping ring," she concluded solemnly.

"How many listings are on this platform?" I asked, still gaping.

"I don't know yet," she replied. "I've only managed to access one page so far, what you see here. I was planning to try to trace the details of the admin of the site, to see if there's any way I can anonymously rat them out to the government. I'm guessing the kids would be in better hands even with the CRAS."

I looked at her, once again impressed by her maturity. "That's really brave of you, Gabby. Are you sure you're taking proper security measures to make sure nobody can track *you* down?"

"Oh, yeah. I don't do anything in the shadows without several layers of encryption."

"Good," I said. Even on the ocean, I worried that if she pissed off the wrong criminals, they could find a way of getting to her. Especially if they were making a lot of money through this kind of operation. I wondered what type of person could stoop to running a site like that. Then I realized it could very well be people who weren't dissimilar to me and my colleagues. Perhaps whose technical operations were even close to Nelson's, and other groups operating out of OH. The only difference was where the children ended up. People who stole them and then, instead of giving them back to their birthparents, sold them. Which was a sobering reminder that anything in this world could be used for good *and* bad.

I hoped Gabby would figure out a way to crack it, because people like that needed to be taken down. And with the time and dedication she seemed to have, I wouldn't put it past her.

But I put thoughts of that site aside for now, because I wasn't sure how much longer I had in here with her, and a different subject had surfaced in my head—one I'd actually been wanting to bring up the moment she mentioned hacking.

"Do you know anything about the government's adoption archives?" I asked. She had obviously spent a lot of time browsing the shadow web, or *in the shadows*, as she referred to it. It seemed possible that she could've read a discussion on it or something. Perhaps seen someone else talking about their attempts to crack it.

But she shook her head. "Nope. I think my mom would prob- ably slaughter me if I tried to touch anything even remotely government-related."

"Oh, yes," I said quickly. "I'm not encouraging you to try. I just wondered if you might have come across anything."

"Yeah, I haven't. Sorry."

The sound of footsteps outside drew my attention away from the screen and reminded me that Gabby's elders would likely *not* approve of what we'd just been discussing.

"Where have you taken her, girl?" I sat up straighter as the familiar voice of the brunette mother drifted in through the cracks in the door. "Few minutes sittin' with a guest and you run off with her!"

Gabby quickly dimmed the screen and turned to look at me with a heavy sigh. "Looks like it's time for you to go."

Her dismay touched me, and I almost wished I could stay a bit longer just for her sake, but I had an idea of how I could ease the blow a little for her. "Hey, are you a member of OH?" I asked.

"Yup," she replied.

"Add me to your circle, then. I'm RobinHood21."

Her face lit up like fireworks. "Oh my God, I will. I'm Gabby-Sails! All one word, same as on my network!"

"Thanks. I can give you my number, too, if you have a way to call me," I added. Honestly, she was a smart cookie, and her computer skills made her the kind of person who could be useful as a contact, especially when the only other tech I was close to was Nelson. Plus, I wanted to know how it went with that kidnapping site.

And if I could help make her life saner along the way, by giving her someone she could talk to, then that was all the better.

"That's even awesomer!" she practically squealed. "I promise I won't call you much."

"It's fine," I said, smiling. "I'd like you to let me know how things go with that site, as well as if you come across anything about the archives during your shadow web crawls."

"Sure thing!"

She gave me a pad and a piece of paper, and I scrawled my number on it. And when I handed it back to her, she pulled me into a hug. I hugged her back awkwardly, given the cramped space, and then she leaned over me to push open the door, and we both made our way out.

Hux and her mother were standing in the hallway, waiting, and the woman gave her daughter a mildly disapproving look. "What were you two doing in there?" she asked with a frown. Hux was looking at me with confusion, too.

"Just hanging out," Gabby replied with a shrug.

"Yup, just hanging out," I repeated, keeping to her version of the truth, as she had now confirmed my suspicion that her mother likely didn't know about her hacking endeavors. "You ready to leave, then?" I asked Hux.

He nodded. "Yeah. All done."

"Okay, great."

Then, just as the woman was leading us back to the living area, the hoard of children came spilling down the staircase and swarmed around us.

"You goin' already?" Rufus asked, wide-eyed, while several of the other kids asked variations of the same question.

"Afraid so," I replied, ruffling his curly hair.

Gabby kept close behind me as we returned to the trap door, then waited as her mother opened it.

"We should touch the dock in about a minute," the woman explained. "So head down and wait for the ramp to open."

"Thanks for your hospitality, ma'am," Hux said, shaking her hand, and then nodding to the rest of the adults still in the room.

"Thanks, ma'am," I echoed, shaking her hand as well.

"No, thank *you* two, for coming," one of the men replied. "This new initiative sounds like it'll be real interesting."

And hopefully also helpful.

Hux nodded, and then the two of us climbed down the ladder, descending once more into the damp gloom.

Gabby and as many of the other children as could fit peered down at us through the hole as we waited for the ramp to fall. I waved one last time to all of them before we walked across the ramp and out of sight. The ramp started withdrawing again almost as soon as our feet had touched the pier, and the ship quickly motored away, back into the darkness.

We watched it go for about a minute in silence, and then Hux turned his back on the ocean. "Let's head back," he said.

I nodded, and we took off at a brisk walk down the pier.

"So what did that girl actually want with you?" he asked,

frowning. "It was pretty weird the way she pulled you out of the room."

"Yeah, about that," I said, having been about to broach the topic with him myself. "Her name's Gabby, and she seems like a smart kid. She had a computer in that little cupboard room and is in the process of designing her own social network for home-schoolers. She's also a self-taught hacker." I proceeded to explain about the kidnapping ring's site she was attempting to crack, and by the time I'd finished, Hux's eyes were wide.

"That's disgusting," he said, the corners of his mouth turning down.

"I know. I'm hoping she'll figure out a way to take it down. And back to the subject of Gabby: I think she could be a good asset to the new portal, so if you've decided to invite her parents, which I'm guessing you have, I suggest you invite her too. Her handle's GabbySails."

"Yeah, I'm planning to invite them. And I'll send off an invite to her, too."

"Good," I said, and then there was a pause as we reached the end of the pier and took off down the station road. "What is their group actually known for in the OH community?" I asked. "I mean, what was it that flagged them as a trustworthy group? How did they earn their reputation?" It was a key piece of information that I hadn't gotten out of Gabby during the brief time we'd talked. We'd ended up getting too sidetracked with her shadow web projects.

"They help fellow OH members, occasionally," Hux replied. "From what they told me, it's mostly people who're in need of emergency hiding places. They let folks on board their boat temporarily, until the dust settles."

"Oh, I see. Well I guess that's brave, to say the least, for them to take that risk of inviting someone into their home."

"Yes," Hux replied. "I think their hearts are definitely in the right place. And they do seem brave, if a little eccentric."

I smiled. "Yeah, well, sharing that small space for decades will probably do that to a person."

He chuckled, shaking his head. "Rather them than me, that's all I'll say."

"I'm guessing back where you're from, you had tons of space to stretch those long legs of yours," I remarked, my eyes dropping automatically to the lengthy strides he was taking.

He gave me a bemused look, his lips curving in a half smile.

"What?" I asked.

"Long legs?"

I shrugged. "They are long, aren't they?"

"Yeah... I guess it's just not a descriptor I'm used to being on the end of, as a guy."

I smirked. "Well, take it as a compliment."

"Okay... And to answer your question, yes. I'd sometimes be gone for days at a time, when hunting for food in the winter."

Our conversation trailed off as we reached the station entrance. We both stopped, and I was turning to look at him, wondering if he had commuted by train today, too, when a ringing suddenly erupted from his coat pocket.

He dipped a hand inside and pulled out his phone, and his face darkened as he glanced at the screen. He swallowed hard, his Adam's apple bobbing, and I couldn't help but feel that this call might be related to the conversation I'd caught him in earlier, the one that had put him in such a bitter mood.

"I'm sorry, Robin," he muttered. "I gotta take this call now. I'll... I'll be in touch about the next visitation tomorrow, in case you want to come again, okay?"

"Oh, yeah, okay," I replied, then watched as he turned on his heel and swiftly crossed the road, pressing the phone to his ear as he headed into the shadows of the parking lot beyond.

My mind once again mulled over what this whole issue could be about, but thoughts of more important things soon distracted me as I walked back through the station barriers. Like that awful kidnapping site. The fact that such things even existed disturbed me deeply. I couldn't bring myself to imagine what it would feel like to have my own child listed there. At least under the CRAS, Hope would have been taken in by a responsible family, who might not give her the love she deserved, but would at least look after her, the way the Sylvones had looked after me (until I was seventeen, anyway).

And I wondered how many other sites like that existed. Sites that we didn't even know about. Especially considering that Gabby's discovery of this one had been pure dumb luck.

The bitter side of me blamed its existence on the CRAS, wanting to believe that it had encouraged a culture of commodifying children, with so many wealthy people "collecting" them. Even though I knew that wasn't entirely fair. Evil like this, in one form or another, had existed since the beginning of written history... though I couldn't imagine that initiatives like the CRAS helped.

But regardless of whose fault it was, the whole subject got me thinking, as I climbed aboard my train and settled into a window seat, that maybe, once we got organized, the portal could have a broader scope. Maybe we could take a leaf out of Gabby's book and target criminals whenever we came across them.

And then I realized, a few minutes into those musings, that we couldn't stretch ourselves too thin. There wasn't an unlimited number of us, nor would we have unlimited resources, and taking on the CRAS alone was a massive task.

We needed focus as a group. So perhaps we were going to
have to leave this kind of work to Gabby's free time after all.

I sighed and leaned back, my eyes glazing over against the
lights whizzing past the window, though the subject lingered in
the back of my head throughout the journey home.

13

I had been so distracted by the evening's events that I almost forgot about the invitation to the new portal that I was supposed to be receiving that evening. I remembered a minute after I stepped through the front door of my cabin, and after using the bathroom and grabbing a bottle of Nurmeal, I settled into bed and logged on to Operation Hood.

The little red number hovering above the messages tab told me that I had two new emails, and I quickly clicked to open my inbox. A small smile played on my lips as I saw that the most recent was a friend request from Gabby. I checked the time it had arrived and realized she had sent it about ten minutes after we left. It came with a little note:

"Hey, Robin. Thanks for visiting us today. Look forward to seeing what happens with Nathan's new project. Hopefully I get an invite along with my parents. In the meantime, I'll keep chipping away at those shadow bastards.

- Gabby x"

I typed a quick reply:

"Thanks for having us. And yes, I hope to see you around in the new portal. Good luck with that project. Keep me posted and stay safe. R. x"

And then I returned to my inbox. I was eager to check the second message, which was indeed an invite to the new portal. It had been sent by one of the admins: ZombieBrainz. I frowned, wondering for a moment if that might be Nathan, but I had no way of knowing, so I proceeded to click on the link provided in the message. It led me to a blank login page. Since no new username or password had been included in the message, I supposed my main OH credentials would work, and I entered them.

They worked. The login page disappeared, and the next screen that flashed up was a familiar interface. Its minimalistic gray-and-brown design was like the main network's, except this was a stripped-down version, with a group forum being the most prominently displayed module.

The site's official opening was supposed to be next Monday, so this had to be a beta version. Nathan must still be working on the bells and whistles, but released it early to get the new recruits in ASAP. And there were already eleven active members browsing the forum. I clicked on the link to add one to that number and found, to my excitement, that there were three conversation threads, all of them with intriguing titles:

"First stunt…"

"Facilities/resources you can put on the table"

"Changing perspectives"

As well as a pinned post at the top:

"Security best practices: READ FIRST"

Before I could click on any of them, however, my phone rang. I leapt off the mattress to fetch it from where I'd left it in the living room and checked the screen. It was Nelson.

"Hey," I said, answering the call. I put it on loudspeaker and set the device down on my mattress.

"Hey," her voice came back, slightly morphed and crackly thanks to our encryption protocol. "I see you logged in to the new portal. You back home now?"

"Yes. You received the invite too?" I asked.

"Yup. I'm logged in and looking at your glowing green avatar as we speak."

"Where do I find the full list of members?" I asked, searching around for it.

"It's just under the—"

"Ah, yeah, I got it," I replied, having just spotted the link at the bottom, beneath the forum.

I blew out as the list appeared. There were eleven active members in the forum, but thirty members in the portal already. Granted, many of those were probably admins, but still, this was *happening*! There had been talk of the portal all week, but actually seeing it in the flesh sent a thrum of excitement through me.

I scanned the list to find that Nelson, Julia, Marco, and the twins had already joined, and were all showing up as online. I frowned when I saw that Jackie wasn't there, but then shook it off. Maybe she had just been busy this evening.

Davine and Noreen were also there, though currently showing as offline, but Gabby and her family were still waiting for their invites, it seemed. Hux had only just recruited them a couple of hours ago, though, so I supposed they'd receive theirs tomorrow sometime.

"Have you checked out the forum yet?" Nelson asked.

"No," I said, quickly navigating back over to the forum. "I was just about to when you called. I'm back in there now."

"I just wondered if you'd read through any of the comments yet under 'First stunt.'"

"Let me go in there now." I clicked on the thread and began to read. A guy (or girl) whose profile name was Zion Rey (handle: LionZion) was the thread starter.

"Obviously, this requires a lot of thought and discussion, but interested to hear everyone's initial ideas on what our first move could/should be, once we're all in here..."

To my amusement, Abe had been the first to reply:

"Something that doesn't get us all killed."

"Yeah, I figured that was kind of a given..." Zion replied, evidently not catching on to Abe's humor.

"A mass robbery of a holding center," a girl (or guy) with the profile name Winter De Ville (SnowQueen) suggested.

"I'd say that falls under the above-mentioned category," Marco had replied, less than a minute after Winter posted.

"Agreed," Nelson had added curtly, along with several others.

And I would agree with them, too. Holding centers were facilities where kids were sometimes kept by the Ministry, when immediate delivery to a family wasn't possible. For example, if they lived in another part of the country, or the paperwork/adoption admin fee transfer was delayed. I'd never visited one, but from what I'd heard, they were always well populated by nurses looking after the children, along with twenty-four-hour security, to prevent kidnapping rings from getting any funny ideas.

Plus, it would be a horribly crude way to introduce ourselves to the world. We stole children, yes, but we also had discrimination regarding which ones we targeted. At least, the people I worked with did. Not only did we have an age limit, but we also only took back what was ours—or more specifically, the families' we were helping.

We needed to project a positive image of ourselves to the mass of people, if they were to take us seriously. If we pulled off a stunt like that, the media would be quick to tarnish us with the same brush as the shady kidnappers and other troublemaking criminals, which would cause more damage to us than good.

Not to mention, what would we do with all the kids, even if we did manage to steal them? If we didn't have access to the government's adoption archives, we'd have no clue whom to return them to.

No, that seemed like a thoroughly stupid and irresponsible idea.

Whatever we did, it had to be intelligent, and staged in such a way that would make it clear to the media, beyond any doubt, that we weren't just your average rebels without a cause, but a serious, organized group seeking to reform, rather than hurt, our country.

How we were going to pull off anything remotely close to that, I still didn't know. I needed more time to think about it, so I decided to shelve it for now, and returned my focus to the screen.

"Hey, you there?" Nelson's voice crackled up from the bed, interrupting me.

"Oh, sorry!" I said. "Forgot you were still on the line. I'm just reading."

"It's fine. Was just curious to hear your thoughts, but I know it's a lot to absorb. We can catch up another time because I gotta go offline for a bit. Oh, and you need to tell me how it went today with Hux."

"It went fine. Another successful visit," I replied, then went on to give her a summary of everything that had happened. As expected, she was horrified to learn about the kidnapping site, as well as intrigued by my description of Gabby, saying that she looked forward to her joining the forum so she could have a chat with her.

Then, once she'd finished asking me questions and I'd told her all I had to say, she exhaled and said, "Okay, Robin. Thanks for the recap. I'll catch you later."

Bidding her goodnight, I cut the call, then looked once more to the screen, continuing to scroll down the page. Several more suggestions popped up, no less rash than Winter's—and in some cases, even rasher, like targeting schools in wealthy areas, or even children's hospitals. All of those got a massive no from me, and I was glad to see that others, including my own team, commenting in the forum shared my disagreement. We needed to do better.

By the fifth page of comments, I was starting to feel over-whelmed by the bombardment of ideas and random trains of thought. The open dialogue was great—it was the first step in the right direction—but I could see that we really were going to need to have some better organization and management of thoughts and ideas if we were to get anywhere. There were only ten or so people even taking part in this discussion right now; I couldn't imagine what it would be like once more joined, and we got into the hundreds.

Realistically, we were probably going to need to meet in person somewhere, at some point, and have a moderated meeting overlooked by an appointed chairman. Online, people tended to be scatterbrained and less organized. But until we trusted each other enough for a real meetup, Nathan would most likely institute some kind of voting system—a modified version of the polls we had on the main network, to allow the most popular ideas to rise to the top and gain the most visibility. I just had to try to be patient and wait until Monday, for when the official site rolled out, and we could really start getting things moving. *Five more days.*

For now, I decided to click out of that "stunt" thread, to give my brain a rest, and check out the list of security best practices.

That thread had been started by the one and only Mr. X, to my pleasant surprise, who was currently showing as offline. Perhaps he hadn't reached… wherever his home was… yet. Or had gone straight to bed when he got in.

I read through the list of security advice, and most of it was obvious to me, thanks to my training from Nelson. All of the guidance basically amounted to the same thing: share information only as strictly necessary. There was one line that caught my eye, however, which might not have been completely intuitive to me:

"We advise you to avoid posting specific information in the Facilities/Resources thread until you have gotten to know this community better. Especially where said facilities/resources could give valuable intel about loopholes to a government mole."

That made sense. I checked the resources thread just to see if anyone had fudged over that advice and posted anyway, but no, it was still bare of comments.

My eyes were starting to droop, the lack of sleep last night and the long day today catching up with me, but I managed to keep them open long enough to scan through the final "Changing Perspectives" thread. It wasn't very long, with the opening being a general statement by a member named Stayhome Dad (hairy_poppins), expressing that the best, and only, hope we had of effecting change was to affect the consciousness of the people, because there had to be only so much external, public pressure that even a leadership as stubborn as ours could take. If enough people rallied together, change could happen.

And as I finally sank into my pillows and closed my eyes, I just hoped that was true.

14

The hours seemed to tick by even more slowly than usual at the factory the next day. The overwhelmingness and general disorganization of the forum played on my mind, making me impatient for Monday to arrive, and I'd also gotten another message from Hux earlier this morning, asking if I was free to meet him outside Trenton Mall at 6:00 p.m. for another visitation. I'd been pleasantly surprised by the location and immediately replied that I'd come, since the mall was right near my factory. Which left me checking my watch so often that even my colleagues started to notice and asked if I had a date or something this evening.

I told them yes, because it wasn't a lie. Despite its teething problems, the early opening of the portal had injected me with an enthusiasm I couldn't shake to continue going out with Hux, and help him recruit the rest of the group's members as soon as possible. So we could actually start *doing* something. After all, every step forward, however small, was a step closer toward my endgame: saving our country and finding my daughter.

And if I had thought my life had regained meaning seven months ago when I discovered Nelson and her team, it was feeling a hell of a lot more meaningful now, regardless of how far we'd actually end up going. My horizons had been broadened, and it made my blood hum.

I raced out of the factory the moment the dismissal bell rang, almost running over my supervisor on the way out, then leapt onto my motorcycle and drove around the corner to the mall, where I found Hux already waiting, sitting on a bench outside the entrance.

He was slouched over, his head resting in his hands, and he didn't notice me even when I parked right next to him. Nor when I dismounted and started walking toward him. It was only when I got within a couple of feet of his bench that he finally raised his head.

And there was no kind way to say it: he looked like crap. Dark circles ringed his amber eyes, which were bleary and slightly bloodshot, while his dark hair was sticking up in at least four different directions.

"Whoa," I said. "Are you okay?"

He leaned back, running a hand through his thick, tousled locks. A halfhearted smile twitched his lips. "Do I really look that bad?"

"You just look... really run down."

He exhaled. "Probably the result of getting less than two hours of sleep last night," he muttered under his breath, then rose swiftly to his feet and cast his eyes up and down the street. "So you parked already?" he asked, changing the subject before I could ask why he had slept so badly.

It made me think back to the call he had received just before I'd left him last night, and the way his face had darkened. I couldn't help but suspect that his lack of sleep was related to it. "Yes," I replied, having no time to dwell on it now.

"Okay. We're going to need to rely on personal transport for our destination today, and I suggest we take my bike."

He led me around the corner of the small shopping center building to a large, shiny, beetle-black motorcycle parked in one of the bays, then opened up the seat and pulled out two helmets, handing one to me while he put the other on. He mounted the bike first, moving as close to the front of the seat as he could to make room for me. Luckily the seat was pretty elongated, and I was able to sit fairly comfortably, my fingers hooking under the safety support beneath my butt. Still, I was unable to ignore my proximity to him, and it sent an embarrassing thrill rushing through me. It was as physically close as I'd gotten to him, and the novelty somehow increased the speed of my already-racing heartbeat.

Trying to put the feeling away, I kept my eyes focused straight ahead as he took off. We headed through the urban area, and when the buildings became sparser, I realized we were heading all the way into the countryside. Soon we were actually trundling through open fields.

I attempted to make small talk a few times, but he clearly wasn't in the mood, so I let silence reign—which wasn't difficult to do anyway, with the breeze whipping against our helmets. Instead, I watched row after row of wind turbines, their rotors glinting in the sparse evening light, until the sun dipped, and the twilight turned them into hulking shadows.

Once we were truly in the definition of the middle of nowhere, Hux turned down a small dirt track, and I noticed in the distance a large, rectangular building with metal walls. It seemed to be some kind of warehouse, and as we drew closer, the words painted on the wall and illuminated by two white spotlights, became clearer: *Burnaby Group, Inc.* We pulled to a stop about twenty feet away from the entrance and got off the bike. I gave Hux a curious look, but his eyes were already fixed on the building, and he started moving toward it.

Once we'd approached within ten feet, there was a loud groan and a side door opened, revealing a tall, thin man wearing a black suit and tinted glasses. It seemed this guy was cagier about revealing his appearance than others had been, which instantly got my guard up, making me wonder what he had to hide.

He beckoned us over, and as we reached him, stepped backward, allowing us through the door, before closing it behind us. Once we were inside, he held a hand out for Hux to shake, but made no motion to shake mine. He seemed tense, anxious to get the meeting over with, and led us swiftly down a narrow, white-painted corridor toward a paper-strewn office, which overlooked a giant storage room... filled with guns of every shape and size imaginable.

Hux and I took seats opposite him, and as they began to talk, it became clear to me that the guy was the owner of a legitimate weapons business. Which would explain his nerves, and simultaneously lessened mine somewhat, now that I had something to pin his caginess on. His jaw kept twitching, and every other minute, his eyes darted reflexively to the door as if he feared someone was about to barge in. In helping us, or even agreeing to meet us, he was putting a lot on the line. Not only himself, but also his company.

I realized that it was noble of him to even consider taking the risk of joining Nathan's new initiative—and perhaps for that reason, the meeting was over quickly, within fifteen minutes. We both gave him our heartfelt thanks when he agreed to sign up. I hoped we wouldn't need to call upon his services much, if at all, and that we could find more nonviolent ways to go about our dealings. But it was comforting to know that we had him and his weapons as backup, should the need arise.

Then, after a few questions of his own regarding confidentiality, and once he was satisfied, he escorted us back out of the building and bade us farewell.

Hux went quiet after that, his mood growing heavy once again, as we got on the bike and headed off. I made a comment about the good progress we, or rather he, was making, with three positives in a row so far, and then I went quiet, too, knowing better than to keep talking, after his reluctance to hold a conversation on the journey out.

Before long, we were back in front of the mall, and I slipped off his motorcycle, about to say goodbye. Then, to my surprise, he got off too.

"You're not heading home now?" I asked, as I handed his helmet back to him.

"No. I've got to buy a birthday present for my sister," he muttered. "It's this Sunday."

"Oh," I said, my eyebrows rising. "That's nice."

He gave me what I guessed was supposed to be a faint smile, but it came off as more of a grimace, and then started moving, and I sped up to walk alongside him.

"What sort of thing are you looking to buy?" I asked, trying to coax him back into conversation as we reached the entrance.

He glanced through the revolving doors, then hesitated, running his tongue over his lower lip as if considering his next words carefully. "To be honest, I don't know," he said. "Back home, we created gifts for each other. I made her wooden toys when she was younger, and then a necklace for her last birthday. But since I don't really have the equipment for either of those options anymore..." He looked at me, furrowing his brow. "Do you have any ideas?"

I blinked. "Me?"

He shrugged. "Yeah. You're a girl, aren't you?"

I smirked. "Yes, but I don't know your sister. I mean, I could try. But full disclosure: I don't have a lot of experience shopping for gifts. So this might be one of those blind men scenarios."

He sighed. "Maybe, but I'm guessing you'll do a better job than me."

I paused, giving him a considering look, and then decided that his statement was probably accurate. "Okay, well... Shall we go inside, then?" I asked.

"Thanks," he replied, with the first genuine smile I'd seen on him all day.

We passed through the revolving doorways and began examining the store windows.

"Does she have a favorite color?" I asked as we passed a clothes store.

"Purple," he replied.

I smiled. "Good taste." It was my favorite color, too. "How about we take a look in this store?" I suggested.

"Sure," he said, and we went inside.

"You said she's ten, right?"

"She'll be eleven on Sunday."

"Okay."

We headed to the children's section, a small area at the back that held only three aisles, and the selection of clothing was uninspiring, to say the least. Mostly essential items like pants, shirts, and jackets. It only took me a couple of minutes to do a sweep and see that there was nothing worthwhile.

"Let's keep moving," I said, leading him back out.

We passed a few more shops, including a chocolatier, but chocolate just seemed too thoughtless. I guessed we could keep it as a last resort, but I wanted us to do better than that.

We went into a toyshop next, but she was too old for most of the items on the shelves, and even the ones that might be suitable, like the stuffed animals, were stupidly overpriced. I didn't feel comfortable suggesting to Hux that he buy them. I didn't know what he did for a living, but I doubted he was rolling in money.

After I had rejected five shops in a row, Hux started to look a little guilty. "Hey, I didn't mean for you to spend so much time on this," he said. "I thought it might just be a quick thing. If you need to go, I'll just try to find something for her myself."

"Um, no. It's okay," I replied. It wasn't that late yet, and I'd said I would give him a hand with this. I wasn't the type of person to be a quitter if I could help it.

"Okay. I just don't want to put you out too much, because it's probably not the end of the world even if we don't find anything." He paused, then, and I suddenly sensed that heaviness from earlier returning. His face darkened and he turned away, his tone going low as he murmured, almost to himself, beneath a breath, "It's not like she wants to see me anyway."

My breathing stalled as I stared at him. For several seconds, I didn't know how to reply. If that was what his phone calls had been about, then I could understand why it had been eating away at him so badly. What had happened between them that they didn't live together? What could he have done to make her so angry with him? And where was she staying now? It wasn't likely to be with a CRAS family, given that he seemed to have the freedom to visit her whenever he wanted, and the fact that he had mentioned a "contact" who I thought would have helped them both escape the government's capture. So I wondered who else it could be.

Whatever was going on between them, it sounded brutal.

"I... I'm sorry," I managed.

He shrugged, trying to act nonchalant again, and failing miserably. His eyes fixed determinedly on the path ahead of us, but he couldn't hide the pain etched across his face.

"Do you mind if I ask... how? Why?"

He drew in a deep breath, a muscle in his jaw twitching. "My sister. She blames me for what happened. For our brother and parents' deaths."

My mouth dropped open and I froze in my tracks, my hand instinctively reaching out to grab his arm. *"What?!* How could that possibly be your fault?"

He shook his head. "It's not, of course. And deep down, I honestly don't think she truly believes it is either. But, my sister..." He exhaled. "She's smart and capable in certain areas, but she was born with a mental irregularity. We were never really able to diagnose what it was, without a professional, but she's always had behavioral issues. She struggles to empathize and has a habit of just clamming up in stressful situations. Cutting herself off emotionally from those around her. The blame she's placing on me, I think it's her warped way of dealing with the pain. I think the trauma of losing our family just sent her over the edge. And I... I've been trying to pull her back. But it's hard." He breathed out heavily. "God knows, it's hard."

I found myself speechless. Whether his sister had a disorder or not, I just couldn't imagine the pain it must be causing him to be blamed for his family's deaths, especially when he was still recovering from the trauma himself.

"I'm so sorry," I repeated, as we reached the last group of stores on the bottom floor. It was all I could think to say.

He set his jaw and stepped onto an escalator. We ascended to the next floor and then continued perusing the shops in silence, though I could hardly concentrate on the items behind the windows after what he'd just told me. My mind dwelled on the issue, and I contemplated asking him about the situation further, but decided it was better to let him lead on this topic. He might just want to change the subject now.

He stopped outside a snack stall. "Thirsty?" he asked me in a low tone.

"I'm okay," I replied. "Thanks."

He bought himself a bottle of water, and we continued walking, with me trying to focus better on the task at hand. But even after roaming through the mall's second floor, nothing was sticking out at me. I suggested we do a check of the third and final floor, and he nodded in agreement.

As we ascended the last set of escalators, I was beginning to think that the topic of his sister issues was past us, but then he cleared his throat again and said out of the blue, "I was out collecting firewood."

I paused to look at him, raising my eyebrows, and saw that his expression had taken on a distant quality, his eyes fixed on the floor in front of us, yet far away. It made me sense that whatever he was about to tell me was for catharsis, and I needed to just stay quiet. So I pressed my lips together and continued scanning the shopfronts, albeit absentmindedly.

"My sister was with me," he went on after a moment. "She and our two dogs. We were out in the woods around the back of our mountain, gathering timber I had chopped the previous night. She was sitting on a fallen tree, talking to me about the dinner she was going to help my mother cook that evening, when we heard the sound of sharp popping.

"I was initially afraid that it was some kind of severe rockslide near our settlement. I caught my sister's hand and ran with her out of the forest, and onto a cliff that overlooked our home. That was when I realized it was gunshots." He paused, his chest heaving out. "Our people had been trying to fight off what they'd thought was an invasion, but stood no chance. Anyone who tried to resist was mowed down. I covered my sister's eyes, not wanting her to watch. And then I picked her up and ran back into the forest. I told her to wait in the hollow of a tree with the dogs and promised I would bring back our brother and parents. She was shaking when I left her, but I told myself she would be okay. I told myself that, somehow, we would all be okay. That this couldn't actually be happening. Our friends and family couldn't be dying.

"My brain went into a haze of panic. All I remember of that climb down to the caves was the fervent hope that I would find my family alive. But by the time I made it down there, the gunfire had stopped, and anyone left in the caves was on their back, still.

"There wasn't time to identify bodies. I had to run to escape the patrol. So I fled back up the mountain, gathered my sister and dogs, and hoped my parents had somehow managed to escape. But we stumbled upon the survivors an hour later, and they weren't among them.

"And my sister was never the same after that. It was the hour she locked herself up and threw away the key. She wouldn't talk to me for weeks, hardly even acknowledged my presence, despite my begging her to. Barely even blinked when we had to leave our dogs behind. And when she was taken in by the group that's looking after her now, she didn't say goodbye. I had already lost her.

"And then, last Sunday when I visited her, something snapped in her and she finally spoke to me. Slapped me across the face and told me it was my fault. That I shouldn't have come back without them. That I should have tried harder. That I lied to her. I guess in a way she's right. I shouldn't have promised her the unpromisable."

He trailed off, resuming his focus on the stores around us and leaving me to process his words. I felt his pain almost as if it were my own, imagining what the last several months must have been like for him. Forced to flee the only home he'd ever known and adjust to the strangeness of mainstream society, while trying to cope with the deaths of his parents and older brother, then being ignored and attacked by the only family member he had left. His own sister.

"I'm sorry," he said after a moment, his voice stronger, shaking his head as if he'd just snapped out of a daze. "I'm not sure why I told you all that... I guess I haven't talked about it in a while."

I breathed in, trying to steady my own voice. "Hux, you feel free to talk to me anytime you want, okay?"

"Okay." He gave me a smile, then turned his eyes ahead with a sigh. "Anyway, as brutal as last Sunday was, I'm actually hoping it's a step forward. I feel like the boil has started to burst, and if I can get her to keep talking, she'll come around. She doesn't really blame me; I know it. She loves me, and I just need to get her to remember that."

"So you're going to go visit her again this Sunday?" I asked, once again wondering where she actually was.

He nodded firmly. "She told her guardians that she doesn't want me to come, but I'm going to. I've *got* to fix her. And besides, it's her birthday."

"Right, of course." I nodded, feeling the urge to give his shoulder a reassuring squeeze. To offer him at least some of the support he'd lacked for so long. But then I reminded myself that he probably hadn't told me any of this to earn my pity, and I wasn't sure if he'd interpret the gesture as that. He'd just let this out to get it off his chest. So I kept both hands to myself, and mentally gave him a little hug.

"Also," he added after a pause, giving me a sidelong glance, "I have to go there anyway on business. Her group is one that's on my trusted list, and I need to talk to them regarding Nathan's new initiative. So if you aren't fed up with me by the weekend, you can see where she's staying. It's the same place where Noreen and Davine's women and children take refuge."

My eyebrows shot up into my hairline. "Oh! Wow. I can really come to see it?" I was *extremely* curious as to how those mothers and children were able to stay in the country without being found out—had been ever since I visited Noreen and Davine's little grotto— because once I got my own child back, I would be faced with the exact same issue. I wanted to be aware of all the options available to me before taking the last resort and fleeing the country.

He nodded, giving me a canny look. "Yes."

And then I blinked. "Wait. I thought you said you couldn't share that info with me?"

"Technically I don't have permission to *talk* about it, per the usual protocol: the location is strictly on a need-to-know basis. But if you come with me on Sunday, it'll be a bona fide visit, and you'll find out for yourself."

"Then I would love to come!" I gushed. "What time are you leaving and what's the meeting spot?" Not that I had any plans for Sunday, anyway.

He chuckled. "I'll send you the details nearer the time."

"Okay. Thanks!"

We both then returned to the matter at hand, as we were beginning to attract stares from security personnel due to the way we were hovering around the shop windows. As I continued searching for a gift, however, more than ever, all the options felt lame. Now that Hux had given me all of this background around her, I wanted to find something deep and meaningful and heartfelt. Something that might, somehow, help the girl warm to Hux.

And I just didn't think I was going to find that here.

We reached the final stretch of shops, and I was about to admit defeat when I spotted something... interesting. It was a narrow stall, tucked right at the end of the walkway, and contained raw materials—reams of fabric and balls of wool. As I approached the counter, I also noticed mending equipment. Needles and multicolored thread, scissors and tape measures. They even had knitting supplies.

My eyes lit up. "Hey, Hux. Come over here!" I called to him, as I realized he'd gotten distracted by a sock stall farther up. If he had even remotely been considering socks, he had definitely been right to ask for my help.

He approached and frowned as he laid eyes on the materials.

"I bet I could make your sis something cool with a few items from here," I said, eyeing the prices.

Hux froze. "You... You'd be willing to do that?" he asked, his eyebrows shooting up.

I smiled at his surprise. "Sure. You could just purchase the materials, which should come to less than ten dollars. Not too bad, right?" I didn't know what I was going to make yet, but I was pretty sure I could come up with something cool once I had some basic materials together.

He shook his head, still looking slightly dazed at my offer. "No. Not too bad at all."

I turned to the woman behind the table and ordered what I needed, stuffing each item into my backpack as she handed it to me. After Hux paid up, we stepped back from the stall.

"That's... really great of you, Robin," he said, finding his voice again as he gazed down at me. "It means a hell of a lot to me."

I shrugged. "It will be a fun personal project for me, honestly. It's been a while since I've done anything creative, and I doubt it'll take much time. So don't sweat it. The only thing is, I might have a few questions for you, once I get home and do some brainstorming for the design. Nothing identifiable. Just a tad personal, so I can make the gift as good as it can be."

"Sure," he said, his face lighting up.

His tension seemed to ebb away as we made our way back down the mall's levels toward the exit, and though we fell into another silence, it was the comfortable type, unlike earlier. I could practically feel the warmth emanating from him. He really did seem touched by my offer, which made me happy. God knew we all needed a little compassion in our lives now and then.

We walked back out through the revolving door, and then Hux turned to face me, his honey-brown eyes still shiny with gratitude. He was presumably about to suggest we head our separate ways when another idea hit me. One so obvious I couldn't believe it hadn't occurred to me right away.

"Hey, while we're on the subject of needles and thread," I said, before he could speak. I quirked an eyebrow. "My offer still stands for that sew job."

A slow grin stretched his lips. Then he shoved his hands into his pockets and rocked back on his heels, feigning consideration. "Well, technically it wouldn't be professional of me to accept the offer, given that I am"—he coughed—"your colleague, as well as, technically, your team leader. But then again, I suppose I've already screwed my professionalism by telling you my whole life story. So heck, why not give you my pants?"

I laughed. "And a shirt."

He nodded. "And a shirt. We'll see how you do with those first." To my surprise, he shrugged off his backpack and pulled out a spare pair of pants and a shirt right then and there.

"Whoa. Had you already been planning to accept my offer today, or what?"

He gave me a wry look. "Nope. I just had a spare set of clothes in there because I wasn't sure where I'd be sleeping tonight, and since we finished earlier than I expected, I've decided I won't need them."

I grinned. "A likely story," I said, taking them from him and stuffing them into my bag.

He gave a little shrug. "It's true."

"Anyway, I'll get to work on them once I'm home, and hopefully you can feel like a new man by Sunday."

"I've given you a lot of homework."

"Ah, that's okay. I can make time at the edges of the day. I'll get your sister's present finished as soon as possible, too. Definitely by Saturday."

"Thanks again, Robin," he said with a genuine smile.

He held out a hand, and I took it. Our handshake seemed to become more of a squeeze than a shake, and I wasn't sure if it was just my imagination, but it also seemed to last a moment longer than required.

When we stepped back, we gave each other a final smile.

"So I'm guessing there'll be another message from you in my inbox tomorrow morning about our next adventure?" I asked.

He grinned. "You can count on it."

15

Thanks to a road accident, I ended up stuck in a load of unexpected traffic, and it took me way longer to get home than it should have. It was 10:53 p.m. by the time I walked through my cabin's front door, but oddly, despite the day having been long and laborious, I wasn't feeling tired.

I couldn't stay up too late, of course, or I wouldn't be able to function properly tomorrow, but I could give myself another hour or so. I was eager to check in with the new portal, and then at least make a start on Hux's clothes. I was guessing that job was going to end up taking less time than his sister's gift, so I wanted to get it out of the way first.

I grabbed a glass of water and a bottle of Nurmeal (I was becoming a bit time-strapped these days) and then sat down at my dining table, pulled out my tablet, and logged in to the new portal.

The first thing I did was check to see how much the members list had grown, and my, *had* it. It was more than double the size it was yesterday, with over fifty members. It made me wonder how many other admins were out there, recruiting people. I didn't remember Hux mentioning an exact number, but there were definitely more new members than we could take credit for.

I was pleased to see that among the new members were Gabby's family, and that "GabbySails" herself was there.

I clicked on the forum to find it thrumming with activity. Half a dozen new threads had been posted, and the "stunt" thread was busier than ever. Like yesterday, though, after browsing through several pages filled with comments, I began to feel overwhelmed by all the different streams of consciousness. (There also seemed to be quite a bit more arguing going on, though I realized after a minute that was mostly Gabby's family amongst themselves.) And it once again made me impatient for Monday. *Four more days.*

I exited the portal because hanging around the threads wasn't going to be very productive until then, and my time was limited tonight. Especially as I suddenly remembered that I also needed to talk to Nelson. I picked up my phone and dialed her number, and was glad when she answered after a couple of rings. I filled her in on how my day had gone, as well as my initial thoughts on the new portal. She agreed with basically everything I said and told me she had already spoken with multiple admins, who assured her that Monday would bring the features we needed. We were just dealing with an early bird version of the portal right now, as I'd suspected.

After wrapping up my conversation with her and saying goodnight, I decided to allot the rest of the evening to my long-lost hobby.

I cleared the table to make room for Hux's pants and shirt, and spread them out over it. Then I fished out the sewing equipment from my backpack and started examining the seams of the clothing. As it turned out, it was a surprisingly simple job. The clothes were an extra-large size as they were, but I guessed he had bought them from some sort of specialized store, because they had also been designed to be adjustable—to accommodate people of even larger sizes, with some easy alterations. He probably just hadn't realized it, or even if he had, hadn't known what to do about it.

There was extra fabric tucked up around the seams, though, which made it easy for me to do an extension job. I didn't have his exact measurements, but I was pretty good at eyeballing things, and by the time I'd finished with both the pants and the shirt, I was confident that he would be a much happier man in them.

The work took me less than an hour for both items, and I was rather pleased with myself, now having some time before sleep to think about his sister's gift.

I decided that a change of scenery was in order, and relocated to my bed, carrying with me what I needed and plopping it down on the mattress. I slipped beneath the sheets and pulled the materials toward me. Like I said, my nanny Sarah had taught me how to create wonderful things with cloth, and I wasn't lying when I told Hux that I was looking forward to the creative challenge. It had been a long time since I'd had a chance to put my skills to use, and doing so brought about fond memories of her, and the way she'd shaped my childhood.

But I had to admit that this was an extra tricky task, given the tension between Hux and his sister. It wasn't a matter of simply creating something pretty. I wanted to try to create something that would help bridge the gap, somehow. Something that would resonate emotionally. Remind her that he was her loving brother and would probably sacrifice the world for her. But how was I going to do that, exactly? I still wasn't sure.

I closed my eyes for a minute, thinking, and then quickly fetched a small pad of paper and a pen from the living room. Returning to my bed, I started to sketch out ideas, but ultimately stalled, and realized that I wasn't going to get much further without some extra help from Hux.

I glanced at the time on my phone. 11:46 p.m. He'd said that after midnight he turned grumpy... so maybe he was still awake? I decided to send a text, just in case, as that was less intrusive than a call, and likely to get a quicker response than an OH message.

"*Hey, you asleep yet?*" I typed, then pressed send.

I waited, staring at the screen, then smiled when his response came back.

"*Apparently not... But you're in dangerous territory.*"

My thumbs worked quickly. "*I'm working on the gift. Had a few quick questions.*"

"*Go ahead. :)*"

"*What's her favorite animal?*"

"*Brown bear.*"

"*And does she have a favorite tree/plant?*"

"*Probably quakies.*"

I frowned. "*Quakies?*"

"*A type of thin tree with yellow-orange leaves.*"

"*Okay. And favorite place?*"

"*The lake... It was bordered by lavender bushes.*"

I paused at that additional bit of information. Interesting. I had lavender bushes growing just near my cabin.

"*Ok, thanks,*" I typed back. "*Think that's all I need for now.*"

"*That wasn't too imposing.*"

I grinned. "*Glad you think so.*"

Though I hadn't asked much, the information he'd given me had actually helped a lot. My brain was starting to buzz with ideas, and I felt a rush of excitement as one in particular came to the forefront.

"*I guess I'll let you go now,*" I added. "*Before you turn into a pumpkin.*"

"*A grumpy-ass pumpkin.*"

I chuckled. "*Talk to you tomorrow.*"

"Yeah. Sleep well."

"You too."

"Goodnight."

"Goodnight."

Grinning, I set aside my phone, then began to sketch a detailed design plan. It was getting late, and I knew I should probably just turn off the lights now, given that it would take me a while to drift off, but I was too excited to not make at least a small start on the project tonight. I couldn't wait to see how the gift turned out. I was a little nervous about how his sister would receive it. But I also had a strong feeling I was on to something.

16

Thursday, Friday, and Saturday passed quickly. In between my stitching work in the mornings and evenings, attending my day job, and accompanying Hux to visitations in the evenings —*and* trying to maintain a decent level of sleep—I barely had time to watch the new portal's progression. Which was good, because each time I logged on, it only made me more impatient for Monday.

The chaos there didn't stop my team from joining in the discussions, although, come Monday, some of them would have less time for that too. Hux had told me that our visit to wherever his sister was staying on Sunday would be the final group on his safe list, after which we'd start reaching out to the riskier prospects in the area. For that, we'd need to call upon at least a couple more members from my team to assist us, security-wise.

In the meantime, Hux and I met with three more trusted groups.

On Thursday, we visited a remote farm, whose owner mentioned that he could help in the form of a supply of food and shelter in his barns, if there was ever an emergency, and then agreed to join the portal (then warned us that he wanted to be more of a background supporter and didn't want to be heavily involved in the discussion).

On Friday we met up with a small group of nomads, all around their mid-twenties, who roamed from place to place in a couple of old trailers. They didn't have kids with them, though they claimed they'd been victims of the CRAS in one way or another, and offered to help as foot soldiers on missions, should the need for extra manpower arise.

Then, early on Saturday morning, we met a forty-something-year-old man who claimed he was a car dealer and could assist us with transport. He mentioned in passing that he'd been directly affected by the CRAS when he was a younger, and poorer, man— and that he'd lost two children to the system, the grief of which led to a breakdown in his marriage. He was a smart, well-dressed guy, but the bitterness in his eyes and voice as he spoke of his past made him seem almost feral. I could practically feel the lust for vengeance burning through him when he requested an immediate invitation to the portal. I was sure that, when the time was right, he would make a good ally, but his mood also left me with the feeling that we needed to be careful, every single one of us, not to be blinded by vengeance. We were playing, or about to play, a very dangerous game here, and none of us could afford to approach this with anything but a cool head.

Which was why it was important to have as many of those as possible within the portal. I knew my team, for all their desire to see the system come to an end, were level-headed thinkers, Nelson in particular. I just needed to hope that there were enough others around to balance out the more passionate folks.

We were done with the car dealer by 10:00 a.m., and I took the early finish as an opportunity to sit Hux down in a little juice joint we passed on the street. Since yesterday, his mood had grown tense again, and while it wasn't nearly as dark as it had been before my offer to make his sister a present, I still sensed a growing unease in him. He seemed to become quieter and quieter outside of meetings, and it appeared to be a strain for him to engage even in small talk. I understood, of course. The last time he'd met with his sister, it hadn't gone well. It had been downright traumatic, and he was clearly afraid of a repeat.

But Sunday was only one sleep away now, and I needed to broach the topic. I'd completed his sister's gift the night before and had it with me in my bag. I'd just been waiting for the right moment to show it to him.

"You okay?" I asked, giving him a look as our fruit juices arrived.

He heaved a sigh, running a hand through his thick, dark hair. "I'm just nervous."

"I understand," I replied, giving his arm a sympathetic pat. "At least I think you'll have a great gift for her. I really think you'll like what I made, and I'm hoping she will too." He hadn't seen the final result yet. I hadn't sent him any photos, nor had I described it, because I'd wanted it to be a surprise so I could see the reaction on his face. A small part of me hoped I could be there to see his sister's reaction, too.

"I'm looking forward to seeing it," he said with a small smile, and then a yawn overtook him and he stretched out his arms, rolling his neck.

It was nice to see him finally comfortable in his clothes. After I'd fixed the first set on Wednesday, they'd fit him nearly perfectly. A *touch* on the baggy side, but that definitely didn't bother him. So he'd given me two other sets of clothes to fix, too.

"Well, that's a good thing," I replied with a grin. "Because I kept to my deadline, and I have it with me right now."

His eyes widened. "Really?"

"Yup. Close your eyes."

"Okay," he murmured. He did as instructed and dropped his eyelids, even as his lips stretched into a crooked smile.

Dipping a hand into my bag, I fished out the present, which I'd embroidered with a design of my own imagination and then stuffed with wool and lavender to form a scented pillow, and set it right in front of him on the table.

"Now open them," I said.

He did so, and his smile immediately broadened. He picked up the pillow, examining the design on the front of it for almost a minute, and when he flipped it over, checking out the design on the other side, his smile stretched even wider and he burst out laughing.

"Oh. I think you're right," he said. "I think you hit the right note here. I… I really think she'll like it."

I smiled back, content that the design had had the desired effect. "Good."

He flipped it over to look at the front again, and then the back, and he chuckled again, before raising it to his nose and inhaling. "Smells amazing, too."

I nodded, even as I realized I needed to use the bathroom. I told him I'd be back in a minute, then left him to a bit of privacy while he looked at the item.

On returning, I saw that his smile had faded, replaced by a contemplative expression. "She's going to wonder who made it," he said, glancing at me as I resumed my seat. "She knows I can't sew to save my life."

I raised an eyebrow. "And? It's still a gift from you. You paid for the materials."

"I know," he said, dropping his gaze back to the gift. He shifted on the seat, suddenly looking a little awkward. "It's just, I was thinking. When we arrive at the place, we'll go to meet with the appointed contact there, first. And after that, I was planning to stop by to see my sister. And, uh, I was thinking you might come in with me, rather than wait outside."

I smiled at his hesitancy, and also couldn't deny that I was rather touched that he would ask. "I would like to, actually," I replied warmly. "If you think your sister won't mind a stranger intruding on the meeting."

He shook his head, sighing. "I mean, she doesn't even want the meeting in the first place, so it's hardly going to make things worse. I'm asking because I actually think the presence of a stranger might help. It's just been me visiting her for the past four months, and..." He trailed off, swallowing. "I guess she's developed something of a negative thought pattern toward that. If you came with me, it might just help to break up that pattern a bit." He shrugged. "Maybe it's a stupid theory, but I don't think it can do any harm. Besides, if you came, she'd be able to meet the genius behind the gift."

"Flattery will get you everywhere." I grinned. "Sure, I'll come."

We took a train the next morning, as he informed me that our destination would be the farthest we'd traveled yet. It was nestled deep in the mountains, apparently, but he didn't say more than that, leaving me in suspense, as he had a habit of doing, until we actually arrived.

After an almost four-hour journey, involving changing trains three times and then getting a taxi to transport us along a winding, mountain passage, we finally reached a breathtaking valley, where some kind of huge compound sprawled, surrounded by a high wall.

I realized only as we drew nearer what it was, my eyes catching sight of a bold sign near the entrance gates, and my jaw dropped.

Orange Grove Convent. For Daughters of Christ.

"Oh my goodness," I breathed. "This. Is. Genius."

A nunnery. They're freaking hiding in a nunnery.

I didn't even know all the details of the relationship yet—or any—but I was already imagining how they managed to get away with this. Our government held holy people like nuns and monks in far too high a regard to ever suspect they would be helping dissidents. Heck, they were the epitome of morality and self-control, qualities governors of the Burchard Regime most respected. And, tucked away out here, right in the middle of nowhere, I could fully imagine that they were able to absorb dozens of people into their large community and keep them sheltered. Not unlimited numbers, of course, but more than Nelson's border contact could ever help.

I wondered, however, what happened to those they hid in the long term. Was the plan for them to literally live here until the day they died?

That didn't seem very practical or realistic to me, and it certainly wasn't something I'd want to force on my own child. Kids would grow up and want to visit the outside someday. And what about the male children? Surely they wouldn't live here through their adulthood?

I couldn't help but wonder if they might have found, or at least be working on, some other loophole or solution for that eventuality.

But for now, I knew a whole lot more than I had this morning, and I was eager to learn more just as soon as I got the chance.

My heart was still pounding in my chest from a mixture of disbelief and excitement when the taxi stopped in front of the sturdy set of entrance gates.

"Be back in a moment," Hux murmured, and then got out of the car and headed over to a control panel fixed on the wall next to the gate.

I rolled down my window, letting in a warm, nearly intoxicating breeze that carried the scent of oranges and flowers, and poked my head out of the car so I could listen in as he buzzed.

"Name and purpose, please," a throaty, female voice crackled out.

"I have an appointment with Sister Isobel. She knows me as Mr. Huxley."

I pulled my head back instantly, suddenly feeling horribly guilty. *Huxley.* Might that be his real surname, which he'd used as inspiration for his fake middle name? I couldn't be sure, but if these ladies were looking after his sister, I guessed it was possible they were on real-name terms.

Shoot. I rolled up my window and knocked my head back against the seat, even as the guilt continued to creep up in me. I hadn't meant to overhear personal information. I was just so curious about this place in general that I'd wanted to keep my ears and eyes open at all times. Memories of my very first briefing with Nelson kicked in, where she'd laid out the reasons why we didn't exchange personal details. If any of us was ever caught by the government—the likelihood of which was only going to increase, given the riskier turn all of our lives were about to take with the new, focused action group—then torture was a very real possibility. Nelson had told me she'd heard of it happening before, though she hadn't given me details of who and when.

But I could believe it. Because enforcers were naturally keen to sniff out other dissidents, and there was no easier way to do that than to have one of their own turn on them. And under the duress of torture, there was no saying what even the most loyal among us would do. Everyone on OH knew that, which was why everyone in the community was so cagey, and there had never been a real effort to band together until Nathan's intervention.

Heck, I wasn't even sure what *I* would do. I couldn't fully trust myself, which was why I was so reluctant to know anything more about people than I absolutely had to. I didn't want to be a liability to anyone, least of all someone I'd come to consider a friend.

I sucked in a breath as he returned and heaved himself back into his seat. Then the gates rattled open and the taxi rolled forward, and I found that I couldn't even look him in the eye.

"You okay?" he asked, apparently noticing my shiftiness. He shot me a glance.

I sighed, not liking the idea of lying to him. "I'm sorry, Hux," I said softly, not wanting the driver to overhear. "But I listened in on what you said just now, to that lady. At least, the first part of it."

His frown deepened. "You mean you caught my surname?"

I nodded, wincing slightly. From the way he'd phrased the question, and from the look on his face now, I guessed Huxley *was* his real name.

He gave me a considering look, then leaned back in his chair, facing forward. I waited with bated breath, worried about his reaction, while the guilt continued to eat away at me.

And then, to my surprise, he merely shrugged.

"It doesn't matter," he muttered, as the taxi came to a stop inside a pretty, stone-paved courtyard within the compound. He paid the driver for the ride and asked him to wait for us for the journey back, and then we both got out of the car.

"What do you mean?" I asked, my eyes drawn to the stunning,

medieval-looking stone buildings surrounding us, even as I frowned at his response. A gorgeous church, whose walls were engraved with murals, loomed directly ahead, and next to it stood a long, low, rectangular building with a concave roof. A community center, based on the sign above the arched oaken door.

He shrugged again at my question, glancing down at me as I moved closer to him. "I mean, you would have likely found out anyway, because the sisters call me that around here. And also, I trust you, Robin."

There was something about the sincerity in his eyes as he spoke that final sentence that made my heart skip a beat. And yet I felt even worse for listening in. Because he shouldn't trust me. Not when I couldn't even trust myself. I felt that none of us ought to place that level of trust in one another, given the stakes.

But I couldn't help but feel touched all the same, and I decided to accept the compliment for now.

"Okay. Thank you," I replied softly, offering him an appreciative, albeit guilty, smile.

"Welcome," he replied, giving me a small smile back, and then he turned and began leading me toward the rectangular building.

17

S tepping through the community center's large doorway, we emerged in a vast entrance hall whose bare stone walls were lined with chairs, and where a modest wooden reception desk stood at the far end. A thin lady sat behind it, wearing a long-sleeved black tunic, just like the six other women I spotted in the hall, some sitting in chairs, some hovering around the perimeter and talking in hushed tones.

Hux led me to the reception desk, and the woman glanced up from the notepad she'd been writing in to set her bespectacled brown eyes on us.

"Mr. Huxley?" she asked.

"Yes, Sister."

"Sister Isobel will be with you shortly. Please take a seat."

We sat down in the seats nearest to the desk, and then waited in silence, our eyes moving between the two main doorways that connected the entrance hall to other parts of the building.

The name Huxley repeated in my head on a loop like a taunt, reminding me of what I'd done... But after a while, I had to admit, my mind started focusing more on the sexy ring it had to it than anything else. I quickly banished the thought as a tall, tan-skinned woman in her mid-fifties emerged through one of the doors and strode toward us, her hair swept back and covered by a white cowl.

Reaching us, her lined face broke out in a serene smile. "Good to see you, son." She spoke with a mild Hispanic accent. "And you, miss," she added with a friendly nod. "Come with me, if you please."

We followed her across the hallway and down a long corridor lined with religious tapestries, before she took a sharp left, and then stopped in front of a pale wooden door. She retrieved a crude iron key from her pocket and opened the door, revealing a small office containing nothing but a desk and three chairs.

Hux and I took seats on one side of the table, and after she'd closed the door, she seated herself on the other side.

"So," she said, a coy smile playing on her thin lips as she shuffled a few papers in front of her before pushing them out of the way. She laced her fingers together and rested her hands on the desk. "To what do I owe the privilege of a meeting with Mr. Huxley?"

Hux cleared his throat, a subtle blush creeping to his cheeks. "Sister, I've come to talk to you about a new initiative that's been in the works for some months now on the OH platform…"

I watched the woman's face as he continued to explain. It was a mask of placidness, and yet there was a sparkle in her eyes that bordered on mischievousness, telling me that there was a lot more to her than met the eye.

By the time Hux had finished, she could barely contain her smile, and she gave him an immediate nod. "This sounds like something that is right up our alley," she announced, leaning back slightly in her chair as she perused the both of us. "In fact, I am surprised Nathan took so long to think of it. We must somehow come together if we've any chance of creating a better future for this country's children. We will help in any way we can."

"Thank you, Sister," Hux replied, letting out a slow breath. "Your support will be among the most valuable that we can get."

She reached into one of her desk drawers and whipped out a flashy pink tablet. "So when do I get my invite?" she asked, quirking an eyebrow.

I stared at the tablet in surprise, while Hux chuckled. "I'll get it sent out as soon as I return home," he said.

"Good. I'm looking forward to seeing what discussions are already going on. This will be the talk of the day among the sisters during lunch and dinner hours, let me tell you. You'd better also send an invite to ImmortalSunshine, Blessed_Jemima, Jesus123, Courageous_Heart—"

Hux scrabbled to pull out his phone as she dictated a long list of handles, punching them all in and then nodding. "Okay. I'll get through them all before tomorrow."

"Thank you, dear." Her focus then switched to me. "And who is this young lady you've brought with you today?"

Hux flashed me a glance. "She's, uh, my colleague."

"I see," she said, eyeing me curiously.

"I'm Robin," I offered, leaning forward to hold out my hand. "Nice to meet you." I was eager to get in a few questions of my own about this place, and I hoped this was my opening.

"And you," she replied, accepting my hand in a shake. "I take it this is your first time visiting here, as I don't recall seeing your face before."

"That's right, Sister. I'm honestly quite in awe of what you've managed to do here. It's very generous of you to put yourselves out like this."

She gave me a solemn look. "It is our service to God. In His eyes, we are all equal, and He has given each and every one of us the right to raise our own. No manmade law should meddle with that. Justice must, and will, prevail by His grace, and we can but play our small part." She then paused, a demure smile tugging at her lips. "In the meantime, I must admit we're having quite the ball running rings around our esteemed governors."

"In what way?" I asked, jumping on the opportunity. I knew these nuns were capitalizing (shamelessly, I might add) on the Burchard Regime's reverence for them in order to keep mothers and children hidden, but I wanted to know more. For example, how grown-up children could be content to stay hidden here forever, plus how they handled the issue of males once they reached adolescence.

She looked to Hux. "I take it you haven't told her much about our activities."

"Robin knows you shelter women and children here," he replied. "Otherwise nothing. Per the protocol."

She sighed, leaning back in her chair. "Okay, well, we don't dish out our secrets unless there's an absolute necessity, so for now let's just say we also have a way of helping adults reenter society, if they wish to."

With that, she pursed her lips, leaving me to wonder if that meant these nuns had found some way to equip people with false identities. Maybe they even had their own sympathetic contact in the government who was able to forge documents. Because people born off the grid would need them if they wanted to have any chance of reintegrating with society.

It hit me then that maybe it was how Hux had gotten *his* ID. I mean, he had to have documentation, because he drove and, presumably, rented a place somewhere.

I could see how this kind of government contact could be incredibly valuable to our action group in a number of situations, and not just for children who needed IDs. It could potentially also help someone disappear, if enforcers ever caught on to them, and allow them to resurface with a new persona.

"I see," I replied slowly, my mind reeling with the possibilities. If Hope and I could somehow get new documentation, then maybe we wouldn't have to leave the country forever after all. I was still a way off from getting Hope back, but it was something to think about. Not just for myself, but for the families Nelson helped, too. They might at least appreciate the choice of staying over fleeing, even if they still chose the latter.

"And now," Isobel said, turning back to Hux and drawing me out of my thoughts. It was definitely a subject for another time, given that Nelson and I would need to earn these nuns' trust over the portal before we could be privy to further information. "I understand you're also here to see your sister," Isobel went on. "Sister Maria said she would escort you, so if we're done here, you can head on down to the reception."

"Thank you, Sister," Hux said, rising to his feet and bowing his head respectfully. We headed to the door, and Hux was halfway through opening it when he stalled. "Wait. Which Maria?"

Isobel chuckled. "You're right. There are far too many of them around here. Sister Maria Fergora is the one you need."

"Okay," he said. "Thanks again."

She moved to the door to see us off, then closed it as we headed back down the corridor.

"Don't you know the way to where your sister's staying?" I wondered aloud, finding it odd that we'd need a guide.

"Yes, I do," he replied. "But it's not considered proper for a man to be wandering around here without an escort."

"Ah." I nodded, supposing it made sense.

Sister Maria F. was already waiting for us in the reception area when we arrived. She was a short, plump woman with a radiant smile and a hearty laugh. She engaged us in small talk all the way through the journey across the grounds, toward the shade of a sprawling orange grove, where several dozen cozy-looking bunga-lows were nestled. Though, I was mostly the one chatting back, as Hux was growing tense again.

When she stopped in front of Number 11, I realized it was our destination—and also doubted that it was a coincidence that the mothers' and children's quarters were in what seemed to be the most naturally shaded part of the compound. The nuns didn't seem to be worried about the government sending a probe out here anytime soon, but with this setup, children could play outside beneath the groves without risk of being spotted from the sky.

Maria F. gave Hux her number and told him to call her when we were done, and then strode off through the grove, leaving us alone in front of the building. Hux took a deep breath, his eyes fixed on the door. This was the culmination of a week of stress and tightly wound nerves, the moment he'd been losing sleep over.

I kept quiet, letting him do his thing, in preparation, and then watched as he walked up to the door and knocked gently, three times. He then stepped away, and I could see the backs of his shoulders heaving from the tension.

Luckily, he wasn't left waiting for long, as a nun opened the door thirty seconds later.

"Oh, good day," she said, her lips stretching into a wide smile, her pearly white teeth contrasting against her dark skin.

"Good day, Sister Gina," he replied with forced brightness.

The woman's face then turned serious, and she threw a glance back through the house over her shoulder. "So, I waited until last night to tell your sister you were definitely still coming," she said in a lower tone. "Since I didn't know how she'd react, and didn't want the news to put her off during the school week." She hesitated, giving Hux a concerned look. "She's in her room and has been cagey all morning. You are of course free to try. And if you want my help with anything, give me a shout."

Hux nodded stoically, while I absorbed her words. *School week.* I guessed that meant the nuns must run a little school for the kids out here.

Gina moved aside, allowing us to enter. Hux headed off down a hallway to our left, and I followed, keeping close to his heels. He stopped at the door right at the end of it, and then hesitated, his hands balling into fists.

I stood back, waiting for him to gather his thoughts and take a few breaths. He shrugged off his backpack and pulled out the gift, then raised a fist and knocked softly against the door.

A minute passed with no answer.

He knocked again.

Still no answer.

He knocked three more times in slow succession, and when the room beyond remained quiet, he tentatively gripped the handle and pulled downward. He entered cautiously, peering around the door and doing a sweep. I watched his eyes settle on something in one corner, and then he slowly left the door and moved deeper into the room.

I followed, entering the room just enough so that I could peer in. I spotted what Hux had: a young girl with straight, thick, black-brown hair trailing down her back sitting at a desk, in front of a pile of books. She was facing the window, a pencil in one hand.

I watched as Hux moved closer, until he was three feet away from her, and then he paused, coughing softly.

The girl still didn't budge, acting as though she didn't hear him.

"Hey," Hux said gently. "It's me." He moved up to her and placed a hand on the back of her chair, then leaned against the desk so he could get a glimpse of her face. "Rhea," he pressed, and I wondered if that was her real name—if he was trusting me with his sister's name too. I *really* wasn't sure how I felt about that, but I pushed the thought aside for now.

"I don't have to stay long," he went on. "I just… I wanted to come wish you a happy eleventh birthday, and I brought you—"

"I never asked for presents," she said suddenly, her voice sharp.

She stood up abruptly and moved over to her bed, flopping onto it and burying her head in the sheets. She hadn't even looked at Hux or seen the pillow he was holding in his right hand.

Hux stalled, clearly recalibrating the situation and figuring out his next move. He glanced at me, and my eyes wandered tentatively back to the girl on the bed. Sighing, he approached the mattress, then sat down on the edge of it, careful to maintain some distance.

"I know," he replied. "But what kind of big brother would I be if I didn't bring you one anyway? Come on, at least take a look at what I've brought."

She remained still, ignoring him.

He swallowed, glancing down at his lap. "Look, Rhea," he said quietly, "I know how bad you're hurting. Because I'm hurting just as much. But you gotta talk about it. You can't stay bottled up like this, or you'll drive yourself insane."

There was a pause, and then she mumbled, "It's your stupid fault."

Pain flickered across Hux's face, and he sucked in a breath, as though recovering from a punch to the gut. Then he nodded slowly. "I promised you something I never should have, and that was wrong. I… I let you down. But it doesn't make what happened my fault, nor does it change the fact that I love you, and that I'm here for you no matter what."

"If you loved me then you'd do what I asked and leave me alone," she bit out.

"That wouldn't be love, Rhea," Hux replied, his voice tight. "And you know it. The more you push me away, the more you're hurting yourself, and I can't allow that to happen. I'm working hard to save up so that one day, you can move back in with me, because I know it's what you want, even if you're refusing to admit it. It's what Mom and Dad would've wanted, too."

"Don't talk about Mom and Dad," she growled. "They'd still be alive if you had just stayed back for them!" Her voice cracked, her cold façade breaking. Her warped version of reality shook me, but I saw now how deep her emotions ran. Like Hux had said, it wasn't that she didn't feel them, it was just that she didn't know how to deal with them, how to release them. They got clogged up inside of her and shot out in all the wrong ways. She was raw and hurting, and it gave me a firmer conviction in Hux's belief that if he could figure out the right button to push, he could free her of all this pent-up toxicity.

Hux's expression darkened, and I could tell that it was taking everything he had to hold it together. "Okay, fine," he managed after a moment, his voice thick. "I'll leave you alone. Though I'm not the only one here. I brought someone with me." He glanced my way.

The statement was enough to spike the young girl's curiosity. She uncovered her head from the sheets and glanced at me, and I found myself gazing into the face of a pretty girl with narrow bone structure, a pert nose, pale skin, and the same deep amber irises as Hux. Her expression was stubborn, yet hollow, with dark shadows beneath her eyes, as though she'd been losing sleep at night, too.

After barely five seconds, she tucked her head back beneath the sheets. "Just leave," she muttered, her cold tone returning. "I don't want to see you or your visitors."

I grimaced. *So much for my presence "breaking the pattern."* I felt Hux had gotten close to something, though, a few moments before, when her emotions had risen to the surface, and now it felt like we were going backward. As Hux shifted closer to her on the mattress, somehow I just knew that attempting a physical route wasn't going to end well. A different idea occurred to me, and before he could reach out and touch her, I waved a hand to get his attention.

He frowned, stalling, and then left the bed and moved over to me. I gripped his arm and pulled him out of the room, back into the corridor.

"I think the harder you push right now, the harder she's going to resist," I whispered, in a voice barely louder than a breath. "Just... why don't you try leaving the gift on her mattress, and then come back out here and close the door."

It seemed like a long shot, and I didn't know that it would help at all. She could just toss the pillow in the trash without even looking at it. But as she was a young girl, I was banking on her at least being curious enough to take a peek.

And if she did that... given Hux's reaction to the design, I felt it would at least encourage *something* positive in her. Something more positive than Hux attempting to manhandle her, anyway.

"Okay," he murmured, his expression ashen as he returned to the room. He went over to the mattress as I'd suggested and planted the pillow down next to her head, then silently left the room, closing the door behind him. He looked back down at me, his eyes widening in question. "And now?" he whispered.

I hesitated, my eyes moving to the closed door. "I guess let's just give her some space."

He nodded reluctantly, and then we both stood silently, leaning against the walls on either side of the door. I knew what I was hoping would happen, but I was afraid to expect it in case it didn't. But then, about a minute later, it did.

My ears picked up on the soft, barely audible sound of chuckling coming from behind the door. I immediately looked up at Hux, a wary smile creeping across my lips. His eyes sparked with hope, and we both inched closer to the door, pressing our ears to the cracks. The chuckling grew a little louder, until it became quiet laughter, and then it became louder still, until we didn't need to press our ears to the door anymore to hear it.

It went on for almost a minute, until it became a full-on belly laugh, and I couldn't help but chuckle quietly to myself, knowing the joke was at Hux's expense. Not that he minded. He was having to suppress his own amusement, too. A grin had spread across his face, and he looked happier than I'd seen him all week.

And then something unexpected happened. The laughter stuttered, and transformed into a confusing combination of guffawing, snorting, and sniffling, and then, to my shock, it morphed into deep, racking sobs.

Hux's smile disappeared as he stared at me, his face a mask of disbelief. "She's crying," he whispered hoarsely.

I nodded back, equally stunned. I hadn't intended for the gift to have that effect on her. I'd only meant for it to make her laugh. But perhaps I shouldn't have been surprised. I knew that laughter could be a powerful thing, and it seemed it had been what was needed to finally budge the stopper that had been trapping her true emotions inside. Her gateway to the grief that was now pouring out of her in waves.

Hux and I sank to the floor, staring at each other. I felt tears prick my own eyes at the sound of her long-overdue mourning, her deep sobs growing louder and more intense. I felt her grief resonate within the very core of me.

Hux's words dried up and he pressed his lips together, and I saw the glistening of tears in his own eyes. I looked down, not wanting to make him feel uncomfortable. We sat there for a while longer, just listening to her weeping, and then Hux rose slowly to his feet, and nodded toward the end of the corridor. I followed him there, and we paused just before the front door.

"It's more progress than I've made in four months," he said, his voice husky as he gazed down at me through glazed eyes. "And I don't want to spoil it by going in there now. We'll just leave her to process things, and I'll see how she's doing next week."

I nodded. I had been planning to suggest the same thing. It wasn't a good idea to intrude now, when she was in the middle of such deeply personal emotions. She needed space and time to mourn, the way she had never gotten a chance to. It would be a long and painful process, but ultimately it would free her.

He moved along the other end of the corridor and stopped outside a kitchen, where Gina was washing up dishes.

"Back so soon?" she asked as she noticed us, a surprised look on her face.

Hux nodded stoically. "I think it went well. She's crying now, and you just need to leave her be for a while. Let things settle."

"She's crying?" Gina widened her eyes in alarm, as if it were a bad thing.

When Hux elaborated on his reasoning, however, she quickly saw it, and gave a bittersweet smile. "Of course."

We took our leave, heading out the door and back into the grove. Hux fished for his phone in his pocket and was about to call Maria, when an urgent shout came from behind us.

"WAIT!"

We whirled around in confusion to see Rhea racing toward us, her feet bare and the pillow still clutched in one hand. Her face was a red and blotchy mess, her long hair flying wildly behind her, and tears were streaming down her cheeks in rivers as she headed straight for Hux.

She launched into his arms and bound her arms around his neck, pulling him close and latching onto him as if she were drowning. "I'm sorry, Jace," she sobbed. "I didn't mean what I said!"

Hux—*Jace?*—staggered back, not from the weight of the slight girl, but from the sheer surprise. She buried her face in the crook of his neck as heavy sobs continued to rack her body, and when Hux... Jace... got over the shock a moment later and hugged her back, I saw that his hands were trembling.

"Hey," he croaked. "Hey, it's okay. I know you—" His voice cracked, as his own dam burst and tears escaped his eyes.

I turned away, giving the two some space as they broke down together, experiencing the moment of shared grief they should have had four months ago. Bending down to pick up the gift Rhea had dropped on the driveway, my lips stretched into a watery smile as I looked at the design again.

On the front was a depiction of the lake that "Jace" had mentioned to me. I'd sewn a round blue basin of water, surrounded by what I hoped looked like quakies—thin trees with yellow leaves (I would've mixed in orange if I'd had the color)— and I'd stuffed the cushion with wool and dried lavender, which I hoped had reminded her of the lavender bushes. The main feature of the design, however, was a big brown bear standing in front of the lake on its hind legs. Its arms were open, as if welcoming the viewer into a hug, and I'd sewn a tremulous smile onto its face.

Above the picture were the simple words: *Happy Birthday.*

As I flipped the cushion over to the other side, my smile

broadened. The background was bare there, unlike the pillow's front design, the sole focus being a portrayal of her brother. His bulky body was stuffed into awkwardly small clothes, and his height was exactly the same as the bear's (I'd taken measurements to be sure). His position was also identical, with his arms spread wide for a hug, and the same apprehensive smile across his dark-bearded face. It was a little too easy to make him resemble the bear, honestly, and I probably grinned a little too much while sewing it.

Above his head were the words: *From your big brother.*

It was a simple thing, and pretty silly, really, but from the way I had sewed it, it was hard not to laugh when you viewed the sides one after the other, especially as the tight clothing struck so close to home. I'd pulled off that depiction pretty well, if I did say so myself.

I was just glad I'd managed to play a small role in fixing something that had been causing pain in Jace's life for so long.

Jace...

I set the pillow back down on a small bench behind me, then stepped away from the bungalow to give them more time and space.

Also, to think about the fact that I now most likely knew his full real name. *Jace Huxley.* It suited him, I couldn't deny that. It had a rugged, masculine ring that was so deeply him. And yet it still unnerved me that he'd placed so much trust in me. It also made me feel a touch guilty that he knew nothing about *me.* Well, he called me Robin, but he didn't know that was my real first name. Just another of the dozens of Robin Hoods within the OH network. Maybe I would tell him, at some point, to even out the balance a little.

I became lost in my own thoughts as I went for a walk among the grounds, sticking to the borders of the peaceful grove, mostly, so as not to venture too far from Rhea's bungalow. I spotted several children playing among the trees, being watched over by their young mothers, and the sight gave me a pang of regret. I couldn't help but imagine, if I'd just done things differently, that I could have been one of those mothers myself, watching my own child play beneath the dappled sunlight.

But it was pointless to lament. I'd had no way of knowing of an alternative at the time. And she was long gone now. The only way I could get her back was if someone cracked the archives, which I hoped, now that we were pooling so many minds together, would be sooner rather than later.

In fact, I made a mental note to ask about it on the forums as soon as I got back home, create a new thread and see if anyone who had already joined knew anything at all. We would be close to one hundred members soon, anyway, at the rate the portal had been growing. And that was one hundred more minds to probe that I'd never had before. I didn't need to wait for the forum's improved functionality to ask a yes-or-no question like that.

I continued wandering and musing for about an hour, my eyes drinking in the spectacular views the valley had to offer, until Jace finally came to me. His eyes looked red and watery, though he had a smile plastered on his face. I glanced toward the bungalow to see Rhea standing in the doorway with Sister Gina, watching and waving.

He made the call to Maria, and then, for a while, neither of us said anything. We waited for her to arrive, enjoying the warm, fragrant breeze caressing our skin, the gentle rustling of the trees, and the occasional laugh of a child tinkling through the quiet groves.

When the sister came into view on the other side of the orchard, he finally turned to look at me. His eyes were shiny and his voice was thick as he simply said, "Thank you."

18

Sister Maria walked us back to our taxi before bidding us both farewell and leaving us to climb into the vehicle.

As we pulled out of the compound and began rolling back through the mountain passage toward the train station, I kept my mouth shut, knowing that anything we discussed could be overheard by the taxi driver. But then I sensed Jace looking at me. I glanced his way and met his honeycomb eyes, which were still warm and glowing with gratitude.

He cleared his throat. "I was just wondering if you had any plans for the rest of the day," he said.

The note of hopefulness in his voice caused an unexpected sliver of pleasure to unfurl within me. I didn't have any plans. And I wondered why he was wondering.

I shook my head slowly, then tilted it to one side. "Why?" I asked.

He leaned back in his seat with a contented sigh. "Well, a few friends invited me for drinks this afternoon, down at a little tavern called the Bullhorn, by the shore. It's about an hour's train ride from here. If you haven't got anything going on, I was going to invite you to come with me. It's a cool place, and I think you'd like it. Drinks would be on me, of course."

I hesitated, the idea frankly sounding crazy appealing. I couldn't remember the last time I'd let my hair down, so to speak. And certainly not with other people. It had to have been before the Sylvones kicked me out.

At the same time, I didn't like the idea of Jace spending money on me. Not after I'd heard him basically admit he was only just scraping by and trying to save enough to support his sister.

He seemed to somehow read my expression, as he added, "The Bullhorn's prices are nothing like the average bars in cities. And besides, I feel like our relationship has been rather one-sided so far... I owe you for that sew job."

A surprise laugh escaped me, and then I found myself nodding, unable to resist what sounded like the perfect escape for this afternoon. "Okay, I'll come," I said. "Though the sewing really wasn't a big deal. Honestly, I enjoyed it."

I glanced down at the shirt and jeans he was wearing—the first set that I had fixed—and thought privately that it had been worth every minute and more that I put in to see him so comfortable.

"All right," he said with a grin. "So I guess it's a date, then."

I smiled. "You said you already threw professionalism to the wind, right?"

He nodded. "Whatever professionalism was there in the first place."

I snorted, and then we both settled back in our seats and spent the rest of the journey watching as the mountains swept past us, followed by the gentler, rolling plains of agricultural fields.

I was pleased with my decision to accept the invitation. Honestly, I was looking forward to spending time with this guy—

I'd grown close enough to him to consider him a pretty good friend in such a short period of time.

I was also curious to meet people he considered to be friends.

As Jace predicted, once we arrived at the station, it took us almost an hour to reach the shore. When we did get there, we headed right for the ocean-facing promenade and walked along it, enjoying the warmth of the early evening sun. Then we traveled down a steep set of stairs that led to a rocky beach.

The Bullhorn, it turned out, was really nothing more than a wooden hut. A large hut— which looked capable of holding at least one hundred people comfortably and had a big veranda that stretched out behind it over the rocks, and partly over the ocean— but a hut nonetheless. Which, honestly, made it all the more attractive to me. As we walked through the main entrance that stood at the bottom of the stairs, I felt a tug of nostalgia. The interior was all wood, from the walls to the floor to the furniture, which gave the place a musty wooden smell that reminded me of my own home. It was crowded, but not uncomfortably so, just enough to give it a cozy vibe. The warm light emitting from the soft orange ceiling lanterns helped with that, too.

Jace led me over to the long counter that wrapped around the bar area, toward four men who were seated there, the oldest of whom looked to be in his mid-thirties. Tall mugs filled high with a frothing liquid sat in front of them, and when one of them spotted us approaching, all four swiveled in their bar stools and stood to greet us.

I hadn't been sure what Jace had meant by "friends"—whether they were colleagues he had met in the last four months, or fellow survivors from his commune back in the mountains—but given that they had the same rugged look Jace had, I guessed it was the latter. Their hair was thick and a touch overgrown, their beards shadowing strong jaws, while their bulky frames looked built to withstand harsh environments. None were quite as tall as Jace, though, so they didn't seem to have clothing issues like he'd had. At least, it wasn't noticeable.

I supposed whatever "contact" had helped Jace get down here, and become involved with OH, had also helped them. He, or she, must have gotten them all out of the area and brought them here, giving them identification and enough to start a life. I couldn't be sure, though, whether they were all part of the admin team too, or even on the network, so I made a mental note to avoid bringing up the subject. I'd just have to wait and see if they did. I *hoped* they were, and I particularly hoped they were admins. Because that would mean they were better connected than me and perhaps even knew things, or had connections, that Jace didn't. And the more contacts I had, the better my chance of stumbling across information about the archives. I mean, for God's sake, how many parents in this country had been affected by the CRAS, and would give an arm and a leg for *any* kind of information about their children, even if they weren't brave enough to attempt to steal them back? *Someone* had to have figured it out.

As Jace and I closed the distance, I pulled my thoughts back to the present, and the four men before us. They were eyeing me with half amusement, half curiosity.

"This is my new friend Robin, from OH," Jace announced, pulling up a seat for me next to the man at the end of the line, and confirming my supposition that they were at least aware of the network.

"Robin, this is Alf, Cloyd, Denver, and Kory." He gestured to each of his friends in the order they were seated in. Closest to me was Kory, a stocky man with ash-blond hair and light blue-gray eyes. He stood about 5'8", which was around my height, making him the least intimidating. Perhaps someone I could begin asking questions. "Friends from back home," Jace clarified.

"Good to meet you guys," I said, shaking each of their hands. Their grips were noticeably stronger than the average shake.

And I wondered in that moment if Jace had just given me their real names, too. Because if so, I couldn't help but think that this was starting to amount to a lot of names I was going to have to try to forget, in the eventuality that I one day found myself strapped to a torture chair...

I shook the grim thought aside, determined to just relax and try to enjoy the rest of my Sunday. God knew, I couldn't live strung up on nerves all the time. Jace seemed to understand that work-life balance slightly better than me, given that he was able to relax a little once he found a person he felt he trusted.

Maybe I ought to take a leaf out of his book. It was just hard, with Nelson's training ingrained in my system. But for this afternoon, at least, I could push it aside. It was just me, Jace, and a handful of his close friends.

Who, if Jace *had* given me their real names, didn't seem fazed by it either. Considering how long they'd known each other, they probably trusted his judgment about people—and, in this case, me.

I had to admit the thought was flattering. As was the fact that he had invited me into his close circle of friends, even if he had provided false names. It felt like a vote of confidence I hadn't received from anyone in a long time. And coming from him... it just warmed me in a way I couldn't quite explain.

I sat down in the chair Jace had pulled up for me, while he seated himself on my other side. He pulled a drink menu toward him, and I gave him a smile when he shared it with me.

"So, what'll it be?" he asked, smiling back. I once again

became aware of those cute indentations at the edges of his mouth and felt myself flush. "Pick what you want," he added.

"Um." Realizing I'd paused to gaze at him a second too long, I quickly switched my focus to the list of options and narrowed in on the cheapest item there. "Apple cider, please."

He raised a dark eyebrow. "Seriously?"

"It's either that or fruit juice," I replied, giving a little pout. "I don't need to get drunk to have fun." Plus, I meant it when I said I didn't want to waste his money.

He chuckled, then turned to the server who had appeared on the other side of the counter. "Two apple ciders, please."

"Nobody said you had to adopt my virtues," I murmured, throwing him a teasing glance when the server moved away to fetch the order.

He shrugged. "Nothing wrong with apple cider."

"It's what we ordered." Kory chuckled from his seat next to me, and I turned to see him smirking at me, one hand sloshing the frothy orange liquid in his mug.

"Oh. Well, aren't you being good boys?" I remarked, seeing the opportunity to start warming the men—and this man, in particular—to me.

"I'd like to say it's 'cause we're angels, but alcohol is just bloody expensive in this country," Denver—a man with mud-brown eyes and raven hair long enough to tie back in a short pony-tail—said. "Even in the Bullhorn."

"Hey, I'm in a good mood," Jace replied. "So if any of you wanna order something fancier, go ahead."

They shook their heads.

"Nah, we wouldn't do that to ya, Jace," Kory said.

"Yeah, careful what you're saying there, Jace," Alf called over. "Give Cloyd a few hours and he'll have you in debt." He clapped the older man next to him hard on the shoulder.

Jace chuckled, then reached out and took one of the two mugs of apple cider the barman had returned with. I reached for my own mug and sipped, finding it surprisingly full-flavored and delicious.

"So how come you're in a good mood?" Kory wondered, shooting him a curious glance.

"Yeah, how come, Jace?" Alf added, angling an amused look at me. "Does it have anything to do with your new friend Robin?"

I didn't miss the way he emphasized "friend," and I suddenly felt a burst of heat in my cheeks. That was *not* what was going on here.

"Actually, yes," Jace replied, before I could think of a comeback of my own. He caught my eye and gave me a broad smile. "Robin helped me fix things with my sister."

"Seriously?" Kory asked, his eyebrows shooting up in surprise.

"That's amazing, man," Denver said.

"How did you do it, Robin?" Alf asked. "Jace's been having problems with Rhea for months!"

I swallowed. Since Alf had used Jace's sister's real name, as well as Jace's real name, I now assumed that my suspicion was correct: Jace had given me *their* real names. And the confirmation that he'd felt close enough to me to do that, combined with all four men's eyes suddenly on me, as well as Jace's, caused my temperature to spike higher.

I waved a dismissive hand, needing to defuse the situation. "Honestly, *Jace* is giving me too much credit," I said, shooting him a look. "He gave me some ideas and I made her a little gift."

They weren't satisfied with that explanation, however, and soon I found myself describing not only the homemade gift in detail, but also Rhea's reaction to it.

"That's hilarious," Kory declared, grinning at Jace. "Her issue was literally solved by laughing at you. I told you you looked ridiculous."

"Hey," Jace growled. "Don't get cocky just 'cause Robin's sitting between us. I can reach around her."

"Speaking of which, you got new clothes or something?" Denver asked. "You wouldn't have been able to reach Kory in any of your old ones."

Jace sighed, then gave me a conspiratorial glance. I pressed my lips together, wondering if he was about to make this even more embarrassing. To my relief, he replied simply, "Robin fixed them. She's got great sewing skills."

"Wow. She sounds like a keeper." Alf blew out with a cheeky whistle.

"Back to the subject of Rhea," Cloyd said, speaking up for the first time and setting his dark blue eyes on me. "I think you're being a bit coy by saying you did very little. Sounds like it was a pretty genius idea."

"It was," Jace confirmed before I could respond, and he sent me a firm look that brooked no argument. "She deserves every bit of the credit I'm giving her."

I rolled my eyes, then dropped them back to my drink and took a long sip. Blowing up my role in Jace and his sister's relationship wasn't exactly helping his friends' misconception of our relationship. But it was pointless trying to keep asserting my modesty when Jace was laying it on me like that.

"So you're all from way up north," I said, changing the subject in an attempt to get this conversation back to something potentially useful. "How are you finding it down here?"

They paused in their drinking for a long moment and glanced at one another, the same deep grimace darkening all of their expressions like a storm cloud.

"In short, they love it here," Jace replied, and I laughed,

grateful he had swooped in to make light of the situation. In hindsight, it had been a dumb question to ask, and I hadn't thought it through in my eagerness to change the subject. For all I knew, these guys had lost family members, like Jace. Plus, they would be feeling the daily grind of working in society, rather than just living in the wild. Sunday was meant for escape, not for thinking about all that, and it had been a crappy way to try to lead our conversation into new territory.

Jace's joke went down well, at least, and they joined me in laughing.

"Yeah," Alf said dryly, his face returning to a grimace as he took another sip from his cup. "Let's just say if we had a choice, we'd rather be back home."

A band suddenly started up in one corner of the hut, causing a distraction, and we all swiveled in our chairs to watch as people began leaving their seats and heading to a makeshift dance floor in the center of the building.

"Ah, music," Jace remarked, turning his seat back around. "This calls for another apple cider."

I snorted as he beckoned the bartender back over, and let him order me another drink too. We then all fell quiet as we listened to the upbeat music, produced by drums, a guitar, and a saxophone, and then a male singer who joined in, pouring out his dulcet tones through a microphone.

It seemed my questioning was going to have to wait.

As the dance floor became more and more crowded, we stood up with our drinks in order to maintain our view of the band and the dancing. Then, after another few minutes, Kory leaned off the counter and speared Jace with a look.

"So, Jace, is this pretty girl standing next to us really just your friend?" he asked, giving me a flattering smile. "'Cause if so, you won't mind if I ask her to dance, right?"

I froze in place, the blood flooding back to my cheeks in full force. My eyes then lifted to Jace for his reaction, and I realized his cheeks were flushing, too. Deeper than I'd ever seen them do before. He avoided eye contact with me, choosing instead to give his friend a hard look.

"Yes, she is my friend," he said gruffly. "And yes, I would mind, because I was about to ask her to dance *myself.*" He turned to face me, finally meeting my eyes with a twinkle of humor, though for some reason, he was still flushing. He shrugged off his backpack, set it down on the table, along with his drink, and held out an arm to me.

Despite being certain that my face was the shade of a tomato by now, I grinned stupidly and set down my own drink, along with my backpack. Heck, who was I to say no to a dance? I took his arm and let him lead me to the dance floor—but not before he cast one last glare back at Kory, who was grinning at us. We found a spot at the border of the dance floor where it was relatively empty, and then looked at each other, stalling awkwardly for a moment.

"So, do you even know how to dance, or was that just a knee-jerk alpha male thing going on back there?" I asked him with a grin.

He smirked. "Put it this way: I've never taken lessons. But maybe you can help me figure it out. May I?" He raised his eyebrows as he lowered his hands to my waist, not touching me until I gave permission.

I nodded, trying to ignore my suddenly racing heartbeat. "Sure. I'll see if I can't teach you," I replied.

I wasn't a great dancer myself, but I was guessing I had more experience than a caveman.

As his hands closed around my waist, my skin broke out in tingling where his fingers grazed it through the fabric, and a hoard of butterflies materialized in my stomach, stealing my breath.

Geez. That was a little more intense than I had been expecting.

Yes, I liked Jace. I wasn't stupid enough to deny that. *But come on, girl, we're just dancing.*

I tried to brush it away and placed my hands on his shoulders, but my heartbeat only quickened, as the motion drew me closer to him, until I could practically hear the blood pounding in my ears. This was the closest we'd ever been; even when I'd ridden on the back of his motorcycle, I hadn't really been touching him.

"So, let's just sway a bit first," I said, needing to distract myself with conversation. "Find a rhythm. And then we can try some more fancy things, like that couple over there."

I pointed to a couple that was doing a particularly complex—and honestly rather ridiculous—waltz-like number, involving the woman throwing her head back dramatically every six steps.

He looked over at them, then back down at me, his face deadpan. "Yeah, right."

I laughed. "You're right, I'm just kidding. We'll stick to swaying. Which is about all I'm capable of anyway."

I dared to lean in a little closer, until my cheek was almost resting against his chest—*almost*—and then started to guide our movements, getting him to follow my steps. We just rotated in small circles around the same spot, hardly getting any exercise, yet my heart continued to pump as if I were jogging.

I glanced to one side, distracting myself with the other couples, while I felt his heart thudding against me. I didn't know where he was looking, since glancing up at his face now would be *way* too awkward, with how close we were pressed together, but I sensed he was gazing at our surroundings too, from the way his chin brushed occasionally over the top of my head.

I looked in the direction of his friends and, to my surprise, saw that only Cloyd remained, sitting in his chair in front of the bar, his mug clasped in his hands, a stoic expression on his face. My eyes scanned the room for Jace's three other friends, wondering where they had gotten to, and then I saw them circling around the other side of the dance floor. In the short time that Jace and I had been dancing, they'd all managed to find single ladies to dance with. Or perhaps they'd gotten lucky with a group of them. Either way, geez, they moved fast.

Looking back toward Cloyd, I took in his darkened expression again and noticed this time that he seemed to be gazing at nothing in particular. His eyes were almost glazed over as he looked toward the dancers, and I couldn't help but wonder if the reason he hadn't joined his friends in picking up a partner was that he had lost someone. Someone he wasn't ready to replace, even for a dance. It might have been a bit of a reach, but his eyes were so haunted, his expression so stiff amidst the lively atmosphere, that his melancholy transferred to me, and made me ache a little inside.

I felt Jace's chest vibrate against me a moment later, and pulled my eyes away from Cloyd, realizing that Jace was chuckling softly.

As we swerved to dodge an incoming couple, Alf, Denver, and Kory flew through my field of vision, and I heard Alf's cheeky voice carry over the noise behind me, "Couldn't let you have all the fun, could we, Jacey?"

"No, you couldn't," Jace replied dryly, chuckling again. And then he added in an undertone, just for me, "I apologize for my friends, by the way. They're incorrigible."

I smiled. "They're pretty awesome, if you ask me."

He sighed. "Well, what can I say? Birds of a feather, and all..."

I chuckled, knowing I wasn't about to argue with that.

19

After about half an hour of dancing, the floor had become so crowded and hot that I was starting to feel more than a little claustrophobic. I found myself subconsciously squeezing Jace, and only realized I was doing it when he tucked his chin against his chest to look down at me.

"Hey," he said softly, frowning. "You okay?"

I loosened my grip instantly, embarrassed. "Oh, yeah, fine," I said quickly.

"It's getting pretty hot in here, isn't it?" he said, and I nodded, glad he was feeling the same.

"How about we go out onto the veranda for a bit?" he suggested.

"That sounds great."

He removed his hands from my waist, and then one of them caught my hand unexpectedly, sending a surprise rush of pleasure through me. His long fingers gently laced through mine as he wove a path through the dancers and toward the back exit, which led directly onto the veranda. Once outside, he let go of my hand… and I found myself wishing that he hadn't.

Get a hold of yourself, Robin. It was stupid to allow myself to feel too much—and I knew it. Hadn't I already learned that it was too easy to lose the people you loved?

We crossed the wooden floorboards to stand on the very edge of the platform that hung over the waves, and leaned against the handrail. I drew in a deep breath of the fresh, salty air, the feel of it in my lungs instantly calming me and cooling my flushed skin, and gazed out toward the dying, blood-orange sun, which had already sunk halfway into the ocean. The afternoon had flown by quickly, and I still hadn't asked any useful questions of Jace's friends. I knew I'd told myself that I'd come here to relax—it was Sunday, after all—but I guessed there were some things my brain just couldn't ever shut off, in spite of how good a time I was having… namely, my daughter. She was always there, embedded into the layers of my consciousness, even when I didn't realize it. And if there was a chance of getting one step closer to finding her, I had to take it. Even on my day off.

Jace's soft cough drew my attention, and I turned to see him staring out at the horizon too.

That cough was a mannerism that I knew well by now. It was a little tic of his, clearing his throat when he sensed there was some tension or wasn't sure quite what to say.

"What is it?" I asked, staring at him.

He turned to look at me, a slight blush returning to his cheeks. "I just…" He sighed, twisting his torso to face me fully. "I meant it when I said that I feel things have been pretty one-sided. You don't know how much it means to me, what you did for my sister and me earlier. What it means to both of us. And I realized how self-absorbed I've been the past week, so wrapped up in my own issues that I barely even thought to ask anything about you or your life. Not that I expect you to tell me anything, of course, it just would have been courteous of me, I guess, to at least ask, given the amount of talking I've done about myself. So…" A small smile stretched his lips. "I guess this is me attempting to be a gentleman now and asking if there's anything you want to tell me about how you came to be connected to OH, or anything else."

The fire returned to my skin under his attention—and at the reminder of his friends' teasing earlier, regarding my involvement with his sister—and I found myself stalling for words for a moment. It was true, he hadn't really asked me anything about myself, but then again, I hadn't expected him to, thanks to my training in Nelson's group. She'd hammered into our brains the idea that we could never give out information that wasn't completely necessary. And my backstory was just that. Unnecessary, so far as our professional relationship was concerned.

Still, I appreciated the gesture, though I had to give it a minute of thought to decide what I wanted to tell him, and in what detail.

I looked back out over the ocean waves, my mind scanning through the past two years. My eyes closed instinctively as I relived the pain in brief flashes of memory, and then I blew out. "I… I found myself without a home, and more or less penniless, a couple years ago. And it caused me to lose someone very close to me. I was a single mother, without adequate means, and the Ministry took my baby daughter." It had been a long time since I had even talked about this, and I hadn't been expecting my reaction, but my voice broke slightly and tears formed behind my eyelids. I had said something about it to Nelson, and teared up then, but that had been around seven months ago. I thought I'd be a little stronger about it by now.

Then again, scars as deep as this probably never healed.

"Oh," Jace breathed.

I turned to look at him again, and saw that he was gazing at me in somber surprise, all traces of humor gone. His Adam's apple bobbed as he swallowed. "I'm so sorry," he said, his voice low.

I exhaled. "It's okay. It's just… It's why I asked if you knew anything about the adoption archives, or anyone who might know something about it. I'm really hoping to get her back."

A look of guilt washed over him. "Well, now I feel like even more of an ass. I pretty much forgot you asked me about that." He paused, gazing at me intently, as if still processing the information. I had never told him my age, and I figured he was trying to guess at it now, since he probably hadn't expected me to be a mother.

"I'm nineteen, by the way. Twenty in a handful of months," I added. It was a piece of information I didn't mind revealing, especially since I knew his full name.

He nodded slowly. "I see. I was wondering." He then looked back out at the ocean, a thoughtful demeanor descending on him. "Well, I'll start by saying that I'm going to ask Nathan and every other OH admin if they know anyone who's ever cracked the archives, or gotten close to cracking them. Honestly, I should have offered to do that when you first asked me about it. I guess I just hadn't realized how personal it was to you at the time. But it's the very least I can do."

My face broke out in a grin, my heart overflowing at his offer, the tears growing dangerously close to the surface again. "That would be *amazing*. Thank you. You have no idea what that means to me. I'd actually been planning to ask your friends about this, thinking they might be admins with connections… Though, like I said, this isn't a game. You don't owe me anything just because I did a bit of sewing for you."

"My friends aren't admins, just regular members. But I'll put them on my list to talk to in any case. And I know," he added, giving me a firm look. "I'll be doing this because I want to."

My heartbeat drummed in my chest at the conviction in his voice, and I experienced a moment of elation so strong, I almost forgot the ground beneath my feet. "Okay, Jace," I managed softly. Then added after a pause, "And I guess you know I know your full name by now."

He nodded, smiling back. "And I absolutely don't mind."

The trust in his eyes filled me with another surge of warmth, which somehow momentarily overcame the tension knowing so much about him brought me, but before I could say another word, two familiar voices cut through the veranda.

"Hey, Jace, there you are!"

"We thought you'd done a runner with the lady!"

We twisted to see Alf and Kory jogging toward us from the tavern, moving through the other couples who had spilled outside for fresh air, and my smile faded some. I liked the guys, but I really could have gone a few more minutes without their raucous energy.

"Don't think you can get away from us that easily." Alf grinned, grabbing Jace's arm and ushering us back inside. "It's time for another round of ciders!"

Jace smiled at his friend, but I could tell it was forced, as we crossed the veranda and stepped back into the bustling tavern. I figured we both could have done with a few more moments alone out there in the quiet.

Once we resumed our seats in front of the bar, the rowdy noise of the crowd and the blaring music seemed to separate us, even though we were right next to one another, and even though I was still beaming inside from his offer. If Jace asked Nathan and the admins personally, they were likely to take the subject much more seriously than if I just made a public post on the forum (which I was still planning to do, anyway), due to his direct relationship with them.

And they were the most connected people on OH. If *they* couldn't find me a lead, I didn't know who could. I would likely be back to relying solely on Nelson, which might not be the end of the world, as she seemed to think she was close to a breakthrough. But it was still a while away, and she also couldn't guarantee it.

Either way, I would hopefully find out soon where, if anywhere, Jace's queries would lead. It felt like a hopeful step forward, regardless.

We stayed at the bar for an hour longer, unable to say much of importance thanks to the crowds and the music, and then finally all stepped out into the night together. Jace's friends walked with us to the station, loud and in high spirits (with the exception of Cloyd, who, although chuckling at jokes, remained the quiet one), and Jace and I didn't get a moment alone again until the train we were riding approached the station where I would catch my connection back home. As I felt the train begin to slow, I stood up and moved toward the exit, waving goodbye to Jace's friends, while Jace followed me to the doors.

I turned to face him when I reached them, glancing up to see his expression focused, his amber eyes gazing down at me intently, almost as if he were still thinking about all I had told him.

And in that moment of goodbye, I suddenly felt the urge to hug him. I wasn't really sure why. We'd spent a long day together, I guessed, and it just felt like the right way to part, especially after what he'd just offered to do for me. I found myself moving in without thinking—at exactly the same second that he extended his arm for a handshake.

We both stalled midway, jolted into an awkward no-man's-land, halfway between a hug and a shake.

"Oh, let's be professional then," I said, stepping back quickly and gripping his hand.

He shook my hand, while his lips curved upward. "Actually, the bear wouldn't object to a hug."

I grinned, then stepped forward again. I slipped my arms around his firm midriff while his arms came around my back, enveloping me in a strong, yet gentle hold. My cheek rested against his chest, and I inhaled the musky scent of him, drawing in a quiet breath. Even after our dance earlier, I hadn't been quite prepared for how good this felt. I used to think Henry's hugs were nice, but Jace's were something else. Like hugging a bear. It was warm and cozy, his body was bulkier than Henry's, and he held me in a way that made me feel completely surrounded by him, the outside world blocked out. I squeezed his waist instinctively, subconsciously wanting to feel him a little closer. My stomach bred more butterflies, and his friends wolf-whistled, but in that moment, I didn't even care. It felt so good, and I wasn't sure when I'd find an excuse to do this again.

"Hey," Jace said softly, his mouth close to my right ear. "The doors are about to open."

"Oh, damn," I murmured, quickly letting go of him and moving backward.

His lips looked a little flushed and his eyes were slightly hooded when I glanced up at him, giving me the impression that he'd relaxed into the hug just as much as I had. "I'll be in touch," he said, clearing his throat and straightening his back with a smile.

"Right," I replied as the doors opened. I stepped out with half a stagger, then turned back to face him with a wave. "Talk to you soon."

He nodded. "Yup. Talk soon."

As the doors closed, I turned and hurried through the barrier, clutching my flaming cheeks. And wondering for the first time if I was actually *falling* for this guy.

20

On returning to my cabin, the first thing I did was race to the bathroom to pee (thank you, apple cider). Then I collapsed on the sofa with a bowl of cereal, thinking about everything the day had thrown at me.

Specifically, Jace.

He had been on my mind throughout the entire journey home, to be honest, and I was still wrangling with my feelings about the subject. On the one hand, I couldn't deny that I liked him. He was cute yet mature, direct yet sensitive, and honest in a way that made me laugh. He made me feel things that I had felt at the beginning of my relationship with Henry. Arguably even more intense.

But still, where the hell was my head?

Getting into another relationship—if Jace was even interested in me in that way—was the absolute last thing on my list right now. Had no right to even be a thought flitting through my brain. Not when we were in the middle of so much. Especially after today, when Jace's trusted list had ended. Things were about to get riskier for everyone, and would require our full attention. I needed to stay focused. Keep my feet on the ground. Not allow them to do another loop around the moon. I'd already done that once and landed with a bump. Literally.

And now I owed it to said bump to keep on task. I owed it to Hope and to every other parent who had lost a child.

So I forced thoughts of that dance and that hug aside for now, along with the way he had made me feel, and resolved to stay on a more productive line of thinking for the rest of the evening.

The first thing I did was pull out my tablet and log in to the portal, which, I discovered, now had a proper name. "OH+" read a new logo at the top of the page. Not terribly creative, but it worked. I navigated over to the forum, to find that it had now tipped a hundred members. The threads were now more crowded and noisy than ever. I scanned the titles of the growing thread list, wondering if anybody had posted about the archives yet, but there wasn't a dedicated post, so I created one, asking the simple question of whether anybody knew about anyone working on cracking them.

I then sat back and munched on my cereal, waiting for the replies to come in.

"*Nope,*" came the first, less than a minute later.

I slumped back with a sigh and continued to monitor it.

Several more "*nos*" followed, as well as a "*you'd be crazy to even try,*" which got on my nerves, to be honest. That was hardly a useful contribution to the thread.

After ten minutes had passed, with five more people replying pretty unhelpfully, I noticed the responses starting to come in more swiftly, and then realized that the post had been pinned to the top of the forum... by Mr. X, who was currently online.

Despite my determination to brush my feelings for him aside, they resurfaced at the gesture, and I opened up the messages tab and typed one to him.

"Thanks. I appreciate that. :)"

His reply came back a minute later: *"You're more than welcome."*

I grinned in spite of myself, then returned to the thread and continued to monitor the responses as they streamed in. Still, however, none of them replied with what I wanted to hear.

The portal wasn't filled to capacity yet, but the fact that not a single one of these people even held a note of hope that it could be done didn't exactly sit well with me. I hoped that Jace's contacts, who surely couldn't all be ex-cavemen like him, but rather actual techies, would come back with a more positive response.

Gabby's reply was pretty much the only positive one among the sea of negatives, albeit not very helpful:

"Don't lose hope, Robin. I know we'll find a way. x"

I smiled, feeling tears rise to my eyes again. She couldn't know how much her wording touched me.

And then a red bubble caught my attention over the messaging tab, indicating that another message had come through.

It was Jace again:

"I asked my friends once they got over their cider high, after you left, and they didn't know anything (though I didn't expect them to, given their lack of connections). But I've now put out the word among all the admins, so we'll see what happens. In the meantime, I have details about visitations for next week, if you still want to come."

"Yeah, I'm in," I replied, with a bit more casualness than I felt. Yes, I wanted to come, but I was also nervous about the kind of people we were going to start meeting. *"You need some of my team too, right? How many?"* I added.

"Three would be good."

I lifted an eyebrow. *"Three? So that would make five of us, including me and you?"*

There was a minute before he replied. *"Yeah. Like I said, these are going to be sketchier. I'm really not sure how it's going to go down tomorrow. You should definitely all come armed. And wearing masks. Just in case."*

I swallowed. *"Okay."*

"I'll send out messages to each of your group and see who comes back. But for now, so you know, we'll be meeting at Bridgeton Main Station. Our destination is just nearby."

My eyes widened as I took in the name. Bridgeton Main Station. *Bridgeton.* It was a small town nestled between swathes of forest, and its main attraction was a giant lake. It was also where I had gone for summer camp as a kid. Where I had met Henry… and where Hope had been conceived.

I blew out, wondering if I was prepared for this. Even if we didn't go near the campsite, I knew the place well, having wandered around the town with Henry on a number of occasions. It held countless memories. Countless heartbreaks. Reminders of what was—and what might have been.

But they say you need to face your fears in order to move past them, right?

I guessed I'd just have to look at it as a character-building exercise, because there was no way I was backing out just because of the location, regardless of the discomfort it might bring me. That would've been the old Robin, the one who retracted into her shell when the world outside grew too big or too dark. Not the new one, who woke up facing each day with courage, and looked at obstacles as challenges—straight in the eye.

At least, that was the person I was *trying* to be. Because it was the person I wanted Hope's mother to be. Even if, right now, she didn't even know I existed, I wanted to be her role model.

Besides, I needed to be ready for when the day finally came.

"I'll come," I repeated, inhaling slowly. *"What time?"*

"We can meet at 7:00 p.m."

I chewed on my lower lip, mapping the journey in my head. I'd take the train there straight after work, so it was perfectly doable. *"All righty. I'll be there."*

I then turned my mind back to the discussion forum, and was about to navigate back to it when a thought occurred to me on the subject.

"Speaking of tomorrow, do we really need to continue expanding this portal's membership right now? I mean, we've already topped one hundred members, just from Nathan's trusted lists. That seems like plenty for an initial mastermind group. Wouldn't it make sense to start smaller, and then expand, once we've done a few first projects together? Guess I'm just wondering why we even need to reach out to the riskier members yet when we already have a solid starting place."

This whole initiative was still very much an experiment, a pilot test. Surely we should run at least one successful mission together—whatever that might be—before letting in another flood of people? And especially untrusted people. I worried that things would become too diluted and crowded, even with better forum functionality in place, which would lead to greater tension and distrust. If we didn't start with an initial solid base of members who'd been given the opportunity to build trust and work together, then it could become just another version of the main network, albeit a bit smaller.

The issue had been playing vaguely at the back of my mind since I first logged in and saw how much it had grown since the day before. I just hadn't given it space to surface, in my eagerness to post about the archives.

There was a pause before Jace responded:

"It's a good question. And I agree. We actually filled up way faster than initially planned. In fact, I just came off a conference call with my team and we weren't expecting such a good response from the initial outreach. Nearly 100 percent of the 'trusted' members we met with accepted the invite. So we don't have to reach out to as many riskier ones, for now.

"Nathan also thinks we should start on a smaller scale, as you suggest. It's standard programming procedure... not that I'd know a lot about that.

"Anyhow, he's shortlisted just a handful of the riskier ones who he thinks could add value, assuming they're real, to our beta base. So our 'risky' list is now way smaller than it was at the beginning. I only have three visitations on my personal list. And we should all be done before Friday, if everything goes smoothly. Then we can close the portal to additions and start serious discussion and planning.

"Side note: full-fledged forum features will be launched tomorrow, around lunchtime."

I read his messages a second time, absorbing his words thoughtfully, and then replied, *"Good news about the features. And okay. So just a few dicey ones. Not too bad, I guess. So this contact tomorrow in Bridgeton. Why did Nathan choose him/her in particular? What does he think they could add that could be truly valuable—resources that none of our current members have access to?"*

"Potentially, yes," he replied. *"All of them have claimed that they have valuable resources they can contribute. We have to verify it, of course, but the one we're visiting tomorrow claims to have access to rare technology that could help with ground missions. I don't have details about what it is yet, but we've had one member confirm they've procured something from him, and that he's legit. One*

member isn't much, of course, not enough for Nathan to put him on our trusted list, anyway, considering how long this person has been a member on the platform. But still, it could just be he (or she) is cagey. They've agreed to meet face-to-face, which is a good first sign."

I took a pause to munch on some more cereal while I thought about it. It still felt like we had a pretty good starting place with just the members we had already, but maybe there was something about this technology that was too valuable to pass up. It was worth checking it out, I supposed. Especially as the guy or gal seemed willing to show it to us.

We'd just need to arrive prepared and expect the worst-case scenario. Which wasn't anything new to me and the rest of Nelson's team.

"Okay, Mr. X. I think I'm gonna have a chat with my team now, see if they've got your invites yet, and touch base with them about tomorrow."

"Okay, Ms. Hood. - X."

Trying to suppress my smile at his signoff, I navigated back to the forum to check on my archives thread. The smile quickly faded, however, when I saw only more negative responses there. I exited the portal with a sigh, then brought up my conference app and dialed Nelson. Everyone seemed to be online, so while waiting for her to pick up, I sent out invites to the others to join the call.

Nelson connected first, however, and I was instantly surprised by how red her eyes and the tip of her nose looked, even through the screen and behind her glasses. I also picked up on a slight croakiness of her voice as she said, "Hey, Robin."

"Hi," I replied, distracted by her appearance. "Have I... caught you at an okay time?" I'd never seen her looking like this before. She always looked so put together and professional.

"Ah, it's okay," she said, sighing. "I just... Something really crappy just happened. One of my friends, she—"

Before she could continue, the twins connected to the line, followed by Marco, Jackie, and Julia, all in quick succession, barely seconds from each other. They all seemed to notice Nelson's face at the same time, and immediately asked her variations of the same question.

She gave a watery smile. "Geez, do I really look that bad? I should've waited to take the call."

"Hey, you don't have to tell us," I cut in, not wanting to make her feel uncomfortable. "We could just get on with talking business, of which there's plenty to discuss."

She shook her head, inhaling deeply. "It's okay. It's just that someone dear to me lost her baby yesterday. It was all so unexpected. She and her partner both had decent jobs and thought they were well above the danger level. And I'd thought so, too." She lifted a tissue to her nose and blew into it. "Turns out the Audit Office disagreed."

My heart clenched, feeling Nelson's friend's pain even though I didn't know her. I'd heard about incidents like this before, when even the middle class could be targeted, if the government's auditing super computer calculated that a family was a net drain on the country. Their system computed exactly how much each family was costing with the services they consumed—hospitals, schools, etc.—versus the taxes they paid. And anyone who became a net cost was in danger of being targeted.

The problem was, those records weren't made public, and although only the bottom 20 percent of the population were supposed to be targeted, nobody could ever be fully certain who that was.

"The worst thing is," Nelson went on, swallowing, "I could have helped them get the kid back. If only I'd known in advance.

They only told me what happened last night, after the fact, because… well… they didn't know anything about what I do on OH. I never told them about my alter ego because I tell as few people as possible, and I didn't think they needed to know. And now I feel like a self-preserving pig for it." She ran her hands down her face, and there was a long pause in which everyone else remained silent, apparently as unused to Nelson's emotional side as I was. And then she finally blew out and spoke again.

"Anyway, I'm making a mess of myself here. I guess it's just all the more motivation for me to crack those archives, eh?" Something hard glinted in her eyes.

I nodded stiffly, my chest still feeling constricted over the news of another child taken. It had the same emotional effect on me every time I heard someone's story, as if I were subconsciously reliving my own.

"Speaking of the archives," I said, wanting to distract both myself and Nelson, "Hux offered to ask around about it, among all his admin contacts. Including Nathan."

Her expression perked up instantly. "Oh, that's good news. Keep me updated on that."

"Of course!" I said. "You'll be the first to know."

"And speaking of Hux," Marco went on tentatively. "You all get a message from him about tomorrow?"

"Ah, yeah," Jackie said, clearing her throat. "He says he wants three of us, in addition to Robin. I was gonna suggest that the usual ground team go with him."

That meant Jackie, me, Ant, and Abe.

When I looked to the twins' screen, I realized that I had been so focused on Nelson that I hadn't paid attention to their faces. And I discovered now that I seriously couldn't tell the difference between them. Ant had gotten rid of his moustache.

"Whoa, Ant!" Marco said, almost choking on his drink as he

noticed at the same time. "You really took my suggestion to heart! Attaboy."

The twins stared blankly back.

"Except you don't know which one of us is Ant, now, do you?" one of them replied after a moment, his voice monotone.

We really didn't. The fact that they were both, probably deliberately, wearing the same plain black t-shirt didn't help, either.

"Oh, my God, that is just weird," Julia muttered, rubbing her temples.

"You asked for it," Twin 1 replied tartly.

Jackie sighed, shaking her head. "He's right. We did."

"You're going to be begging for that 'stache back by the end of the week," Twin 2 said smugly, folding his arms over his chest. *Presumably* Ant.

Jackie rolled her eyes. "Okay, I agree. The mustache was better than no moustache. Grow it back."

Both of them broke into contented smiles.

"I knew we would wear them down," Twin 2 muttered.

"All right," Nelson said, looking mildly amused, and much cheerier than she had a few minutes ago. "Let's get back to the matter at hand. So it will be the ground team tomorrow. Have y'all got everything you need? Enough bullets, etc.?"

Everyone nodded. She had given me a gun, along with ammunition, once I'd officially joined her team, and I kept it in a little box beneath my bed. I presumed she'd done the same with the others, as I'd seen her topping my colleagues up with ammunition.

"All right then," she said, giving one long, final blow into her tissue before tossing it away. "Let's get on another call tomorrow night, after you get back. Oh, and Robin, how did things go today with Hux?"

I took a deep breath, knowing it was kind of a tricky question. I hadn't asked for permission from the nuns to talk about their operation, and they seemed to want to keep it under wraps as much as possible, so I just described my day in vague terms, while making a mental note to ask at some point if I could share the info with Nelson. Their facility was a good thing for us to be aware of, in general. Not just for my own child, but in case we ever wanted to provide it as an option for the families we helped.

I also avoided mentioning the tavern date Jace had invited me on afterward, with his friends. I really didn't feel like telling them how chummy I was becoming with him. I knew it would lead to some annoying comments, from the twins in particular, which would only serve to put me further on edge about the subject.

So after telling them all I wanted to tell, I wished them good-night and took my leave from the call. I wanted to get an early night so I could pack in some extra sleep for tomorrow and make sure I had my wits about me.

Because it was going to be tense. On a number of different levels.

21

I was the first to reach Bridgeton Main Station the next
evening, my gun stowed in my belt beneath my coat, my mask
stuffed into my jeans pocket. I would put the latter on once we got
closer to our destination.

I had arrived about fifteen minutes early, so I went and sat on a
bench opposite the barriers and watched as people spilled through,
trying to ignore the waves of nostalgia that were already beginning to course through me. I remembered meeting Henry here a
number of times, the first of which had been the evening of our
second date. I'd been sitting on this very bench when he'd stalked
over to me from the barriers, trailed his fingers through my hair,
and caught my lips in his. He'd stood me up, pressed me against
the wall, and kissed me like we were the only people in the
station.

I closed my eyes, the flashback making my heart race even
now, my lips tingle from the ghost of his touch. I couldn't deny
that I still missed him sometimes… missed *that*. The fire. The
longing. The *need*. The way he'd whisper "baby" in my ear and

rest his hands on the small of my back, pulling me flush against him. The way he'd drop slow kisses down my neck and caress my earlobe with his lips, his warm breath tickling my bare skin and lighting me up from the inside.

The way he'd make me feel like I was both flying and falling at the same time.

The falling had been hard. So hard. But God, I couldn't lie to myself. I missed the flying. It felt like a long time since I'd had someone close in my life.

My traitorous mind instantly took me back to those few fleeting moments I'd spent in Jace's arms recently, and although I knew I ought to push it aside, somehow I just couldn't. My mind lingered there, settling into that close space between his heartbeat and mine, and reminding me of how much I'd wanted him.

I snapped my eyes open, needing to regain a grip on reality. I'd known coming here would take its toll on me, in one way or another, but I hadn't expected it to be like *this*. I'd already been over the situation regarding Jace in my head and decided where I stood. Right now, I owed it to Hope to avoid distractions, at least until I fulfilled my promise to her and got her back.

And I knew just how distracting new relationships could be.

Going off with some other guy right now (assuming Jace was even interested in me in that way) just felt wrong. Like I was being irresponsible as a mother, showing Hope she wasn't my first priority. And God knew she *was* my first priority. She wasn't just the love of my life, she *was* my life, and I would feel incomplete until I got her back.

I also didn't know if I was emotionally ready to open myself up to another person, even leaving aside the big gaping hole Hope's adoption had drilled through me. Henry leaving me might not have hit me as hard as Hope's absence, but it had still hurt. We had been close, albeit not as close as I'd once imagined. We'd brought life into this world together, after all. And his decision to leave had left a scar on me. I didn't blame him, or even really hold a grudge. I understood our relationship hadn't been mature enough to endure the ups and downs that life can sometimes throw at you, and pain is just the risk you take when you make yourself vulnerable to a person.

But, still, I wasn't ready to board another rollercoaster ride, just yet. Even if it did end up in a brighter place. The journey was too daunting right now. It made me exhausted to even think about it. My emotions had been hung up to dry during the past two years, and they needed more time to straighten themselves out.

And yet... even while I told myself all of this, that dull ache in my chest remained, the emotions this station had once held for me still infusing my consciousness. I decided I needed to go outside —get away from this bench, in particular—because I wasn't feeling like myself. And it was the nostalgia's fault. But just as I was standing, I spotted Jackie striding through the barriers. She wore a long black coat and had a large hood pulled up over her head, casting shadows over her face, and I latched on to her as a distraction.

Catching her attention with a wave, I watched her stride over. "You okay?" I asked, my eyes automatically falling to the scar on her cheek as she sat down on the bench. It looked much fainter than it had the last time I had seen it up close.

She nodded tensely, her eyes darting around the station. "Yup," she said, then dug a hand into her coat pocket and pulled out a black head mask. She tossed it to me, and I caught it, frowning.

"Got me a new mask," she said, a tad smugly. "Feel that material. It's way tougher. Can't be nicked by a blade, so no bastard is ever gonna go pulling a fast one like that on me again."

"Oh," I said, gazing down at the mask as I unfolded it in my hands. My fingers squeezed at the material, and it definitely felt tough, like some kind of rubberized fabric. "Where did you get it?" I asked.

"That's a bit of a secret," she replied, giving me a conspiratorial glance. "But I'm going to try to get some more of it, so the rest of you can get new masks, too. With all the extra danger we're about to involve ourselves in, I figure it's about time we had upgrades."

"Thanks," I said, handing the mask back to her. "That would be great."

"What would be great?" We heard the voice of one of the twins from above us, and we both looked up to see the duo standing over us. We had gotten distracted and missed them coming through the barriers, and my brow furrowed as I realized Ant already had his mustache back.

"What?" he asked. "Cat got your tongue?"

"Oh, my God," Jackie said, realization dawning in her eyes as she slapped a palm to her forehead. "Don't tell me that thing was fake all along."

Ant reached for the mustache and tugged at it, peeling it off in one swipe, and I burst out laughing. "No wonder it looks so stupid!"

"So does this mean you can't grow a mustache either?" Jackie asked.

"No," Ant replied curtly. "It just means we like to keep you on your toes."

He then handed the mustache to his brother, who pasted it over his lip. "I'm Ant, actually," Abe… Ant said.

Jackie and I stared at them.

"Okay," she muttered. "Just one of you keep the damn mustache, or you're gonna put us in a freaking psych ward."

Just then, my eyes caught Jace's head bobbing above the

crowd of people who had just arrived on a train and were surging through the barriers. And the feelings I'd been trying to distract myself from returned, forcing me to work doubly hard to beat them back. I decided the best way to do that was to act as if nothing was bothering me, because nothing *should* be bothering me, and I stood up to wave, catching his attention and beckoning him over.

As he strode toward us, he gave me a warm smile… which did more than I cared to admit to my insides. And then his eyes fell on my comrades. He looked them over curiously. After all, it was the first time he was seeing Jackie without a mask, and the first time he was seeing the twins at all.

"Mr. X?" Ant asked, his eyes bugging slightly as he took in Jace's imposing form. The twins were tall, but they were like wiry reeds compared to him.

Jace nodded, a good-natured smile quirking his lips. "That would be me, at your service, though feel free to call me Hux," he added, his voice low. And for some reason, he looked at me as he spoke his name, which caused another round of light fluttering in my stomach. I glanced away quickly, cursing my flushing cheeks.

I was making today way harder than it needed to be by not getting a damn grip on myself.

The twins both reached out a hand, and Jace shook them one at a time.

"Well, you're a bit different than what I expected," Abe admitted.

Jace chuckled. "Yeah, I get that a lot."

"You a personal trainer or something?" Ant murmured, frowning at Jace as he looked him up and down.

"Um, no," Jace replied, his expression amused. "Can't say I am."

"Look at you two, man-crushing already." Jackie scoffed as

she held out her own hand to Jace. "Please ignore the children. They don't get out very often."

"We just admire a good beard when we see one," Abe clarified, his eyes lighting on the thick, dark stubble around Jace's jaw.

"Well, thanks, I appreciate that," Jace replied, fortunately seeming to catch on to the twins' sense of humor quickly. He then looked out past the station doors toward the street. "Shall we get going then?" he asked, clearing his throat.

I managed a smile. "Yeah, let's."

As eager as I was to leave the station, due to the particularly intense memories it held, once we were out on the streets, my nostalgia just increased. This whole area had been my old stomping ground, and I found myself hanging back a bit from the group as we walked, feeling the need for some space.

Jace seemed to somehow pick up on my change in mood, and he shot a look back at me, though thankfully, the twins kept him distracted with their chattering as we walked across town, and I wasn't forced to deal with his proximity.

Luckily, our destination wasn't far away, either, and that finally presented me with the meaty distraction I needed: today's task. Because after fifteen minutes, we had found our destination road, a wide street close to the edge of the vast lake, which was, to my additional relief, pretty far away from my old summer camp. I couldn't even make out the camp from the side of the bank.

The road we were on now was lined with large, wood-paneled vacation homes, and it was clear that whoever we were visiting was wealthy, if he or she owned one of them. Though I doubted they would invite us directly to their real home. More likely, they had a short-term lease on it. Still, it would cost a decent chunk of change even to rent one of these things.

About halfway down, Jace stopped and pointed to one of the houses at the end of the road. "That's the one," he said softly, his eyes focused on the building. "I'm gonna suggest that two of you stay back here, to serve as backup, while the other two and I go up to the door."

When Jackie volunteered to go with him, I did too, since the two of us were usually a team, and the twins agreed to hang back. Jace then dipped into his bag and gave the twins a comm device each. He handed Jackie and me small clip-on comms, which we attached to the insides of our coat collars. If there was some kind of emergency, it would allow us to immediately call for help, and our comms were also equipped with sensitive microphones, so the twins could listen in on the conversation to gauge how things were going and decide whether they needed to step in.

Once the comms were figured out, we all put on our masks, and the twins slunk into the shadows of a copse of trees that lined the road to watch, while Jackie, Hux, and I approached the house. When we reached the front gate, we eyed our surroundings cautiously. All the blinds were drawn on the windows of the three-story building. A soft light glowing around the corners of a window downstairs was the only sign that somebody might be in.

We walked up to the front door, and my hands reflexively balled into fists as the three of us exchanged a glance. None of us knew what was going to be waiting on the other side. After another long moment, Jace drew in a breath and rang the doorbell.

Loud barking instantly erupted on the other side, making me jump, and we all stepped backward, creating some distance between us and the front door as heavy footsteps sounded behind it. Then came the noise of heavy bolts being drawn, and the door swung open. A tall, thickset man appeared on the other side, wearing a full-head balaclava mask and restraining a large German Shepherd.

"Mr. X?" he asked, his voice low and gravelly.

Hux nodded.

"Give me a minute," the man muttered.

He retreated with the dog, and we heard another door opening, and then closing, the dog's barking instantly getting quieter, before the man made his way back to us. He pulled the door open wide, gesturing for us to come inside.

We accepted the invitation tentatively, stepping over the threshold while continuing to look around. My hand hovered discreetly near where I had my gun tucked, ready to reach for it at a second's notice.

We moved through an entrance hall lined with pine flooring, and into a large living room, the decor of which confirmed that this place was most likely rented. It was pretty bare and way too neat, and held very few personal touches, the walls adorned only by the odd generic painting of the lake.

The only thing that caught my eye as being out of place was a tall object at the far end of the room, covered in a white sheet.

But our eyes were quickly drawn away from it by the man, as he walked into the room behind us and looked each of us over from behind his mask. He had dark brown eyes, I realized, beneath the ceiling spotlights, and judging from the lines surrounding them, he was in his early fifties.

"Mr. Montague," Jace said, holding out a hand. I was guessing the name was fake, given the rental arrangement he had made here. If he wasn't going to let us into his real home, he definitely wasn't going to tell us his real name.

The man took Jace's hand and shook it.

"I want to thank you for agreeing to meet with me," Jace went on politely. "I know it requires a level of trust."

"That's quite all right," the man replied, though he looked at us with an air of suspicion. Which was somewhat comforting, just like Jace's suspicion had been when I'd first met him. If this guy was genuinely feeling as cautious as us about this meeting, it was a decent indicator that he was worried about us being government moles, which at least made it likely that he wasn't one. "I want to be involved in this initiative, however I can be," he continued. "And I understand that it requires some physical verification... and for me to prove to you what I can offer." He gestured to the sofas. "Feel free to take a seat."

I realized then that Jace must have already given him a briefing about the initiative because, since he'd had so little activity on the platform, Jace needed him to show us what he had to offer upfront, during the first meeting, so we could figure out whether he was the real deal or just a timewaster. It had to be part of the more thorough probing for the less trusted members that Jace had mentioned earlier.

"Is that it?" Jace asked, his eyes on the sheet-covered object.

The man nodded, then walked over to it. He gripped the sheet and tore it off in one swift motion.

And what stood beneath the fabric made my jaw drop.

It was some kind of metallic suit. Its body was designed to mirror a human body, cover it from head to toe, including the hands and fingers, and it was made of some kind of dark gray metal, while its head contained a black, tinted visor for the eyes. My mind was already beginning to buzz with ideas about what it could be, and how it could be useful, when the man cleared his throat and announced, "This here is an exo-suit."

He pressed a button on the shoulder of the suit, and the front of it opened up, revealing a hollow space within. He turned back to face us. "Would any of you like to volunteer for a demonstration?"

The three of us looked at each other, and I shrugged. "I don't mind, I guess," I said. Jace definitely wasn't the best person to try out new, and potentially complex, technology, as he was still getting used to things like tablets and websites (plus, unless the suit was adjustable, he wouldn't fit), and Jackie wasn't exactly jumping to volunteer.

Jace frowned. "You sure?"

"Yup," I murmured. I didn't really feel comfortable about the idea of stepping into a piece of foreign metal equipment, offered by a guy we didn't even know we could trust, but someone had to volunteer to move this meeting forward if we were to get this potentially useful toy on our side.

I walked tentatively up to the machine suit, and Mr. Montague gestured for me to turn around. I did so after a brief moment of hesitation, and then, casting a fleeting look at Jackie and Jace, stepped backward into the suit, placing my feet in the hollows of the machine's feet. I pressed myself back, slotting the rest of myself into the vacant space of the suit, and felt soft padding behind me. The hands and fingers of the suit were also hollow, allowing me to slide my own through them, as if they were gloves. The man then pulled two straps around my torso, fastening their clips in place, and stepped back.

I blew out. So far, so good, it seemed.

"Now, the inside of the suit is fitted with sensors that track your body's movements," the man explained. "Soon enough, it actually begins to feel like it's just an extension of your own body. Once inside, you simply start moving as usual, and the suit will respond. May I close this?"

"Um, okay," I murmured, my nerves returning to me as he pressed the button on the shoulder. The front of the suit swung closed, sealing me inside, and I held my breath, afraid that claustrophobia might set in in such a small, confined space. Not to mention, I had no idea yet how to get back out.

Trying to force myself to relax, I stared straight ahead through the visor, at the two familiar sets of eyes watching me from the sofa, and reminding me that even though I was alone in this suit, I wasn't alone in the room.

"Good," the man said.

I could still hear him clearly through the suit; his voice was just a touch muffled. There was also definitely some kind of ventilation system, as, thankfully, it didn't feel stuffy.

"You will feel a button near your right index finger," he went on. "Press that, and it will unlock the suit."

I did so quickly, and the front of the suit popped open. *Thank you.*

"To close it again, simply press the same button again," he instructed.

I pressed it again, with more confidence now that I knew how to open it back up, and the machine obeyed.

"Now, take a step forward."

At this, I stalled, worrying I was going to trip. It all still felt very unintuitive and alien. But I moved my right leg forward tentatively, expecting myself to lose balance, and the machine instantly moved with me. And as I continued to put one foot slowly in front of the other, it kept up with my movement, until I had walked all the way over to Jace and Jackie.

That was surprisingly easy.

"Perfect," the man said. "Now walk back to me."

I did so, and then he proceeded to ask me to demonstrate a few other movements, such as bending my arms, neck, and fingers. The entire machine was remarkably responsive and flexible—and also surprisingly quiet. Other than its metallic feet against the floor, it didn't make a sound when I moved. I could totally see how it would feel like a second skin after a while.

And my mind went back to mulling over the potential uses that a piece of equipment like this could have...

But he wasn't finished with the demonstration yet.

"One last thing. Let me show you how to extend the legs," he said.

My eyebrows rose. "Extend the legs?" I asked.

He nodded, and proceeded to instruct me to press another button, once, with my right big toe.

As soon as I pressed it, there was the sound of clinking metal, and then the hard soles beneath my feet glided upward, until they had raised me two feet in the air. Glancing down, I saw that wide metal stilts had extended beneath me. They were somehow stored within the thick soles of the feet, giving me a significant height advantage. Though I had to admit, this felt a bit unsteady. I didn't want to find out what it felt like to fall over in one of these things.

"The suit can go quite a bit higher, if you keep holding that button," he explained, "though obviously we can't try that indoors. The height thing does take some getting used to, but it's pretty easy to master with practice."

He showed me how to set the legs back to their former size, with a quick nudge of the same button, and then how to extend the arms. It involved activating another button, near my left foot, which made the hands shoot out, the metal encasing distancing from my fingers. The suit was so cleverly designed, though, that even though my hands were no longer within the machine's hands, sensors within the frame still picked up on my finger, wrist, and arm movements, meaning the experience of navigating much longer arms was not that much harder from a technical standpoint. The physical movements were more or less the same. It just required a lot more concentration when you suddenly had an arm span of six feet.

Finally, I pressed the button to open the suit, unstrapped myself, and stepped out, my legs feeling a little wobbly on the wooden floor as I got used to my real body again. I glanced toward Jackie and Jace, who were still gazing at the piece of equipment, their eyes wide and impressed.

Jace then stood up and walked over to us to examine the suit more closely, and Jackie followed suit. "Well, this is interesting, to say the least," he murmured.

"I'm glad you think so. The suit was originally designed for construction workers," Mr. Montague explained, taking a seat in an armchair as he watched us eye his equipment. "Which means they're sturdy, can carry heavy weights effortlessly, and can take hits from heavy objects like bricks and other debris. They should be more or less bulletproof, including the visors, though I can't say I've tested them for that purpose, so I wouldn't want you to hold me to that. They're primarily meant to enhance the strength and ability of a human in the workplace. They can also be adjusted to fit any size or shape of person," he added, looking to Jace. "So, I'm guessing you can already start to see how something like this could be useful."

I sure as heck could. Completely bulletproof or not, I'd feel a lot safer wearing one of these on whatever missions might lie ahead of us. Especially if they involved ground work. They not only provided protection and supernatural strength, but also an extra layer of concealment, in addition to our masks. The metal feet were noisy, but perhaps they could be customized, padded so they made no more noise than regular boots.

Jace finally returned to his seat, while Jackie and I remained standing by the suit, and he set Mr. Montague with a hard look— one that told me he still didn't fully trust the guy, and it was time for round two of the vetting process. Which I was glad for, because in spite of how cool this piece of equipment was, I didn't trust him yet either. *How does he happen to have this suit? How many does he have? Why is he so willing to turn it over?* were just a few of the questions running through my brain.

"How many of these things do you have?" Jace began.

Mr. Montague gave a casual shrug. "I can be flexible, depending on the mission. When the time comes, if you let me know the number you need, I'll see if I can meet it."

"Okay," Jace replied, though he was still frowning. "And how do you have access to the suits?"

The man blew out, crossing his arms over his chest. "I'm sure you understand that I'm not comfortable giving details. But what I can tell you is that I'm in the construction business, and I have a finger on the pulse of emerging technology within the industry."

"And why is it you want to help us, put yourself out for us in this way?" Jace asked, gazing at him intently, and I mentally gave him a thumbs-up for asking my most pressing questions.

At this, the man gave a bitter laugh. "I wonder if you'd ask me that question if you thought I was poor."

I frowned, not quite catching his drift. It seemed that Jace didn't either, as the crease between his eyebrows deepened. "Actually, I would've asked the question regardless of what I thought your income might be," he replied tentatively, eyeing him over, as if trying to make sense of the man.

Mr. Montague shook his head, sighing. "Ah, I didn't mean to snap at you, boy. I'm just sick of people judging each other based on money in the bank, is all. It's not just the poor who hate today's culture. Not that I can blame anyone for holding a prejudice against the upper class. It's what happens when we have government of the rich, by the rich, for the rich."

Jace nodded slowly.

And then, to my surprise, the man suddenly reached for the base of his shirt and pulled it up, revealing his bare abdomen. Across it ran a massive scar, starting from the corner of his right hip and connecting to the base of his ribs. It looked like, however the original injury had been caused, it could've easily been deep enough to rip his insides out. And yet he had somehow survived.

The man dropped his shirt, leaving us all staring at him. "Curious to know how I got that?" he asked.

We all nodded, transfixed by the older man.

He gave a dry chuckle. "I was one of the early protestors, back in the day. Back when I was young and foolish. Joined the riots during the beginning of the CRAS, and let me tell you, the cops were not gentle with us. An officer sliced me right open with a spiked baton. Was a miracle I survived." He paused then and leaned forward in his seat, his expression now dead stern. "I show you the scar not to boast, but to impress upon you that I am serious. I might come from a more privileged background than most, but I have always been a fighter for equality. For basic human rights. And I wish to do something about our country's state of affairs, even in my older age."

He fell quiet then, and I glanced at Jace and Jackie, whose eyes were wide as they stared at the man, their lips slightly parted. Their expressions mirrored exactly how I felt inside—utterly taken aback by the passion of this man. It made me feel guilty for doubting him, yet it warmed me at the same time. It was further confirmation for what I had always hoped was true: that there were many others like us out there, willing to stand up for what they believed in, from all walks of life.

It took a while for anyone to say anything, and it was Jace who finally broke the quiet. "I see, sir," he replied, coughing his throat clear. "And I am sorry to call your integrity into question. But I'm sure you understand that we must be careful. As you appear to know better than all of us, there are lives at stake here."

Mr. Montague nodded grimly. "Oh, I understand."

"Then I hope you won't mind me asking why you've shown so little activity on OH, given your desire to help?" Jace asked.

The man sighed, running a hand down his masked face. "It's what happens when you have a family, lad," he replied. "I can't be as reckless as I used to be, not when I have a wife and children. After the riots, I settled down. Took over my father's business. Can't say the fire in me ever left, but it got smothered by responsibilities. Then I stumbled upon OH a few years back and joined on a whim. But it's been hard to know whom to trust, and like I said, I can't put myself at risk the way I used to. Which was why I was so pleased when you reached out to me," he concluded, the corners of his lips lifting slightly.

Jace nodded slowly. "Okay," he replied after a beat. "I suppose that makes sense."

I watched the man closely as he waited for Jace's next question. As convincing as his story sounded, of course, we still couldn't be certain that he was telling the truth. The scar could be from something else—or heck, even fake—but I was getting a good vibe from him. And I really wanted to trust him. The fact that he had shown up with serious technology like the exo-suits at least seemed like a good indication.

I looked back to Jace and watched as he pulled out his tablet and scrolled through what was presumably a list of notes. Then he stowed the pad away and lifted his gaze back to the man.

"Okay," he said, blowing out. "I think those are all the questions that are relevant for now. I'll discuss the meeting with my team, and if all goes well, will send you an invite sometime tomorrow."

"I suppose that's fair enough," the older man muttered. "Though, just for the record, I'll never ask for personal information about any of you, or even another physical meeting. So even if you don't fully trust me, I'm happy simply to lend the tech. Just a thought to keep in mind. It'll give an old man a lot of satisfaction." He gave us a wan smile.

Jace nodded appreciatively. "I understand. And thank you. It's generous of you, sir."

And then we all rose to our feet, and the man led us to the door. He opened it for us, allowing us back onto the porch.

"Safe journey home," he said, his expression turning tense, his eyes darting about the street once more, as if he was worried someone was watching.

"Thanks again," Jace replied.

"Have a good night," I said warmly.

He cast me a gentle smile back, his gaze weary yet glistening with a spark of hope. "And you, dear. God bless," he said softly, and then he was closing the door, fastening it with the heavy draw of a bolt.

22

After we reunited with the twins, we all headed back to the station together. Thanks to our comms setup, Abe and Ant had heard the whole conversation, and the only thing they wanted to be filled in on was details of what the suit looked like. The five of us went over how we thought the meeting had gone as we retraced our steps through the town, and everyone seemed to be of a similar mind, including Jace.

Mr. Montague appeared to be legit.

By the time we had reached Bridgeton Main Station, we had pretty much discussed all angles that any of us could think of, based on the brief conversation, and were just about ready to part ways, when we realized that the barriers had been closed. The station had been shut down for maintenance this evening. All of us had apparently failed to notice the warning sign earlier, which was lit up on the station's notice screen.

Which meant we had to walk to the next nearest station, which was about half an hour away, on the other side of Bridgeton.

Which presented another annoying opportunity for my nostalgia to resurface.

I'd been able to distract myself pretty well since we left the station, thanks to the intrigue of the meeting, but as we set off on another walk, delving deeper into the town, we began to pass places that were more familiar to me—from Henry's and my favorite ice cream shop, to a theater where we'd watched our first movie together—and I found myself falling silent again, needing to be in my own space as I grappled with the same damn feelings that rematerialized from earlier, while my colleagues continued to chat around me.

Henry's gone, I told myself firmly. *He's not coming back. He's probably even met another girl by now.*

And I don't need another guy in my life. Not now. Probably not for a long time. I don't have room for him. He'll just bring in his socks and underwear and scatter them over my floor. And I don't have time to pick them up.

That was the thing about nostalgia, I needed to remind myself. It could be both a gift and a curse. It made you only remember the good things about people and places of the past, glossing over the not-so-good as if they had never existed. Everything was rainbows and unicorns, kisses against the sunset and lovemaking on the beach.

Which was great when you wanted to look back on your life, in your old age, and remind yourself of all the nice times you'd lived through.

But it wasn't so great when you were trying to move on from something. It dragged you back, reminding you of what you were missing out on, infecting you with feelings that were irrational, and yet near impossible to shake. Because somehow, it made you believe that you could experience them again, without all the bad stuff that was fundamentally part of the package we called life.

The reality was, once you got past the starry-eyed first-date and honeymoon phase, relationships were hard work. And you had to really, really be sure about your partner before you ventured into one, if you wanted to stand any chance of coming out the other end of it unscathed.

I exhaled, shaking my head and running a hand down my face.

As soon as I got out of this town, I knew all this stuff would go away, and I could be back to normal in a day or two. So I just had to hold out a little bit longer, until we reached the next station.

My silence attracted Jace's notice once again, however, and, after about ten minutes of me hanging back, he retreated from the conversation with Jackie and the twins to walk by me, causing my breath to hitch involuntarily.

I liked the guy, but I really didn't need him in close proximity right now. Then again, that was my exact problem. I liked him. *I friggin' liked him.*

"You okay?" he asked, casting me a sidelong glance.

I forced a smile, keeping my eyes on the path ahead. "Yeah."

"Okay. You just seemed pretty quiet all of a sudden."

I pressed my lips together. "Mm-hm. This place just holds some memories for me, is all."

"The good kind, I hope," he remarked.

I shrugged, wanting to keep playing it cool, in the hope that I could fake it till I made it, that my external mood would infect my actual inner state. "Think high school summer romances."

His eyebrows rose. "Sounds scandalous."

I laughed, in spite of how close his remark came to the truth. "Yeah," I replied, shooting him a look. "Maybe I am the scandalous type."

A smile tugged at his slightly uneven lips. "I'd never have guessed."

"Then you still know very little about me, Mr. X," I replied primly, switching my gaze back ahead, as I was well aware by now what those little dimples at the edges of his mouth could do to me.

"Clearly..." he said.

As we rounded a corner, passing a music shop Henry and I had hung out in a few times, I felt a sudden twinge of guilt and abruptly felt the urge to add, "You do know my first name, though."

Jace looked at me in surprise, raising an eyebrow. "Robin?" he mouthed, and I nodded. "Your *real* first name?"

"Mm-hm."

He frowned. "Oh. Okay."

I could tell he was wondering why I'd suddenly decided to tell him, and to be honest, I wasn't sure either. The fact that I was feeling a bit jumpy right now, in my attempt to force confidence and chill in front of him, might have had something to do with it, causing me to overcompensate. Because honestly, getting closer to him by sharing personal information was the last thing I needed to do.

And yet, I just felt it was fair to him. As a friend. It had been playing on the back of my mind for a while, ever since I had learned his full real name, because it didn't sit right with me that the balance was tipped completely on his side. I somehow felt more comfortable in our professional relationship knowing he knew at least something more about me.

Besides, he was already calling me Robin, so it hardly felt like a huge step.

"Thanks, I guess," he said after a moment, still eyeing me curiously. "I appreciate the trust. Though you didn't have to tell me."

"I know," I replied. "It just seemed fair."

"Okay." He nodded slowly, and then returned his eyes to the

sidewalk ahead. "Well, I suppose I have it easier than you, not needing to remember to switch your name in public."

I chuckled. "Yup."

"Oh, and speaking of names," he added. "On a different note: I haven't heard back from any of my contacts yet with an affirmative about the archives. And I know that the community response hasn't exactly been great, but I'm still hopeful someone will come back with something."

"Okay," I replied, grateful for the change of subject, but also feeling a throb of disappointment. I hadn't really expected him to come back with an answer so quickly, though, as he had only put out the word last night. And I appreciated him taking this so seriously.

His statement also reminded me of the developments on OH+ that were supposed to have taken place today, which would finally make it easier for us to begin serious action planning.

And with that to focus my mind on, now I couldn't get home soon enough.

I managed to keep thoughts of Jace mostly at bay on my journey home, with my brain anticipating the new portal (leaving Bridgeton helped with that, though I knew it would take at least a day or so for the nostalgia to fully wear off), and on reaching my cabin, I flung myself onto the sofa with my tablet before even getting any food or water. I logged on to OH+ and was thrilled to see that the changes had been made as planned. There had been little tweaks implemented all over the site to make it run more smoothly and intuitively, but the one that caught my eye was the most important one: a poll module right above the discussion forum.

I navigated into it and saw that, to my surprise, it was completely empty of submissions. There was a "new submission" button right there, clearly visible for all to see, and I'd thought that people would be all over this feature—eager to begin posting suggestions for our next move and taking votes.

And then I saw a pop-up notice on one side that explained how the poll worked:

"Enter a succinct description of how you believe we could begin taking action as a group. Your idea will go through a moderating period, then be reviewed by our administrators, to ensure that it is within the realm of reason, and then each submission will be sent out via private message to each member of the group. They will have an option to select yes or no. At the end of this process, submissions will appear within the poll area, and in this way we will see which ideas are the most popular, and are worthy of further discussion.

Please be patient as we go through this process. It may take several days for a submission to show up. And please do vote on all ideas. Every voice matters.

Submission deadline is this Saturday for the first pilot mission, so be sure to send us your idea by then if you have one. After the winning idea has been chosen, focused discussion will start.

Yours,

The admin team."

I finished reading and immediately checked my inbox, but no new messages had come through yet, so I guessed whatever submissions they'd received so far were still in processing. The admins had been extra busy recently, after all, not just with working on this new portal while maintaining the main OH network, but also on the in-person groundwork the team was doing.

That didn't mean I was going to wait to get my suggestion in.

I set down my pad, thinking. This seemed like a pretty logical way to go about this. Now I just needed to figure out what I wanted to submit. I'd thought about it some before, and figured that whatever we did first should be something that painted us in a positive light before the public, something that inspired trust and respect, and showed we were not only good guys, but motivated and organized. A force to be reckoned with. But how could we do that? It was what I had to begin hashing out now. I needed to come up with a solid idea, or at least an example, that could be a starting point for discussion.

I closed my eyes, and was just falling into concentration when my phone rang, startling me. I scrambled to pick it up and saw that it was an unidentified caller.

"Hello?" I said, answering it.

"Hi, Robin, this is Gabby," the girl's voice crackled through at the other end of the line.

"Oh," I replied, surprised. "Hey, Gabby! How are you doing?"

"Okay, thanks. Hope I'm not disturbing you?"

"No, it's okay. I just got home."

"Okay. I guess you already logged in to the portal and saw the changes?"

I looked back to my screen. "Yeah. In fact, I'm just thinking about what to submit now under the poll section. Have you submitted anything yet?" I wondered.

She sighed. "No. I've just been thinking about it, too... You know that trafficking ring I've been trying to hack? I still haven't managed to crack it, but imagine if everyone on this platform put their minds together on a way to get in. We could bust it in no time. I know it's not directly related to OH's main objective of ending the CRAS, but it's just really been bugging me. *Somebody* has to do something about those monsters."

I paused, an idea hitting me hard and fast. I hadn't thought of that site, per se, but I suddenly realized how it could cross over to my line of thinking. Start with something good, and possibly unrelated to our main agenda, to begin inserting ourselves into the public's consciousness.

"You're right, Gabby," I said slowly, the cogs beginning to whir in my brain. "Even regardless of what we're trying to achieve here, something has to be done about that site."

I'd bet we had enough techy minds to hack their system within a day or two, maybe even a few hours, if we joined together. And if we went about this right, we could end up killing two birds with one stone.

"I'm so glad you agree!" Gabby replied, sounding excited. "I was thinking it could be a great first exercise in working together, even leaving aside the kids we would have helped."

"Is that why you called, by the way?" I asked. "To share your idea with me?" I was eager to get back to full concentration, now that, thanks to her interruption, the first inkling of a solid plan was beginning to form in my mind. But I didn't want to cut her out.

"Um, yeah," Gabby said. "And to give you an update on how I was doing with the site, since you asked. Also, I figured I'd see how you were doing with all of your other visitations."

"They've been going pretty well so far, actually," I replied. "Mr. X just has a couple more on his list, and then we should be ready to close the portal, to begin working on an actual mission. Apparently, all admins should be done by this Friday."

"That's exciting!"

"Yes, it is," I murmured, drifting back into my musings. "Well, I'm gonna work on a submission now," I said after a pause. "You've given me a good way to pitch something that I've already been mulling over, and I'm actually thinking we could submit a pitch jointly. How about I send it over to you for feedback once I've hashed it out?"

"Oh, sure! That would be awesome, because I wasn't really sure how to word the idea."

"Okay, keep an eye on your inbox."

"Will do! Bye-bye!"

I ended the call, then picked my tablet back up and began to compose the submission. There was a limit on words, so I had to be concise, but after about an hour of thinking and rewording, I finally sent it off to Gabby. She got back to me within five minutes with a "YES, THIS IS PERFECT!" and a string of thumbs-up emojis, so I went ahead and hit submit, signing it with both of our names.

I was pretty happy with the end result, but time would tell whether others thought the same. For now all we could do was wait.

23

For the first time since I'd started going out with Jace, I had an evening off. He confirmed to us via private message that the second appointment wasn't until Wednesday (with the third set for Thursday), and with that, I had an entire night to myself.

I thought I might enjoy having the evening free, but I found myself wishing that I was out doing something. Moping around the cabin allowed my mind one opportunity too many to return to Bridgeton, and the memories that had resurfaced there. The feelings the place had dug up hadn't left me yet, either, as I'd hoped they would. Instead they lingered, simmering just beneath the surface of my consciousness, and bubbled up whenever my mind wasn't deliberately focused on something else.

Which was annoying, because I didn't want to keep feeling awkward around Jace. He was my colleague, and this foolish crush I had on him was making it even more difficult to focus on the task at hand, adding to the tension I was already feeling by going out on these uncertain missions. I had to get over it. And I would. I probably just needed to give myself more time.

And in the meantime, I'd keep acting like I wasn't swooning over him every time he glanced at me.

This evening, the main problem was that there wasn't much more to do on the OH+ portal to distract me, given that we were waiting for the poll results to emerge. I did have a number of submissions to vote on starting to trickle into my inbox, which was something, but it didn't take very long for me to go through them. Most of them were recycled ideas that I had already seen bandied about on the forums. They were less rash than they had been in their original state (most likely rethought in order to get them through the admins' moderation), but all seemed to be rooted in short-term vengeance, rather than long-term thinking. I just hoped that, when people saw Gabby's and my suggestion, they would be able to see past their bitterness and recognize that it could make sense from a strategic point of view.

After logging out of the portal, I just ended up getting an early night, catching up on some extra sleep for the next day, in case we got back late. The appointment had been set at another remote location, in the countryside, which, according to Jace, we could still reach by train.

And I was glad for that, because a motorcycle journey would've been tedious, and I had been spending way too much on fuel recently.

Once the end of the workday arrived the next day, I headed straight for the nearest station, and, after a couple hours' journey, reached Yew Station, located in the small village-like town of Appleburn. I was both surprised and relieved to find that everyone had already arrived, because waiting around would've only made me feel uneasy—not just from the fact that I would've felt pressure to make small talk with Jace, but also because it would've allowed more opportunity for tension to build up for today's meeting.

As it was, I was able to immediately launch into action, because as soon as I approached them, we took off into the night.

It wasn't long before Jace was veering us away from the town, and along a seemingly endless road that wound between fields of wheat, with a disconcerting lack of lampposts. They were stretched too far apart to shine light on every stretch of the road, and Jace ended up pulling out his flashlight to help illuminate the way.

To say I was nervous about tonight's location would have been an understatement. I sensed the nerves stretching around all of us, even Jace, who kept glancing uncertainly down at the map on his pad, as if wondering whether it might somehow be leading us the wrong way. For all we knew, we were walking right into a trap, and although we were armed, we had no idea how many people might be waiting for us at our destination. Or whether they were government moles.

"You sure we're going the right way, Hux?" Ant asked warily, after fifteen minutes of walking along the dimly lit road.

Jace swallowed, then nodded. "Per the GPS."

"And what is this person, or people, supposed to be offering us that's worth the risk of us coming out this far in the dark to see them?" Abe asked, his angst mirroring his brother's.

"He/she wouldn't say, exactly. Same deal as with Mr. Montague. Said they didn't want to disclose details until we'd met face-to-face, but it's supposed to be some other kind of technology. Said it could be particularly useful during stealth missions. So we'll just have to see." He paused, glancing at each of us. "Unless any of you don't feel comfortable about this and want to turn back now. You're free to, of course."

We all glanced at each other with a firm look that said, "Nope, we're in this together," and kept walking, swallowing back our nerves and fixing our sights on the road ahead.

Once Jace's GPS announced that we were approximately ten minutes away, we paused to pull on our masks, and then prepare our guns. I retrieved mine from my bag and slipped its cool frame into my pocket, keeping my fingers wrapped around the handle for easy withdrawal.

This was a much dicier situation than Bridgeton had been, and I found myself wishing we were wearing Mr. Montague's suits for this already. Even if the contact wasn't a government mole, they could easily just be regular thugs, looking to rob or do who knew what to us. And, out here, nobody could hear us shout. There was no saying how long it'd take for cops to reach us.

Not that we'd dare call the police anyway.

I tried to keep my brain on a more optimistic line of thought as we took a left turn off the road and down a dirt track, which was completely devoid of light, except for a warm orange lantern glowing at the end of it.

As we neared the light, a small building came into view behind it, and Jace cut a beam across it with his flashlight. It was an old chapel, judging by the steeple and stone slab walls, and had been abandoned many years ago, based on the many holes punched into the stained glass windows. The smallest flicker of light spilling through from one of the ground-level windows caught my attention, and I pointed to it.

Each of my colleagues followed my gaze.

"Seems like someone's home, at least," Jackie muttered.

"So, I'm thinking same protocol as last time," Jace said, his voice whisper soft. "Everyone okay for the twins to play backup again, or you wanna switch things around?"

"I'm okay to go in," I replied. "Up to you, Jackie."

She nodded curtly. "I'm okay with it. They just owe us next time."

The twins exchanged a look, and then Jace was distributing the comm equipment again. Once we were all set up, he unlatched the wooden gate and eased it open, just enough for him to squeeze through. He gestured for Jackie and me to follow, while the twins ducked down behind the stone walls.

It was eerily quiet as we moved through the overgrown yard—which I quickly realized was a graveyard, as my foot connected with a low headstone. Jackie cursed beneath her breath as she almost tripped on one too, and we tried to stick to the narrow path that wound in between the weeds toward the entrance.

Then Jace was approaching the heavy oak door and knocking his fist against it hard, three times. And then we were all holding our breath and waiting.

I counted the seconds in my head. Thirty passed, then sixty, then ninety, and I was about to suggest to Jace that he knock again when I heard the whining of metal, and the doorknob twisted. It made me jump, as I hadn't heard the slightest sound of footsteps on the other side, and when the door creaked open, I was equally taken aback by the figure that stepped into view.

It was a small woman. A small, *young* woman, wearing a patchwork dress with a woolen shawl clutched around her shoulders. She was probably not much older than any of us, and yet there was a weariness to her features that aged her. Her blue eyes were dull, her mouth downturned, and a small scab ran across her lower lip. The skin around her jaw was oddly slack, her face holding a pallid, sickly hue.

Her thin lips stretched into a crooked smile as she laid eyes on us, and when she spoke, her voice was raspy, like that of a heavy smoker. "Ah, Mr. X and friends. I was worried you might've bailed on me! Come in, come in."

She staggered slightly as she stepped backward, away from the door, revealing a brown bottle clasped in one hand.

None of us budged as we cast uncertain looks at one another.

I didn't know who this woman was, but it seemed obvious that she was a waster. And I couldn't imagine what value we'd get out of this meeting. Still, I wasn't picking up on any imminent danger from her yet, so I supposed that since we'd come all this way, we might as well hear her out.

Jace and Jackie seemed to conclude the same thing, as they started to move after the woman through the door, and I took up the rear, careful to keep the door slightly open before following them through into a cavernous hall lined with dilapidated benches. All items of worship seemed to have been removed long ago, the walls stripped of decorations, leaving the place an empty, echoing shell.

I shivered at the chill draft wafting through. It felt a lot colder in here than outside.

The woman angled for a door in one corner of the chapel and pushed it open, leading us through to a small service room lined with candles. She'd turned it into some kind of temporary bedroom, judging by the sleeping bag rolled out in one corner, and a camping stove surrounded by a small pile of canned food.

At least, I assumed it was temporary. I couldn't imagine living in this place full time.

"Sorry, I got no chairs in here," she said roughly, gesturing to the floor around the stove. We all remained standing while she plopped herself down on her sleeping bag with a huff. "Suit yourself."

"Um, Ella," Jace finally spoke. "What is it exactly that you have to show me?"

Her blue eyes narrowed on him, and then a cackle bubbled up from her throat. "I'm sorry, I lied to yeh. Ain't got no special stealth tech to offer, or any tech at all! But I do got myself. Pamella Pomfry, at your service. And that's not a fake name, by the way. It's the one my parents cursed me with." She cackled again.

I exhaled, figuring we'd definitely seen enough by now, though my heart ached for the young woman. I didn't know what had driven her to this state, but I could only imagine that her past was tragic. Nobody deserved to live like this.

Still, we were just wasting our time at this point.

It was just one of the risks that came with the job, I supposed. Sometimes the meeting would end up being a dud. Though duds were better than death traps, so there was that, at least.

Jace sighed and started to back away. "I'm sorry, Ella. In that case we have to leave."

"Wait!" She shot to her feet so abruptly, she was practically a blur as she latched on to Jace's right arm. She tugged him back into the center of the room, panting under the strain of pulling the large man. "Please, wait!" she said, a look of urgency streaking across her face.

She sounded so desperate that we couldn't help but stall. A part of me felt terribly sorry for her, though another part couldn't beat back a creeping suspicion that began to unfurl within me. She seemed to *really* want us to stay.

Could this be some kind of trap?

I looked nervously to Jace, who extricated himself from her gently, gripping her shoulders and guiding her back down onto her sleeping bag. He then rose to his feet, frowning down at her. "What is it?" he asked firmly.

"Just hear me out, mister," she rasped, pinching the bridge of her nose while continuing to take deep breaths, as if trying to force herself to focus.

Jace nodded slowly, and then glanced at Jackie and me. Still half-fearing that this was a trap, I moved back to the door and peered out into the dark chapel. It was ghostly quiet, as before, the only movement a large spider weaving its web against a nearby windowpane.

I returned to the room and nodded at my colleagues, and then we sank down to the floor to be level with the woman. It just felt wrong to be towering over her when she wanted to tell us something.

"Okay, we're listening," Jace said finally, setting her with a stern look. "Go ahead."

She nestled deeper into her corner, slipping her legs between the folds of the sleeping bag, then leaned back against the cold stone wall, her rheumy blue eyes glistening in the candlelight. "Let me tell you a story," she said after a moment, her voice deep, calmer. "There was once a young girl... let's call her Mella... and she fell in love with a young boy. Let's call him Sammy. She was sixteen and he was seventeen."

She paused and took a swig from her bottle, and a shiver crept up my spine at the way her story had started.

"Sweet sixteen," she crooned, smacking her lips together as she set her bottle between her legs. "They lived in the same fancy neighborhood and went to the same fancy private school, and they'd known each other since kindergarten. Close friends all through junior high, and then lovers through high school. They were the perfect match, everyone said. Even their parents adored little Mella and Sammy as a couple."

I let out a breath at the slight diversion the story had taken compared to mine, having been afraid for a crazy second that it might have been some kind of setup—that by some bizarre twist, she somehow knew my story and was going to out me or something here—and then I brushed all thoughts of my own history aside and refocused on the woman.

Her eyes seemed to glaze over for a moment as she stared at the wall, before she gave a hacking cough, and then continued, "So, they did what everyone expected them to do, as soon as they hit the legal age. They got married. They had a gorgeous wedding, surrounded by their friends and family. Mella looked like a princess in her frilly white gown, and Sammy looked like a freakin' stud in his shiny black tux. Everyone rained down gifts and cards, wishing them a long and healthy life.

"After that, they went on their honeymoon. A three-week skiing trip up in the mountains, courtesy of their parents. And then, woohoo, before you knew it, the girl was growing a friggin' bump. Funny what happens when you put a boy and girl together, huh?" She guffawed, then hiccupped, brushing at a bead of spit that had fallen onto her chin.

Then her smile faded suddenly. "Only, it wasn't so funny once the baby was born." Her breathing grew slow, belabored. "You wanna know why?"

I pressed my lips together, already guessing the answer. Assuming the story she was telling us was true, somehow, the baby had probably been confiscated, like mine had. Maybe her family had fallen out of fortune, or something, and her reason for wanting to be involved with OH+ was the same as mine: to act out against a system that had hurt her.

Though, she hardly appeared to be in a position to help us; I didn't even know how she got access to a computer or the internet, and by the looks of her, she could barely help herself. I guessed this chapel couldn't be her full-time base, and she probably just wanted to feel useful, somehow.

None of us answered her question in the affirmative—especially not me, who didn't want to hear another traumatic tale of a child being prized from their birthmother, as it only ever reminded me of my own history—but the woman continued anyway.

"Because he had severe medical problems that not even the specialist doctors could fix." Her voice dropped to barely a whisper, her eyes growing haunted.

And I suddenly realized that I had probably gotten the wrong end of the stick. In fact, I didn't know where this story was going now.

"You wanna know why?" she went on, and I found myself holding my breath at the sheer look of pain flickering in her irises.

A pin-drop silence fell about the room, stretching out for several long moments as she rose slowly to her feet, her hands balling into fists.

"Because little Mella and Sammy never should've been a mommy and daddy," she whispered finally. "Little Mella and Sammy shared the *same* mommy and daddy."

Before I could even process her words, her hand shot out for one of the candles and she threw it across the room, missing Jace's head by less than an inch as it smashed into the wall behind him. A shriek of anguish tore from her throat, and she bent down for the metal stove, picking it up and hurling it blindly.

Jackie shot to her feet just in time to avoid being crushed by it, and then the three of us were racing from the room. She wasn't trying to hurt us, I was sure, but the girl had clearly lost her mind.

And I realized that I couldn't blame her.

My stomach roiled as we fled the church, a deep sickness settling there and threatening to overwhelm me as I processed what must have happened, her reason for hating the CRAS. She had *found* a long-lost family member, in the worst possible way. It made my own reasons pale in comparison. We pounded down the pathway toward the gate, her howling following us out into the night, her pleas for us to come back ringing in my ears and making my hands tremble.

We kept running, picking up the twins on our way back to the main road. Even though I wanted to go back and help her, I didn't know how. None of us were qualified to deal with her level of problems, and certainly not tonight. She needed professional help. Though, if she came from a wealthy family, as her story had indicated, then something told me her parents would have already gotten her that.

No, what she needed was for that to never, ever have happened, I told myself, an angry fire burning through my veins. What had happened to her and her brother was a rarity, something I had never even considered before, but something I was sure as hell adding to my list now. It was an additional reason we could draw on if ever we needed to persuade others to help us end the CRAS. Because this was inexcusable.

Something like this *never* needed to happen. All Ella and her brother had needed was an open archive, so they could've known who the hell they were, and where the hell they'd come from.

The anger remained burning within me long after her cries had faded into the distance, drowning out all coherent thought and conversation. Until there was nothing but eight words repeating in my mind, in rhythm with the pounding of my feet:

We have to end this. We have to.

24

We were all feeling shaken the next day, so much so that Jace suggested he push our final appointment to Friday, to give us all a bit of breathing space to recover. And I was grateful for it. My sleep had been fitful that night, the vision of that poor woman darting in and out of my dreams, and the following day I barely had an appetite.

The next evening, we met up at a station a couple of towns away from where I lived. None of us spoke of Pamella, though her story still glimmered in all of our eyes, haunting us.

We walked in mostly silence along several residential streets with lower-middle-class dwellings, donning our masks as we moved. We stopped when we reached a small laundromat, closed at this hour, and crossed to the other side of the road, eyeing it cautiously. It was our destination, according to Jace, where we were due to meet a group who claimed they could offer us some other kind of equipment that would be of use—details to be revealed once we arrived. But after our experience in the chapel, I was feeling extra nervous about who they might actually be.

"I think we need to take the side door," Jace said quietly, moving along the sidewalk to get an angle on the side of the building, where there was another entrance farther back.

"If you and Robin wanna stay back this time, we'll go in with Hux," Abe spoke up, looking between Jackie and me without a single trace of humor in his eyes. He seemed to genuinely want to give us a break after yesterday's scene, and while they'd witnessed it too, in a way, over the comms, it hadn't been nearly as intense or disturbing for them as it had been for us, face-to-face with the woman's raw emotions.

So Jackie and I accepted the boys' offer, and Jace quickly distributed the necessary gear. "We can wait around the side of that building," she said softly, pointing to a narrow alleyway that cut through the blocks on this side. It would be a good option, as it was almost opposite the laundromat and would provide us with a good view of the side entrance.

Jace nodded firmly, and before I could ask them to be careful, he and the twins were heading off across the road. Honestly, I felt a little guilty about staying back, when Jace was still going in, given that he'd been through exactly what we had the other night in the chapel. Still, none of us knew how this was going to go down; for all we knew, Jackie and I would end up going in anyway.

So I might have been feeling guilty too soon.

Jackie and I walked to the alley and crouched down, keeping close to the wall of the corner building, and set our focus on listening. The men were still within view, just reaching the door, and I could hear their heavy breathing on the line. Their nerves stretched my own, even though I wasn't the one potentially walking into imminent danger this time.

Jace rang a doorbell fixed to the wall on one side, and then the three of them took a step back and waited.

Nothing happened for a minute. No sound of anyone scurrying to reach the door on the other side, just the men's continued uneven breathing. A minute stretched into two, then three, and Jace tried again.

But still nobody answered.

"You sure they definitely got your message about shifting the meeting to today?" one of the twins mumbled.

"Yes," Jace whispered. "The contact confirmed with me and said it was all right."

"Then why aren't they answering?" the second twin muttered.

They waited another minute, and then Ant's hand moved to the door handle, as if on impulse. He gripped it, and to my surprise, there was an immediate creaking sound and the door gave way.

"Whoa," he breathed. "They left it off the latch. In fact, it looks like the lock's broken."

The three men paused for a long moment, staring at the now-ajar door as if wondering whether to trust it.

"I'm not sure," Jace replied, his voice pitched low and a touch tight. "But I suggest we go in with our guns ready."

The twins looked at Jace and nodded, and then all three men were reaching for their weapons, clicking the safeties off, and holding them at their sides. They moved in, Jace taking point, with Ant at the rear, and a couple seconds later, all three were gone from sight.

I gave Jackie a nervous look, which she returned. Then I hunkered down lower and closed my eyes, needing to block out all external distractions and focus only on the noises in my ears. For now, it was just their increasingly tight breathing, and slow footsteps on what sounded like some kind of sleek flooring. I imagined them in my mind's eye, walking down a corridor, stopping at the junction of each off-shooting room and looking inside.

It probably wasn't far off, given that I could make out the low groan of a door opening every now and then.

They kept moving in silence, and then suddenly, Jace cursed.

Fear bristled through me at the alarm in his voice, and the twins quickly joined him in cursing. They hadn't gone in with earpieces, per protocol—it could set potential allies on edge if they thought we'd arrived with an elaborate setup—so we couldn't talk to the men, only hear what was going on.

I looked to Jackie, my heart quivering. There were no gunshots, and none of the men were shouting, or even running yet, from what I could tell. But their reaction to whatever they had just seen wasn't sitting well with me.

"You think we should—?" I began to ask.

"Search those other two rooms," Jace said suddenly, cutting me off midsentence.

I pursed my lips and continued listening as the footsteps sped up, and I heard a couple more doors opening, followed by what sounded like shuffling papers and the gliding of drawers.

"Empty," one of the twins said finally, his voice uncharacteristically shaky.

The other twin confirmed the same a moment later.

"Jackie, Robin," Jace said. "In case you're wondering, we're okay. The place is clear, but... Well, maybe you want to see this for yourselves. Then again, maybe you don't."

I was already springing to my feet, unable to stay in the dark any longer. Jackie followed quickly behind me, and we crossed the road, racing along the side of the building and slipping through the side entrance.

We arrived at the beginning of a long, dark corridor, not unlike what I had pictured in my head. Except it was more of a dump than I had imagined, the paint on the walls and doors peeling, the ceiling patchy with mold. We passed several rooms on either side of us, filled with shelves and office furniture, as we went toward Jace and the twins, who were standing outside a room at the opposite end of the corridor.

They were frozen in place, staring at whatever lay beyond, and barely even registered us as we pushed past them to get a look.

And when I got one, I understood why Jace had said I might not want it.

This end room was larger than the others, and it felt like I'd just stepped onto the set of a gangster movie. Tables and chairs had been upturned, shelves knocked over, hundreds of pieces of paper scattered about the floor... and the pale green walls were absolutely splattered with crimson. As though someone had been shot multiple times, from multiple directions.

Or multiple people had died in here.

The floor and furniture had been sprayed with blood too, puddles still moist and glistening beneath the beam of Jace's flashlight. The place was bereft of bodies, but the scent of death hung heavy, making my stomach churn, my throat gag.

I stepped back, exhaling sharply and bracing myself against the corridor wall. Then fear gripped me. The scene was so fresh, it meant that whoever was responsible might still be in the area.

"We should get out of here," I managed.

"But what the hell happened?" Jackie whispered, clutching her stomach.

"We don't know," Ant replied. "Maybe they were involved in some kind of gang feud. Maybe someone else wanted what they were offering us. Maybe—"

"Enforcers were here," Jace said suddenly, and our eyes all shot to him in alarm.

He dropped to a crouch by the door's threshold and scooped something up from the floor. Rising to his feet, he turned the object over in his palm, and my blood froze.

It was indeed the badge of a law enforcer, its smooth silver surface engraved with the flag of our country, a unique officer number etched into the base of it. The fastener at the back of it looked slightly bent, damaged enough to slip from a uniform.

"Let's go!" Jackie hissed before my brain could even fully process the sight.

Jace dropped the badge, and we turned and ran back down the corridor, slipping out into the night. I was the last outside and closed the door behind us, before we took off at a fast jog back along the street toward the station.

Whoever those OH contacts had been, and whatever they'd been doing or had to offer us, they'd been sniffed out. They must have taken a misstep, become lax in their security or skipped a protocol or two, somewhere along the way. Because I was positive that it was more likely to be their blood on the walls than the cops'.

A chill settled into my core as I realized we were a day too late. But then again, maybe someone somewhere up above was looking out for us. Because if we'd gone ahead with yesterday's meeting as planned, our blood could have very well been splattered there, too.

25

The vision of the crimson-smeared office bled into my dreams that night, much like the crazed woman had two nights before, and I woke up the next morning in a cold sweat, convinced that enforcers were closing in on my cabin. I'd heard them picking at the lock of my front door in my nightmare, but as I fully rose to consciousness, I realized that what I'd heard was less the sound of picking and more of scratching, accompanied by a familiar whining noise.

I breathed out heavily, brushing the sheen of sweat from my forehead with the sleeve of my pajama top. *It's okay,* I assured myself as I climbed out of bed. *You're fine.* I headed straight to the door before doing anything else all the same and peered through the peephole, just needing to convince my subconscious beyond any doubt that it wasn't the police.

Spying my semi-regular wolf visitors through the hole, I opened the door and walked out, trailing my fingers through their soft fur while they jumped up at me. I sank down on the small bench that lined my porch and gazed off into the distance, continuing to pet the animals absentmindedly.

We'd had two meetings go wrong in a row now, which was starting to feel like a bad omen, after all the positive, easy meetings I'd been in on at the start. And last night had been a visceral reminder that none of us were ever far from death on this tightrope of a life we'd chosen to lead. It brought me a renewed wave of respect for Nelson's protocols, and an increased determination to abide by the training she had given me.

We couldn't take our safety for granted, couldn't afford to become lax even in the slightest. Because once you became loose about one thing, it could easily spill into another area, until soon, you were making reckless mistakes and painting a bright red target on your back.

It also triggered a fresh spike of guilt about knowing Jace's and his sister's names, as well as some regret for sharing mine.

But what was done was done. All I could do was be more careful about what I overheard in the future. Regardless of the fact that I trusted Jace and he trusted me, we should have followed protocol. Because the government had very little patience when it came to criminals these days. Enforcers weren't supposed to shoot us outright without a trial, of course. Most likely, whoever had been shot back there hadn't cooperated, or had done something to prompt the officers to react with violence. But the fact remained: even if we weren't shot onsite, it wouldn't take long for the judicial system to get to the bottom of our crimes and put us to death if we didn't keep our trail clean after they tried to get information out of us.

From what I'd studied of history, the death sentence hadn't been doled out so freely in the past. That was something that had changed over time, as administrations argued that it would save lives in the long run, because people would become more afraid of committing crimes in the first place. *Be heavy-handed with the few to save the many* was the logic.

And the system worked, to a certain extent, I supposed. Crime was down overall in our country compared to previous decades. At least, per the reports I'd seen.

It just wasn't so marvelous when you were potentially on the wrong end of it.

Anyway, I was glad today was Saturday. I didn't have any plans to go out. My mind and emotions needed a break from the stress of the last few days.

Leaving the animals, I went back indoors and got myself some breakfast, then sat down at the table with my tablet. I logged in to the portal to find my inbox spilling with more voting requests, and was just going through them when I noticed a message from GabbySails with just a subject line in all caps: "CHECK THE POLL SECTION!"

My heart skipped a beat as I navigated there. It had finally populated, with over a dozen submissions, and I almost choked on my milk when I saw whose was right at the top.

Mine and Gabby's.

With ninety-two votes. That wasn't far off 100 percent of the platform's members. I gaped at the screen, stunned, and wondered for a moment if my eyes were deceiving me. I'd hoped our proposal would get a good response—at least enough to make it onto the poll list as an option—but I hadn't been expecting *this*.

It brought a renewed surge of hope in me for the people of this platform, knowing that they'd voted ours above the more sensational and instant-gratification ideas, which revolved around coming out of the gate by directly attacking the CRAS and its elements.

And it was also humbling, and a little bit off-putting, to feel so many virtual eyes on us, sitting up there right above everyone else's ideas.

Submissions were still coming in, so I guessed it was possible we would be overturned before the poll closed to new entries by the end of today, but at least for now there seemed to be no danger of that happening. The other submissions had received substantially fewer votes; the one in second place—a suggestion to organize an online petition for the end of the CRAS and try to get it to spread virally—only had fifty-four.

Honestly, that didn't sound like a terribly difficult thing to organize and would probably only take a small team of techies to put together. I couldn't really see it having legs, though, given that most people didn't take online petitions seriously, especially as many would choose to sign anonymously. And even if it got up to a million signatures, what would happen, exactly? I was sure there had been petitions of that sort before that hadn't gone anywhere. Still, there was no harm in making it a side project if we had the people and resources, especially as it was probably the least risky idea possible.

It seemed that others agreed with me, though, that we had to strike a balance between safety and risk in order to draw the kind of attention we needed to stir people. We didn't want to come off as reckless, but we also had to show that we were ready and willing to make things happen, and weren't just a bunch of dreamers.

And hopefully, the idea Gabby and I had presented would be a good starting point for that.

I clicked on our submission and read it over again:

"1) Hack into an auction site run by child kidnappers and trace the ringleaders.

2) Capture evidence of their activities and rat them out to the government.

3) Somehow record proof of our actions, so we can submit evidence of our involvement to the media and leak it on other online channels, to begin seeding public awareness of us as a group. (We will obviously need to think of a better name than OH to go by, for the public. Maybe RAM, Reform America Movement, or something along those lines?)

4) All while keeping ourselves safe, of course."

My eyes lingered on my last point. The advantage of a mission like this as our "opening statement" was that we were not putting ourselves directly in the line of fire from the government. Things were bound to go wrong during our first project working together as a group, and I felt like this would minimize our risks, while still allowing us to achieve meaningful results.

We would be helping the justice system do its job, in fact, by rooting out a band of heinous criminals. It was an act that would also be universally supported by the public, regardless of political views. The main thing we'd need to be worried about, safety-wise, was retaliation by the criminals themselves. Which, as a collective, I was pretty confident we could handle. Especially with the resources we'd managed to gather during the past couple of weeks.

We'd still need to keep our identities carefully hidden, of course, when ratting the criminals out to the government, because the RAM (or whatever we ended up calling our movement) would not be doing this kind of "non-offensive" work forever. Our ultimate target was the CRAS, and soon, we were going to be focusing all our efforts on taking it down hard.

Which was basically the equivalent of prodding a nest of wasps.

I sank into contemplation for the rest of the day, watching as new poll submissions came through and monitoring our submission's status in the list. Over a dozen more trickled in, making thirty in total by the end of the day, when a notice was put up informing us that submissions were now closed, but voting would remain open until the end of Sunday. So there was still a chance late voters could topple our position.

But by midnight on Sunday, that still hadn't happened, and ours emerged as the winner by a long shot.

Barely twenty minutes after midnight, all of the threads in the main forum relating to other ideas were shifted over to a new "off-topic" section and a new thread was created by one of the admins stating that the main discussion area was now specifically designated for talks relating to the winning poll idea.

Which meant, I guessed, that the first stage had finally begun.

I felt nervous, knowing that if anything went wrong during the course of our actions, I would feel responsible. Half of it was Gabby's idea, but half was also mine, and I was the one who'd packaged and submitted it.

Someone had to shoulder that responsibility, though. And since my submission had caught the most wind, I guessed it might as well be me.

26

The next few days went by in a blur of discussion and activity on the OH+ platform, which contrasted starkly with the other half of my life—the monotony of the factory.

On Monday, I woke up to several PMs from my group, congratulating me on getting my submission selected as our first project. They were all enthusiastic about it, to my relief, and it gave me an extra boost of confidence that things would work out.

Then I noticed a message had come through from Jace, too, and my pulse spiked a little as I clicked it open.

"Hey Robin, good job. Couldn't have thought of a better idea myself.

X."

A smile immediately unfurled on my lips and warmth burgeoned in my chest, my brain unable to miss the absence of the dash he usually put in front of his initial... And then I mentally slapped myself.

Nope. Nope. Nope. Nope. We're not going there again.

It hadn't been difficult to find distractions over the past week, given the tension and stress it had brought us, and luckily, they were only going to increase now that the ball had gotten rolling.

There was definitely an "unluckily" in there somewhere, too, but I chose not to focus on that for now, my immediate gratitude being not having to deal with those exhausting emotions.

I just needed to keep keeping things together.

Which thankfully wasn't too difficult, because beginning Sunday night, people started discussing the first step: hacking the site and trying to trace an IP location. If we couldn't find an address, or some other clue that could lead us to the criminals' location, then our plan would basically fall flat. At least, in terms of PR. Yes, we could figure out a way to pass on the site's direct link to enforcers, but we could hardly claim involvement in busting them, or gain the kind of public exposure we needed for that basic act.

We had to take things a lot further for that.

Which was why I was praying that the team of six hackers that had formed by Monday morning—including Nelson and Gabby (who had somehow convinced her mother to let her be involved) —would figure it out. Nelson had been nominated the leader of the IT team, and I found myself glued to video chat for the next couple of days, keeping in constant contact with both Nelson and the rest of the team, so I could get immediate updates whenever they made any progress.

Honestly, I was frustrated that I wasn't a hacker myself and couldn't be more directly involved. I knew this was only prep work, and that I was going to be knee-deep in the actual mission soon enough. But still, it made me impatient, because most of their updates didn't mean much to me, since I didn't understand the ins and outs of coding or hacking sites. And I probably started getting on their nerves with all the questions I was asking.

But their general mood remained optimistic over the chat, and

I almost squealed with excitement when Wednesday evening came around and Nelson finally announced that they had managed to find an IP. Which I took as a good first sign. The fact that they'd been able to figure out the security pretty quickly might indicate that these were cowboy-type criminals who didn't have either enough resources, brains, or patience to do things thoroughly. Which could mean the chances of them being a serious threat to us for the latter part of our plan would be smaller.

The IP pointed to a location in the suburbs of Belmore, which was a prosperous city farther up north, toward central America, and about a three-hour flight from my group's general area. Further investigation narrowed it down to an actual address.

Which left the next step clear: scouting and schematics.

We had to be sure that the property was real, and if so, get an understanding of the place. Because even if it *was* real, we still had to retrieve evidence that whoever lived there was definitely behind the criminal activity. Nelson informed us that the group we were hunting might have used the IP of an innocent person, which was why, after verifying the address, we were going to have to send in a ground team to breach the actual property.

But first things first.

Given that Nelson already had access to an aircraft, and we had the equipment required to draw up schematics remotely, she put our group forward to handle it, and Julia, Marco, and I ended up leaving together on Wednesday evening. It didn't really require two people to do the aerial scans—Julia could have managed it alone—but I needed something to do with my fidgeting hands, so I offered to play assistant.

It took us just under three hours to reach our destination, and by the time we did, it was pitch dark, which was our plan. It made it easier for us to fly undetected. Once Marco gave the go-ahead, I helped Julia deploy the drone, and she navigated it over what was, indeed, a real property.

It was a long, rectangular building with a corrugated roof, and when Julia began capturing snapshots of it with the drone, they automatically flashed up on the little screen fixed to the passenger cabin wall, revealing more details. From what I could tell, the building seemed to have once been some kind of factory or processing facility but had now been repurposed as an office.

It was also set back from the road, enclosed in its own small compound, and surrounded by what looked like a high barbed wire fence, outside of which was a large parking lot that seemed to be shared by several other office-like buildings in the vicinity. Beyond that was a field, a bit of forest, and then farmland. Nothing too interesting.

My eyes were quickly drawn back to our target property, when Julia pointed out movement around it, suggesting multiple security guards. Which was disappointing, to say the least. Based on how relatively stress-free our IT team's probe of their online site had been, I'd been hoping that security around their physical site would also be relatively lax.

But perhaps they were old school like that.

Still, we returned home that night with a lot more clarity about our target than we'd flown out with, and I woke up on Thursday to find a new post in the forum started by Julia titled "*STEP 2: Accomplished.*" She'd included all the aerial photographs and the X-ray schematics from our trip in the post, and there was already a flurry of activity as a result.

I clicked it open and scrolled down to begin reading the responses, and saw that Nelson had replied first:

"*I and the rest of the IT team tried to get intel on the owner of this property, but we're coming up blank. Can't see any records other than it's owned by a corporation: IIC Holdings, which we can't find info on.*

That said, for the purposes of the ground mission, I suggest we operate on a 'guilty until proven innocent' basis. We go in looking for, and expecting, evidence. And if we find none, then, well, we go back to the drawing board."

I nodded to myself in agreement. There was a chance the criminals could have been spoofing the IP, but I figured it was just as likely that our IT team had found a loophole in their cyber security, and this *was* their real base of operations. It was going to be a tricky job, and we had to go in there like hound dogs, with clarity and single-minded focus. Mission: search for evidence, regardless of whether or not it existed, rather than having our minds clouded by doubts of their potential innocence.

I scrolled farther down the page to view the other responses, and saw people already leaping on Nelson's advice and discussing the next step: infiltration and retrieval of evidence. Which was understandable. Everyone was eager to push on and get our first success under our belt. But I wasn't done re-absorbing the information Julia had posted yet, so I set my pad aside for a moment, needing some space to think.

Judging by the size of the building, and the fact that it was encircled by high fences and monitored by security guards, we ought to arrive with a largish ground team, just in case things took a turn for the worst and we needed backup, or extra people to create a diversion. We also didn't know what hours these kidnappers kept—whether the office was even guaranteed to always be empty of workers at night—so we had to account for the possible presence of people within the building, too, not just outside it. Which made things even more tricky.

But not impossible.

I believed we'd managed to gather a smart and varied pool of people together over the past couple of weeks. Now it was time to put us all to work.

We hashed out a plan over the rest of the week, including discussing the various types of evidence we might find there, and consequently, the sorts of things the ground team needed to look for when gathering volunteers. I, of course, threw my hat in the ring, along with Jackie, Abe, and Ant.

And then I found myself absently scanning the rest of the list for Jace, to see if he had volunteered as well. But I couldn't find his name there, which I found a little odd. I'd been under the impression that he'd wanted to be in on this project, from start to finish, given his heavy involvement in recruitment. I hadn't seen him around the forum all that much over the past couple of days, either, now that I thought about it. But maybe he was just taking some time off before the big day. He'd been under a lot of pressure recently, too, with our visitations. Arguably more so, since he'd been our team leader.

Anyway, I reminded myself firmly, it wasn't exactly my business. So I put it out of my head and focused on things that were.

Once our plan was more or less solidified, I posted a brief summary of the main points in a new thread, and one of the admins pinned it to the top of the forum, so everyone could easily get a bird's eye view of it while we continued to hash out details.

It read:

"*Step 1) Ground volunteers arrive at the site at designated time.*

Step 2) Split into two teams, one frontline and one for back-

up/decoy purposes, and approach building.

Side note: Front line will approach building from the roof, by aircraft; backup by foot.

Step 3) Frontline team begins recording footage and gets in undetected. (Cameramen: Ant and Abe.)

Step 4) Stay undetected (with help of decoy team, if necessary) while retrieving evidence that proves the property's connection to the shadow site.

Step 5) Get out.

Step 6) Submit evidence/address to enforcers ASAP (IT team) and then leak edited footage to press + every online news/viral social channel we can think of (again, IT team).

Note: Ant/Abe are also in charge of video editing and will brand the final footage with the name RAM (Reform America Movement) and block font logo we agreed on in the branding poll."

I exhaled as I finished reading. It didn't seem like all that much, when broken down into simple steps, but I knew this was going to be anything but easy. Each of these steps was crucial. If we failed at any one of them, the best-case scenario we could hope for was our plan blowing up in our faces and all of our work being for nothing.

Worst case: we'd pay with our lives.

The frontline team, which I was going to be a part of, needed to include at least one tech, since whatever evidence we found was unlikely to be written on stray pieces of paper. It would be in the computer systems. I'd been worried at first that Nelson was going to volunteer herself—I always got jittery at the thought of her being in the line of fire, given that she had always been (and still was) the only person I knew who'd made any progress with the archives—but four others from our IT team stepped in quickly instead, including Gabby. (Gabby's mother was quick to shoot that down, however, leaving us with three options.) Which meant Nelson was going to be part of the remote team.

Once we had discussed every other detail we could think of on the forums and analyzed every resource that was available to us in the gradually populating Resources and Facilities section, we came to the next obvious step: meeting each other.

I'd gotten a decent idea of everyone who was going to be involved in this sting based on the hours of discussion I'd spent with people on the forum over the past week, but the ground volunteers still needed to meet before the actual day, in order to get comfortable with one another. It was a necessity if we were going to trust each other enough to cooperate efficiently on this mission, and would also give us the chance to hash out some finer details face-to-face. We'd all wear masks, of course, just like we would during the mission itself, but putting eyes and a voice to the cyber personalities was a vital human part of the equation.

Especially because we didn't trust each other 100 percent yet. I was praying we didn't have any moles in the group after Nathan and the admins' vetting process, but the danger was there. And as Jackie had so succinctly put it, it would only take one mole to bring us all down.

It was a chilling thought, given how comfortable I'd started to grow with folks on the forum, but it was also a point I couldn't afford to forget. Not with our most recent, graphic reminder of what was at stake here.

Meeting in a more casual, low-risk environment beforehand was important, even if it just made us all feel a little easier about the situation, and the team we'd be working with.

So, come Sunday evening, I found myself closely monitoring the discussion thread that was dealing with potential meeting venues. I made several suggestions myself, while trying to be mindful that these people came from all parts of the UNA. I was in the middle of responding to another member's suggestion, which I believed to be too far north to be fair to most members, when my phone rang.

I rolled out of bed to snatch it up from where I'd left it charging on the floor, and to my surprise, the caller ID read... Mr. X. My heartrate increased a fraction as I stared at the screen, wondering where he'd been all this time, and why he was calling me. He'd never called my phone before, not even when we'd been going on visitations together, so it struck me as odd that he'd be calling me now.

Then the thought occurred to me that he could be finally getting back to me with good news about the archives, and I quickly answered it with an enthusiastic, "Hey, Hux!"

"Hey," he replied, in a tone that was considerably less lively than my own.

"What's up?" I asked, frowning.

"I, um. I heard back from my last contact about the archives this evening."

My heart plummeted at his tone, and I instantly braced myself for the disappointment I knew was coming. "And none of them could help," I finished for him with a sharp sigh, not wanting to drag it out.

He exhaled. "Yeah. I'm... I'm really sorry. I was hoping at least someone would come back with a lead, but people are scared to even try poking around government-owned cyberspace."

And I didn't blame them, considering that it could warrant the death penalty.

Still, I struggled to bite back the disappointment. I'd known from the start that the chances were slim, but it had been hard not to get my hopes up. When I'd joined, I couldn't help but see this portal as a new and exciting potential gateway into the archives, with how many additional people I'd have access to.

But maybe the portal still wasn't big enough to include that one special gem.

In the meantime, I guessed there was still Nelson. And perhaps I shouldn't be too despondent, given how hopeful she was about having gotten closer to a way in.

"Okay," I said, trying to put a lid on my conflicting emotions. "I really appreciate you asking around anyway."

"I know it's not good enough, though," he replied, sounding genuinely annoyed.

"Yeah, well…" I swallowed, unable to keep from being touched that he'd been taking this so seriously, while also feeling frustrated myself at the lack of leads. "There's probably nothing more we can do right now. Maybe someone or something else will come up in the coming weeks." I realized I hadn't told him that Nelson was working on the archives and was about to add it to try to make him feel better about the failure, when I remembered her rule: no unnecessary information. So I decided against it. "Anyway, speaking of the coming weeks," I added, wanting to change the subject for both of our sakes, "what do you think of everything that's been going on?"

I hadn't made much of an effort to speak to him recently, for various reasons, but I was genuinely curious to get his take on how everything was unraveling. To be honest, it all felt like it was happening so quickly, I was still in a state of processing it myself.

"You didn't see I volunteered for the ground team?" he asked, sounding mildly surprised.

I frowned. "No," I replied, wondering how I could have missed him there.

"Well, I guess I came forward a little later than everyone else because of, uh, family commitments. But yeah, I'm part of the team."

"Ah, I see," I replied, guessing he'd added himself since I last checked... and realizing this meant I was probably going to see him again in a few days. The initial meeting was probably going to take place in the earlier part of next week, specifically Wednesday, because it was a public holiday for the entire nation. Even the factories would be closed, so it seemed like the perfect opportunity, given that many of us would have to travel hours to the meeting venue.

"That's cool," I added quickly, realizing I'd left too much of a gap after my initial statement. Because it was cool. It was just fine.

My mind then latched on to the latter part of his first statement, and it was on the tip of my tongue to ask how things had been going with his sister since our visit—I knew he was supposed to see her on Sundays—when I swallowed it back, reminding myself that, even though it seemed like harmless information, since I already knew about his sister, it was unnecessary, and asking would be breaking protocol, which I needed to stay in the habit of *not* breaking.

So instead I changed the subject again. "What are your general feelings about this, anyway?" I asked. "Positive enough to volunteer to be on the ground, but... anything else?"

"Well, I don't think there's going to be anyone on this mission who's not feeling nervous, but I'd say my optimism outweighs the negative. I seriously think this will be a good way for us to build trust with one another, as well as seeding some trust with the public."

"And how does Nathan feel about how everything's playing out?" I asked, still wondering which of the admins Nathan actually was.

"He's excited and optimistic, like the rest of us."

"Good," I said, blowing out, and then falling silent.

There was a long pause, then, in which I wondered if Jace was going to say something else. Whether the news of the archives had been the only reason he'd called me. But if he had been about to say anything, he apparently thought better of it.

"Okay, well, I guess I'll let you go now," he said, clearing his throat. "I'm sorry again. If there's anything else I can do, let me know. And I'll keep my ear to the ground regardless."

"Thanks, Ja—Hux," I said, quickly correcting myself. I didn't want to use his real name over the line, encryption present or not.

"You're welcome," he replied, and then hung up, leaving me to push thoughts of him aside again, along with my disappointment about the lack of archive leads, and return my focus back to my tablet… and the small beginnings of a rebellion that was gradually taking shape.

27

By Tuesday, we'd finalized the venue—an empty warehouse on an industrial estate in the suburbs bordering Tucklons City—and Wednesday morning found me getting ready to leave. The rest of Nelson's group and I were traveling together, given that we had access to an aircraft—and Nelson was coming too. Since she'd become one of our main strategists, she wanted to meet some of the members of her IT team and get a feel for our action group as well. She wouldn't be coming with us on the day of the mission, but would be involved remotely by providing technical support and advice should the need arise. So she needed to know who she was going to be dealing with.

It had been the car dealer guy on Jace's trusted list, "Marty Bales," who came forward with the venue. He'd said the storage space belonged to a contact of his, and that he could arrange to give us access to it. And he was who I spied first when we reached our destination.

I'd just climbed out of the aircraft when I spotted him standing outside the entrance of the large, windowless gray building. He was wearing a mask that concealed his bald head, but I recognized the short, portly form of the forty-something-year-old, as well as his intense, low-pitched voice as he addressed another small group who'd arrived a couple minutes before us.

I wasn't sure how to feel about him being at the meeting today, honestly. Jace's and my visitation with him hadn't exactly inspired me with confidence about his character; he'd been too high-strung for my liking, with an emphasis on vengeance that had made me uncomfortable. I wasn't sure that his motivations truly aligned with what we, as a group, were trying to achieve here: a steady, well-balanced mindset that would allow us to make plans and decisions based on logic, rather than emotion. Still, unless he was an excellent actor, he was fully committed to bringing the CRAS down. Which should be enough of a qualification for providing us with a safe meeting spot.

All the same, I wasn't planning to let my guard down.

I glanced around at the small parking lot we'd touched down in, opposite the warehouse, as I waited for the rest of my team to disembark. Strips of reddish sunset streaked the cement walls, while dark shadows were beginning to swell in every corner. The area was mostly devoid of vehicles, which made sense. The rest of our team was probably parking closer to the city and walking the rest of the way to the warehouse, so that they didn't reveal their plate numbers.

As if on cue, my eyes caught movement to the left of us— more dark-clothed figures approaching the building on foot—and I felt the sudden need to check my mask. My hands went instinctively to my face, feeling at the fabric, and then I breathed out slowly, trying to calm my nerves.

So much could go wrong in all of this, but so much could go right, too, and in this moment, I had to try to focus on the latter. Because this meeting was pivotal for the future of OH+. It would basically determine whether Nathan's entire idea would fly or fall, whether we could actually come together and cooperate as a group... or not. If we couldn't muster the courage to meet in the flesh, then nothing would ever come of all the work we'd put into building up the platform. And the CRAS would march on.

"You think that's what Mr. Montague sent the suits in?" Jackie whispered, pointing to a truck that was parked adjacent to the warehouse.

"I guess," I murmured, not sure what else it would be for.

In addition to checking each other out in person, we'd also realized that this meeting was an opportunity to familiarize ourselves with the tech we were planning to use during the mission, and that included Mr. Montague's suits, among other things. Luckily, he'd been able to arrange for some on short notice —using that truck, apparently, because I didn't know of any other resources that would have required such a large vehicle. If they existed, I hadn't been told about them yet.

"Okay, folks," Nelson said suddenly, disembarking from the aircraft a few seconds after Marco. "We ready to go in?"

"Ready as we'll ever be," Julia muttered.

Sucking in a deep breath, I took the lead with Jackie, remaining conscious of the gun tucked beneath my coat. With hindsight, I realized I would have been more comfortable if the meeting was being held out in the open, rather than in a concealed space. It would have made for an easier escape if anything went sour. But it was a little late for that now, as we'd all agreed to it already.

Plus, outside had other disadvantages. For instance, we couldn't try out the equipment we'd brought with us and would run the risk of being seen or overheard by security guards or late-shift workers on the industrial estate.

Nope, we were just going to have to suck this up.

We lined up behind the small crowd that Marty was letting in one by one and waited tensely for our turn. I sensed nerves radiating off the people surrounding us, too, given the lack of conversation, and it was a relief when it was finally our turn to face the man.

"Log in, please," Marty murmured, his dark blue eyes giving us each a furtive look. Since I was nearest to him, he handed me his pad first, with the OH+ login window pulled up. I bit down on my lip, experiencing the same moment of doubt as when Jace had asked me to log in on his device. Technically, there wasn't much damage a person could do to me even if they did get access to my account, due to the lack of personal information there. But still, the idea of Marty wanting to capture our logins for some reason made me feel uneasy, even though I didn't know why he'd want to do that.

Pushing the doubt aside, I punched in my details and showed him the successful login. He nodded once, then logged out and handed his pad to the next person: Nelson. He remained standing in front of the entrance until he'd approved each member of my group and ticked our handles off in his register, and then he stepped aside, allowing us to enter.

The building's interior was nothing but a single, long, high-ceilinged room. A line of white plastic tables had been cobbled together and arranged to run down the center of the space, along with several dozen plastic chairs, and I was surprised to see half of them filled already. We'd been angling to get here earlier than the appointed meeting time—it was due to start in half an hour—to allow for some time to get comfortable with the environment. But apparently we hadn't been the only ones with that idea.

Before I bothered too much with the people who were already seated at the tables, my eyes moved instinctively around the room, scoping out potential exits. There were three, from what I could make out: the main entrance we'd just come from, one emergency exit in the center of the wall to my right, and another emergency exit at the opposite end.

"Let's try to sit toward the back of the room," I told my team softly, discreetly gesturing toward the exit at that end. I wanted us all to be near a door, just in case anything went wrong and we needed to make a rapid escape, and as the seats closest to the other two doors were taken, the farthest end of the conference tables was our best option.

"Good idea," Marco muttered. He'd been about to reach for a random seat closer to us, and now immediately adjusted his trajectory.

As we made our way down the long room, squinting against the fluorescent strip lights that lined the ceiling, I switched my focus back to our fellow meeting attendees, and suddenly spotted Jace in a chair near the end of the tables. His bulky form was unmistakable. The only reason I hadn't seen him right away was that he was hunched over, engaged in some kind of conversation with two shorter, though similarly built, men, who sat on either side of him. There were eight chairs in a row free just near them, and since my team was heading straight for them, I guessed that was where we were going to sit.

Which was fine, of course.

Though subconsciously, I hung back a little, wanting to see if any of my team would take the seats closest to Jace and his companions—who, I realized as we approached, were his friends Kory and Cloyd, judging by their familiar voices. My team ended up leaving a seat free right next to the shorter man, and rather than deliberately sitting all the way on the other side of the line my comrades had formed, which would look weird, I took it.

Especially since Kory had already spotted me.

"Hey," I said in a low tone, my eyes on the table as I lowered myself into the chair.

Kory nudged me in the shoulder. "Hey, stranger. Hux didn't mention you were coming along."

At that, I snuck a glance at Jace, and tried not to notice the way his amber gaze warmed on spotting me.

He then rolled his eyes at Kory. "It's not exactly any of your business."

When he looked back at me, I could tell he was smiling behind his mask. "Good to see you."

"And you," I replied, smiling broadly back—perhaps a little too broadly. But damn, it *was* good to see him. I'd gotten so used to being with him every day during our visitations, and now that I was seeing him again after so long, I had to admit I'd missed him quite a bit over the last week.

But there didn't have to be anything wrong with that. You could miss a person while still staying at "just friends" level. You could still do a lot of things, actually. I didn't need to get hung up about this. And I was determined not to.

"Oh, hey, Mr. X," Nelson said, peering around me from the seat on my other side.

He broke eye contact with me to give her a friendly nod back. "Hey."

Nelson then turned to face the center of the table and leaned in to me, asking in a quiet voice, "You know those guys with him?"

"Uh, yeah," I replied softly, turning toward her—and remembering that I had omitted a large chunk of that particular Sunday during my report. "Yeah, I... They're cool," I concluded, deciding that was all she needed to know.

She smirked. "Okay."

"What are your handles, by the way?" I asked, swiveling in my seat to look between Kory and Cloyd, genuinely curious. I'd had no idea his friends were going to be involved with the ground mission, and given that I didn't know their handles, wondered if I might have interacted with them on the forum recently without even realizing it.

"LumberJack. Just Jack for you," Kory replied with a grin, and I frowned at him, not remembering seeing him around.

"Hairy_poppins," Cloyd muttered.

This time, my eyebrows rose. "Oh, Stayhome Dad!" I said, a grin splitting my face. I couldn't have forgotten that handle if I'd wanted to, and I remembered now that he'd started that wise "Changing Perspectives" thread a while ago, when the portal had first opened. I'd also seen him around on the boards since. I had to wonder at his choice of name, though. Had he managed to escape the mountains with his child, or children? And was he somehow still able to look after them, even now?

Or perhaps his choice of name was more wishful thinking than a reflection of his reality, and I was reading too much into it.

Either way, the questions slipped from my mind as a loud noise came from the door at the middle of the room. Two masked men had just stepped through it, sharing the weight of a large, familiar object covered in bubble wrap. Some other men entered, also carrying a metal suit, and both pairs leaned the machinery up against the wall before tearing the wrapping off to reveal the shiny silver surface beneath. I watched the men exit, then reenter a few more times, until ten suits were standing proudly against the wall.

The crowd around us murmured in awe—it was unlikely any of them had laid eyes on this kind of technology before—while I continued watching the door. The men were now carrying in armfuls of guns and ammunition, along with an interesting selection of stealth and decoy equipment, ranging from smoke bombs to piles of spare face masks. They laid everything down on the floor next to the suits, and once they were done, dusted their hands off. One of the men closed the side door up again.

I let my eyes trail over the impressive array of equipment. The idea was to not only do a real-life tally of everything we had, but also to distribute some of the equipment today, so that it would be one less thing to worry about on *the* day, which was going to be stressful enough already.

Nelson had volunteered us to transport the suits to the site of the mission, because our stealth aircraft was going to attract less attention than a truck, and although it was pretty small, it'd be able to fit them with some creative use of space. The rest of the small items would be distributed evenly to whomever could carry them, and we had to trust that nobody would just steal them, because I imagined that a lot of this stuff could go for a hefty price. But then, that was the whole purpose of this meeting: establishing trust.

The front door creaking broke my train of thought once more, and I looked toward that side of the room to see Marty now inside, slipping his pad into his shoulder bag and closing the door behind him.

"Has everyone arrived now?" a deep voice with a southern lilt spoke up from a chair closer to the main entrance. A tall, slender man rose to his feet. He had dark skin and light brown eyes, from what I could make out through his disguise.

"Yeah, everyone's been checked off the register," Marty replied, then pulled up a spare seat and sat down.

"Good," the other man said. His eyes swept up and down the table, which was now almost filled to the brim, with just over forty people (based on the count I did). Not everyone here was going to be on the ground during the mission, but everyone had been involved in some way or another with the operation, either in the lead-up preparations, equipment previsions, or just strategy discussion and formulation. They all had a right to be here.

This was our team.

"For those who don't yet know, I'm Zion Rey," the tall man said bluntly.

A round of soft ohs swept around the room, including one from me. He'd been one of the first to post in the forum after it was set up—on the thread calling for suggestions about what our first collective project might be—and I'd seen him around the forums a lot since then. I'd wager he was one of the most active members. He'd offered to be chairman and moderator of the meeting and had been coordinating with the key organizers in our group to come up with a schedule.

"So, per the agenda we agreed on, we're going to start by introducing ourselves to each other—by our profile names, of course," Zion went on. "So we can begin to get a little more comfortable in each other's company. Everyone still on board?"

The question was met with murmurings of agreement, and I nodded. It was the logical place to start.

"Okey dokey, then let's take fifteen minutes to stretch our legs and mingle." He gestured for us all to rise to our feet, and we did so.

Though, to be honest, I was feeling awkward as hell. I had never been the type of girl who found it easy to go up to, much less strike up a conversation with, strangers. And doing it in these circumstances, when I didn't even know who the person was behind their mask, was stomach-churningly uncomfortable. Still, I steeled myself against the discomfort as best I could and tried to be a good sport.

I cast one furtive glance around at my team to find Nelson, Jackie, and the twins already sauntering off to find some new person to speak to, and I started toward the other end of the hall, figuring I might as well throw myself in at the deep end. From the corner of my eye I noticed Jace making his way slowly around the other side, eyeing people tentatively, and I had to stifle a grin. Somehow, I doubted he was a natural "mingler" either.

My focus drew away from him quickly when a tall, broad woman walked up to me and held out a hand.

"SnowQueen, aka Winter De Ville," she announced with a small smirk, gazing down at me through slate eyes. I remembered her from the early days of the forum too, as someone who had suggested one of the rasher ideas for our first step. And as someone whose comments and replies to other people's posts tended to be on the brash side in general.

"Hi, Winter. RobinHood21," I replied, accepting her hand in a shake.

"Gah. That's the second Robin in the room. Let's hope there isn't a third!" She gave me a playful wink, then strode off and continued to mingle with the crowd.

I couldn't help but gaze after her for a moment, finding her friendly manner at odds with her bullish online persona. Then again, I supposed we all came off differently online, where it was all too easy to misconstrue tone and jump to conclusions.

I continued walking, only to stop again a few seconds later when I almost bumped into Marty. I'd been meaning to talk to him anyway, just to be polite and say thanks for arranging the facility, and I was glad that he'd presented me with an easy opportunity. I looked into his blue eyes and saw a swell of tension behind them, the vulnerability of which made me feel a bit more comfortable about him in general. Because it was a natural emotion. This facility might not belong to *him*, but it was supposedly his contact's, which meant he could potentially be tracked if any of us were dickish enough to rat the location out. Or if a mole got in.

It was good of him to offer, honestly, because trying to meet at a more public third-party venue, like a conference room in a hotel or pub, would have been difficult for a number of reasons. It would look ridiculously fishy if we all showed up in masks, to start with, and we'd hardly be able to spread out our equipment like we were doing here.

Marty scrutinized me for half a second, his eyes narrowing, and then there was a flicker of recognition in his irises, and his expression lifted. "Robin," he said, sounding pleasantly surprised, and I nodded, shaking his hand.

"Thanks for offering to host this. It means a lot to all of us."

He gave a nervous laugh. "No problem. Let's just keep our fingers crossed that it all goes well." He gave me a small pat on the shoulder, and then he was walking past me.

I continued making my way across the room and managed to introduce myself to eight people I didn't remember seeing on the portal, before Zion called for us all to take a chair again.

"Okay, we've spent enough time on that for now," he announced, raising his hands for everyone's attention, and we bustled around the table to resume our seats. "There'll be time after the meeting for more socializing. Next on the agenda is equipment. We'll get that out of the way, and then we can move on to finalizing mission details. Any objections?" No one had any, or if they did, they didn't make them known, so he continued. "We'll begin with the suits then. Ground team, make your way over."

Over a dozen people rose from their chairs, including myself, Jackie, Ant, Abe, and Jace and his two friends. Not all of the ground team would be wearing the suits during the mission, but there was no harm in all of us knowing how they worked. I noticed that six manuals for the suits had been dropped on the floor beside the weapons, and stooped to pick them up, before handing them out.

Keeping two back, I moved to where my group was standing, along with Jace and his friends. I handed one to Jackie, while Jace and his friends peered over my shoulder to look at mine. Mr. Montague had given us a demonstration, so I knew the basics of how the suits worked, but there wasn't any harm in getting a refresher. Especially for those who hadn't seen or experienced the suits before.

Before long, I had Kory walking around in a suit. He was a little shaky, but improved quickly. It gave my companions the boost they needed to give it a try, too (though I noticed Jace hanging back from volunteering), and they took turns trying out the available suits, while I had another try myself. Practicing without looking at the manual, I began walking around the room and getting a better feel for how stealthy I could be in it.

"Come to Mama!" Jackie's voice said from behind me, and I turned to see her clunking toward me, her metal arms outstretched, and laughed. I didn't often get to see the lighter side of Jackie, and it was nice to witness it every now and then. She was obviously having a lot of fun in these things, and I imagined a broad grin plastered to her face behind the tinted visor.

"Hey, Robin," Kory's voice came from my right. I glanced over and saw that he was still hogging his suit, apparently having too much fun to give someone else a turn. "Wanna dance?" His visor was popped up, so I could see the cheeky smile on his lips as he cast a look at Jace, who was still hovering around the edges of the room.

I smirked, deftly tamping down the memory his question evoked, and watched as Jace gave a deep eye roll. "Um, maybe later," I said.

I had to admit, this little exercise felt like it was really helping to break the ice in the room. Even those who weren't part of the ground team had gathered around us, amused expressions in their eyes as they watched us navigate in the suits. The tension seemed to be slowly ebbing, which I hoped would continue throughout the rest of the evening.

Because I *really* wanted to trust these people. God knew, there were so few of us to begin with. People who were not only brave enough to be part of a network like OH, but also willing to take action. With such small numbers, our only hope of achieving anything lay within how well we could cooperate with each other, and for that, trust was *the* most important thing.

So far, so good, at least.

After I'd walked around in my suit for a few more minutes, and saw that Jace still hadn't gotten into one, I cautiously made my way over to him, knowing that he would sense what was coming.

"Hey, big guy," I said with a grin, popping my visor open so he could see my face, or at least my eyes and mouth. "Why do I get the feeling you're avoiding me?"

He gave me a tentative look. "Yeah. I'm just not sure if this is going to work for me."

I smiled. "Well, Mr. Montague said they could be adjusted to your size, so how about we try?"

Before waiting for his answer, I popped open the front of my suit and stepped out. After taking a moment to steady my knees, I looked up at him with a broad grin. "I'll help you."

He heaved a sigh, an expression of deep reluctance turning his lips downward.

"Don't look too enthusiastic," Kory called, and I turned to see him watching us with amusement through his open visor.

Jace shot him another disparaging look, but then conceded,

unfolding his arms from his chest. "All right," he muttered. "Do your worst."

Smiling triumphantly, I went about setting the suit to his size, with the help of the manual. First I tackled the height, and then the width, until it looked like there was a comfy enough space for him to slot into.

"Okay, be my guest," I said, gesturing for him to step in.

He gave me another reluctant look, but then turned and backed into the space. I helped settle him in, pulling the straps across his broad chest, and then showed him how to close the front. He sucked in a deep breath, as if fearing he was about to be deprived of oxygen, before sealing himself inside.

"Okay," I said, trying not to laugh. I could understand why a guy like Jace found this to be an uncomfortable experience. I mean, he was still getting used to tame things like tablets and websites. The suit had been quite unnerving even for me the first time. "Now let's try to get you moving."

I began to give him instructions, running him through the basics, and though his movements were jerky and hesitant at first, he got the hang of it surprisingly quickly, which proved to me how intuitive these really were. They were designed for construction workers who didn't have time for complex manual study, and just needed something to get the job done. Hopefully they would be as easy for the entire team.

It could literally save our lives if everyone was comfortable inside of these, and ready to go at a moment's notice.

I followed Jace around the room, wanting to make sure that he felt supported in his foreign new body. Not that I would've been able to do much for him if his six-foot-four, metal-clad body suddenly went tumbling, but I didn't need to mention that.

After ten minutes, I was happy to see that his grimace had turned upside down, and he was smiling.

"Okay," he conceded, giving his metal arms and fingers a flex, popping his visor closed, and then opening it again. "This is pretty damn neat. Though I still worry about flexibility. We're obviously not going to be as dexterous in these as we would be without them. And I'm not sure I want something weighing on me and slowing me down."

"Try running in it," I said, pointing away from the crowd and toward an emptier area of the warehouse near the back.

He did as I suggested, positioning himself apart from the crowd and moving into a jog... and then, as his confidence grew, a full-out run. The clunking of his feet on the floor was loud—there was a thin layer of rubber on the metal soles for grip, but it wasn't enough—so we were definitely going to have to do something about that. But his movements were amazingly fluid, which was the main thing. Granted, those metal fingers weren't going to be great for detail work, like picking locks or using a keyboard, but that was why the plan was for not all of us to be wearing them.

He flipped his visor open, a contemplative expression in his eyes as he reached my side again. "You're right, they're fast, and don't decrease speed as much as I thought. And I think—"

Whatever he was about to say was cut off by a sudden sharp popping sound, and a split second later, the ceiling lights went out, plunging the warehouse into pitch darkness.

28

Everyone's reaction was the same for a long moment. Complete silence reigned around the large room, as if we were all waiting for the glitch to be over and the lights to turn back on. But they didn't.

My nerves immediately spiked, and I found myself moving instinctively toward Jace, my left hand slipping into my pocket for my phone, my right moving to my gun. I woke up my phone screen to create some light in the room, just as a dozen others had the same idea. A scattering of small, rectangular screens illuminated their immediate areas, though it didn't do much to beat back the shadows.

"Marty?" Zion's deep voice spoke up. "Think you could check out what's happened to the lighting?"

We all gazed around expectantly, trying to make out our host in the shadows, but I couldn't find him, and if he was present, he wasn't answering.

"Maybe he's in the bathroom," someone suggested. "It's around the side of the building."

Four people took off toward the middle exit, and I heard one of them pulling down on the door handle. But it wasn't followed by the creaking of a door opening. Instead, there were several sharp exhalations, followed by, "Try the other doors. This one's locked."

My heart beat faster as Jace and I hurried toward the exit at the end of the room, which was closest to us. Jace reached it first, his metal hand gripping the handle and thrusting downward while I cast light with my phone. But this one was locked too.

"All exits are locked!" a shaky voice announced from the other end of the warehouse.

"Marty?!" I called out, unable to keep the tremor from my voice. I couldn't believe it. I'd had an uneasy feeling about him from the start, but I hadn't really thought it would actually *come* to anything.

Oh, God. Why the hell did I let my guard down? How could I have let myself get so far from the exits? If I'd been paying attention...

Half a dozen others began calling his name too, and more people flooded to the doors, taking their turn in trying to open them.

Meanwhile, my worst fears blossomed to life in my mind, as the darkness continued to press in on us, the sounds of people trying to force the doors growing louder. Was Marty a rat working for the government? Had he been acting since the beginning? Playing along so he could get us all in one place? He had been on Nathan's trusted list, and other members' experiences with him, as well as Jace's and my meeting with him, had all been positive. But of course, as Jace had already warned us, the vetting process was nowhere near bulletproof. We had all been taking a calculated risk in coming together at all.

And now I was terrified that it had just blown up in our faces.

"We gotta force this door!" I whispered to Jace, my voice choked. For all we knew, the cops could be closing in as I spoke. And if we didn't get out in time, they'd catch us all like sitting ducks, snuffing out any chance of a rebellion before it could even get off the ground. The thought made my throat dry up, my eyes sting with fear and regret, and the vision of that bloodstained office returned to my mind.

I turned to see that Jace had already begun trying to force the door, his metal fingers attempting to wedge between the double doors, searching for leverage. I had just whirled back around to scan the room, looking to beckon another suited person to help him, when a speaker crackled to life from somewhere overhead, and a familiar voice boomed down.

"Do as I say, and nobody needs to get hurt."

I held my breath in the stunned silence that followed his statement.

Then, it was as if a tide of anger slammed into us all at once, and the warehouse erupted in shouting.

"MARTY? What the HELL is this?" Zion's furious voice rose above the din.

"If you quiet down," Marty's voice crackled back, "then I can explain."

"Just open the doors, you son of a bitch!" Jackie yelled from about ten feet behind me.

"I will," Marty replied, his voice eerily calm. "The moment you agree to get out of those suits and line them all up in a neat row by the wall, along with all your weapons. Then you can all walk out of here."

The blood rushed to my face, my head tilting automatically to scan the ceiling for cameras, even though it was too dark for me to spy them now.

This wasn't happening. Couldn't be.

And yet, I couldn't think of another explanation. He was turning us over. Disarming us, and then handing us to the enforcers, who were probably careening through the air and streets right now, heading directly for us. I imagined his bald face, his eyes burning with what I'd thought was vengeance at the time —the desire, no, the *need* for change. Clearly, he was burning with something, but it wasn't anything in our favor.

"To hell with this!" Jace resumed his attack on the door while my eyes snapped toward the pile of guns. I raced over to grab one of the larger ones and was about to rush back to try to blow the door open when a peppering of bullets sounded by the main entrance, followed by a sharp cry of pain.

Panic surged in me as I whipped my head toward the sound. The door was still closed, but a man was on the ground, gripping his right thigh and writhing in agony in the pale light of several phone screens.

"Don't try to blow the doors!" a woman shouted from that end. "The bullets bounce!"

I cursed, my grip on the gun I'd picked up instantly slackening. What the hell kind of doors *were* these?! Marty had to have been prepared for this. Heck, for all I knew, this very warehouse was government-owned, the doors reinforced to military standards.

"Don't try to get out," Marty's voice boomed down again. "It is futile. Set aside the suits and the weapons, and then the doors will open."

Icy fear slipped down my spine. We had to get out of here. Now.

My eyes desperately searched the cavernous room for another solution. Jace had now been joined by two others in suits, Jackie and Kory, and they were working together to try to get through the door. But if bullets couldn't put a dent in the doors, I feared their efforts would be in vain too.

I scanned the room frantically, willing there to be another way out of here... and then a thought struck me. Where *had* Marty gone? We had all been distracted by the suits, yes, but the doors of this warehouse were noisy. And none of us would have let our guard down enough to be oblivious to them opening and closing. I, for one, would have noticed, in spite of how far away I'd drifted from them.

So where was he?

I moved closer to the edge of the room, holding my phone out in front of me to cast light on the walls. There were only three external doors—that I was sure of. But could there be something else? Something I'd missed during my initial sweep?

A memory sparked in me, and I sped up to a run until I reached one corner of the rectangular room, on the right side of the main entrance. I remembered noticing a metal beam there, during my initial sweep, that rose up through the ceiling. I hadn't thought anything of it, but desperation had a way of making my brain remember little details that had seemed unimportant at the time, and when I got close to the metal beam, I realized that its interior was hollow, one of its edges comprised of horizontal slats, and there was a gap just large enough for a person to fit through and enter the space within.

It could be climbed. And even if this wasn't how he'd escaped, maybe it would lead to the roof, or give us some other way to flee this building.

I whipped out my phone and dialed Jackie's number, knowing it was a faster way of communicating than racing back over, and the noise in the room had reached a feverish pitch that was far too loud to shout above. I heard her phone ring out across the room, where she was still helping Jace and Kory attempt to open the door, and saw the flash of her screen as she picked up, and then her voice was loud in my right ear.

"Robin, wha—"

"To your left, there's a metal beam. It's actually a ladder if you look closely. There are beams on each side of the room. Grab guns and get people to start climbing. I think it's how Marty left the room." And if he was still up there, and hadn't escaped via some hatch leading outside, then it could be dangerous, which was why we needed to be plenty armed.

I made hurried calls to Nelson and the twins, telling them to do the same, and soon the crowd was dispersing, sweeping up weapons and racing for the chutes, including the one I was about to climb.

My limbs jerked to life, and I began swinging myself up the ladder, not wanting to slow anyone down.

The ceiling was high, but it took less than a minute for me to reach the top, adrenaline lending fantastical strength to my body. I poked my head up through the hole in the ceiling where the ladder connected, to find that it led to a dimly lit loft, and I clambered out onto one of the large metal beams that crisscrossed the loft's floor.

I couldn't see any signs of exit hatches from here, and it was as empty as the level below. Except in the center, where I saw a small, square structure. A control room?

My heart pounding, I raced toward it, the soles of my boots clanging over the metal and making more noise than I would've liked. I heard people following me, their legs pumping just as quickly, and then spotted more flooding up through the other three openings. We all had our sights on the small structure in the center, and it became a race along the crisscrossing beams to reach it.

Having had the head start, I arrived first, and was about to press my ear to the door when it shot open suddenly and Marty staggered out, a gun clasped in one hand. He yelped in alarm as those of us who had reached him raised our guns toward his head, and then I was being pushed aside, a tall man darting past me and knocking the gun from Marty's frozen hands with a sharp chop of his forearm. I grabbed the gun from where it fell, then moved into the room after the man, who was forcing Marty back in.

It was some sort of small control room, as I'd prayed it might be. Two counters lined the edges of the space, one holding several switchboards, another holding screens that showed night-vision views of the dark warehouse below. Marty must have been watching us via the cameras, and realized we were closing in on him... but why on Earth had he locked himself in here with us in the first place? There appeared to be no way to escape the building via the roof, so this seemed incredibly shortsighted on his part.

The tall man slamming Marty down against the floor drew my attention, and I watched as he locked him in place until the shorter man whimpered in pain.

"P-Please! Don't hurt me!"

"You'd better tell me now how to unlock those damn doors!" the tall man growled, and I realized it was Zion.

"Th-The green one! S-Second panel from the door."

I stared at him in confusion, surprised that he'd give up so easily. Then Zion cast a glance back at me, and I hurried to the panel, seeking out the green button and slamming it down.

"Don't shoot me!" Marty gasped.

"You deserve it, you rat bastard!" Zion hissed. "How long till the cops are here?"

"I didn't call the cops!" Marty wheezed, as Zion pressed the butt of his gun harder against his neck.

"The doors are open!" a voice shouted from behind us, distracting us all for a moment from Marty's statement.

We paused to listen, and sure enough, I could hear the sound of the doors being yanked open. I let out a small sigh of relief, then turned back to stare at the man. Zion, and everyone else who'd piled into the room to see what was going on, gazed at him too.

"You're lying," Zion spat.

"Go see for yourself," Marty rasped. "I swear, no cops are on their way. Go outside. Nobody's coming!"

"Then what the hell were you playing at?" A growl came from behind me, and I realized it was Jace—now out of his metal suit. His chest heaved as he glared at the shorter man, who was still struggling beneath Zion's weight.

"If you want the truth, I'll tell it to ya: I was going to call the cops, but you didn't give me a chance." Marty gave a weak, bitter cough. "Got into a nasty bit of debt recently, and the opportunity was too tempting to pass up. You know the kind of bounties enforcers dole out these days for dissidents? That, combined with all those suits downstairs, could have cleared my debt. I figured I could scare the lot of you outta them, then call the enforcers."

"You son of a bitch," Zion spat, giving Marty's head another slam against the floor.

My pulse spiked. He probably *was* lying about having called the cops, and was now just trying to keep us here as long as possible so we'd get caught. In which case we had to get out while we still had the chance.

But then again... another part of me believed that he really was just that incompetent and hadn't gotten around to calling them yet. I mean, this whole plan had been pulled off piss-poorly, and the guy was a pathetic mess now. Sure, he had some fancy doors downstairs, but locking himself inside the building with us? It was laughably bad. It had only been a matter of time before one of us spotted those chutes and climbed up here, like I had. It stank of the act of a desperate man, and desperate people didn't make for good planners.

But still, we couldn't be sure.

"Well, if what you say is true, you're a real moron, aren't you?" Zion muttered, lifting the butt of his gun and driving it down hard against Marty's temple.

The shorter man's body went limp instantly, and Zion shot to his feet, a deep scowl darkening his eyes.

"We need to get out of this building and check the area," he grated out. "Now."

29

Well, most of us.

W e piled downstairs and out of the warehouse, crouching down in the shadows and listening, waiting, watching for any indication of enforcers approaching. But it turned out Marty had been telling the truth, and we'd just managed to prevent him from calling them. They never came, and after an hour, we mustered the courage to go back into the building.

Well, most of us.

The guy who got injured left with his two friends, along with a handful of others who'd been spooked by the whole incident. But the bulk of us decided to stay.

Going home would be admitting defeat. Throwing in the towel with the entire OH+ project. Because if we couldn't even come together for a meeting, how were we ever going to pull off a mission together? How were we going to start pushing back against the system that had torn apart so many lives, or apply pressure for the changes our country so desperately needed?

And if we didn't, who would? The CRAS had been going for over two decades already, and it stood to reason that it would only continue if nobody took action to stop it. Granted, I didn't know how any action we took was *actually* ever going to change anything. It seemed like an insanely behemoth task, and I probably needed my head examined for even dreaming that we could ever have any kind of effect on the course of our nation.

All I knew was that someone had to try. That *I* had to try. Pushing back against the system that had wrecked my life was the only thing that gave me true purpose, the only thing that kept me sane. And given that I didn't see many others stepping up to the plate, it might as well be us, even if it meant starting with baby steps. Or even fetus steps.

What had just happened with Marty had been scary. Terrifying, in fact. He'd been one phone call away from ending us all. But he hadn't accomplished it, and we were still here, all in one place. I simply couldn't bring myself to leave, and I was glad to see that plenty of others felt the same way.

So after locking Marty's unconscious body up in the back of the empty truck, we finished doing a tally of our equipment, then reseated ourselves around the tables and tried to continue the meeting as if nothing had happened. Zion said he'd take responsibility for wiping the rat's pad and figuring out what to do with him, and in the meantime, we just needed to keep him from running away or eavesdropping.

Although everyone was clearly shaken, the rest of the evening proved to be surprisingly productive. We hashed out the finer details of our plan, and by the end of the meeting, I found myself feeling much closer to the members of the group than I had before Marty had switched off the lights, even though I still didn't know any of their faces. I guessed it was because we'd all just been thrust into a majorly stressful situation, and we'd cooperated and pulled through it together. It was a good drill, I supposed, as far as team-building was concerned, even if our nerves could have done without it. I also realized, as we sat around the table talking, that it had inadvertently distilled our group. The flakier people had chosen to leave, which I hoped had left us only with serious, genuine action-takers.

So perhaps we had something to thank Marty for after all. I was just grateful that he had shown his true colors quickly, leaving us with what was hopefully now a solid team we could rely on.

I *really* hoped so. Because I didn't know that we could survive another disappointment. We were determined, but we also liked being alive.

And because, by the end of the meeting, we'd set a date: this Sunday. Four days. No delays, no dropping out. It wasn't a lot of time, but that was because we didn't want to leave a large gap in between the meeting and the big day. The plan and schematics were fresh in our minds after this evening, and now that we had all the equipment we needed, we had to get it over with ASAP.

So all I could do was cross my fingers and hope for the best. We might not be confronting the government directly with our first project, but there were still any number of things that could go wrong on the day.

Because if I'd learned anything during my months of going out with Nelson's team, it was that no plan survived first contact.

Over the course of the rest of the week, I found myself wishing that we had set the date earlier—heck, even Thursday. Because with each day that passed, the knot in my stomach grew tighter.

The worst thing was that I had nothing with which to distract myself. No evenings with Jace. Nor any work from Nelson (our next kidnapping had been pushed back at least another two weeks, to give us time to work on the mission with OH+). And everything that needed to be done in preparation for the mission had basically been done already. I found myself hanging around on the private forum thread ZombieBrainz had set up just for the ground team, but that ended up making me feel worse. I could practically feel the nerves of my fellow group members seeping through the screen, from the tone of their responses to the types of last-minute questions they were asking. So I eventually stopped looking at that, too, and resigned myself to browsing the web and trying to distract myself with TV.

Until, on Saturday afternoon, the sound of a text coming through broke the monotony. I padded over to the other side of my living room to get my phone, expecting it to be Nelson or someone else from my group wanting to discuss some last-minute issue. I widened my eyes when I saw it was from Jace.

It was... a pleasant surprise, given that we hadn't spoken to each other since the meeting on Wednesday. We hadn't been talking much via PM or text in general, recently, since I stopped going out on visitations with him.

Drawing in a quiet breath, I tapped the message open.

"Hey. I asked Nelson if I could get access to a suit today. Want to get some final practice before the mission. I'm headed to the Roundhouse this evening. Wondered if you felt like joining me."

I raised an eyebrow, finding the idea instantly appealing. I knew that tonight was going to be the worst in terms of stress, as the night before the big day, and this seemed like the perfect distraction. Not to mention, it would also be useful; I definitely wasn't as proficient with the suits as I could be, and considering the fact that they were a key part of our strategy for tomorrow, more practice could only make me feel more confident about the whole thing.

Plus... I wanted to get over this Jace thing. Like, completely over it. I was getting better around him, I figured, though there were definitely still moments of awkwardness. And I had to admit that the thought of being alone with him again made me feel apprehensive. Which was why I needed to overcome it. And the only way I was going to do that was to face it head-on. Neither he nor I was going anywhere, so we were going to be colleagues and members of the same group for the foreseeable future. I had to practice *not* feeling awkward around him, until I didn't feel awkward around him at all. Because it was too much of a professional distraction.

Practice makes perfect, right?

"Sure, I'll come," I replied a moment later, with a firm nod of my head. *"What time will you be there?"*

"8 p.m. Apparently there's a park just nearby. I figured we could practice there."

"Ah, yeah, okay," I replied, picturing that park in my mind. It had a vast grassy area and would most likely be deserted at that time of evening.

"Cool. See you then."

I put the phone down, narrowing my eyes at myself in the mirror. *I can do this.*

I spent the remaining hours of the afternoon outside, trying to enjoy a brisk walk in the woods surrounding my home. The fresh air always did have a way of calming me, though my nerves were tight with thoughts about tomorrow as soon as I stepped back into the cabin. I indulged in a long shower to wash the sweat of the walk away, wanting to feel fresh for the evening, and then left the cabin again and made the journey to the Roundhouse on my motorcycle. It was definitely one of the closer locations Jace had asked me to meet him at in recent weeks, and the journey didn't take long.

On arrival, I parked some distance away and headed straight for the back of the pub's building. The door leading to the hidden parking area had been left slightly ajar, and I stepped through, spotting Jace instantly. He was standing on the ground in front of the aircraft's open side door, in the middle of taking one of the suits from Marco.

"Well, well, well. Look who's here," Marco remarked, spotting me as I approached.

"Hey," Jace said, turning to face me as he set the suit down on the ground, that boyish smile of his lighting up his unmasked face.

"Hey," I replied brightly, clearing my throat and feeling determined not to let it throw me off. I made my way over to stand next to him. "Could you hand me one of those babies, too?" I asked Marco.

He'd just been reaching down to grab a bottle of water but turned at my request and gave me a considering look. "Depends on how nicely you ask," he replied primly.

"Pretty please with three cherries on top."

"Make that marshmallows," he said, before lugging one toward me. I reached out to grasp it as soon as it was close enough and gently set it on the ground next to Jace's.

A moment later Marco was dropping out of the aircraft and closing the hatch. He tossed me the keys. "You can lock up after you're done. And leave the keys with Cianna. She's working late tonight. Nelson or I will collect them from her later."

"Got it," I said, stuffing the keys into the pocket of my jacket and zipping it up. "Cheers, Marky, see you tomorrow."

"Yeah. Oh, and don't mess up the soles of those suits. Julia and I spent a whole night on those modifications."

"Ah." I glanced down at the feet of the suits and saw that, indeed, an extra layer of rubber had been applied to them to soften the noise of footsteps. Which would make me feel a whole lot more comfortable wearing them in any secretive situation. "Of course we'll be careful," I said. I gave Marco a squeeze on the shoulder as he passed, then turned my attention back to Jace.

He gave me another brief smile, then dropped his gaze to the suit. "Thanks for coming out," he said.

"Oh, it's fine," I replied coolly, setting my eyes on the suits as well. "I could do with some more practice, too. So, um. How do you suggest we get over to the park with these things?"

He shrugged. "It's only about five minutes away. Marco suggested we head out the back entrance of the compound. Apparently it leads to a narrow alley that connects directly to the park."

I nodded. "Makes sense."

A quiet fell between us as I shrugged off my coat and Jace took his off, though I wanted to think it wasn't the awkward kind of quiet, as I helped him adjust his suit to fit him. His fingers accidentally brushing over mine, as we both moved to push the same button, sent an unignorable tingle up my arm, but other than that, I figured I was doing well. Especially considering our proximity.

Eventually I climbed into my own suit, and we pulled our coats over the suits and the hoods high over our heads, so that if we did pass anybody, we wouldn't look *quite* so weird. There wasn't much we could do about our metal legs and feet; hopefully people would think we were on our way to or from a costume party or something. Or were just really drunk. At least we wouldn't sound so clunky in them now.

We kept our visors up, allowing the fresh night air in as we left the compound and walked briskly down the alleyway, our footsteps amazingly soft against the pavement. And sure enough, the alley bled into the park.

Jace immediately set his sights on the large field, which held several frames of high monkey bars and other strength-training apparatuses designed for adults. There were no lampposts nearby, but it was a clear night, and the light of the moon was ample for our purposes.

"You thinking what I'm thinking?" he asked in a low tone.

"I think so," I replied with a grin, glad that my mind had something solid to focus on for the evening. One of my motivations for coming here had been to force myself to get more comfortable around Jace, but awkward silences could occur around anyone if neither party had proper engagement. These park toys were a meaty challenge we could both sink our teeth into, allowing me a distraction for the moments when that awkwardness did resurface.

My confidence that this evening was going to go well further bolstered, we took off at a jog toward them, our metal feet crushing the grass and sinking into the soft soil with every step. We stopped when we reached one end of the monkey bars, and I took a step back, letting Jace go first. He drew in a deep breath, flexing his fingers, and then positioned himself directly beneath the first bar, before leaping upward. His aim impressed me as his hands connected with it, but then they lost grip a second later, and he came thudding back down.

He sighed, shaking his head ruefully.

"Hey, second time's the charm, right?" I said with a grin. I knew he was still uncomfortable with this kind of high-level technology, despite how well he'd gotten the hang of the suits' mechanisms, and I wanted to encourage him to develop his confidence. It was going to be super important tomorrow; the workings of the suits needed to come as second nature to us because we wouldn't have the mental bandwidth to worry about them, with so many other moving parts and things on our minds. Like getting ourselves out of the building alive.

Bending his knees slightly, Jace tried again, and this time, to my pleasure, his grip held.

"Woohoo!" I whistled.

He grunted in response, then swung his legs slowly back and forth, until he'd built enough momentum to reach for the next bar. When he gripped it and transferred his weight, his hands held firm again, and I moved forward to stand at the side of the frame, staring as he progressed through the line to the final bar.

"Whoa," I said as he touched back down on the ground. I actually hadn't expected him to get through all the bars in one shot. Rubber wasn't built into the suits' fingers or palms (though we were supposed to be equipped with handgrips tomorrow), so they could be a little touch and go. But he'd impressed me. Maybe he had a natural affinity for physical challenges like this, thanks to his upbringing in the wild.

He straightened and threw me a triumphant-bordering-on-cocky look. "Your turn."

I raised an eyebrow. "After that performance? You trying to embarrass me or something, Mr. X?"

He gave me a smirk, then stepped back and watched as I climbed up the slats in the side of the frame—not able to reach the bars by jumping directly from the ground, like he was able to.

To be honest, I *was* actually feeling a bit pressured after his performance. Like this had suddenly become a bit of a competition. I didn't usually consider myself the competitive type, honestly. Except when it came to sports. Back in school, I'd been the girl who would rather get her eye gouged out trying to get a ball through a loop than step back and let another player try. And I guessed that side of me was resurfacing now, although I wasn't even sure where it had come from. Perhaps it had stemmed from the family I'd grown up in, where high achievement had been expected. Or maybe I'd inherited it from one of my biological parents.

THE CHILD THIEF

Either way, right now, I was going to see exactly how well I could stand up against a caveman.

A controlled smile unfurled on my lips as I focused on gaining a solid enough stance on the frame. I took a moment to try to gauge my aim at the bars as best as possible, and then launched off.

I cursed as I missed, and landed on the ground with a thud, just as Jace had done the first time.

"Hey, second time's the charm, right?" Jace quipped, and it was my turn to shoot him a rueful look, before climbing back onto the frame.

"I got this," I remarked. I focused again before leaping, but failed a second time, my fingers slipping off the bar. "Gah!"

Jace chuckled as I mounted the frame a third time, and thankfully, my hands had now caught on to the technique, and I was spared the embarrassment of another fall. Soon I was swinging across the frame, my metal fingers clanging over the bars while the muscles in my arms strained. I was now determined to make it all the way across like Jace had. And I did, about thirty wobbly seconds later.

Jace broke out in a metallic round of applause when I dropped to the grass and, grinning, gave him a small curtsy. "Told you I could," I pouted.

"I never doubted it," he retorted.

I chuckled, then glanced at the next apparatus—some kind of tightrope walk—feeling determined to conquer this one, too, and in fewer tries. "Shall we continue?" I asked.

Jace nodded, and we jogged over to it.

I let him go first again, wanting to see how he coped with it before I gave it a try, and he ended up having a little more trouble with this one, given his heavier build. Okay, a lot more trouble. It took him seven attempts to make it across successfully, and by the time he finally did it, we were both laughing. Hard.

"There's some stuff bears just aren't good at," he muttered, brushing his hands against his coat, and I laughed again, the memory of Rhea's gift resurfacing in my mind.

On the subject of Rhea... for some reason, it felt like forever since we'd visited her. Even though it had only been a handful of weeks. Then again, it somehow felt like forever since I'd met Jace, even though it had been less than a couple of months.

"So, your turn," he announced, bringing me back to the present, and I shook my musings aside.

He crossed his arms over his chest, raising an expectant brow. Which, again, I found a little bit intimidating. He'd sucked at this, so he didn't exactly have a leg to stand on when it came to judging me, but still, I felt the urge to not fail in front of him.

"Okay, mister. Watch and learn," I murmured. I walked up to one end of the metallic tightrope and carefully positioned myself on it, my hands closing around the barriers on either side.

Once I got going, placing one leg painstakingly in front of the other, in a near-perfect line, I realized that, to be fair, it *was* pretty tricky, even with the rubber soles. We didn't have quite the same mobility and control over our balance as we had without the suits, which made this quite a challenge, so I was proud of myself when I got to the other end on my first try. And I let Jace know it.

I gave him another curtsey, stooping a little lower this time. A bit too low, actually, because I suddenly lost my balance and went tumbling forward.

My hands shot out instinctively, digging into the soil and easing my fall, and a soft laugh escaped my throat once I got over the initial shock. It had been a gentle landing, though I could definitely see how falling in these things could hurt, if one tumbled a larger distance or from a different angle. Our torsos were strapped in, keeping us in place to a certain extent, and there wasn't padding throughout the interior. You could certainly get bashed about if the fall was too violent.

As it was, I doubted I'd get more than a slight bruise. Though Jace clearly didn't realize that, as he came rushing over, a concerned look on his face.

"Hey, you okay, Robin?" he asked, bending down and holding out a hand.

I accepted it, my metal fingers entwining with his, and let him help me back to my feet. And suddenly I found myself less than a foot away from him, my face mere inches from his, his deep, honey-brown eyes glistening with concern in the moonlight.

"Uh, yeah. Thanks," I managed, my suit suddenly feeling too warm for me, my lungs lacking breath. I forced a smile, needing to diffuse that serious expression on his face. But for some reason it remained there, those deep amber pools locked on me.

What was probably only a handful of heartbeats stretched out and felt like a full minute, and I wasn't sure if I'd imagined it when his gaze dropped for a flicker of a second to my lips.

All I knew was that I needed to step back. Now.

I did so more abruptly than I'd intended, turning sharply away and catching the tip of my right foot in the soil. I stumbled into an awkward stagger as I found my footing, only just avoiding falling over a second time, and then forced out a laugh, needing to make light of it all, even while my temperature escalated.

"Seems like you should've been the one to give *me* lessons on these things," I said, feigning another laugh. I set my focus on the next obstacle along, desperately needing another distraction. I didn't want to say it had been a mistake to come here with him, when I'd been having such a great time. But that had just been a little too intense for comfort.

"So, the next one?" I suggested, injecting strength into my

voice. "We're kind of slacking." I shot a glance and a smile back at him, needing to reassure myself that the moment had passed for him too, but while he returned my smile with one of his own, I sensed it was just as forced as mine.

"Oh, yeah. Sure," he replied, and I did my best to ignore the slightly disappointed note in his tone—because it could very well have been my imagination playing tricks on me again.

And that was all we needed. Another distraction.

The next obstacle was several lines of stepping stones, which grew farther apart the farther you went along the course, and on reaching it, we each boarded a line each and started to move along the stones. But things got a little too dicey once we neared the end, where the stones were unreasonably far apart, and I decided to drop out, not wanting to risk damaging the suit, or myself, before the big day tomorrow. I'd done enough stumbling for one evening.

Jace decided the same, and then I suggested we experiment with speed a little, before calling it a night. There were other obstacles we could've tried, but it was getting late, and I was starting to feel the urge to return home. We had a big day tomorrow, and we ought to be well rested.

So we agreed to half an hour longer, and set about walking, jogging, and sprinting across the grass. It only took about fifteen minutes for me to start panting hard, however, and I sank to the ground, needing a few moments to catch my breath. Jace joined me for a break and seated himself a few feet away from me, his long legs stretched out in front of him.

"That was a good 'un," I said, leaning back on my hands and fixing my gaze determinedly on the stars.

"Do you know how often the suits need to be recharged?" Jace wondered in a low tone.

"They're recharged automatically via movement, from what I

read in the manual," I replied, thrilled to latch on to the subject. "They don't need to be plugged into a power source unless they haven't been used for ages. Which isn't the case with the ones Montague sent along. Apparently the batteries need to be changed every five years, but judging from the manufacture dates on the soles of these, we won't have to worry about that for a long time. They're only, like, less than a year old. There's some kind of maintenance required, too, I think, once every few months, both to the battery and to the suit in general. Though, again, we shouldn't need to worry about that. I'm pretty sure Montague will be handling it."

I trailed off, realizing I was spouting out more information than he probably wanted.

"I see," Jace murmured after a moment, and from the corner of my eye, I caught him frowning slightly, then leaning back on his hands too. "Well, I guess that's pretty swell."

"Yeah. They are pretty cool, aren't they?"

I dared to look back at him, and he nodded, his amber gaze holding mine for several long heartbeats.

And then his lips were slowly parting.

"Robin, I..." he began, his voice low.

And my face snapped instinctively back toward the open field. I held my breath, his tentative tone making my whole body still, the hairs at the back of my neck stand on end. Whatever he was about to say, I both desperately did and didn't want to hear it. Which confused the hell out of me.

But then he heaved a sigh, and I realized that my reaction had been too abrupt, too hostile. More so than I'd wanted it to be. Even though I *had* wanted to pull away.

And I sensed that now, whatever he'd been about to say, I wouldn't get to hear it.

"I wanted to wish you good luck for tomorrow," he concluded, his voice roughening some, and confirming my suspicion. "I know we'll see each other before things go down, but it'll be rushed. So, yeah, good luck."

I let out the breath I'd been holding, feeling simultaneously relieved and intensely disappointed. Whatever had been on the tip of his tongue, it obviously hadn't been that, and while I really had no right to feel anything but glad I didn't have to deal with it... God, I didn't know how to help it.

I nodded slowly, trying to beat back my conflicting emotions, and finally daring to face him again. "And you," I said, pushing out a smile.

But he wasn't looking at me now. His eyes were on the ground, his hand picking absently at a tuft of grass by his thigh. And I feared right then that I might have hurt him.

Could he really be feeling something for me, more than just friendship? Might he have had an ulterior motive for inviting me out here this evening, just as I'd had one for coming, and wanted to talk to me about... something?

What had he been about to say, before I'd so tactlessly cut him off?

I worried now that I would never know. Even though it shouldn't have worried me, because I'd already decided to cut him out.

And yet, another part of me, the part closest to my pounding heart, couldn't help but fear that I was making a huge mistake.

30

That night was rough. I tossed and turned, willing myself to fall asleep, but my evening with Jace haunted me. The way he'd acted differently after I'd done what I'd done. The way he'd avoided eye contact. The way we'd parted on a more awkward note than I'd even thought possible.

I'd gone to see him to decrease the tension between us, not increase it, dammit! I didn't know how I'd managed to let things go so badly.

But I didn't have time to unpack it now. Not before tomorrow. Maybe not ever.

The plans for the mission burning through my brain didn't help my insomnia, either. I kept going over it, running through all the things that could go wrong. I had to keep reminding myself that this first mission wasn't in direct conflict with the government. That we were just dealing with regular criminals, and that it would all be worth it in the end. Not only for the children we would help, but for furthering our plans. Because we would have taken our first step together as a group, proving that we could work with each other.

But no amount of sweet-talking could ease my nerves that night. It didn't matter how well prepared we thought we were. The truth was, we had no idea what we were up against, or what it would look like when we got there. And we didn't even know how the people around us were going to react to it. I had never been part of such a large operation before, and I didn't trust it. There was too much that could go wrong.

Especially given that I was part of the frontline team, the ones who would be breaching the building first and risking our lives.

It must've been close to 5:00 a.m. by the time I finally drifted off, and I let myself sleep in, hitting snooze on the alarm more times than I cared to admit, knowing that I desperately needed the rest for the mission, when my brain and senses would have to be razor sharp.

I wasn't due to leave until 4:00 p.m., and I slept as close to that hour as possible before climbing out of bed and getting ready. I showered, and, once I'd slipped into my most flexible set of black clothes and pulled my hair back into the tightest bun I could manage, I prepared my backpack. Then it was time to lock up the cabin and drive to the Roundhouse, where I was due to meet my colleagues.

The sun had begun its steady descent toward the horizon by the time I arrived, a few minutes late, thanks to a little traffic. I headed around the pub to the compound at the back, and found my team already there, leaning against the aircraft. And given the way their eyes snapped toward me, they were all just as high-strung as I was.

Everyone except Nelson, who was going to be providing technical support remotely from her office, was there, and they lost no time in bundling into the ship once I arrived. I followed, trying to focus on my breathing as we seated ourselves among the exosuits, and Marco took off. I looked to the pale faces of my colleagues, noting the shadows beneath their eyes. Even the twins were like deflated balloons compared to their usual selves.

"Oh," Jackie murmured suddenly, after about ten minutes of silence. She reached a hand into her backpack and pulled out a fistful of black masks, which looked identical to the new one she'd been wearing during our last outing.

"Here, I managed to get these for you," she said, handing them to Ant, who was sitting closest to her, and gesturing for him to pass them around.

"Oh, thanks," Ant mumbled, taking one and then passing the bundle on to Abe, who tossed one at me.

"Thanks," I said, catching it, and feeling glad that I had something tangible to distract myself with, if only for a few minutes. I traced a finger over the tough fabric, the sturdiness of it comforting me, and then pulled it over my head, trying it on.

"Feels a bit more stifling than what we're used to," Abe muttered.

Jackie nodded. "Yeah, that's kind of the price you pay for having a sturdier material."

I flexed my facial muscles beneath the fabric, discovering that Abe was right. But I would get used to it soon enough. I was going to be wearing a suit, as were Jackie, Ant, Abe, and the rest of our agreed-upon ground team, and while we would obviously keep our tinted visors down, extra camouflage underneath was important. Because none of us knew what was going to happen once we hit the ground. It was a new experience for all of us, and from what I'd gleaned from the other members, none of us had ever pulled off such a large operation before. Everyone had previously only worked in small, few-person groups, doing their own little projects.

I sat back and tried to get some rest, thinking that it might help me prepare for the mission, but the hours felt like they somehow compressed themselves, and before I knew it, Marco was saying that we were there.

I gazed through the window and saw swathes of inky blackness stretching out beneath us, with the glow of orange lights a haze in the distance. We were meeting in a rural area on the edge of the estate where our target building was located, so that we would have somewhere safe to touch base before moving in. And the darkness made this a perfect landing spot. We hovered directly over the border of one of the fields for a moment, and then Marco began to lower the aircraft. My stomach flipped—and not just from the jolt of gravity. This was it. Stage one of our plan, upon us, almost before I even realized it: regrouping and breaching the building.

My hands gripped the arms of my seat hard as we landed with a soft thud, and then all of us were shooting to our feet. Jackie, Abe, Ant, and I rushed to the suits while Julia began to work on preparing one of the drones, getting ready to stay behind with Marco and guide us from the safety of the ship.

Being closest to the hatch, I opened it, and found the rest of tonight's team already waiting outside, huddled in a tight-knit circle, some of them having driven vehicles into the field from the road that ran nearby. As almost two dozen eyes fell on me, my hands instinctively rose to my head, feeling the need to double check that my visor was down, even though I was wearing a mask beneath it. I was much more confident with the people we were working with now than I had been before, but my nerves were jittery with the possibility that something might go wrong. I wanted to make sure that my face was covered. That I was unrecognizable.

Then I spotted Jace at the back of the crowd, towering over everyone else, and I quickly looked away. I couldn't tell if he had spotted me yet, through the darkness (and even if he had, he probably couldn't tell it was me beneath the suit), but either way, I didn't have the time or emotional bandwidth to dwell on him.

Jackie and I got to work passing suits to some of the folks standing in the field, while they handed three large black bags bulging with equipment to us, and then Jace, Kory, Zion, Winter, and Austin (a tall, skinny guy who was our frontline tech) joined us in the ship, as we had planned. My colleagues and I backed into one corner to allow room for them as they fetched their own suits and began climbing into them, and then we started strapping the equipment we'd need to bandoliers and fastening them around our waists.

After a minute, I found myself glancing over at Jace despite myself, knowing that he might be having trouble customizing his suit to fit. But then Kory stepped in, and I let out a breath and leaned back against the wall.

I realized that I probably *should* try to break the ice with Jace a little, before we touched down, given that we were going to be working closely together. But now didn't seem like the right time, in such a small space, and with people still fitting into their suits. It was all we could do just to find somewhere to stand, even after having offloaded some of the suits.

But we managed, and five minutes later, Marco was closing the hatch again and the aircraft was rising.

The team we'd left on the ground was the decoy/backup team, and they would be making their way over to the site on foot to pull off their part of tonight's plan. We estimated it would take them about ten minutes at a fast jog. Which meant Marco could take his time finding a decent angle at which to hover above the large factory-turned-office. We soared silently over the dark fields until we reached the orange glow of streetlights, and as the building came into view, a chill ran down my spine. It, and its barbed-wired compound, suddenly seemed much more intimidating than when I'd last seen it, and my heart beat even harder when I caught a glimpse of two security guards outside leaning against the interior of the barb-topped wall and talking.

Thankfully, the clouds were low and dense tonight, the moon nowhere to be seen, and the aircraft in its silence would blend in with the darkness, unlikely to draw attention. Especially as Marco began navigating it out of view of the guards, at an angle, using the building's wide roof to act as coverage for us.

My eyes moved to the field beyond, and I noticed the subtle glimmer of flashlights. Our decoy team was swiftly approaching, and Marco seemed to notice it too, as the aircraft rose slightly, giving us all a better look. Once they had reached the shadows of the outer perimeter of the parking lot beyond the compound, it was time for the next stage: moving in.

I clenched my fingers within the suit, then rolled my neck and shoulders, trying to relieve some of the tension there, while Julia made her way to the hatch and ordered us all to stand back. She wasn't wearing a suit; none of the techs were. The bespectacled girl called Alexy was here to assist Julia with aerial surveillance, so she didn't need one, and Austin, who was going to be entering the building with us, had decided that the suit wouldn't allow enough dexterity for the IT work he was probably going to have to do. Julia and Alexy crammed into the front corner of the ship while the rest of us did our best to get out of their way, and a moment later Julia had opened the hatch and launched her drone into the air.

I could feel only a small whisper of the night breeze waft

through the ventilation of my suit, but it was a welcome sensation. Sweat was already beading on the small of my back, in spite of the moderate temperature.

I watched through the window closest to me as the drone silently positioned itself closer to the roof, and then began doing a round of the perimeter. Julia was being careful to keep it within the boundaries of the roof to keep it from being spotted from the ground.

Perhaps the trickiest thing about today was that we couldn't knock out the electricity, per Nelson's usual protocol. Because the X-ray had shown lots of computers in this place, and that was where we suspected we would find the evidence we required. We needed them fully functional if we were going to find what we were searching for.

Not having the electricity blacked out made everything even *more* dicey, because it took away our element of surprise. It also made me a whole lot more grateful for the extra protection the exo-suits provided us. They gave us a much stronger chance of getting out of there alive and unrecognized.

"Okay, begin final preparations," Julia announced softly, as she finished doing a loop of the roof with the drone. Her gaze was on a little screen on the other side of the passenger cabin wall, where the X-ray details were beginning to populate, though I couldn't make it out properly from where I stood.

Following her instruction, I dropped my eyes to the belt around my waist and pulled out two rubber handgrips, sliding them over the fingers of my suit, and then I opened my visor briefly to attach the comms equipment to my ears and around my neck.

Once everyone had announced that they had done the same, one of the twins pulled a lever to lower the winch from the ceiling, then beckoned over the first volunteer. We glanced at one another for a moment, tension radiating from each of us, and then the bulky form of Winter De Ville raised a hand. She was closest to the winch, so it made sense for her to go first, but I admired her bravery all the same. Glancing down at the long, dark roof, I knew being the first to touch down would be the most stressful. We were fairly certain that there were no security cameras on the roof itself, but just gaining a firm grip on the slanted, corrugated metal surface could be a challenge in these suits. We'd come prepared with rubberized grips, but still, we'd never tried this before.

Jackie helped Winter hook up, and then the larger woman was moving backward. Reaching the edge, she crouched down and lowered her legs into thin air, then surrendered herself to the line. The winch creaked slightly under her sudden weight, which, combined with the weight of the suit, had to be considerable, and Julia lowered her at a slow pace. I let out a sigh of relief when Winter's feet softly made contact with the roof, and she immediately leaned all her weight against the roof's slant, her rubberized fingers reaching down and finding purchase. She pulled herself up to a higher point, until she looked like she felt comfortable with her positioning, and then unhooked the line from her belt and allowed Julia to pull it back up.

Jackie was next in line, and managed to land as silently and gracefully as Winter, followed by the twins, Austin, and then Zion and Kory, until it was just Jace and me left, the two of us automatically shuffling closer to the winch as the aircraft emptied.

Jace's visor looked in my direction, and I got the feeling that he sensed it was me. I was about to take the opportunity to wish him good luck when he held out a hand, gesturing to the line.

"You wanna go next?" he asked softly, and I nodded, swallowing back my words.

I guessed I understood why he wanted to be the last one down.

He was the largest, and a part of me was sure that the worry had to be playing on his mind that the thing might break.

"Break a leg," I said quietly, hooking myself up to the line.

He nodded. "You too," he murmured, and it irked me a bit that I couldn't see his expression. I'd have liked to know if there was any humor there at all in that moment, as it probably would have done something to ease my nerves. Not just about our situation, but in regard to him.

But that was going to have to suffice, I supposed.

Because then I was backing away, toward the edge of the aircraft, getting on all fours and lowering myself down slowly, legs first—until I felt confident enough to let go.

31

The line jerked as I dropped several feet, and I gripped it tightly to steady myself, trying not to worry about the slight creaking sound the winch had made. I tilted my head down, focusing on where I was going to land, and was ready for it when my feet hit the slanted, ridged surface. I mimicked the actions I'd watched the others take, leaning all my weight into the slant, and then slowly climbed up to a higher level, where the two sloped sides of the roof joined and the surface became level, seating myself next to the twins.

I then looked back up and watched tentatively as Jace came into view. He lowered himself down, his legs gradually dangling off the edge of the aircraft, but then he let go, lurching downward with a sudden jolt that made my heart leap into my throat. The slack of the line caught, pulling him to a stop midair, but I still winced as the winch made its loudest protest yet. I doubted it would break—after all, it had supported the weight of as many as four lines at once before—but the noise was more than we could afford to be making right now, and I prayed nobody in or outside the building had heard.

I watched with bated breath as Jace lowered himself the rest of the way, at a painstakingly slow pace, and exhaled when his feet finally hit the roof's surface. It took him a moment to get secure on the corrugated slats, but then he was climbing up toward me, his palms and feet making thankfully little sound. Once he'd seated himself next to me, he detached the hook from his belt, allowing the winch to suck it back up.

Now that we'd all made it down okay, I turned to my right to look at the twins and saw that they were already prepared with their night vision cameras.

"Okay, I'm gonna do a quick intro now," one of twins whispered. "So smile, everyone."

He fumbled with a button on one side of the camera, then began to do a quick sweep over each of the hulking forms crouching on the roof.

"Just be careful not to get Nelson's aircraft in view," Jackie muttered.

"I know. And now I've got to edit out the sound, too," the twin shot back.

I rolled my eyes, then watched as the second twin did a sweep with his camera as well, capturing the greater area that surrounded the building. As a group, we'd debated a couple of things regarding this video footage idea, the first being whether it would be wise to get our exo-suits on the shots. Some had raised the concern that they could possibly be traced back to Montague and his company, but when we asked him, he said that there were many of them in regular usage, and that there wouldn't be any risk of these being traced back to him specifically. Second, we'd discussed whether the twins ought to wear them at all, given the risk of the metal heads hampering their vision, and the metal hands hampering their camera-operating capabilities. But they'd practiced with them and decided they were comfortable enough to wear them, too.

Which had been a relief, because I didn't want them walking around without any protection. Not if we could help it.

Which left Austin as the only one down here without a suit. He'd been uneasy at the idea of going without the extra protection —still was, from the nervous glimmer in his eyes—but the hands on the suit just weren't suitable for the kind of precise hacking work he might have to perform once we got into the building and reached the computers. So we'd arranged for a bulletproof vest for him, which was better than nothing. But I still didn't like it.

"Okay, we're done," Twin 2—the one farthest from me— announced, and I pulled my eyes away from Austin to see the brothers attaching the camera straps higher on their arms, to free up their hands for climbing.

A moment later, Alexy's voice crackled in our ears. "Launching Drone 2."

I glanced up to see it soar out from the aircraft's interior, then swerve instantly away from the building and its compound. Her job was to keep an eye on the surrounding area and watch out for anyone else approaching the property from the outside. It was important, not just for those of us going into the building, but also our backup team, who were currently crouching in the shadows of the adjacent parking lot.

"Okay, we talk over comms from now on," Zion's whisper came through our ears. "And let's get moving." He rose slightly from where he had been crouching on the other end of the line and began making his way toward one of the three skylights fixed into the metal roof. From what we had been able to tell from the X-rays, these openings led directly into an attic, which would make for the easiest and most discreet entrance into the building.

Each of us moved after him, choosing caution over speed, knowing that one slip could result in us tumbling off the roof. Going quickly would also mean making more noise, which we couldn't risk, especially when we knew there were security guards outside. There could also be people within the building, though we were still waiting for Julia or Alexy to confirm that. We stuck to the flat, top area of the roof as much as we could until we reached the skylight closest to us—and also farthest away from where we'd seen the two guards standing in the compound.

"How're things looking inside, Julia?" I whispered, knowing we needed her feedback before we attempted entrance.

"Um, pretty still right now," her voice came back. "Then again, people could be sitting in chairs and working, or even resting, so keep your wits about you. I'll keep you updated."

I inhaled. We still knew very little about who these people were, or what they might be doing in this place. We also didn't know what they might do to us if we got caught. I just knew that we couldn't afford for that to happen.

Winter and Zion reached the skylight just as Julia ended her transmission, and positioned themselves on either side of it. Jackie handed them the cutter she had been carrying in her belt, and I pressed my lips together. We weren't sure if the windows way up here were rigged to the alarm system, but we had to hope that cutting through the glass itself wouldn't trigger it even if they were. Otherwise, we were basically screwed.

Winter grabbed the cutter and set to work, her metal hands gripping the object hard. I watched with a tight stomach as she slowly, painstakingly cut around the edges, making the glass looser and looser, until the pane became dangerously close to caving in and shattering on the floor beneath.

But she paused just before that could happen. "Okay, I figure we're thirty seconds away from the glass breaking, if I continue cutting," she muttered. "Team Decoy, do you hear me?"

The deep voice of Cloyd, who had volunteered to manage the backup team, came back. "Yup. And we're ready."

"Okay, you need to activate in thirty seconds, counting from NOW."

Winter immediately switched the cutter on again and pressed it once more to the shaky glass. My gut clenched harder as she continued slicing, and I counted down the seconds in my head. *Twenty-five. Twenty. Fifteen. Ten. Five...*

BANG.

BANG.

BANG.

A series of explosions erupted from the parking lot, so loud I didn't even hear the glass shattering when it dropped, and we all froze, listening to the sounds of confused voices drifting up from the compound. Then came the noise of hurried footsteps. I was just thankful that the sounds hadn't been accompanied by a blaring siren; it meant shattering the window hadn't triggered any alarms.

Julia's voice swiftly returned to the line. "Okay, I got good news and bad news. Bad is, there are definitely people inside the building. Good news is the decoy seems to have distracted them. I see at least three figures on... varying levels... moving away from your end of the building and toward the parking lot. So now's your chance. Go. I'll keep you updated on their movement."

We didn't need telling twice. Winter was the first to drop through the hole, followed by Zion, Jackie, Kory, Austin, and the twins, with Jace and me taking up the rear, due to our natural positioning in the line. We found ourselves landing on a solid, dusty cement floor, in a low-ceilinged attic that seemed to span the entire length and breadth of the building, and was scattered with piles of discarded hardware, from cracked monitors to broken keyboards to ancient-looking hard drives. I noticed everyone eyeing the heaps as we passed them, as if each of us might be wondering the same thing: whether there might be any evidence up here in the attic itself. If there was, we might not need to venture downstairs. But the equipment looked more or less like trash, so we hurried past it.

Suddenly Zion came to a stop up ahead, causing the rest of us to slow down. "We'll take this trapdoor down," he grunted as he bent down and heaved at a hatch, attached to which was a foldable ladder.

Winter knelt to help him, though the door seemed to open without much trouble. They lowered the ladder, and then the man and woman were disappearing through the open hole, and the rest of us were moving to stand around it and gaze down into what appeared to be a dark hallway.

Zion and Winter had their guns out in front of them as they looked left and right. And then, apparently satisfied that the coast was clear, Zion nodded and gestured for us to climb down after them.

Jackie lowered herself first, being closest to the top of the ladder, and the rest of us followed quickly afterward, trying to make as little noise as humanly possible. I went before Jace, then watched as he climbed down after me, nervous at the noise he might make, but the rubber modifications on our soles really did seem to be doing wonders, and he made it down with minimal sound.

I turned my attention to the front of the line, which had already begun to move—Zion, Winter, and Jackie taking point, with Austin trailing them, while the twins, a few steps behind him, had begun to film again. None of us knew how long our decoy team was going to be able to keep the guards and other occupants of this building distracted. The plan was for the cherry bomb explosions to lure as many people outside as possible, to investigate, at which point the team was supposed to set off a round of smoke bombs laced with sedative gas, to cause further confusion and ideally take out a few men in the process. Which would hopefully give *my* team the time we needed to discover and retrieve evidence.

But the strategy was a shaky one, to say the least. We had to hope that a) nobody in the surrounding area saw the smoke from the building, assumed there was a fire, and decided to call the fire department, and b) nobody in the building itself saw our setup for the decoy that it was, evaded the smoke, and called for backup. We were banking on nobody being ballsy enough to call the cops, given what we suspected went on in this building, but either way, we had to hurry. Especially since there were CCTV cameras dotted about the ceiling.

We just had to hope that nobody was monitoring this floor right at this moment.

I hung back from everyone for a second to throw a glance over my shoulder, needing to reassure myself that nobody was following us, even though Julia was supposed to be alerting us to any movement coming our way. The hallway was still empty, though, so I set my sights ahead again.

We had a backup plan for how to deal with people who evaded the sedative and either returned to, or remained in, the building, but I really hoped we could avoid that. In any case, until we heard back from Julia with an update on movement, all we could do was focus on our next step: getting to a computer terminal. One that would have the kind of data we needed.

The front of the line came to a sudden stop, with Zion, Jackie, and Winter peering into two open doorways, one on either side of the wall, before spilling into the one on the right. I glanced through at both rooms as soon as I reached them, and saw that they were empty offices. I entered the right-hand room and watched tentatively as Austin did a sweep of it, examining monitors and ducking beneath desks. He stopped when he reached a bay in the center of the room that held a large CPU, which seemed to be hooked up to multiple monitors.

"Let's try this one," he murmured, taking off his backpack and kneeling. He pressed the power button, fumbled in his bag for a mini drive, and plugged it into the machine, before pulling out a clunky-looking handheld device.

We all waited around him, watching tensely. My eyes flitted between his fingers punching the handheld's small rubber buttons and the lines of coding spilling across its narrow screen—and the open doorway. We wanted to avoid closing it, not just for fear of it creaking, but because we needed to hear any noises coming from the hallway.

"I'm starting to see movement coming in your direction," Julia's voice suddenly crackled through, making my skin crawl. "Looks like two people. They seem to be on a lower floor, so probably not an immediate threat, but yeah. Hux, Robin, and Jackie: you'd better follow through on that backup plan, pronto."

"Got an ETA, Austin?" I asked in a strained whisper, a pit of dread opening up in my stomach. I'd prayed it wouldn't come to this. That we'd be able to swipe the evidence we needed before people in the building became a problem. But I couldn't say that it was unexpected, either. I'd known the chances of all of them venturing outside and getting caught by the sedative were slim.

But that didn't stop my palms from sweating. If Austin thought he was going to be longer than another couple of minutes, it meant we had to take them out ASAP. If they were going to call for backup, we were most likely already too late to stop them, but we were hoping backup wouldn't be immediate. And with Alexy monitoring the surrounding roads, we should have ample warning of approaching vehicles. In the meantime, we could neutralize anyone inside the building, so Austin could complete his work without any immediate threat.

At least, that was the theory. One that was based on a few more "shoulds" and "hopes" than I was comfortable with.

The wiry man at the computer gave no response to my question, but his thumbs started working faster. He was under enough stress as it was, and likely didn't appreciate me laying on more pressure, but I couldn't help it.

After a long moment, he finally replied in a hoarse whisper, "Okay, good news and bad news. Bad: security is a lot stronger than I'd hoped. No way I can breach the system with this hand-held. Good: I've managed to establish a remote connection to Nelson, so she can take it from here."

His voice then cut off in my earphones, and I quickly flipped my visor open to change channels on the comms, realizing that was what Austin was doing, to connect with Nelson.

"Nelson, you got my transmiss—?"

"Yup, I see what you've done," Nelson's voice cut through his question. "Will deploy all the horsepower I got and try to breach ASAP. Switch on a monitor so you can follow my progress. I'll relay whatever data I find, and Abe can film."

With that, she cut off, and I switched back to our communal channel before closing my visor. Austin immediately moved to do as Nelson instructed, switching on the screen of the monitor nearest to us, but as much as I wanted to stay and watch Nelson begin to dig through their system, Jace, Jackie, and I had to go. This process sounded like it was going to last more than a couple of minutes.

Which meant we had to take care of the people who might be

coming straight for us. Preferably before they could make trouble. I just hoped there really were only two of them.

Jace's visor was already tilting in my direction, telling me he understood. We headed to the door, Jackie—and one of the twins —following swiftly on our heels.

I whirled on the twin, raising my eyebrows, even though I knew he couldn't see them through my visor and mask. "Abe?" I asked.

"Ant," he muttered.

"What're you doing?"

"My job," he remarked. "Abe can more than cover what's going on up here. I want to capture more of this place on film. Who knows, we could even come across some low-hanging fruit."

I sucked in a breath, knowing that his words made sense; we weren't expecting there to be low-hanging fruit in this place in the form of physical evidence, like documents lying around, but it would be shortsighted to completely discount the possibility. And once we managed to take down the remaining hostiles, we might have a bit of time to look around, while we were on the lower levels of the building—and Ant could record it all, in case we *did* stumble across anything pertinent.

Still, I didn't exactly feel comfortable with the idea of Ant tagging along. It was one extra person exposing themselves to the line of fire, because I didn't doubt that the people in this building would be armed. And the fact that half of his brain was going to be distracted by filming didn't help my nerves.

But I wasn't his mom, and it wasn't my place to try to dissuade him. So I pushed the worry away and walked the rest of the distance to the door's threshold, where Jackie and Jace were waiting. Jackie's visor fixed on Ant for a moment, as if she shared the same concerns as me, but she didn't comment, and then the four of us were stepping out into the hallway.

"Let's switch to our own channel," I murmured, as tense whispers from the room we'd just left entered my ears. I figured we could all do without the distraction of their nervous conversation now that we were venturing into unknown territory. We could check back again in a bit to gauge their progress, and Julia and Alexy had the ability to override all of our channels, so we weren't in danger of missing an important announcement from them.

My companions nodded, and we briefly flipped open our visors to make the switch to channel three.

"I see four of you moving," Julia's voice crackled in our ears as we began to walk again.

"Ant's tagging along with us," I replied.

"Okay. Developments: the two people I spotted earlier seem to have convened in the same room. Which should hopefully make things easier for you. Hard for me to tell exactly which floor, but judging by how blurry and obscured their forms are, I'm guessing the bottom floor. Possibly even the basement."

"Okay, got it," Jackie replied, and then Julia disconnected again.

There was a pause as the four of us looked at one another, knowing that this was it. And, in spite of the tense atmosphere, I suddenly wished that we'd kept our visors open, that I could get a true read on their emotions in that moment. Particularly Jace. I'd been in my fair share of life-threatening situations since I started going out with Nelson's group, and although we wore masks, I'd gotten used to always being able to look into their eyes—and hadn't realized how important that was until now. Even if they only reflected my own anxiety, it felt like an important human part of the equation when heading into uncertain danger. To be able to sense that we were all in this together, to see that we were all going through the same emotions. Staring into a bunch of dark, flat visors seemed horribly impersonal, and left me feeling needy for a sense of grounding.

But this was seriously not the time to get melodramatic, and if anyone else was feeling the same, they didn't comment on it, so I shoved it aside and kept moving.

We walked slowly down the corridor at first, but after half a minute, as if all remembering at once that our targets were supposed to be way downstairs, we dared to speed up a bit, at the risk of making a touch more noise, until we reached a staircase and an elevator about three quarters of the way down the hallway.

And I thanked God for the option of a good, old-fashioned staircase, because there was no way I would've wanted to risk taking an elevator—not just from the noise of the cables, but from the fear of who might be standing there when the doors opened.

Jace took point, and I followed right after him, then Jackie, with Ant at the rear with his camera. We crept down the stairs more painstakingly than we'd walked along the corridor, since they were trickier to navigate quietly, and when we reached the bottom of the flight, on the next level down, we found that it connected directly to the next set of stairs. The pattern repeated itself all the way down the building, until there were no more stairs to climb, and I realized that we had unwittingly reached the basement already.

We paused at the bottom of it, our ears as alert as they could be within our suits. It was dark, except for a handful of dim service lights punched into the ceiling at intervals. The corridor here was also shorter than that of the levels above, and overall it seemed a little too quiet. I was about to suggest we check the floor above us first, but then Jace suddenly started moving, away from the stairs and toward the right-hand side of the corridor.

As we followed him, I realized that his gaze was set on a metal door that had been left ever so slightly ajar, about seven feet down. A soft white light, almost imperceptible beneath the ceiling lights, was escaping through the cracks around its edges. He stopped in front of it, gesturing with one hand for us to approach with caution. As he placed his head near the crack, we followed suit, and I realized what Jace had somehow heard: a faint murmuring drifting through from the other side.

Given that none of the rest of us had noticed it from the staircase, I was highly impressed by his sense of hearing, even through the suit, and wondered if it was a side effect of having been brought up in the wild. But now wasn't the time for irrelevant questions, so I refocused on the matter at hand.

I squinted in concentration, trying to make out the words of the conversation, but the voices were too indistinct. The only thing I knew for sure was that they were men, due to the depth of their tones.

I bit my lip and leaned back so I could face my colleagues. "Definitely men in there," I breathed. "Suggestions for how we approach this?"

Jackie reached for one of the smoke/sedative bombs that she had strapped to her belt. "One of us pulls the door open, and I throw it in," she whispered. "We hope it disables them before they can shoot, but keep sheltered out here until we're sure. Then we go in and disarm them."

I nodded, my mouth feeling dry, and looked to Jace, hoping that he'd be comfortable with that—I mean, it seemed like the quickest and safest option, given the circumstances.

If his curt nod was anything to go by, then he was.

And then Jackie turned to Ant. "As for you. You just... do your thing back there, okay?" She pointed vaguely toward the staircase. "Don't come near the door. You'll only get in the way and probably end up getting shot or something."

"Well, thanks." Ant scoffed.

"What Jackie's saying is don't try to multitask," I cut in. "If you wanna help, put the camera down first. Otherwise, stay back."

He gave a huff but did as we advised, moving back until he was level with the staircase, before defiantly pointing his camera at us.

Exhaling, I resumed my focus on the door—and Jace's hand, which was inches away from opening it.

32

G ripping my gun, I shoved my back against the wall while Jackie prepared the bomb. Once her index finger was firmly looped through the ring, she pulled the pin and hissed to Jace, "NOW!"

He yanked the door open with one firm tug, and Jackie hurled the bomb. It left her hand, disappearing from my view, but before she could take a step back for Jace or me to push the door closed again, the sound of sharp popping erupted from the room. Bullets sprayed out through the doorway within a split second, and the next thing I knew, Jackie was clutching her gut and staggering backward.

"Jackie!" I gasped, rushing to her while Jace dropped to the ground and gripped the edge of the door, forcing it closed with a violent slam.

Her back hit the opposite wall and her visor tilted downward, gazing at the area of her suit where her hands were clutching. I grabbed her arms and pulled them away, dread gripping my heart in an ice-cold vice. Montague had said the suits should be more or less bulletproof, but he hadn't guaranteed it, and I feared the worst as my eyes fell on two deep indentations in the metal.

But then I realized with a gasp of relief that they were just that. Indentations. The suit had been strong enough to withstand the bullets. Just about. If the shooters had been closer... I shuddered to think that they could have sunk right through.

But right now, this meant Jackie was simply in shock.

"Th-They moved so fast," she whispered, and I could see that her hands were shaking even through the suit.

"I know," I replied, clutching her shoulder. I was in a state of shock myself at how quickly they'd reacted. They'd fired within a split second of the door opening, which was a faster response than I'd thought possible.

But maybe they'd seen us approach via CCTV. Heck, maybe this was the camera room, and they'd convened here after realizing the decoy was fishy, to see what else was going on in the building. They could have been watching us the whole time. The only other explanation I could come up with was that these men were no ordinary security guards. That they were *highly* trained, because reflexes like that just weren't something that came naturally. Which would mean we'd have to hope—

THUD. THUD. THUD.

I whirled back around to see Jace gripping the door's handle and shoving his weight hard against the surface to keep it from opening—along with Ant, who'd abandoned his camera. It sounded like the men were attacking the other side with some kind of heavy, blunt object, and the door shuddered worryingly in its frame.

"We gotta keep it closed!" Jackie said, her voice regaining some of its strength as she hurried to the men.

We both joined them, but there wasn't much space left for us to press ourselves against it. Jace, who was clearly doing most of the heavy lifting, was strong enough to prevent the men from getting the knob turned and getting out that way, but I feared how long the rest of it was going to hold up. The door was made of metal, but the way it was starting to quiver in its frame from the force of the men on the other side sent a chill racing down my spine.

Then the thudding stopped.

PING. PING. PING.

We all ducked reflexively, realizing they were now shooting bullets.

"Those sons of bitches," Ant breathed, he and Jace somehow still able to maintain a decent pressure against the door from their lowered positions.

I cursed. None of the shots had made it through to our side yet. But I had no idea the caliber of the guns they held, or how long the door's metal could withstand it. They were clearly trying to get us to back away from the door, but we couldn't do that! Once they got out, the danger would be amplified, without any doors in the way. Not just for us, but for our team, if either of these guys managed to flee and make it upstairs. Besides, the gas from Jackie's bomb should be kicking in at any moment. We just had to hold out.

"They're desperate," Jackie whispered, her voice admirably steady as she voiced my own thoughts. "We just gotta stay strong a bit longer."

Still, each bullet hitting the surface made me fear for Jace's and Ant's lives, given the shooters' now close proximity, and as the long, nerve-wracking seconds bled into ten, then twenty, I clung to Jackie's words, telling myself that they were true.

And then finally, they became so. The bullets lessened in frequency, the rolling beat becoming more of a pitter-patter, until they'd faded completely and sputtered out with two heavy thumps.

Ant and Jace held their positions against the door, but Jackie and I dared to rise from our crouched positions.

"What if they're just pretending?" I whispered, my heart still hammering against my ribcage.

Jackie hesitated. "They could be, I guess, but the gas really should have gotten them by now. They held out long enough."

Still, we waited another couple of minutes in silence, Jace maintaining his pressure on the door, and then Jackie gently laid her hands over the men's shoulders, gesturing that they should move backward. They did so, albeit reluctantly, and I worried about Jackie approaching the door again; despite her apparent quick recovery, her nerves would still be shot from her previous fright. So I stepped forward and gripped her arm, tugging her backward. She tilted her head in question, but I ignored it, continuing to pull at her until she was out of my way, and then approached the door in her place.

"My turn to go first," I muttered, not bothering to look back for her reaction. I set my suit into non-ventilation mode temporarily, to avoid breathing in the gas, then tightened my grip around my gun and held it in front of me. I guessed we could have just turned back now, returned to our group upstairs, but it felt wrong to leave without verifying beyond a shadow of a doubt that our job here was done, and they were down.

I slowly pulled down on the handle, and my heart beat hard at the sight of the hairline crack, and then thundered as I widened it. My index finger twitched, ready to pull the trigger at the slightest movement, but all remained still in the room beyond, and then I'd opened the door wide enough to glimpse the two limp bodies sprawled facedown on the floor, their guns scattered around them.

"*Looks* like we're clear, but I'm going in to check. If you wanna follow, remember to switch your ventilation off," I whispered, then moved in through the wisps of smoke to snatch up both guns.

Jace and Jackie spilled in after me and immediately rolled over the men's bodies, double-checking to make sure they were definitely out and searching them for other weapons, and I moved in closer to get a proper look at them for the first time.

They were both tall—I estimated around six feet—and thickly built, and wore nondescript black uniforms. From their relatively unlined faces and lack of gray hair, I guessed they were in their late thirties, though one of them had several scars crisscrossing all the way from his jaw to the base of his neck, which seemed to confirm my suspicion that these were seasoned fighters.

Whether they were just hired security or actually a part of this kidnapping gang remained to be seen, but this was a pleasant piece of bonus intel, to be able to get actual faces on camera.

Ant whistled, and I glanced over to see him crouching down with his camera a couple of feet away, doing a slow sweep of the men. "Gonna get these bastards good," he muttered.

I nodded, then turned to survey the rest of the room while Jace and Jackie bound the men's hands and feet together with wire—wondering whether there *were* camera monitors in here. We didn't have much time to hang around, as I was near certain that backup would be on its way, but neither Julia nor Alexy had given us a warning yet, and I didn't want to pass up the opportunity for a quick look around for other potential intel while we were all the way down here. I wanted to know, in particular, why the men had chosen to convene in this room, which more or less appeared to be another office, like the ones I'd seen upstairs. Because I couldn't spot any monitors. At least from what I'd been able to make out through the smog, which still hung heavy, and would take a while to dissipate through the open door.

I approached the nearest table, running my metal fingers gently over the surface as I walked around it. Seeing that it held nothing but unused monitors and IT accessories, I moved to the next one along, which seemed to hold more of the same. Except... I slowed as my eyes fell on a stack of folders propped up next to the monitors at the end of this table. It was the first substantial bit of stationary I'd spotted in this place, aside from the odd pen or blank pad of sticky notes. Which had led me to believe we likely wouldn't find evidence outside of the computer systems. But maybe I'd been wrong.

Excitement thrummed through me, and I hurried to the pile and grabbed the first folder, pulling it open.

And what I saw inside made my jaw drop.

Print-outs of children's faces. This folder was bulging with headshots—and so were all of the folders in the stack, by the looks of it. And not just any headshots. I quickly began flipping through them and saw that the pictures were all of infants. Newborns. And then I noticed the little emblem that watermarked the lower right-hand corner of each of them.

"Guys, check this out," I managed, hardly daring to believe my eyes.

When they came rushing over, I laid a shaky forefinger on the watermark. It was an insignia I recognized all too well: a black cross, entwined with a serpent.

The symbol of the Ministry of Welfare.

"Whoa," Jackie gasped. "What... What are these doing here?"

There was a long pause as my mind raced, and Ant got a closeup of the print-outs. What *were* these pictures doing here? How had these criminals managed to print them out? These looked like they were from the government's archives. That was what the mark was for, to mark the prints as Ministry property.

Which could only mean that...

"Do you think they've somehow hacked the archives?" Jace whispered, and I turned to stare into his dark visor, my heart doing somersaults in my chest.

A burst of excitement coursed through me at the prospect that they could have. Hell, scratch that—*must* have. How else could these records be sitting here?

"Maybe access to the archives is what's helping them pull off this whole operation," Ant whispered. "I mean, helping them decide which kids to target for their site, and their location, and so on. The Ministry has access to every kid born. They mark the ones that are up for confiscation. And this site…"

My eyes shot back to the unconscious men on the floor, and I suddenly felt the urge to race over there and slap them awake. Because, God, these people had the answer. The answer I'd been so desperately seeking. The answer I'd give literally anything to obtain.

They had the key to getting my Hope back.

Jackie and I seemed to be of one mind as she looked back at the men too. I knew she'd lost younger siblings some years back, so we were both dying to finally crack the archives. This was the moment we'd both been waiting for. We still didn't know if this duo was part of the kidnappers' operation, or just hired security for the building, but I was itching to try to force some answers out of them.

The problem was, we had no means of resuscitating them. Slapping wouldn't work. The gas would have them out cold for at least another hour, and we hadn't brought any smelling salts with us. Which meant we'd be gone long before they came to.

Unless…

I looked to Jackie, wondering if she was thinking what I was thinking. Could we somehow take one of these men with us? Jace was tall and strong enough to carry one, especially with his suit, and we could keep the guy drugged, tied, and blindfolded on the aircraft so he wouldn't be a danger to us. We'd come with extra sedatives. And if it turned out he had no answers, or proved to be too difficult a nut to crack even after interrogation, then we could just dump him somewhere, let him go. Given the infinite upside, I couldn't see any downside to the idea.

My lips parted and I was a split second away from voicing the suggestion when Julia's voice suddenly spilled into our ears, causing all other thoughts to evaporate from my head.

"Um, guys. If you've dealt with the hostiles, which it looks like you have, I suggest you head back upstairs. Now. Nelson's found something."

Her voice then cut off, leaving my heartbeat racing.

Maybe Nelson had discovered a clue within the computer system itself. Which could mean we didn't need to bother with these men after all.

"Let's see what she's got," Jackie whispered, then gripped my arm and pulled me toward the door, gesturing for the men to follow.

33

We moved up the stairs at twice the speed we'd come down them, knowing that the building was, at least temporarily, free of hostiles, and arrived back in the room with everyone else within a few minutes.

Everyone was standing frozen around a monitor. Realizing they would all be switched to Nelson's channel, Jace, Ant, Jackie, and I quickly made the switch as well. I needed to work harder to find a position where I could see the screen, because unlike Jace and Ant, I wasn't tall enough to see over people's heads. I managed to nestle my way in between Zion and Kory, finding a place to kneel on the floor, and pulled Jackie through to sit next to me.

As I stared up at the screen, my excitement increased—because it displayed a photograph of an infant, with the Ministry's watermark, just like the ones we'd found downstairs. Maybe Nelson was on the case already!

But when her voice came through my ears, her tone was… less enthusiastic than I'd hoped it would be.

"This little girl," she said hoarsely. "I... I know her."

I frowned in confusion. "Um, I'm sorry, Nelson," I spoke up. "Robin here. We've just rejoined the crew upstairs. Could you fill us in?"

"Uh, yeah," Nelson replied, sounding distant and lost in intense thought. "I... I managed to force my way into the system, and I'm still going through it, but... I stumbled on a bunch of folders containing Ministry photographs like this one. Each of the folders was labeled as either 'Potential,' 'Upcoming,' or 'Recent.' And I happened to spot this kid in the Recent pile." There was a long pause, in which I could practically hear the blood pounding in my ears.

"And?" I urged. "Those labels sound similar to what I saw on the front-end webpage Gabby managed to access, so are these folders part of the site's backend database? Kids that're in their catalog?"

Or could those categorized folders be pulled directly from the Ministry's servers—marking the kids' CRAS status, so the kidnappers knew where the kids were in the various stages of the Ministry's processing? It could potentially be either, and I needed to know.

"Um, I'm not completely sure yet," Nelson replied, clearing her throat. "They're not part of the site's direct database, because I'm still digging for that. But they're clearly connected somehow. I found the folders in the general system files.

"And like I said, I know this kid. Remember how I told you about my friend who lost her child, just recently? Well, this is *that kid*, unless I'm hugely mistaken. And I... I don't think I am. Those jade eyes are distinct. And combined with that little black tuft of hair and slightly cleft lip, I recognized her instantly."

My gut clenched. "Oh, God. And you found her in the Recent folder? Could that mean the gang has taken her?" The thought of *anyone's* child being on the systems in this building made me queasy.

"Um, no. Not necessarily," Nelson replied. "It's what I've just been thinking about. I mean, the Recent folders contain way too many children for them to possibly target them all. And I mean *way* too many. There are probably thousands of them, combined. There's no way this gang could pull off *that* scale of operation without the government closing in on their asses.

"I think it's more like they've somehow pulled these folders directly from the archives, and that they're categorizing the kids. Maybe those who are predicted to be on the list for adoption are under 'Potential.' Then those whose parents are likely to sooner become ineligible to keep them 'cause they've fallen below the threshold could be 'Upcoming.' And those who were recently taken could be 'Recent.' Which would explain why my friend's kid was tagged in the last one."

"And if this group has access, it means they've figured out how to crack it," I breathed, as she confirmed my second suspicion regarding these folders. "And they've downloaded data from the server. What else have you found in the system? Any names or addresses? Any data at all that goes back past Recent—like, the past couple of years or so?"

I knew the questions spilling out of my mouth were purely selfish now, and not directly related to the task at hand—which was, first and foremost, to retrieve the evidence we needed to rat this group out—but I couldn't help it. Julia or Alexy could be calling at any moment telling us we had to leave. We'd been in the building about fifteen minutes already. And Nelson might not have enough time to figure out how they'd managed to break into the archives if she was still fishing through system files. It also might be too late to go back for one of the unconscious men. So if there was even the smallest chance that Hope could be on the system, I just wanted Nelson to grab all the data she could and run. I imagined that she had to be thinking along the same lines, given her own lost child. And judging by how intensely the rest of the group was listening, most of us had a vested interest in those archives.

"I'm still digging through," Nelson murmured. "Though, it doesn't look like they have older data on here. Maybe it's less useful to this group, considering the site they're running. But give me a bit." She fell quiet again, plunging us back into tense silence, and I prayed she would find it. Granted, even if there was older data, it didn't guarantee Hope's would be there. They might not have downloaded entire databases. But still, this felt like the closest I'd ever come to capturing a lead on her, and I wasn't about to let it go easily.

Hope's adoptive family's address could be on these systems, which would mean all I'd have to do would be to swipe her back, as I'd done with so many other children over the past seven months. And then I—we—could get out of this life entirely. Run and hide. Maybe get over the border. Or heck, even join the nuns for a while, and see how staying in the country worked out for us. We could ask them to get us fake IDs, which could allow us both to start our lives afresh. Hope was still so young, not even two years old, so she would adapt, and I knew she'd remember me once I held her in my arms again, even if she'd forgotten my face while she'd been away. She'd see my hazel eyes in hers and remember how my kisses felt. She'd have grown so much since I held her as a tiny newborn, and I'd get to find out if she had developed the color of my hair or Henry's.

The idea became so palpable in my mind, my eyes prickled with tears from just how badly I wanted it. I could finally step off this crazy tightrope. Go back to normal. With the missing piece of my life restored.

I glanced anxiously at the clock hanging on the wall and watched the seconds tick by, while wringing my metal hands. I counted one minute, then two, before Nelson's voice finally returned.

"Oh," she said softly. "This is... odd." Her tone had shifted from pensive to mildly nervous.

"What?" I asked, along with several others, anxiety twisting my stomach.

"I'm looking at an offline backup of their shadow site. I finally stumbled across a full database. And it's... it's not an auction site, like we thought."

"Huh?" Jackie said.

"What do you mean?" I asked.

"Then what is it?" Winter demanded.

In response, the image of the child disappeared from the screen, and a webpage flashed up in its place. I shifted closer to the monitor to get a better look... and realized that it was a long submission form, requesting the visitor to input details ranging from "Age (in months)" to "Ethnicity" to "Eye Color."

"There seems to be no system in place to make actual bids," Nelson went on. "Looks like they're running more of a fulfillment service than anything else."

"Meaning interested parties fill in the sort of kid they're looking for and then the gang goes to find some family to rob?" Kory whispered, his voice thick with disgust.

"Well, they clearly take orders using this form," Nelson replied. "And I'm guessing whatever intel they've managed to pull from the archives is helping them narrow in on the right kind of kid."

"But Gabby and I saw a list," I said, confused. "We saw a page of listings, which indicated they had 'inventory' already."

"That's true, but I haven't seen a lot of pages like that,"

Nelson replied. "Maybe they do have some kids on hand, or within easy reach. But there's clearly a major 'to-order' component to this, too. It seems to be the main feature of the site."

"And how come you didn't realize this earlier?" Zion wondered.

"The IT team didn't dig this deep into the site; once we managed to scrape the IP, we decided not to risk breaching the servers further in case someone detected a probe and it blew our cover for the big day…"

She trailed off again, and although I was curious to learn about the ins and outs of how this group worked, I really hoped she was just going to focus on the archive data now. I was pretty sure we had ample evidence to bust these criminals already, and I needed to get *something* from this excursion. *Anything* that could push me one step closer in my search for Hope. It felt like we were so near to something, it was maddening.

If she didn't find something on the system soon, I was going to need to reconsider going back downstairs and asking Jace for help with one of the—

Nelson's sharp cuss sliced through my train of thought like a knife.

"Look at this," she breathed, and the next thing I knew, the submission form on the screen had vanished, to be replaced with a spreadsheet populated by names and addresses.

"What is it?" Jackie asked, popping the visor of her suit open and squinting at the small font that formed the entries on the sheet.

"I found it in a folder marked 'Orders Fulfilled.' Look at the addresses," Nelson hissed.

I frowned, feeling both confused and shaken by the urgency in her tone, then took a leaf out of Jackie's book and popped my visor open too, so I could see more clearly. Though I only needed to do a brief sweep to realize that all the addresses belonged to wealthy neighborhoods.

"And?" I asked, still feeling pretty confused. I mean, the idea of wealthy people ordering these kids was disturbing, but it didn't exactly come as that much of a shock to me, given that only rich individuals could afford to buy kids in the first place, and—

"Lena's listed there," Nelson said hoarsely.

A pin-drop silence followed her statement, and then several of us whispered at once, "Lena?"

"Lena Dunton. My friend's baby, who was confiscated by the Ministry. Nine rows down. Note the 'Date of Collection.'"

My eyes scanned the rows and columns and came to rest on the girl's name, and then the date: May 7, 2105. "It's the same day the Ministry came for her," I breathed, my mind scanning back to the date Nelson had told me about the kid being taken. She'd said it had happened the night before we talked, and that matched this very date. The implication took several moments to sink into my brain, but when it did, it hit me so hard it knocked the air from my lungs.

The gang and the Ministry had supposedly "collected" this girl on exactly the same day. Which meant that...

"So wha-what are you saying, Nell?" Abe asked, his voice shaky.

"That the *Ministry* could be behind this whole operation?" Ant whispered. "That we could actually be looking at the Ministry's archives, rather than someone who hacked into them?"

Just him voicing the question made me want to shake my head, shoot the notion down outright, even though it had been on the tip of my own tongue. It just seemed... so far-fetched. So crazy. So impossible.

Nelson sucked in a breath. "I don't know. And I'm sorry, I didn't mean to get all alarmist on you here. All I'm saying is, look at what's in front of you. I guess there are other explanations, but it struck me as a disturbing coincidence. Maybe I'm just being paranoid."

"But *how* could the Ministry be behind this?" Austin blurted out. "I mean, even theoretically. If they were, for starters, there's no way we would have gotten into this system so easily. Just think of how tight the security is around the archives. You can barely even poke at it without risking a squad team coming down on you!"

Nelson suddenly let out a sharp breath. "Unless..." she whispered, then trailed off once more. She went completely silent for ten agonizing heartbeats, and when she spoke again, her voice was laced with sheer terror. "Oh, no. No, no, no, no, no. Guys. You need to run. Get out of there. NOW!" She practically screamed the last word, and my heart jumped into my throat.

"What?" I gasped, panic already jerking my limbs into motion.

"Get back to the aircraft and get the hell out of there!"

"Nelson? What the hell is going on?" Zion barked as we all leapt to our feet at once and raced toward the door, several of us almost bumping into each other as we clustered to get through it. Zion's voice was firm, but there was a tremor to it that betrayed his fear.

"The freaking Ministry *is* behind this, because what I just discovered is a snare protocol!" Nelson panted, sounding as if she were scrambling around her office in preparation to evacuate as well. "Proprietary government software that's designed to trap brazen hackers. It detects attacks and allows the unsuspecting intruder entry in order to infect their connection with a virus that reveals their location—and will also send out an alert regarding the nature of the breach. Which will most probably include details like whether a system has been tampered with physically. And pinpoint the exact system's locale." She swore again, her words making it hard for me to even breathe. "The snares are set up around the archives too, which is how I know about them. But I know to *expect* them there!" she went on. "It's why I've never attempted to brute-force the archives. God, I should've been more alert. I'd recognize the coding any day, but I had no reason to look out for it! No reason for it to even be on my radar!"

"Wait," I stammered, desperately trying not to give in to full-blown panic. "But you were using encryption, right? Sure, the system may have sent out an alert that it's been breached *locally*, but how could *you* be at risk, Nelson?" Just the thought of her being in danger sent my heart racing a hundred miles a minute. She couldn't be. She was far too important. To all of us.

"I didn't have adequate security to prevent a virus of that kind," she breathed back. "Hell, I didn't even have my usual layers in place. It would have slowed me down too much in breaching the system, and we had to be fast. I had no idea I'd need all of them. I didn't think we were dealing with the friggin' government!" Her voice rose to a hysterical pitch that made the hairs on my body stand on end.

"But it doesn't make sense," Jackie shot back as we pounded along the corridor toward the attic entrance. "You already probed their shadow website, days ago. If the government really is behind this, how come a squad didn't come down on you right then and there?"

"Maybe because we didn't dig aggressively enough to trigger it," Nelson panted. "Like I said, none of us attempted a brute-force attack. And given how deep the site's hidden in the shadows, it's possible security is less sensitive there than usual. It was a complete fluke that we even came across it in the first place… But whatever the case, you'd better believe they're coming for us. You guys *and* me."

Panic finally claimed me, and the slew of curses that had been on the tip of my tongue since laying eyes on the spreadsheet escaped my lips.

The government was coming for us. *Enforcers* were coming for us. Or someone even worse.

"No, no, no," I gasped as we bundled back up the ladder to the attic. This couldn't be happening. *How* could it be happening? What was the Ministry doing running a site like this?

The Ministry's primary purpose was to enforce the CRAS. And the CRAS was only instituted to solve the country's economic problems. Not to become a mail-order system designed to serve the rich.

If that was what this was.

Right now I couldn't think of another explanation, and the pit of my stomach hollowed out, giving way to a feeling of deep sickness. How many kids were being taken from their birthparents in this way? How many other sites might the Ministry have like this, floating around the shadow web?

And more importantly, were all of these kids being targeted *with just reason?*

I couldn't help but think back to Lena and her parents. How Nelson had been so confident they'd been in the safe zone. Heck, even the parents had thought so. And yet the Audit Office had disagreed. The Audit Office, who refused to make their records public.

Could it be that Lena had just happened to match some wealthy couple's criteria? That her parents might *not* have been part of the 20 percent of the population that was deemed to be a net drain to the country?

That the Ministry had just been looking for an excuse to rob them of their child?

They'd still been lower middle class, which meant, on the surface, they appeared to be within a safe level per the scope of the system. And, like I said, nobody could know for sure, because the Audit Office didn't make their records public. I guessed, in reality, they could have been part of the bottom 50 percent, and we wouldn't actually know.

But, even if all this was somehow true—that the Ministry had become a servant of the rich rather than of the people—the question remained: *why?* It was a question that had been bugging me for a long time. *Why* did the rich want so many kids? *Why* had Mr. and Mrs. Sylvone not been satisfied with two, three, or heck, even four? *Why* did the wealthy seem so obsessed with the idea of increasing their number of adoptions?

I needed to know. But trying to figure it out while attempting to flee the imminent arrival of a government death squad probably wasn't the best idea.

"How long d'you think we have?" Ant managed as we pounded across the attic floor toward the broken skylight.

"They would have gotten an alert a few seconds after I breached the system," Nelson replied. She was panting more heavily now, and it sounded as if she were running, too. "Which was, what, fifteen minutes ago, give or take? Which means it won't be—"

Whatever she'd been about to say was overtaken by a strangled cry, and a second later, her line went dead.

"Nelson?" I croaked. "NELSON?!" I stalled in my tracks, my whole body shaking. "NELSON?!" I screamed.

But the line remained silent.

My heart skipped a beat as a wave of panic crashed over me. Goosebumps prickled my skin like electricity, and tears stung my eyes. But before I could fully process what could have just happened to her, another line crackled to life in my ear and Julia was screaming at us.

"STAY AWAY FROM THE ROOF! THEY'RE HERE! YOU
ALL GOTTA GET OUT ANOTHER W—"

The line cut out.

"Julia?!" I shouted, as we all came to an abrupt halt.

"Government stealth aircraft!" Zion hissed. He'd gotten
closest to the skylight, his gaze angled toward the dark sky
through the open window. "Several of them. They're closing in!"

Adrenaline shot through me like a bolt of lightning and I
whirled on my heel, almost slamming into Jace, who'd come to a
stop a foot behind me. "Go!" I gasped, and then he was turning
too, his legs pumping across the dusty floor as he raced back to
the trapdoor.

We flung ourselves down the ladder, skipping rungs and
jumping most of the way to the floor, then sprinted along the
hallway to the stairs. Any thought of maintaining quiet flew out of
the window as we pounded down them, our heavy footsteps as
loud as thunder as they echoed off the walls.

Jace stopped at the ground floor, just before the fourth flight
of stairs that would lead us to the basement, and when we
diverged from the staircase, my eyes lighted on the exit at the
end of the hallway. The door was open, thanks to whoever had
left the building earlier to investigate the noises in the parking
lot.

"Ventilations off!" I shouted, realizing that the gas would still
be out there. The last thing any of us needed right now was to
inhale that sedative mist.

Snapping my visor back down, I realized my suit was still in
non-ventilation mode after our entry into the basement office, so I
charged ahead, the sound of low clicking surrounding me as the
rest of my team made the switch.

Only, Austin couldn't, I suddenly realized.

I swore, stalling at the exit just as Jace and I reached it. I whirled to face the rest of my team, who caught up with us seconds later. "The gas. What about Austin?" I panted.

"I'll carry him!" Zion grated out. "Just keep the hell moving!"

Before Austin could get a word in, either of objection or approval, the tall man grabbed him by the middle and flung him over his shoulders in a fireman's lift. "Grip's too tight!" Austin yelped.

"Sorry," Zion grunted, loosening his metal fingers around him some. I heaved a quick sigh, grateful that Zion would carry Austin to safety, even if he did pass out.

Assuming we could get to safety.

"We gotta make it across the parking lot, then across the field to the forest," Winter panted from the back of the group.

We all nodded hastily, knowing it was our best option. There was a wooded area on the other side of the field, which would give us coverage, and beyond it was a clearing where we'd agreed to regroup after the mission, or if anything went seriously wrong. Marco, Julia, and Alexy were clearly preoccupied right now and unable to scoop us up immediately, but if we got to the shelter of the trees we at least had a chance of escaping the squad, especially in the dark. And maybe our aircraft could circle back and pick us up later.

I had no idea what was happening to our decoy team at this point, but they should have had the same idea.

Jace and I turned back to face the exit and raced out, straining our suits for speed in a way we'd never done before. We shot out through the open compound gate and spilled into the smoke-choked parking lot, and I prayed the rest of our team had gotten Julia's warning, too. Because it was too late for me to double check. I couldn't open my visor to switch channels until we were out of range of the gas, and—

My thoughts froze at the sound of boots hitting the ground.

Boots that didn't belong to my team. It sounded like they were some twenty feet behind us, but when I threw a glance back over my shoulder, I couldn't see the source thanks to the smog. I could barely even see Jace, who was running a handful of feet beside me.

"Squad's landed!" Kory shouted.

An explosion of bullets pierced the night, and I heard the terrifying ping-ping of the gunfire colliding with metal. Terror gripped me at the sound of Winter's surprised cry ringing out from behind, but I couldn't afford to look back. I had so little visibility ahead of me, and it took all the concentration I could muster just to avoid smashing into cars. If any of us slowed now, capture or death was guaranteed.

But as another round of gunfire resounded through the parking lot, I felt two sharp pings in my back, and was forced to swerve off course. I ducked and darted at a crouch for a car a few feet to my left, hoping to get a few seconds of coverage. But then my right foot collided with something thick and heavy, and I lost balance. I spotted the unconscious man lying in my path a moment too late, and I tripped and fell, landing hard against my side.

"Robin?!" I heard Jace's anxious voice in my ears but didn't have the breath to respond. It was the first time I'd experienced falling over properly in one of these suits, and it was worse than I'd imagined. Pain blossomed along the entire right side of my body, which had borne the brunt of my impact with the metal frame, and my forehead throbbed where the edge of the visor had smacked it.

Clearly, you really weren't supposed to fall over in these things. Especially not at the speed at which I'd been running. And I also realized, as I dragged in a breath and my lungs burned, that non-ventilation mode likely wasn't supposed to be paired with frantic respiration. I was running out of oxygen. Fast.

Gritting my teeth against the pain, and the white spots dancing before my eyes, I forced myself back up. But before I could continue running, something flew at me from behind and caught me around the lower back, knocking me to the ground again. A fresh wave of pain coursed through my body as this time I landed facedown. And it was quickly followed by panic when I realized what had slammed into me.

Turning over as much as I could and staring down, I found myself gazing at some kind of metal pincer device. Large enough to envelop my midriff. And it had snapped closed around me. Fear poured through my veins; I'd never even *seen* one of these things before.

I let out a cry of alarm as I tried, and failed, to pull it apart. My angle was all wrong. I couldn't get the leverage I needed, even with the strength my suit afforded me. I couldn't even reach for a weapon, either, because the thing had covered my belt.

I twisted back around to face the direction of the field, and rose to my feet, intent on getting away—but an invisible force yanked me backward. I snapped my gaze down to the pincers in horror, realizing that *they* were the force. Like some kind of powerful magnet, yearning to return to its counterpart. Yearning to return *me* to their counterpart.

"No!" I gasped, calling on every ounce of willpower I had and straining against the pincers. But my attempts only seemed to trigger an increase in their strength, and I tripped again from fighting the heavy pull.

And then it was too late. Two deep shouts alerted me to enforcers approaching, and I heard a flurry of footsteps picking up their pace. I continued to struggle. The fight in me hadn't left. But when I shot a glance over my shoulder and saw the outlines of two men through the smog, I knew it was hopeless. At their speed, combined with the pincers pulling me, they'd be upon me in five, four—

Gunfire erupted, and I snapped my eyes shut reflexively against the bullets hitting, and possibly piercing, my suit, from how close they were now. But then I realized the noise had come from the opposite direction, and I dared to open my eyes again to see the hulking form of Jace leaning against the hood of a car and opening full bloody fire.

The surprise was enough to force the men backward and send them scrambling for shelter, giving Jace the few seconds he needed to leap over the car and race toward me. Shoving his gun into his belt, he grabbed both sides of the pincers and pulled at them with all the strength his suit could muster. They creaked against the tension, and then snapped back with a sudden clang.

And then I was free of them, and Jace was gripping my hand and tugging me forward, back into the race for our lives.

"Thank you," I managed, trying to ignore the painful protest of my limbs and head as I forced my body back to full speed.

"Wait till we're out of here," he breathed.

And I knew he was right. I didn't know what had happened to the rest of our ground team, or Marco, Julia, and Alexy. The gunfire had scattered us, and I couldn't make out the aircraft in the sky. Fear constricted my chest at the thought of any of them being captured—or worse—and I prayed that they were all somehow okay. Most of all, I prayed Nelson was okay. Because if she wasn't...

The implications of everything that had happened in the past quarter hour finally crashed down on me.

The woman was still my only hope of cracking the archives, in spite of all the people I'd come across in the portal over the past few weeks. None of them had even gotten close compared to her.

And if she'd been captured, and they found her hard drives...

We'd be back to square one. No, worse than square one. Because if they found the drives, they'd be able to address every vulnerability she'd ever flagged, every note she'd ever made, and use it to make their security even tighter.

Which would basically make getting Hope back an impossibility.

The realization made my knees buckle, and I would have tripped again were it not for Jace's hand shooting to my arm and yanking me back upright.

"Focus, Robin," he said, his voice firm, and yet not sharp, giving me the uncanny impression that he somehow sensed what my emotional state must be.

And I knew he was right, and I nodded, instantly contrite. It was hard to focus, to swallow back the fear and worry, but I had to.

Because we still had to get ourselves out of here alive.

READY FOR THE NEXT PART OF ROBIN'S STORY?

Dear Reader,

I hope you enjoyed *The Child Thief*!

Book 2 of the series, *Deep Shadows*, releases on July 15th, 2018. Visit: www.bellaforrest.net for details. Or the direct link to the book is: **www.forrestbooks.com/TCT2p**

I look forward to seeing you there!

Love,

Bella x

P.S. Sign up to my VIP email list and I'll send you a heads up when my next book releases: www.morebellaforrest.com (Your email will be kept 100% private and you can unsubscribe at any time.)

P.P.S. I'd also love to hear from you. Come say hi on Facebook:

Facebook.com/BellaForrestAuthor. Or Twitter: @ashadeofvampire

READ MORE BY BELLA FORREST

THE CHILD THIEF

Brand new action-adventure/dystopian series!

The Child Thief (Book 1)

Deep Shadows (Book 2)

THE GENDER GAME

(Action-adventure/dystopian. Completed series.)

The Gender Game (Book 1)

The Gender Secret (Book 2)

The Gender Lie (Book 3)

The Gender War (Book 4)

The Gender Fall (Book 5)

The Gender Plan (Book 6)

The Gender End (Book 7)

THE GIRL WHO DARED TO THINK

(Action-adventure/dystopian. Completed series.)

The Girl Who Dared to Think (Book 1)

The Girl Who Dared to Stand (Book 2)

The Girl Who Dared to Descend (Book 3)

The Girl Who Dared to Rise (Book 4)

The Girl Who Dared to Lead (Book 5)

The Girl Who Dared to Endure (Book 6)

The Girl Who Dared to Fight (Book 7)

HOTBLOODS

(Supernatural romance)

Hotbloods (Book 1)

Coldbloods (Book 2)

Renegades (Book 3)

Venturers (Book 4)

Traitors (Book 5)

Allies (Book 6)

Invaders (Book 7)

A SHADE OF VAMPIRE SERIES

(Supernatural romance)

Series 1: Derek & Sofia's story

A Shade of Vampire (Book 1)

A Shade of Blood (Book 2)

A Castle of Sand (Book 3)

A Shadow of Light (Book 4)

A Blaze of Sun (Book 5)

A Gate of Night (Book 6)

A Break of Day (Book 7)

Series 2: Rose & Caleb's story

A Shade of Novak (Book 8)

A Bond of Blood (Book 9)

A Spell of Time (Book 10)

A Chase of Prey (Book 11)

A Shade of Doubt (Book 12)

A Turn of Tides (Book 13)

A Dawn of Strength (Book 14)

A Fall of Secrets (Book 15)

An End of Night (Book 16)

Series 3: The Shade continues with a new hero...

A Wind of Change (Book 17)

A Trail of Echoes (Book 18)

A Soldier of Shadows (Book 19)

A Hero of Realms (Book 20)

A Vial of Life (Book 21)

A Fork of Paths (Book 22)

A Flight of Souls (Book 23)

A Bridge of Stars (Book 24)

Series 4: A Clan of Novaks

A Clan of Novaks (Book 25)

A World of New (Book 26)

A Web of Lies (Book 27)

A Touch of Truth (Book 28)

An Hour of Need (Book 29)

A Game of Risk (Book 30)

A Twist of Fates (Book 31)

A Day of Glory (Book 32)

Series 5: A Dawn of Guardians

A Dawn of Guardians (Book 33)

A Sword of Chance (Book 34)

A Race of Trials (Book 35)

A King of Shadow (Book 36)

An Empire of Stones (Book 37)

A Power of Old (Book 38)

A Rip of Realms (Book 39)

A Throne of Fire (Book 40)

A Tide of War (Book 41)

Series 6: A Gift of Three

A Gift of Three (Book 42)

A House of Mysteries (Book 43)

A Tangle of Hearts (Book 44)

A Meet of Tribes (Book 45)

A Ride of Peril (Book 46)

A Passage of Threats (Book 47)

A Tip of Balance (Book 48)

A Shield of Glass (Book 49)

A Clash of Storms (Book 50)

Series 7: A Call of Vampires

A Call of Vampires (Book 51)

A Valley of Darkness (Book 52)

A Hunt of Fiends (Book 53)

A Den of Tricks (Book 54)

A City of Lies (Book 55)

A League of Exiles (Book 56)

A Charge of Allies (Book 57)

A Snare of Vengeance (Book 58)

A Battle of Souls (Book 59)

Season 8: A Voyage of Founders

A Voyage of Founders (Book 60)

A Land of Perfects (Book 61)

A SHADE OF DRAGON TRILOGY

A Shade of Dragon 1

A Shade of Dragon 2

A Shade of Dragon 3

A SHADE OF KIEV TRILOGY

A Shade of Kiev 1

A Shade of Kiev 2

A Shade of Kiev 3

THE SECRET OF SPELLSHADOW MANOR

(Supernatural/Magic YA. Completed series)

The Secret of Spellshadow Manor (Book 1)

The Breaker (Book 2)

The Chain (Book 3)

The Keep (Book 4)

The Test (Book 5)

The Spell (Book 6)

BEAUTIFUL MONSTER DUOLOGY

(Supernatural romance)

Beautiful Monster 1

Beautiful Monster 2

DETECTIVE ERIN BOND

(Adult thriller/mystery)

Lights, Camera, GONE

Write, Edit, KILL

For an updated list of Bella's books, please visit her website:
www.bellaforrest.net

Join Bella's VIP email list and she'll send you an email reminder as
soon as her next book is out. Visit: www.morebellaforrest.com

CPSIA information can be obtained
at www.ICGtesting.com
Printed in the USA
LVHW011522081220
673630LV00004B/724

9 781947 607392